THE SHOGGOTH
CONCERTO

THE SHOGGOTH CONCERTO

A Fantasy with Pseudopods

John Michael Greer

AEON

Published in 2024 by
Aeon Books

Copyright © 2019, 2024 by John Michael Greer

British Library Cataloguing in Publication Data

A C.I.P. for this book is available from the British Library

ISBN-13: 978-1-91595-201-1

Cover art by Margaux Carpio
Typeset by Medlar Publishing Solutions Pvt Ltd, India

www.aeonbooks.co.uk

CONTENTS

CHAPTER 1

THE SONGS OF SHOGGOTHS

Thunder rolled in the night off behind Hob's Hill, rattling the windows of the little apartment. Startled, Brecken Kendall got up from the piano. A glance out the window showed a clear sky spangled with autumn stars, the hill looming up black and hunched close by, and a tiny shape with two red lights—a helicopter, Brecken guessed—circling slowly above it. She shook her head, then saw what might have been a faint flash of light from behind the hill, heard the rumbling sound again a heartbeat later.

Partridgeville weather, she thought. It still doesn't make a bit of sense. She went back to the piano, sat on the bench, forced her attention back to the tricky bit of Telemann she had to have down cold before Wednesday. Mismatched, brightly colored sweats imperfectly hid the gawky angles of her body, clashed with the light brown of her skin; long black hair that never could make up its mind whether it was curly or wavy spilled forward over her face, got pushed back behind her ears with an irritable gesture. As she surveyed the score, her teeth tightened on her lower lip, an old habit. She splayed out her fingers, shook them, and started playing again.

Half a dozen of the notes jarred as she hit them: the old upright piano had already begun its inevitable drift out of tune. Brecken did her best to ignore the sour notes, played the difficult passage over and over again until the mechanical details of playing the piece finally got out of the way and the music started to come through.

Now, once through from the beginning—

Thunder rolled again, hard. She gave the nearest window a dismayed look, even though she didn't need to face whatever weather might be on its way, and there was nowhere else she needed to be until her first class in the morning. Something about the sound put a chill down her back, though she couldn't tell what or why.

You're stressing out over nothing, she told herself. Stop it. She drew in a breath, pushed her hair back behind her ears again, played through the whole piece with as much concentration as she could find. One more roll of thunder sounded, but she made herself keep playing.

By the time she'd worked out all the difficult passages, the thunder had stopped. The staccato rhythm of the helicopter sounded loud for a minute or two, faded into silence, and that was that. She glanced up at the tacky plastic clock on the wall in the cramped little kitchenette that filled one corner of her apartment, blinked in surprise at the time: it was almost midnight, much later than she'd thought. It was a good thing, she reflected, that she didn't have neighbors to pound on the walls or the ceiling.

Her shoulders complained as she got up from the piano bench. She rolled them forward and back, shook her hands and stretched her fingers until the stiffness went out of them, then went to the futon that filled most of one end of the little apartment's ell. A brisk pull on the frame slid it from its daytime state as a sofa to its flat nocturnal shape. Though the thunder had unsettled her, the silence of the night once it was gone seemed oppressive. As she got ready for bed, she could not shake an uneasy sense that something terrible had happened.

* * *

She was up before dawn the next day, and put in an hour of flute practice before getting oatmeal going for breakfast and checking for texts and emails on her phone. After the meal she plunged into the day's homework, trying to get far enough ahead that she didn't have to feel guilty about doing something else that evening.

In the pale light of morning, the apartment looked like exactly what it was, a detached garage that somebody retrofitted to cash in on the market for student housing when Partridgeville State University began to ride the postwar boom. The floor sagged visibly in the middle where a trench left open to allow car repairs from underneath had been bridged over with plywood and third-rate lumber. Cheap wallboard painted off-white defined the walls and ceiling, and old stained linoleum covered the bathroom and kitchenette floors, replaced elsewhere by a carpet that had been burnt orange a long time ago and now just looked burnt: that was as far as the interior decorator's art had gotten with it. The apartment had only three virtues: the rent, which was low; the neighborhood, which was green, quiet, and far enough from campus to keep visitors scarce and the party crowd at a good distance; and the lack of anyone living on the other side of its walls, floor, and ceiling, which meant that a music student could practice at all hours without having to compete for the always overbooked practice rooms on campus.

From outside the apartment still looked like a garage, complete with a rollup door facing the alley, though that had been nailed shut for decades. Garbage cans and recycle bins lined one wall: one of each for Brecken, for Mrs. Dalzell the landlady, and for the two tenants on the upper floor of her house. Normally the cans stood in a row like so many tin soldiers, but at quarter to ten, when Brecken finally put on street clothes, loaded her tote bag, and left for her first class, all the garbage cans had been knocked over. Mrs. Dalzell was bustling around with rubber dish gloves on her hands, picking up refuse from the neatly mown grass. An odd acrid odor, like nothing Brecken recognized, hung around that end of the yard.

"Oh, good morning, Brecken," Mrs. Dalzell said. Hair dyed boot-polish black was her one concession to vanity, contending with baggy jeans, a shapeless green sweatshirt, and a wrinkled face the color of underdone toast. "Did you hear anything out here in the small hours? Something got into the garbage cans. I hope we don't have to deal with those raccoons again."

Brecken got halfway through saying that she hadn't heard raccoons before Mrs. Dalzell said, "Oh, and you got a package slip from the postman yesterday." She handed it to Brecken, who gave it a casual glance and then a second, appalled look. The postal clerk had written the sender's zip code on the pink form, and it was Uncle Jim and Aunt Mary's in Harrisonville. A package from Aunt Mary any time from July through the runup to Christmas meant—

Brecken tried to shove the idea out of her mind. Before she could manage the feat, Mrs. Dalzell started talking again, this time about an article on the Partridgeville *Gazette* about sewer rates, and it took deft maneuvering for Brecken to leave for her classes. She ducked through the narrow gap between Mrs. Dalzell's house and the house next to it. That put her on Danforth Street, which ran down the long slope from the foot of Hob's Hill to the university campus.

As she shouldered her tote bag and started walking, she could see Partridgeville spread out before her in the morning. To the south, Mulligan Wood stretched from Hob's Hill to the distant pine barrens, Belknap Creek flowed green and silent through the oldest part of town to Partridge Bay, and on the creek's far side the low uneven mass of Angell Hill rose up, with the First Baptist Church white and gleaming at its crest. To the north, a long arm of Hob's Hill covered with pines swept around to the sea, shutting out the view toward Mount Pleasant. Straight ahead, due east along Danforth Street, neatly squared blocks of postwar housing gave way to strip malls and apartment buildings, then to the stark concrete buildings of the university, and finally to the old downtown. Beyond that, Partridge Bay met the Atlantic in a narrow gap between rocky breakwaters, and the Mulligan Point lighthouse thrust up toward a gray sky. An ordinary American college town, with an ordinary university that happened to have a better than average music program: that was what Brecken's high school counselor had called it, and if there was more to it than that, Brecken's time there hadn't brought her within sight of it.

She didn't let herself look back at the great dark mass of Hob's Hill. The thunder of the night before still troubled her, for reasons she could not name. She kept on walking until the cyclopean buildings of the university surrounded her and she veered toward Gurnard Hall.

That was the music department building, a tall bleak shape of concrete and glass rising up on the far side of a courtyard paved in concrete slabs. Glass doors opened off the courtyard into the ground floor, where some architect's whim had put a big open space with a scattering of chairs and tables. The Cave, music majors called it, and it deserved the label: a great dim space in which echoes fluttered about like bats. If you knew who was who, you could figure out at a glance the shifting territories where different factions and subsets gathered, and if you listened to the music from the loudspeakers high overhead—all of it chosen by a student committee in long contentious meetings—you could track the ebb and flow of competing fashions.

Poorly lubricated hinges moaned as Brecken came in through one of the glass doors, looked around The Cave, headed for a table right up against a bare concrete wall on the other side of the space. She was most of the way there before someone sitting at the table spotted her and called out, "Hey, girl!"

"Hi, Ro." She got to the table, pulled up a chair.

Rosalie Gibbs-Templeton grinned up at her. Short and plump, she exuded energy from every pore. Purple extensions in her black braided hair swore acidly at the colors of a loud blouse, found more congenial company with the dark brown of her skin. "What's up?"

"Not much," Brecken admitted.

Rosalie wagged a finger at her. "Girl, don't give me that. You got to live the dream."

"I've got to get through this semester first," said Brecken, propping her elbows on the table and her chin on her hands. "And so do you."

Rosalie made a skeptical sound in her throat, Brecken rolled her eyes, and they both laughed. They'd spent the previous school year, the freshman year for both of them, sharing a dorm room in the soaring mass of Arbuckle Hall. Though they'd moved into apartments of their own for their sophomore years, they still ran together more often than not.

The loudspeakers high above, which had been playing something quiet and classical, suddenly spat out a saccharine voice over the top of a drum track, squealing something about love. "Great," Rosalie said, rolling her eyes. "Sky syrup." That was her term for pop music played over PA systems. "You got Music Ed today, right?"

"Eleven-thirty," Brecken said without enthusiasm. Introduction to Music Education I was rapidly becoming her least favorite class that semester. "Not—"

"Hi, Ro." Another young woman veered around a circle of students not far away, came over to the table. "Hi, Breck. How's things?"

"Hi, Donna," the two of them said, not quite in sync.

The newcomer pulled out a chair, flopped down into it. Donna Tedeschi was a freshman that year, petite and olive-skinned, with black hair bobbed short. "Who's responsible for that atrocity?" she said, glancing upward at the mewling from the loudspeakers.

"Don't you dare blame me for it," said Rosalie. "I was just asking Brecken here whether they showed her yet in music ed class how to teach singing."

That got a grin from Brecken. "Not yet," she said. "But I can ask Boley this afternoon whether that's a shoggoth song." That got her startled looks, and she went on. "That's what today's lecture's on: shoggoths."

"Well, isn't that special," Rosalie said in a withering tone. "That's those Lovecraft monsters, right? They probably sing better than she does."

* * *

"Shoggoths," said the professor at the podium, a tired-looking man in a tweed jacket. Ragged gray hair and ragged gray beard framed a pale and sagging face, tried and failed to lend dignity to weary movements. Around him, the cavernous lecture hall soared to dim heights; fewer than a third of the seats below were filled. "One of the most distinctive monsters of twentieth century fantastic literature. You've probably encountered them in pop culture, anime, online fan fiction." He shook his head. "Forget all that. It's not what we're talking about."

It was probably a good lecture the first time Professor Boley gave it, Brecken thought, and tried to imagine him as he must have been then, young, energetic, eager to pass on his own enthusiasms to his students. Since then there had been too many years, too many repetitions; the lecture reminded her of one of those dismal gigs where the same piece of music had to be played over and over again until all the life had gone out of it. She tried to stay interested, reminded herself that she needed the General Studies credit.

"Three stories published in the 1920s and 1930s introduced shoggoths to readers," Boley said. "'The Thing in the Twilight' by Randolph Carter, 'At the Mountains of Madness' by H.P. Lovecraft, and 'The Piper at the Gates of Hell' by Philip Hastane. The first of those is in the anthology, and all three of them are linked on the class website."

Though she'd read all three stories earlier that week, she dutifully wrote down authors and titles in the battered spiral notebook in front of her—another old habit, that, from the days when all the money she could scrape together had to go for her music, and a computer of her own was one of many things she'd done without. Once that was done, she spared a moment to glance at the young man in the seat next to hers. He was watching Boley intently; his bushy eyebrows, the one dark presence on a light face framed with blond hair, were drawn together in concentration over pale blue eyes; his hands hovered over a tablet keyboard, and his lips folded together so that the little tuft of blond beard on his chin bristled.

"None of them invented shoggoths," Boley went on. "Remember that it was standard practice for authors of the fantastic at that time to borrow freely from archaic mythologies and obscure occult literature. In this case all three got it out of *The Secret Watcher* by Halpin Chalmers—they mention that in their letters. One of the papers on next week's reading list, 'The Sources of Lovecraft's Lore' by Miriam Akeley, gives the quotations."

The young man next to Brecken typed at a feverish pace. For her part, Brecken noted down the title of the essay, resolved to read it. She'd have to write a term paper for the class, and hadn't yet come up with a suitable topic.

"So. Shoggoths are protoplasmic blobs six to fifteen feet in diameter—our authors don't agree on size. They were created a billion years ago as a slave species by another set of monstrous beings, the Elder Things, who we'll talk about a little later this semester. They look a little like heaps of iridescent black soap suds, but they're not fragile. They have green luminous eyes that float to the surface, look at you, and then sink back down. They're parthenogenetic females, by the way, and reproduce by budding. They have a language of piping notes over a wide range. Carter says they have a harsh smell, Lovecraft says they smell fetid, Hastane gets florid about it without actually describing it. Chalmers doesn't say anything about a smell at all. Put it all together, and you've got the concentrated essence of pure hideousness."

Boley warmed to his theme, and his face flickered with the last embers of whatever passion had gotten him through his doctorate and landed him a teaching job at Partridgeville State all those years ago. Brecken lost track of his words, though, for his comment about the voices of shoggoths sent her thoughts slipping away down more congenial paths. Piping notes over a wide range, she thought. Start with G below middle C, say, pop up an octave and a fifth to D, drop back down to a pert little trill around D an octave lower and then tumble back down to G in a cascade of sixteenth notes; then do the same sequence again a fourth higher; then— Her pen darted across the paper, sketched out the first half dozen measures of a piece of music. She caught herself, spent a moment feeling guilty, forced her attention back to the lecture.

"Chalmers was a local boy," Boley was saying. "He was born and grew up right here in Partridgeville. He didn't go to PSU, I'm sorry to say, but that's because it was still Partridgeville Agricultural College back then and didn't have much to offer an art historian with a taste for occultism. Dartmouth for his B.A., Harvard for his M.A. and Ph.D., and then to the Manhattan Museum of Fine Arts, ending up as curator of the archeological collections: that was his route. As far as anyone knows, Lovecraft and Hastane never met him; Carter did, but then he knew everybody who was anybody in the New York art scene."

"So. Chalmers came back here when he retired in 1926, and he died here the same year. More precisely, he was murdered here. It was pretty ugly. Whoever did it—it's still an open case—stripped him, bashed him around, cut off his head, and smeared the corpse with some kind of blue gel, to make it look like he was killed by the Hounds of Tindalos, which were monsters Chalmers himself wrote about. You can get more of the details from articles on the class website, but I don't recommend clicking through unless you've got a strong stomach."

The lecture rambled on, and the echo of vanished intellectual excitement that had tinged Boley's voice for a short while faded out into sounds made by rote. Brecken's thoughts slipped back to the musical theme she'd sketched out. She wondered if she'd be able to use it for any of the assignments she had to turn in for Composition I that semester. Playing with musical ideas in the privacy of her own mind or her own apartment was one thing, but the thought of having to compose something for others to hear and judge made her apprehensive to the point of queasiness. Stop it, she reminded herself. You can't get a bachelors' degree in music from Partridgeville State, no matter what track you're on, without two semesters of composition.

"The shapeless," Boley said finally, as the hands on the clock above him pointed to 12:20. "The thing that lacks name, definition, form. To our authors, that's the essence of terror—and it still frightens us today." His voice trickled out into silence, and he stood there blinking like an owl in sunlight as the clock let out a sudden loud click.

Students surged to their feet and headed for the door. Brecken waited until the young man next to her started to get up, then stood, leaned toward him, kissed him on the cheek. "Looks like you got something out of the lecture."

He smiled his usual smile, a slight upward twist at the ends of his mouth, let her take his hand. "Yeah, surprisingly." With a shrug: "Something I can use for my studies."

They followed the other students out into an echoing hallway where footfalls and voices rang off bare concrete, and then out the building's main doors onto gray concrete slabs. "Still free tonight?" he asked her.

"Jay," she said, chiding, though she smiled to soften it. "Of course I am."

"Just thought I'd check." She mimed a swat at him. Laughing, he parried it, said, "Well, you never know."

On the far side of the square, Gurnard Hall rose up gray and stark. They went through one of the glass doors into The Cave.

"Do you mind if we swing by Buzzy's on the way?" Jay asked her.

She did, but not enough to say anything about it. "We can do that."

"Great." He gave her a quick squeeze, a kiss. "See you at quarter to six."

"I'll be waiting," she promised, and watched him cross The Cave to the elevators.

Outside the wind had picked up, and drove long gray shreds of cloud across a pale sky. Brecken huddled into her coat and hurried across campus to the main post office, mailed her weekly letter to her mother, and then got in line. It took ten minutes standing in line and two more waiting at the counter to make her worst fears come true. Yes, it was a package for her from Aunt Mary, with a half dozen rainbow-glitter stickers on the brown paper wrapping to prove it, and this time of year it would have to be—

She did her best to silence uncharitable thoughts and trudged the twelve blocks back up Danforth Street, hauling the package under one arm. For some reason, two identical gray SUVs with tinted windows were driving along different streets near Hob's Hill at walking speed, but neither of them paid her any attention and she promptly forgot them. When she got home, she noticed that the garbage cans had brand new bungee cords in eyeburning colors holding them shut. The acrid odor still hovered faintly over the cans: animal repellent, Brecken guessed.

She got inside her own little space as quickly as she could, went to the kitchenette, gave the package a wan look, and then got a pair of scissors and opened it. Brown paper and a lightly dented liquor box gave way to masses of crumpled paper, to a plastic insulating bag, and then to four loaf-shaped packages neatly wrapped in foil and wax paper, still apparently frozen, with the dread word "zucchini" neatly misspelled in permanent marker on each one.

She really does mean well, Brecken thought disconsolately. It was true, too. Aunt Mary had the best of intentions, but it was a family joke that she couldn't boil water without giving it a scorched taste. Her zucchini bread did its best to rise to that high standard, with considerable success. Maybe, she thought, I should leave it outside overnight to drive off the raccoons.

Tempting though the thought was, she put one loaf out to thaw on a plate, told herself that maybe this batch would be better than the others. The three remaining loaves went into the freezer, and the box and packing material went into the recycle bin. Then it was time to leave for the library, so she had a shot at getting her homework done before she went to meet Jay.

* * *

Buzrael Books—Buzzy's, in Partridgeville State slang—was a hoarder's dream and a bibliophile's nightmare, a labyrinth of narrow aisles, stark fluorescent lights, floor-to-ceiling shelves of bare wood, and quirkily sorted books crammed into six rooms above the Smithwich and Isaacs jewelry store on Central Square. A tall narrow door, a long narrow stair, and another narrow door at right angles to the first led into it. On the far side of the door, a gap barely straight enough to be called an aisle led between a sales counter cluttered with oddities and a floor-to-ceiling display of garish twentieth-century paperbacks. Brecken rarely went past the counter; her sense of direction wasn't good, and she'd gotten lost in the labyrinth more than once.

Once he came through the door, Jay plopped his backpack on the sales counter without a word and headed off into the dim corners of the bookstore. Brecken gave the proprietor, a bent white-haired man with a gnome's face, an apologetic look; he returned a wry glance over gold-rimmed glasses, put the backpack behind the counter, then returned to sorting through a stack of leatherbound volumes with titles in unfamiliar scripts. Brecken glanced idly across the assorted books and objects on the sales counter before going further in. It was a time-wasting maneuver, one of the ways she handled waiting for Jay to finish hunting for books, but this time her eye caught on a photocopied page of handwritten words and music.

She picked up the sheet, considered it, and her brow furrowed. The writing listed phrases and single words, and next to each was a short, neatly drawn bit of musical score, treble and bass clef both. At the top of the sheet, for example, the author had written *I will not harm you* in front of two measures of fast, lilting notes that ran from G below low C to F sharp above middle C and back again. Brecken hummed the two measures, glanced over the other entries on the sheet.

"Ah." The proprietor had risen noiselessly and come down the counter to where Brecken was standing. "An interesting find, that. Do you recognize the handwriting?"

"No," Brecken admitted. "Should I?"

"Perhaps. Halpin Chalmers had a certain local notoriety once upon a time."

She blinked in surprise. "The writer?"

"Ah, you've heard of him. Yes. These photocopies—" His gesture took in the sheet in Brecken's hand, and a stack she hadn't noticed a short distance away, under a hardback volume with yellowing pages and an ornate dust jacket tattered at the edges. "—they came to us from an estate sale last week." With a curious look she couldn't interpret: "It's supposed to be a lexicon of sorts—a list of the songs of shoggoths and their meanings. Interested?"

"Maybe," said Brecken, glancing again at some of the bits of music. The echo of her conversation with Rosalie that morning made her just a little uneasy. Still, shoggoths or no shoggoths, some of the pieces looked as though she might be able to use them as themes for her composition class homework. "How much are they?"

"A dollar for the lot," he said. "Not much market for that sort of thing these days."

Brecken agreed to the price, then went to the bin of fifty-cent cookbooks next to the counter and sorted through them. She found two that looked worth trying, added them to the photocopies and went fishing in her purse for the money to pay for them. She had just tucked her purchases in her tote bag when Jay came back from the stacks with an old book in one hand and a smile on his face—not his usual smile, but a tense smile that bent his whole face around it. It wasn't a pleasant expression at all, and it made Brecken uncomfortable.

He dropped the book on the counter in front of the proprietor, who glanced up at him after a moment, took the book, opened it, closed it again. "You're fortunate to find that," he said.

"Yeah, I know," Jay said, and pulled a wad of bills out of his pocket.

"Not the sort of thing that comes into stock very often," the old man said. He considered Jay, handed back the change and the book. "Not at all."

A few minutes later they were on their way down the stairs. "Find anything?" Jay asked.

Brecken had already weighed her answer. If she told him about the Halpin Chalmers papers, she knew, he'd want to borrow them, and if that happened her chances of seeing them again in time to use them for her composition class weren't good. Once she was done with them, on the other hand, they might make a good birthday present. "Just a couple of cookbooks." She glanced at him. "You found something pretty good, though."

"Yeah." The tense unpleasant smile returned. "A book I need for my studies. Something really old and really rare." He didn't say anything else about it, and she let the subject drop.

* * *

By the time they reached his apartment she'd gotten him talking about the gigs he'd lined up for their musical group over
the winter break, and the smile she disliked so much went
away and didn't come back. They went up a narrow flight of
stairs lit only by a single bare bulb, ducked down a narrow corridor lined at intervals with unmarked wooden doors. Brecken
waited while he fumbled with his keys, followed him in once
the light inside went on.

Jay's apartment was a cramped irregular little space with an
unmade bed in an alcove at one end, a big open space in the
center with no furniture at all, and a ramshackle kitchen at the
other end with a bathroom not much bigger than a closet opening off it. He dumped his backpack and coat on the floor and
settled on a chair at the kitchen table; she set her tote bag near
the door, hung her coat on a hook on the wall nearby, went to
the cupboard and the fridge and assessed the contents with a
practiced eye. "Spaghetti?"

"Please," he said with his normal smile.

"Sure thing." Water splashed into the biggest saucepan she
could find, went to heat on one of the stove burners, and she
sat down across the table from him. "We'll have to do a grocery
run sometime soon. You're out of way too much."

"Yeah, I know." Then: "Breck, I don't know what I'd do
without you."

"I've got a pretty good idea," she said, teasing him, but still
blushed at the praise.

They talked about classes and gigs, the other members of
their ensemble, the latest gossip from the music department,
and a new arrangement she was working up for "The Carol
of the Bells," while the water heated, the pasta boiled, and the
contents of a jar of spaghetti sauce went into a pan to warm.
A salad would be good, she thought, but the refrigerator didn't
offer any help there; two glasses of cheap red wine joined dinner on the table, and that was all.

Afterwards, they talked a while longer and finished the
wine, and then Jay got up, took her hands in his, drew her to

her feet, and started kissing her. She let him lead her to the unmade bed, helped him take off her clothes, held him as he thrust into her clumsily for a while and then shuddered and lay still.

Maybe five minutes later he was sound asleep, and starting to snore. Brecken extracted herself from the bed, gathered up her clothes, and went to the cramped little bathroom to wash up and dress. Jay didn't like to be touched while he was sleeping and he liked to be alone when he woke up in the morning, and so even though she wanted nothing more than to settle down next to him on the bed and pull the blankets over them both, that wasn't an option. Love, she thought, looking at him with a smile she tried to convince herself was heartfelt. It is what it is.

The door clicked behind her as she let herself out, picked her way down the ramshackle stairs to the street. Outside the wind whistled down Partridgeville's streets, flung a few petulant raindrops as it passed. Brecken walked as quickly as she could to Prospect Street, where sodium lights blazed down and an assortment of nightspots and cheap restaurants offered refuge in case of trouble. Prospect to College, and then College to Danforth and the long straight uphill run toward the dark mounded shape of Hob's Hill: it was a familiar route, familiar as the pensive mood her trysts with Jay so often awoke in her.

Such thoughts led in directions she didn't want to face just then, and so she called to mind the photocopies she'd bought at Buzzy's that evening, the pages the proprietor had so preposterously called a lexicon of shoggoth songs. Her memory for music was keen enough that she didn't need to glance at the sheets to remember some of the snippets of melody on them: the lilting notes that were supposed to mean *I will not harm you*, a fast sequence of trills for *I wish to talk*, a passage with a haunting quality that meant *we live beneath the ground*, and more.

She whistled them as she walked, turned them over and over again in her mind, tried to see ways in which she could use them as themes for upcoming composition class assignments. The sequence *I will not harm you* was particularly sweet; it really was a pity, she decided, that none of the Baroque composers had made it the theme of a bourrée or a gigue, one of the dance-music forms they'd turned into a mainstay of the eighteenth-century repertoire. She could hear in her mind the way it would sound on the piano, the crisp allegro tempo, four beats to the measure, the first beat accented but not too much.

The last blocks of Danforth Street slipped past in that pleasant way, and Brecken went through the gap between houses to her door. The lock turned noiselessly—Mrs. Dalzell must have oiled it again, Brecken guessed—and let her into her apartment. Inside, dim light from the alley streetlamp filtered in through the shades, splashed murky shadows over the furnishings. She reached for the light switch, turned to the kitchenette and Aunt Mary's zucchini bread.

The bread was gone. That was the first thing that registered. The plate where she'd left it to thaw was still there on the counter, with foil and wax paper wrappings spread open on top of it, but the bread itself had vanished. An instant later she saw what else was in the kitchenette, and she forgot all about zucchini bread for the moment.

It crouched on the linoleum, a hideous, blobby, gelatinous-looking mass maybe five feet across and three feet thick, iridescent black in color, with six pale greenish eyes scattered across the surface facing her. As Brecken watched in stunned silence, two of the eyes receded into the mass of the thing, and four more emerged and blinked open. All the eyes were wide, and all of them stared straight at her.

CHAPTER 2

THE THING ON THE LINOLEUM

B recken stood there for a long moment, frozen into place. The thing on the kitchenette floor stared at her with its wide pale eyes, trembling visibly, then drew itself together. Its motion reminded her suddenly of an animal about to spring.

Panic set her heart pounding. She tried to think of something to do, anything, but the only thing that came to mind was the absurd notion that she was looking at a shoggoth. All at once she recalled one of the little scraps of melody from the photocopy, the one that was supposed to mean "I will not harm you," and because she couldn't think of anything better to do, and because the thing on the kitchenette floor looked so much like a shoggoth, she whistled it aloud.

The thing seemed startled. Three more eyes blinked open on the surface facing Brecken, stared at her. Then the thing darted away in a motion so quick and evasive she couldn't keep track of it. An instant later it had vanished.

Brecken stood there motionless for some time thereafter. Just then, taking even a single step toward the kitchenette was the last thing on earth she wanted to do, and it didn't matter whether what she found there proved that the thing had actually been there or not. She drew in a ragged breath, made herself go into the kitchenette anyway. The thing really was gone, if it had ever been there. At first, the only sign of its apparent presence she could find was the empty plate and wrappings on the counter. Then she caught a half-familiar scent, recognized it after a moment as the odd acrid odor she'd smelled around the trash cans earlier that day, and noticed that a glass she'd filled with water and put in the sink that morning was completely empty.

She walked back to the futon, slumped down onto it, stared at nothing in particular for what seemed like a long time. The thing couldn't actually have been there, she told herself. Things like that don't exist. Shoggoths don't exist—not outside of stories by old-fashioned fantasy authors like Carter, Lovecraft, and Hastane. Not in the real world, and certainly not in a rundown student apartment in Partridgeville, New Jersey.

After a while she got up again and made sure the zucchini bread really was gone. The wrappings, she noticed, looked as though someone had cleaned them—not a single crumb remained. She dropped the wrappings into the trash, breathed a sigh of relief, then felt guilty and made herself get another loaf of Aunt Mary's regrettable zucchini bread out to thaw.

Lacking anything better to do thereafter, she went to the piano and tried to drown out her thoughts with an hour of hard practice: a flurry of warmups and etudes, and then straight into the second book of Bach's *The Well-Tempered Clavier*, one prelude and fugue after another, until the serene mathematics of Bach's music brought the world back into something like its proper shape. After that she rewarded herself by getting out her flute and playing until sheer tiredness made her stop. More than once, while the clear bright notes of the flute filled the apartment, she had to push aside the uncomfortable feeling that someone was listening to her, but by the time she pulled the futon out and settled down to sleep, she'd managed to forget that passing fancy.

A solid night's sleep, another hour of flute practice, and the rest of her morning routine made her feel better still. By the time the morning sun chased off the last scraps of mist and streamed through her eastern windows, she had convinced herself that she must have imagined the thing on the linoleum. The only discord in that comfortable conviction was the hard fact that a loaf of Aunt Mary's zucchini bread had vanished without a trace. She pondered the second loaf, still in its foil wrapping, and thought of a simple test.

She got a plate and a bowl, unwrapped the loaf, put it on the plate, filled the bowl most of the way with water, and set both on the kitchenette floor. There, she thought. When I get home tonight and both of those are still there, I'll know the whole thing was just nerves or something. Conscience reminded her that the bread would probably be too stale to eat by then, and so she grabbed her purse and tote bag, and headed for the door before second thoughts could interfere. Besides, she told herself, if something really did eat the loaf, maybe it needs another meal.

Outside, the morning air was cold and damp, tinged with salt from the harbor. The slopes of Hob's Hill blazed red and gold with autumn colors, and for some reason three more identical gray SUVs with tinted windows were driving slowly around the neighborhood, as though looking for something. She walked down Danforth Street past the usual morning traffic, cut across the lawn in front of Mainwaring Hall, crossed the concrete plaza to Gurnard Hall, and reached The Cave half an hour before her composition class began. She veered past a knot of students debating some detail of the latest postmodern reinterpretation of music theory, and crossed to the table by the concrete wall. "Hi, Ro."

Rosalie glanced up at her from a chair tipped back precariously against the wall. "Hi, girl. Where were you last night? I tried to call you around eight."

"Over at Jay's," Brecken admitted.

A momentary silence told her what Rosalie thought of that—no surprise there. "Well, you missed a good time. You've haven't met Barbara Cormyn, have you?" Before Brecken got halfway through shaking her head, Rosalie had turned to another young woman nearby. "Barb, this is Brecken Kendall, my BFF. Music education track, plays a mean flute, *and* perfect pitch."

Barbara Cormyn was a willowy blonde with big blue eyes that seemed stuck in a look of perpetual surprise. She shook Brecken's hand. Perfect pitch, imperfect everything else, Brecken wanted to say, but didn't.

Rosalie chattered on. "You know the jazz singer Olive Kendall?" Brecken gave her an embarrassed look, but she went on anyway: "That's her grandmother." She turned to Brecken. "Barb's performance track, plays half the instruments that exist."

"Oh, stop," Barbara said. "Reeds and piano, mostly." She had a breathy high-pitched voice that made her sound like a movie star.

"And flute, and guitar," said Rosalie, grinning. "And I don't know what else."

Barbara rolled her eyes, turned toward Brecken. "That's really wild, that you're Olive Kendall's granddaughter. Did you get to study with her at all?"

"I'm not much of a vocalist," Brecken admitted, "so mostly I learned from Grandpa Aaron. He was her pianist—that's how they met."

"That's sweet," Barbara said. "Rosalie was telling me about the Rose and Thorn Ensemble—you're both in that, right? I'd love to hear you play."

"I don't know what Jay's got booked for us next," Brecken said. She glanced at Rosalie, who looked away with an irritated expression. "I'll find out, though."

"Will you? That'd be great." The soft blue eyes didn't lose any of their surprised expression, but something moved beneath that, precise and implacable as machinery.

"There won't be a lot until winter break," said Rosalie then. "You know how it goes."

"Well, yes. Are you going to be here all break?"

"Oh, yeah," said Rosalie. "My folks are trying to talk me into going to Guadalajara with them, but I'm going to make a career in music. You got to live your dream, right?"

"That's the spirit." The soft eyes turned to Brecken. "You?"

"I'll be here," Brecken said. She hoped the other girl wouldn't ask why—she didn't want to have to explain to a stranger why neither of her parents could give her a place to stay for the holidays. Fortunately, Barbara simply nodded and smiled.

"I'll probably see you around then. I'll be here." Then, glancing at her cell phone: "Gotta run. It was nice meeting you, Brecken."

Brecken said something polite and watched her hurry off.

* * *

"Anything," said Professor Toomey. "Absolutely anything at all." He leaned forward, propped his chin on long folded hands; his long brown face creased in an amused smile. Most of the students in the room gaped at him as though he'd sprouted a second head. His eyes moved this way and that, unreadable, surveying them all.

Composition I met on the top floor of Gurnard Hall, in an architect's afterthought of a room with odd angles everywhere and equally odd acoustics. A baby grand piano sat over to one side of the space; chairs scattered at random across the smooth concrete floor made up the rest of the furnishings. Tall windows on one end of the room looked out toward Hob's Hill.

"There's a lot of structure to the craft of composition," the professor went on. "That's important, don't get me wrong, but it's not the be-all and end-all. There's also your own personal voice, your own personal vision. We're going to give some time to that. All of you know your way around music; all of you know at least one kind of music inside and out—otherwise you wouldn't be in this class. That's why the assignment for your first original composition is wide open. Any style, any form, any genre, any tradition—whatever. Compose a short piece in it. That's your assignment."

Dead silence filled the room for a moment. Then, inevitably, Julian Pinchbeck broke it: a stocky young man in a sports jacket, chinos, and loafers, with a booth-tanned face and blond hair he'd painstakingly trained to billow up like Leonard Bernstein's. "So something really far out on the bleeding edge, like postspectralism, would be acceptable."

"Yes," said the professor.

"How about metal?" That was from a tall young woman with bright pink hair, dressed in a black t-shirt and ripped jeans, whose name Brecken hadn't gotten around to learning, whose talent she admired and whose music she couldn't stand.

"Yes."

Half a dozen other fashionable musical genres got named and approved in the next few minutes. Then, in a gap, a thin tense voice from the back row asked, "What about a fugue?"

Heads turned. "Yes," said Professor Toomey, before anyone else could speak.

That conjured up an even deeper silence.

"Oh, and there's one other thing," the professor said then. "You're not just going to compose a piece, remember. You're going to perform it, right here, for the class to critique. If you need backup musicians, get them. If you need instruments other than that—" His gesture indicated the piano. "—bring them. That's up to you. Performances will begin one week from today, first come, first served; those of you who've gotten something scheduled with me before class starts that day will get an extra five points. Without composing this and your final project and performing both of them here, you can't pass this class. Got it? Excellent." His smile gleamed again. "That's all. See you Thursday." He got to his feet, glanced around the room again, left the classroom.

As soon as he was gone, Julian Pinchbeck stood up and sent a glare toward the back of the room. "A fugue? Are you serious?"

"The professor said anything," said the voice from in back. Brecken turned in her seat, glimpsed the speaker between two heads: tall and rangy, his lean face hunched toward his shoulders, dull brown hair in an unfashionable cut. "Tell me how that excludes fugues."

Pinchbeck rolled his eyes. "That's not the point. As a musical form, the fugue is stone cold dead. Its possibilities got used up centuries ago."

"In your opinion," said the young man in back.

"It's not just my opinion," Pinchbeck snapped back. His voice always rose in pitch when he got pedantic, and it was rising now. "Composers dumped the fugue in the late eighteenth century because it couldn't say the things that needed to be said. Going back to it now is a total waste of time." Three other students started talking at once, but Pinchbeck's voice rose above them: "Classical music is dead. It doesn't speak to anyone any more."

"In your opinion," the young man in back repeated.

Brecken glanced from one to the other, uncertain. She'd heard a hundred times, more, the same rhetoric Pinchbeck used: classical music is dead, it doesn't speak to anyone any more—

Rosalie, shaking her head, pushed through the crowd, grabbed Brecken's sleeve. "Come on," she said. "They'll be at it all day." Brecken let herself be pulled toward the doors.

It speaks to me. The words she hadn't said followed her out into the hallway.

Two of the three elevators that reached Gurnard Hall's top floor were out of order, and the third had a crowd waiting around the door. Rosalie glanced at Brecken, motioned with her head toward the stair, and Brecken followed. Plenty of others were headed the same way. The big metal door, painted an impressively ugly shade of blue, swung open.

Memory stirred as Brecken started down the stairs: a great E flat major chord bursting out of the near-darkness of an opera house on an afternoon twelve years past. She'd been sitting between her grandparents, shocked into alertness by the music, the harsh details of a troubled childhood washed away for a moment by the sound.

Footfalls echoed in the stairwell, beating a leaden bass rhythm on concrete. Voices raised in conversation carried on an ungainly melody line above them. Brecken barely noticed the sounds. In her mind, an orchestra played the adagio measures at the start of the overture to Mozart's *The Magic Flute*. She'd listened, puzzled and fascinated. Then—

All at once the second violins took off scampering in a flurry of notes as adagio gave way to allegro. The first violins leapt in to join them after four measures, the bassoons, the violas and the cellos after seven more. She'd sat there with her mouth open, clutching the arms of the seat, scarcely daring to breathe, the effervescent delight the music brought seemed that fragile. Then the whole orchestra took up the same theme fortissimo, crashing over her like a wave, and she'd sat there shaking in sheer exhilaration, all but drowning in the impossible glory of it.

After it was all over, they'd gone to an old-fashioned café half a dozen blocks from the opera house—it had been a Sunday matinee, the kind where opera companies park second-string vocalists to give the regular cast a break, but if the old gods of nature in all their eldritch might had risen up singing in the opera house, they couldn't have had a greater impact on Brecken's world. There, in a window booth over sandwiches and fries, with the promise of an ice cream sundae hovering in the near future, her grandmother asked her what she'd liked best about *The Magic Flute*. Was it the comical bird-man Papageno? Was it the romance between Tamino and Pamina, the majesty of the wise Sarastro, the perilous beauty of the Queen of the Night?

Then her grandparents had listened with raised eyebrows as Brecken tried to explain, within the narrow limits of a seven-year-old's vocabulary, that it was the music, not the story or any of the characters, that had shaken her to her core. They'd given each other startled looks—she remembered, with almost photographic clarity, the expressions on their faces.

"Earth to Brecken?" Rosalie said then. They were at the bottom of the stairwell, with other students streaming past them into daylight. Brecken blinked, managed an apologetic smile. "Sorry," she said. "I was thinking."

"I figured," said Rosalie. They went out the door onto the bleak gray square, and Rosalie asked, "Got anything scheduled tonight?"

"Homework and practicing," said Brecken. "Of course."

Rosalie laughed. "I know, dumb question. If you finish up before eight or nine, give me a call, okay?"

Brecken promised that she would, and said something polite. Rosalie did the same and headed off at a sharp angle.

It speaks to me, Brecken repeated to herself, and all at once glimpsed the perfect answer to Julian Pinchbeck's smug dismissals. Since she could do anything for that first composition assignment, why not compose a short piece in one of the standard Baroque forms, a declaration of loyalty and love to the music that mattered most to her?

Enticing, the idea hovered in the air around her. As she considered it, she recalled the sequence of notes headed *I will not harm you*, the one she'd picked up from the photocopies and whistled at the thing she hadn't seen in the kitchenette the night before. Her pace slowed to a standstill as she turned it over in her thoughts. It really would make a fine theme for a bourrée, she decided. If only she knew the bourrée form well enough—

Then, all at once, she realized that she did know it well enough. All the Baroque pieces she'd practiced and played, all the music theory she'd studied in high school and in her freshman year, had already handed her the tools. It was just a matter of using them—and if there were details she needed to learn, she knew where to find them.

Yes, she thought. I can do this. She turned, set off for Hancock Library.

* * *

The loaf of zucchini bread was gone when Brecken got back to her apartment, the bowl of water was nearly empty, and a very faint trace of the acrid scent hung in the air. She stared for a moment, then shrugged and put the plate and bowl in the sink. If something was getting into the apartment to eat the zucchini bread, she decided, at least it wasn't leaving a mess.

She had more important things to think about, though, and plopped down on the futon as soon as she'd shed her coat and sorted out the contents of her tote bag. A notebook full of staff paper made a prompt appearance, along with a mechanical pencil. All the way up Danforth Street she'd had fragments of her bourrée playing in her head, and getting them written down before she lost them was the one thing that mattered.

By the time she'd copied down everything she remembered, she'd already decided to arrange the bourrée for piano—it would work as a flute solo, no question, but the melody begged for richer harmonies and a bass line. At first she could only see a few of the ways the fragments fit together, how the bass notes she'd sketched out for one passage in the first part could be developed to fill gaps in some of the other passages, how the middle notes could weave their own textures between the melody and the bass. She wrote, erased, scratched out false starts, and then all at once she could see the bourrée as a whole, turned to the next blank page, and wrote it out from beginning to end in such a rush that she snapped the pencil lead four times.

Now, for the test that mattered.

She was on her feet and halfway to the piano before she realized she'd left the notebook sitting on the futon. Retrieving it, she sat on the bench, stretched her fingers, shook out her hands, drew in a deep breath, and began playing. She stumbled hard the first time through the first part, pushed through, and then caught the rhythm of the bourrée and played the rest of it without trouble. A second time through, a third, and it sounded exactly the way she'd imagined it, filled the little apartment with its own bright elegance.

The last notes faded into silence. Brecken sat on the piano bench for some minutes afterward, feeling a little dazed, a little—what? She couldn't find words. It was done; it was—

Hers. Not hers like something she owned, hers like a breath, a voice, a child.

She shook herself, then, and finally thought to glance at the clock on the kitchenette wall. It was almost eleven o'clock. Somehow four hours had slipped by while she'd been writing the bourrée. It was far too late to call Rosalie, of course, so she got up unsteadily from the piano bench, went to the kitchenette, and split the next half hour between cooking a pot of rice, heating up red beans and collard greens from bowls in the refrigerator, and washing two breakfasts' worth of dishes. Eventually a good-sized bowl of red beans and rice and a smaller bowl of buttered greens accompanied her back to the futon.

Once both bowls were empty, she sat back, tried to clear her head. She ought to put in another hour of piano practice, she told herself, but it felt just then as though every drop of music had been wrung out of her. Instead, once she'd emailed Professor Toomey to tell him she had a piece finished for the composition class assignment, she pulled the futon out flat and got the quilts spread out on it. She had to struggle to find the energy to get ready for bed, and once she lay down and pulled the quilts over her, she fell asleep almost at once.

She had a curious dream somewhere in the small hours, though. In the dream, as in reality, she was curled up on the futon in her apartment, her quilts heaped over her, and she

happened to be looking through the darkness toward the kitchenette. Something dark and shapeless crouched there, gazing
at her with pale phosphorescent eyes.

* * *

"My cousin Rick emailed me a link to the website," Rosalie
said. She was wearing an even louder blouse than usual, and
Brecken suspected she'd chosen it to match her mood. "The
idea is the meaning of your family name predicts your future."

Donna rolled her eyes. "Yeah, right."

"No, seriously, give it a chance. Do you know what your
name means?"

"It's the Italian word for 'German,'" said Donna. "What it
means is that one of my dad's ancestors took a wrong turn in
the Alps somewhere. I'm not going to repeat the mistake."

Rosalie sighed, turned to Brecken. "Help me, okay? Do you
know what Kendall means?"

"No," Brecken admitted, "and that's not what it was originally. Grandpa Aaron changed the spelling. It used to be
Kandel—that's a Jewish name, but I don't know the meaning."

"Your grandfather was Jewish?" Donna asked.

Brecken nodded. "Grandpa Aaron was a Jewish pianist
from Brooklyn, Grandma Olive was a black jazz singer from
St. Louis, so of course it was love at first sight. They started
out doing gigs together, then got married and had my dad.
My mom's Irish and Armenian on one side and nobody's quite
sure what on the other."

"Wow," said Donna. "How do you even decide what church
you're going to get married in? Or synagogue, or whatever it
would be?"

"Your whole family's Italian?" Brecken asked.

Donna nodded enthusiastically. "Oh yeah. Not just all
Italian, all from Abruzzo, and most of 'em from the town of
Pescara. My aunt Giannina gets teased all the time for being a

foreigner because her family's from Chieti, which is like from here to Mount Pleasant."

"You two aren't cooperating," Rosalie said.

"Nope," said Donna, and checked the time on her cell phone. "And we've got about six minutes to get to class, too. See you!" She gave Rosalie a sly smile, got up and headed off across The Cave. Rosalie sighed in exasperation, checked her own phone, and launched herself toward the glass doors, leaving Brecken to shake her head and go to Intro to Music Education I.

Fifty minutes later, she was wondering whether her class in music education made no sense, or whether she was just too stupid to understand it. Professor Neal Rohrbach had curly brown hair and a vague pink face; he talked smoothly in a tenor monotone, but everything he said heaped abstraction on top of abstraction until Brecken was left trying to guess how any of it related to teaching people how to play music, or if it had anything to do with that at all.

After that she had an hour of study time, then The Fantastic In Literature at 1:30, where Professor Boley talked about the philosophy of the Lovecraft circle. "Indifferentism," he said, and once again Brecken could almost glimpse the embers of the enthusiasm he'd once put into his lectures. "That's what Lovecraft called it, but he didn't invent it. It was in the archaic texts he and so many other authors of weird tales read so avidly: the *Necronomicon*, the *Book of Eibon*, the *Seven Cryptical Books of Hsan*, and so forth. Their idea was that the universe doesn't care about us. It doesn't even notice us. What's more, it doesn't mean anything—or if it does, and we're unfortunate enough to find out what the meaning is, it turns out to be so unhuman that it shatters our minds and drives us mad."

"That vision of a universe that's fundamentally hostile to human existence pervades their work. You'll find it especially in the way they interpreted the gods they borrowed from those same archaic texts—Tsathoggua, Cthulhu, Nyogtha, and the rest of them. All of the weird-tales authors of that period liked to pretend that these Great Old Ones were the old gods of nature, the realities behind all the figures of the old mythologies. But these gods don't care. Their concern for you is about on a level with your concern with the bacteria on the soles of your shoes. The same theme of indifferentism: the universe really is out to get you."

Brecken made the mistake of glancing at Jay just then, and saw the smile she hated playing over his face. She forced her attention back to the lecture, and wondered: how can the universe be indifferent to us and hostile to us at the same time? If the Great Old Ones really don't care, doesn't that mean they can't be bothered to be out to get us?

She brooded over that as she went home, got her laundry together, and took it to the laundromat on Meeker Street, where she sat working on her music education assignments while the washer and dryer did their work. After another quick trip home, she headed out again, went through the old downtown to her weekly piano lesson in an clapboard-sided house on Dexter Street at the foot of Angell Hill. Ida Johansen, her piano tutor, was a mousy-looking woman with hair that had once been blonde and was now mostly colorless, who filled in the gaps in an inadequate pension by giving piano lessons and playing organ Sundays at the First Baptist Church, and whose living room was almost completely bare of decoration except for a framed piece of embroidery saying, in faux-Gothic script, 𝔜𝔢 𝔤𝔯𝔬𝔴 𝔱𝔬𝔬 𝔰𝔬𝔬𝔫 𝔒𝔩𝔡, 𝔲𝔫𝔡 𝔱𝔬𝔬 𝔩𝔞𝔱𝔢 𝔖𝔠𝔥𝔪𝔞𝔯𝔱. Her teaching was uninspired but systematic, and Brecken left after her hour with a page of useful comments in Mrs. Johansen's minute handwriting, and two other passages in the Telemann concerto to work on.

The walk back from Dexter Street took her past Central Square and the door of Buzrael Books, and though she had plenty of other things to think about, her mind kept straying back to the vanishing loaves of zucchini bread. Of course the thing she thought she'd seen Monday night couldn't be responsible, she told herself, because things like that don't exist—but a raccoon would have left more of a mess, she'd seen their treatment of garbage cans often enough to be sure of that, and why would a human being who got into the apartment two days running have taken only a loaf of zucchini bread and a drink of water each time?

She was nervous enough when she got to the door to her apartment that it took her two tries to get the key into the lock, and three fumbling motions to turn on the light. The third loaf was gone, and so was the water. Brecken considered the empty plate for a long moment, then shook her head, put it and the bowl in the sink, and got the last loaf of zucchini bread out to thaw. The thing she'd imagined, or hallucinated, or dreamed in the kitchenette Monday night—it couldn't possibly have been real, she told herself.

Could it?

An unwelcome thought tried to remind her that even the hungriest hallucination couldn't actually eat three loaves of Aunt Mary's zucchini bread. Another thought, just as unwelcome, found it improbable that anything, hallucinatory or otherwise, could accomplish that feat. She tried to shove both thoughts aside, went to the futon, sank onto it and closed her eyes.

Moments passed, and then a soft slippery noise whispered across the room from the direction of the kitchenette. It sounded unnervingly as though something was sliding across the linoleum. Brecken shivered, though the evening was still warm, and thought: I am *not* going to open my eyes. I don't care what—

A low unsteady piping sound shattered her resolve. She opened her eyes, and wished at once that she hadn't.

There the thing was, on the floor of her kitchenette again: shapeless, iridescent black, and horrible. It watched her with pale green eyes that emerged from the gelatinous mass and then sank out of sight. The acrid scent came from it, faint but definite. Panic seized her; she opened her mouth, but all that came out was a little squeaking noise. Then she remembered that the thing's piping might be speech.

Without taking her eyes off the thing, she reached with a shaking hand for the stack of photocopied papers on the end table next to the futon. That particular trill—it was on the first page, she thought she remembered. A quick glance confirmed that. It was a question: ♪*Why?*♪

She glanced up from Chalmers' notes. The thing was still there. It piped a longer sequence of notes, in equally unsteady tones, through a mouthlike orifice that appeared on its upper surface and then disappeared again. She glanced reflexively at the papers in her hands, saw enough of the other motifs to guess at the meaning: ♪*Why do you help me?*♪

It's talking to me. The thought circled around and around, the only coherent thing in the utter confusion that filled her mind. Something that can't exist is talking to me. Belatedly, she realized that it probably expected an answer. Pages rustled as Brecken fumbled through the lexicon, and whistled the only answer she could think of: ♪*I think—you need—help.*♪

The thing responded at once: ♪*Your people hunt and kill my people.*♪

It took a few moments for her to decipher the piping, but then Brecken stared, horrified. She flipped through the lexicon again, and managed to whistle an answer: ♪*I—didn't know.*♪

She looked up from the papers again, to see the thing staring at her with no fewer than twelve wide pale eyes. After a long moment, it piped in shaking tones: ♪*Then I thank you for food and water.*♪

That left Brecken even more unnerved than she'd been, and she replied with an impulsive promise: ♪*There—will be—more.*♪

♪*I—I thank you.*♪ The thing turned and fled in a sudden blur of motion. This time, Brecken was able to follow its route: a zigzag dash across the linoleum to the open space below the sink, then suddenly down, through a gap in the flooring that seemed far too small for it. A faint noise told of its descent into the trench under the apartment.

All at once, Brecken realized that she was trembling from head to foot. She drew in as deep a breath as she could manage, then another. The thing was right there under the floor, she knew, had probably been there for days. It was—

A shoggoth. That, at least, she no longer doubted. The description she remembered from Professor Boley's lecture was too close a fit to what she'd just seen, except for the matter of size, and so were the descriptions in the stories she read: the shapeless body that looked like a mass of bubbles covered by a smooth gelatinous-looking surface layer, the iridescent black color, the pale greenish eyes that appeared and disappeared, every detail was right.

Her imagination offered her unpleasantly vivid images of the shoggoth slithering up out of the crawlspace in the middle of the night with some unthinkable purpose in mind. It was when she tried to think of the unthinkable purpose, of course, that the whole fantasy fell apart. If it had meant to devour her as she slept, say, it could have done that already; instead, all it seemed to want was Aunt Mary's zucchini bread and some water to wash it down.

The sheer absurdity of that fact conjured up a little shaken laugh, but there was something about the encounter that felt far too serious for laughter. The creature had been frightened and desperate, she felt sure of it, not threatening—and there were those inexplicable words: *your people hunt and kill my people*. There was no shoggoth-hunting season anywhere Brecken had ever heard of, but she suspected the creature was telling the truth. That implied a cascade of things she didn't even want to think about.

After a moment Brecken got off the futon and crossed to the kitchenette. Though the shoggoth looked gelatinous, the floor where it had been was clean and dry, and so were the edges of the gap in the flooring through which it had disappeared. The creature had left behind no scent at all, for that matter. Considering the gap, she wondered what it was doing under her floor, and how it had gotten there. I'll ask it next time, she decided.

Would there be a next time?

She found, to her considerable surprise, that she hoped so.

CHAPTER 3

A LEAF IN THE TORRENT

The next morning, Brecken set out the last loaf of zucchini bread and another bowl of water on the kitchenette floor before leaving for campus. All the way along Danforth Avenue, as houses gave way to strip malls and then to the glass and concrete of the university, her mind circled giddily around the bizarre encounter she'd had the night before, the frightened creature hiding under her floor, the strange whistled conversation they'd had.

She got to The Cave with scarcely enough time to meet Rosalie, ride the elevator to Gurnard Hall's top floor, and find a seat. Professor Toomey came in while she was still fumbling with her tote bag. He went to the podium and said, "Julian, Molly, Brecken, can I talk to the three of you for a moment?"

That left Brecken flustered for a moment, until she remembered that she'd emailed him about the composition assignment. She got to the podium a few moments after Julian Pinchbeck and the girl with pink hair did.

"I want to thank all three of you for letting me know so promptly about your projects," the professor said. "Ironically, you all left out one detail—the names of your compositions. If you want to give those to me now I'll put you down to perform first thing next Tuesday."

"Mine is titled 'Obsidian Ellipsoids,'" Julian said airily.

35

The pink-haired girl, Molly, gave him an amused look. "Mine's 'Marty's Blues.'"

The professor's eyes, unreadable as always, turned toward Brecken. She drew in a breath and said, "Bourrée in B flat."

Both of the others glanced at her then. Julian looked as though he'd discovered a slug in his salad; Molly looked as though the slug had suddenly started singing to her, and she liked the tune. "Very good," Professor Toomey said. "You're set for Tuesday."

Rosalie gave her a long startled look when she sat down again. "You've already got something done? Girl, you're way ahead of me."

Brecken gave her a smile and a shrug, and Professor Toomey started lecturing a moment later, sparing her the need to go on. There wasn't really much she could say, she reflected later: how could she explain the sudden rush of certainty, the way her initial fumblings flowed together and called the bourrée into being, the dazed wordless sense of release once it was done?

The fifty minutes of class slid past, and she and Rosalie headed out the door and went down the stair to the plaza. "Doing anything this afternoon?" Rosalie asked her.

"Just studying," Brecken said. "I've got a flute lesson at seven."

Rosalie grinned. "Can you handle company? Donna's coming to my place in an hour, when she gets out of her music theory class—we've both got to catch up on a bunch of work." When Brecken gave her a dubious look: "There'll be chicken quesadillas."

That got a laugh from Brecken. "Okay," she said. "But I'm going to hold you to that."

"You do that," Rosalie said. "I've already got all the fixings." With a sudden grin: "I'm going to remember those quesadillas when I'm living on ramen and sleeping in fleabag hotels."

* * *

Down Danforth to Church Street, over Church to the far side of Central Square: Brecken knew the route to Rosalie's apartment as well as she knew the way to her own. Only a few minutes passed before they got off the elevator on the fourth floor of a big modern building, turned left, and went down to Rosalie's door, which unlocked with a keycard. Inside was a pleasant one-bedroom apartment with windows and a balcony looking out over Partridge Bay, art prints on the walls, furniture that hadn't yet seen the inside of a secondhand shop. A photo on the wall near the kitchen explained the relative luxury: Rosalie's parents, Dad in a Brooks Brothers suit, Mom in an elegant silk dress, beaming down vicariously on their youngest child.

Once coats and hats found their way onto the bed, Rosalie made a beeline for the kitchen and waved aside Brecken's offer to help, so Brecken settled down on the sofa with her music education textbook, a notebook, and a pen. As she started trying to get the chapter on learning theory to make some kind of sense, assorted sounds came out of the kitchen, followed by the groan of the oven door shutting.

"There we go," said Rosalie, coming into the living room. "Ten minutes to quesadillas."

Brecken gave her a sly look. "Unless Georgianna knocks on the door."

Rosalie choked. "Girl, don't even think that too loud." She fetched a bulky textbook from a stack on a coffee table, slumped into an armchair facing the couch. "You know perfectly well that half the reason I bailed out of Arbuckle Hall was so I didn't have to keep on hiding that damn toaster oven from her. I know, that was her job, but still."

Brecken didn't argue, and Rosalie flipped open the textbook and settled down to study. Other than quesadillas, nothing interrupted them until the door buzzer sounded an hour later and Rosalie flung herself toward the intercom. "Donna?" The intercom squawked at her, making sounds incomprehensible to Brecken. "Sure thing, girl. See you in a bit." A pause, thumb on the button, and then Rosalie unlocked the door and headed for the kitchen again.

The door opened a few minutes later, letting Donna in. "Hi, Ro. Oh, hi, Breck. I didn't know you were coming to our little soirée." Grinning: "You better have something to study."

Brecken raised her textbook in both hands. "Done."

"Get her to help you if you run into trouble with the music theory, Donna," Rosalie called out from the kitchen. "She's really good."

"I hope so," said Donna, and flopped onto the couch with an exasperated sigh. "Can you explain what the big deal is about tonality? Kaufmann spent the whole class talking about how it doesn't matter any more blah blah blah, and never bothered to explain it."

"Sure," Brecken said, setting the textbook aside. "Think of 'Twinkle, Twinkle, Little Star.'" She whistled the melody of the first two lines. "You start on C, spend the first line going up a fifth to end on G, and then the second line goes back down to end on C. C's the tonic, right? That means it's home base for the melody. You leave home base, go to a note that's in some kind of harmony with it, then return to it."

"Yeah, I get that," said Donna. "So?"

"Next two lines." She whistled them. "They go toward home base but don't actually get there. Your ear expects that next step and doesn't get it—and then you repeat the first two lines again, and you get the resolution. So everything in the melody moves around that home base."

In the kitchen, clattering noises spoke of a baking sheet meeting an oven rack, and the oven door groaned again. "Ten minutes to quesadillas," Rosalie said, and came out to join them.

"Okay," Donna replied. "I get that—but there's got to be more to it than that."

"Of course there is," said Brecken. "You can do all kinds of things around that home base, and the other notes that harmonize with it. Listen to Bach and watch how he dances around home base. But the home base, the tonic, is always there and everything comes back to it."

"That seems pretty arbitrary," Donna said then. "Why bother with it?"

"Because it's what makes music go somewhere and do something," said Brecken.

"But that's arbitrary too," said Donna.

Brecken tried to think of a response; unexpectedly, Rosalie came to her rescue. "Do you want some chocolate ice cream on your chicken quesadilla?" she asked Donna.

"Ew."

"That's arbitrary too," said Rosalie, grinning. "It still matters."

"Okay," Donna said after a moment. "Okay, I think I get it." Her expression contradicted the words, but she turned to Brecken and said, "Thanks."

"You're welcome." When no more questions appeared, Brecken picked up her textbook.

Time passed, quesadillas appeared and disappeared, and more time passed. Brecken read the chapter from her textbook twice, took copious notes, and once again wondered if the people who'd written it had ever tried teaching music to human beings. Then it was on to the next round of readings for her literature class, two stories by Giles Angarth, a third by Amadeus Carson, and half a dozen poems by Edward Derby. By the time she finished the last of those, an unnerving sonnet about a nameless king in tattered yellow robes, evening was near and a dense fog was flowing in from Partridge Bay, turning the streetlights into smears of orange glare and the powerful lamp of the Mulligan Point lighthouse into a blurred momentary radiance.

"Okay," Rosalie said then. "My brain's full." She got up, turned on the lights. "One more round of quesadillas, coming up." She headed for the kitchen.

"Where were you Monday night?" Donna asked Brecken. "You missed a good time."

"I had a date with Jay." Brecken busied herself putting her textbook back into her tote bag, and tried to ignore Donna's look.

"I bet he made you cook dinner."

"I like to cook for people."

Donna rolled her eyes. "Breck, he's just using you. You know that."

"That's really unfair," Brecken told her, reddening.

"No, it isn't."

"Yes, it is," said Brecken. "And it's pretty rude of you to say that about Jay when he went out of his way to bring you into Rose and Thorn."

It had been the wrong thing to say, she knew that at once, and the sudden wince that crossed Donna's face confirmed it. Donna fell silent, glowering. In the kitchen, the oven door groaned. A moment later Rosalie came back into the living room, glanced from one of them to the other, and said, "What's gotten into you two?"

"I was trying to talk to her about Jay," said Donna.

"Don't go there," Rosalie told her. "Just don't."

"I know." In a scornful tone: "Don't get between Brecken and her strays."

"That's really mean," Brecken said, feeling stung.

"Seriously, Breck," Donna said then. "Think, will you? I mean, do you really want to introduce someone like Jay to your folks?"

Brecken stood up, grabbed her tote bag. She heard her own voice, thin and brittle, as though it came from a distance. "My mom's in prison," she said, "and my dad's been dead since I was five, so I won't be asking them for advice. You know what? I didn't ask you for advice either." She turned sharply, headed for the door, remembered just before she got there that her hat and coat were sitting on the bed, veered over to the bedroom to get them.

"Brecken—" Rosalie said in a pleading tone, coming toward her. Brecken shoved past her and bolted for the door.

* * *

Moments later Brecken stood on the sidewalk in front of the apartment building, with the fog flowing around her. Her anger had guttered out, turning as it always did into shame. She managed to keep herself from bursting into tears, though it took an effort, and started along Church Street with no particular destination in mind. An old bitter memory circled in her mind. The other children in her elementary school, cruel as only children can be, liked to taunt her by calling her "broken Brecken"; she hated the gibe, but after a quarrel it inevitably came to mind. She always ended up feeling defective, a thing fit only to be flung aside.

She had most of an hour and a half to spend before her flute lesson, and as she reached Central Square and she fought her way back to calmness, she thought of one way to help spend it. The second floor windows above the old Smithwich and Isaacs jewelry store shone out into the murk, and the door at the foot of the long narrow stair was still open. A moment of indecision passed, and then she was on her way up the stair and into Buzrael Books.

For all she could tell, the proprietor hadn't moved a muscle since she and Jay had left the store Monday night. He sat in the same old-fashioned wooden office chair, sorting through what looked for all the world like the same stack of leatherbound volumes with titles in strange scripts. He glanced up at her the moment she came in, though, and asked, "Can I help you?"

"Actually, yes," she said. "I was wondering if you have any books on shoggoths."

He gave her a long look over the top of his gold-rimmed glasses, and then said, "That's an unusual subject." With a laugh that sounded like dry leaves crackling: "What do you have in mind? Care and feeding?"

Taken aback, Brecken gave him a flustered look, then thought of something to say. "It—it's for a paper. I'm taking a class on fantastic literature this semester."

"Ah," said the proprietor with the glint of a smile. "Yes, I may have something for you. Just a moment, please." He extracted himself from the chair, vanished into the depths of the bookstore. After a moment keys jingled, and door hinges let out a long shrill moan.

Minutes passed. Brecken looked over the books scattered on the sales counter, sorted through the bin of fifty-cent cookbooks again, and then turned to the floor-to-ceiling rack of twentieth-century paperbacks on the wall facing the counter. Glancing over them, she spotted a cover image that made her draw in a sudden sharp breath: a scantily clad woman starting back in horror from a black iridescent blob with pale greenish eyes. The shoggoth looked quite a bit larger than the one she'd seen in her kitchenette the night before, but otherwise could have passed for a painting from life.

The title of the book was *Daydreams and Nightmares* and the author was Philip Hastane. A glance at the table of contents showed "The Piper at the Gates of Hell" among the stories within. The book only cost a dollar, so she took it with her when she heard the hinges of the unseen door moan again, and the proprietor of the store came back to the counter carrying a stout hardcover in a faded dust jacket.

An amused glance moved from the cover of the paperback to her face. "I see you have a good eye for shoggoths," he said, and held out the hardback. "This may be somewhat closer to what you're looking for, though. Halpin Chalmers has quite a bit to say about shoggoths. There's marginal notes and underlining, I'm sorry to say, but if all you need is a reading copy for your paper, why, this ought to do."

Brecken took the volume from him, opened it. The marginal notes were in blue ink, in a neat old-fashioned handwriting. A glance at the front cover confirmed the title and author—*The Secret Watcher* by Halpin Chalmers—and a second glance inside showed $5 penciled in on the flyleaf, which seemed absurdly cheap. "Thank you," she said.

"You're very welcome." He ducked back behind the counter, went to the cash register. "One thing, though. You mustn't show this book to your boyfriend."

Brecken gave him an unfriendly look, but his gaze, unyielding, met hers above his glasses. "It wouldn't be good for him, not at all. Do I have your promise?"

Before she quite knew what she was doing, she'd given the promise, paid for the books, and headed back down the stairs into the darkening evening. At the bottom of the stairs, she shook herself, turned and looked back up at the brightly lit windows of Buzrael Books. The tense way Jay had smiled when he'd found the other book Monday evening came to mind, and she wondered uncomfortably if the old man was right.

That got her thinking again of the photocopies she'd gotten that same night, and that started her mind chasing after scraps of melody. She started walking again up Meeker Street, as much from habit as anything else, and by the time the lights of Hancock Library came into sight through the fog she had an elegant little piano etude in E flat sketched out in her mind. A glance at her cell phone showed that she still had an hour before her lesson. She went into the library, sat down at the first table she could find, got out her notebook and started writing the etude.

* * *

She was almost late for her flute lesson, but "almost" was the operative word. Evelyn Dobshansky, a retired professor from the university, gave flute lessons in the living room of her home just east of campus; she answered Brecken's knock as usual with a smile and a few words of greeting, and the two of them plunged into an hour of rigorous work on one of Bach's flute sonatas, which did a good job of clearing away the last of Brecken's wretched mood.

On the walk back up Danforth Street, the salt breeze off the harbor blew cold and crisp, driving the fog away and leaving Brecken exhilarated, and her new etude played itself over and over again in her mind. The quarrel with Donna still stung, but music had worked its usual magic for her, and pushed the discomfort off to a distance where she didn't have to feel it quite so acutely.

When she finally let herself into her apartment, though, her first glance was toward the plate and bowl on the kitchenette floor. Both were empty, as she'd expected, but that brought up a question for which she had no ready answers: with Aunt Mary's zucchini bread gone, what was she going to feed the shoggoth?

That she would feed it wasn't in doubt. Her promise mattered, to be sure, but that wasn't the only thing that did. The creature was obviously terrified, and the fact that it was hiding under her apartment suggested all too clearly that it had few other options. The difficulty remained that she had no idea what it could eat, no notion if there was anything on the subject in the strange book she'd just purchased, and no one she could ask—with the obvious exception.

After minutes of indecision, and a long careful reading of Chalmers' lexicon, she went to the kitchenette, knelt by the sink, and whistled ♪I wish to talk.♪ Then, guessing that moving further away would be less threatening to the shoggoth, she got up and backed away, sat on the floor beside the piano bench, reached for the lexicon, and waited.

Minutes passed. Then, with a soft rustling noise, iridescent blackness swelled under the sink, flowed outwards. The shoggoth piped, ♪I thank you again for food and drink.♪

It took Brecken a few moments of fumbling with the lexicon to find the proper response. ♪It is a little thing♪, she said.

♪*But I don't have—any more of the—*♪ There was no word in Chalmers' notes for "zucchini bread," but it was simple enough to find words that would do. ♪*—the thing I gave you. I want to know—what else you can eat.*♪

The shoggoth stared at her with eight eyes for more than a minute. ♪*You gave me food and water,*♪ it said slowly, ♪*and you did not have to. You could have told those who wish to kill me where I hide, and you did not. Now you wish to know what I am able to eat. I do not understand.*♪ In a low trembling whistle: ♪*Today my name is Drowned In The Torrent.*♪

The thought that the shoggoth was hiding to save its life put a shudder of cold horror through Brecken, but the last sequence of notes pushed that aside for the moment, made her blink. ♪*Was your name—something else yesterday?*♪

The creature seemed baffled. ♪*I had no name yesterday. How can there be a name when there are none to hear it?*♪

Brecken took that in and tried to make sense of it, without much success. Other things demanded attention first, though. ♪*You can—hide here—as long as you wish.*♪

In a sudden desperate wail of notes: ♪*Why?*♪

♪*Because—I've been alone—and scared too.*♪ And it was true: a cascade of wretched memories tumbled through her mind, bringing back times she'd had to hide from bullies at school, from her mother's boyfriends and drunken rages. She thought of the way that her grandmother used to scoop her up in her arms and hold her, and blushed as she realized that, hideous as the shoggoth was, part of her wanted to do the same thing to it.

The shoggoth in question regarded her in silence. Minutes passed. ♪*I am grateful for what was given, but—but I would welcome more food,*♪ it said finally, in a low piping tone.

♪*You're hungry,*♪ Brecken guessed.

Lower still: ♪*Yes.*♪

♪*What can you eat?*♪

♪*If it was once alive it is food,*♪ said the shoggoth. ♪*But—but a soft thing would be welcome.*♪ The way it piped the final word reminded Brecken of how desperate the creature had seemed the night before. She found herself wondering whether shoggoths found humans as terrifying as humans found shoggoths, and realized that she didn't find this shoggoth terrifying at all. It was too obviously frightened to be frightening.

♪I can make something soft,♪ she told it. ♪But the place where you are is the place where I make food. May I come closer?♪

♪Yes.♪

She got to her feet, moved with deliberate slowness into the kitchenette, watched the shoggoth slide warily to one side. Something soft, she thought. The cupboard wasn't particularly well stocked just then, but it had several boxes of macaroni and cheese, and that would probably do. She decided to make a double batch, filled the biggest saucepan she had with hot water from the tap, got it heating on the stove.

A glance back over her shoulder showed the shoggoth huddled in the far corner of the kitchen. ♪Is there fire in that?♪ it asked, staring at the electric stove.

♪Not really.♪ She considered the creature, ventured: ♪You don't like fire.♪

The answer came with an note of panic that startled Brecken. ♪No!♪

While the water came to a boil, she went to the refrigerator, looked for soft things. A big bowl covered with plastic wrap turned out to contain a batch of vanilla pudding she'd made the previous Saturday and then managed to forget. That'll do, she thought, and busied herself with the rest of the preparations for a dinner for two, aware all the while of the shoggoth's transitory eyes watching every move she made.

Finally she filled two bowls with mac and cheese, two more with pudding, and got out two spoons before she recalled that shoggoths probably didn't use silverware. Two glasses of water completed the meal. Lacking a table, she set the dishes on the floor not far from where the shoggoth waited, sat on the carpet across from it, and whistled, ♪It's ready.♪

The shoggoth slid onto the carpet, approached the bowls and the glass, and gave her a wide-eyed look. She motioned at the food, then picked up her own bowl of mac and cheese and started eating. That was apparently the encouragement the shoggoth needed; a pseudopod flowed out, scooped up a little of the mac and cheese, enfolded it.

♪It is good,♪ it whistled.

Brecken smiled and nodded, then realized that the shoggoth probably couldn't interpret that, glanced at the lexicon, and whistled back, ♪I'm glad.♪

♪It is very good.♪ The shoggoth paused, and then slid forward and flowed into the bowl, engulfing the remaining mass of mac and cheese. When it flowed back, the bowl looked as though it had been washed. Brecken kept eating in her less efficient way, and the shoggoth watched her. After a time it said, ♪Can you only eat through that one place?♪

Brecken had a mouth full of mac and cheese just then, so a few moments passed before she could whistle an answer. ♪Yes. We're like that.♪

♪That is so strange,♪ said the shoggoth.

She finished her mac and cheese and started on the pudding, and the shoggoth tasted its share with a pseudopod. ♪This also is very good,♪ it said, and engulfed the contents of its bowl.

♪There's more if you want it,♪ said Brecken.

♪I am well fed,♪ it replied. ♪I thank you.♪ After a pause: ♪I will hide now.♪ It began to slide across the floor to the space under the sink, moving more slowly than before.

♪In the—♪ She couldn't find a word in the lexicon for "morning" or "sunrise," and had to improvise. ♪When light comes back I'll make more food. I'll speak to you.♪

♪I—I thank you,♪ it repeated, in piping tones that sounded dazed. It reached the gap in the flooring, slid through a little awkwardly and vanished. Brecken stared at the gap for a long while. It was only then that she realized that she hadn't smelled the acrid scent at all.

She dealt with her bafflement by washing the dishes. When those were finished, she went to the piano, sat down, played her new etude twice, then got out an eraser and changed a dozen notes that didn't work. There were other things she ought to practice, she knew, and more work for other classes she ought to do. Once she was finished with the etude, though, she went to the futon, picked up her copy of *The Secret Watcher*, and opened it.

A black and white photograph of Chalmers faced the title page: lean, hollow-cheeked, intent, the face of a medieval ascetic. The title page itself had a curious geometrical diagram on it, a pattern of circles linked by lines. She paged past the table of contents to the first chapter, "The Two Realities," and read the quotation at the top:

> *There are two realities, the terrestrial and the condition of fire.*
>
> —*William Butler Yeats*

The condition of fire, Brecken thought, tasting the phrase. The dizzying intensity she'd felt surge through her as the bourrée finally came together felt like a condition of fire. Was that what Yeats had in mind? She filed the question, having no way to answer it.

From its first lines, however, the chapter plunged into a complex argument laced with terms that Brecken didn't know— the doels, the Alala, the Secret Watcher, the scarlet circles, the kingdom of Voor—and the neat handwritten notes down most of the margins simply added to the obscurity, with references to books and people she'd never heard of. Brecken was tired enough that none of it seemed to make any sense at all. She ground to a halt at something called the riddle of the Alala— "Find me the place where the light goes when it is put out, and find me the place where the water goes when the sun dries it up"—and sat there trying to parse that for a while, then rubbed her eyes and paged ahead to the end of the chapter. The last lines read:

> But the Alala pertains only to those beings who were part of the order of the cosmos from the beginning, those beings in whom curve and angle unite. There are other beings who were never part of that order, the creations of the created. Such are the shoggoths spoken of in a certain very ancient Arabic book, the formless ones that dwell in darkness, and such also are the dread beings that guard the threshold between curved and angular time, which will be considered later. Yet there is one greater than these: Nyogtha, The Thing That Should Not Be. Of him much will be said in a later chapter.

That left Brecken completely at sea. She turned to the index, trying to find everything it had to say about shoggoths, but the words blurred together as she tried to make sense of them, and after a few minutes she closed the book, put it in the bottom drawer of her dresser so that Jay wouldn't see it if he happened to come over, and went to bed.

* * *

The next morning, as the rising sun gilded the upper half of Hob's Hill, she put her flute away after a solid hour of practice, got a double batch of oatmeal cooking, paged through the lexicon again, and whistled a greeting down toward the space under the sink. A few moments passed, faint sounds came from below, and then the shoggoth flowed up from the crawlspace and sat on the linoleum, considering her.

It really wasn't that horrible to look at after all, she decided, and the only scent she noticed from it was faint and not unpleasant, a little like the odor of Brie cheese. Its outer layer caught stray glints of sunlight and turned them into dim opalescent splashes. Where the light was clear, she could see the shoggoth's eyes sliding out from some deeper layer, among the clusters of black bubbles, and returning again. ♪*Food will be ready soon,*♪ she told it.

♪*I thank you,*♪ it replied. ♪*Today my name is Leaf On Wet Stone.*♪ Brecken took that in. ♪*Is it different every day?*♪

The shoggoth seemed nonplussed. ♪*Yes, of course.*♪ Then: ♪*Do you keep the same name from one day to another?*♪

♪*Yes, of course,*♪ Brecken whistled, startled by the question. A moment's reflection, though, left her doubting that matters were all that obvious. ♪*Each of us gets a name when—*♪ There was no word for "born" in Chalmers' notes, so she improvised again. ♪*When we start being. It isn't changed very often after that.*♪

♪*How very strange,*♪ said the shoggoth.

The oats got to the right consistency, and Brecken dressed them with brown sugar and half-and-half and dished them into bowls. Those, coffee for her, and water for her guest—what effect caffeine might have on a shoggoth wasn't something she wanted to find out the hard way—went on the carpet. The shoggoth sat closer to her this time. As before, it waited for her to begin eating, tasted the food tentatively, and then engulfed it. ♪*It is very good.*♪

♪*I can make some more for you if you want,*♪ Brecken whistled.

♪*I thank you, but—but I am well fed now.*♪ The piping tones wavered, as though some strong emotion moved through the creature.

They finished the meal in silence. As she sipped her coffee, Brecken thought of something she'd been wondering since the shoggoth's first appearance on the kitchenette floor. ♪*Can I ask a question?*♪

♪*Yes.*♪

♪*I have—*♪ The lexicon didn't provide her with the word for "read" or anything else having to do with writing, and she decided that finding out whether shoggoths were literate could wait for another time. ♪*I have heard that your people are big.*♪ She gestured at the walls of the apartment. ♪*Big enough to fill this place.*♪

♪*You have heard of the greater ones.*♪ The shoggoth considered her through pale eyes. ♪*My people are not among those, or even among those of middle size. We were small even in the very old times, before the times of hiding, and I am small among my broodmates. We—*♪

All at once the shoggoth began to tremble, and a sharp bitter scent tinged the air. In a sudden shrill tone: ♪*Why do I say we? There is no we. They are all dead, all dead, I have seen the flames and tasted the smoke of their burning, and I am alone, alone, alone—*♪

Appalled, Brecken reached out to touch the shoggoth: an act of raw instinct, as though she'd meant to comfort a terrified child. An instant later she caught herself, but by then her hand rested on it. It felt as cool and dry as the skin of a snake, as smooth and shapeless as water.

Eight eyes popped open, stared at her. For a frozen moment neither of them said anything. Then, for want of anything else, Brecken whistled, ♪*Leaf On Wet Stone,*♪ hoping that its name would calm it. If anything, the opposite happened; the shoggoth trembled even more violently, and something that felt like ambivalence tensed within it to the breaking point. It wanted and it feared—what?

A moment later she guessed what it might be. It took an effort to push past her own reluctance and fear, but she leaned forward, used her free hand to shove the empty dishes aside and, with the other, gently pulled the shoggoth toward her. It stiffened, and then the stiffness broke and it flowed to her, draped itself heavily over one of her folded legs like a shapeless lapdog, settled trembling against her belly and side. She made herself put her arms around it, the way her grandmother had done for her so many times, and held the creature as it shuddered.

Minutes passed and the shaking gradually subsided. Finally a speech-orifice appeared on its upper surface. In a piping low as a whisper it said, ♪*I should not trust you.*♪

That confirmed one of Brecken's guesses. ♪*My people did it, didn't they?*♪

♪Yes.♪ After a moment: ♪*Do they hunt and kill each other too?*♪
She drew in a breath, made herself tell it the truth.
♪*Yes, sometimes.*♪

One eye gave her a horrified look, closed again. The creature huddled against her.

Brecken glanced up at the clock on the kitchenette wall. She had nothing that day but Intro to Music Education I at 11:30, and she'd planned to devote the morning to study, but there was no reason she couldn't do that and still put some time into comforting the terrified creature. After a few more minutes passed, she whistled, ♪*Leaf On Wet Stone.*♪

An eye blinked open, looked up at her.

♪*If we could move there—*♪ She glanced at the futon, saw its gaze follow hers. ♪*—it would be more comfortable for me.*♪

♪*I should not trust you,*♪ it repeated in the faintest of whistles, but it slid off her lap, freeing her. She turned, moved slowly across the floor to the futon, keeping one hand in contact with it, and it moved with her, clumsily, as though its strength had given out. When they reached the futon she braced herself for an effort, guessing that the creature weighed about as much as she did, but it surprised her, flowing up onto the futon like a waterfall in reverse; the frame creaked beneath its weight. She sat down within easy reach of her tote bag and books, and the shoggoth waited until she was still and then slid close, tentatively at first, then slumping onto her lap, clinging to her. A pseudopod probed the quilts, pulled ineffectually at one end.

♪*Are you cold?*♪ Brecken asked it.

♪*No.*♪ It shivered. ♪*Unsheltered. I—I—*♪ The shivering grew more intense.

She pulled a quilt over and got a fold of it settled atop the shoggoth, then put her arm around it. It stared up at her again with three wide baffled eyes, but the trembling gradually stopped, and the sharp scent faded out. Most of its eyes sank out of sight, leaving a few to surface and sink in a drowsy rhythm, seeming to see nothing.

As carefully as she could, she fished her copy of *Fantastic Literature: An Anthology* out of her tote bag, and had to suppress a laugh: was there anything in it as fantastic as the thing sprawled over her lap? Still, she opened the volume one-handed and set it on her unencumbered knee. Before she started the next item in the book, "An Ode to Antares" by Theophilus Alvor, she took a few moments to consider the creature next to her.

This is a person, not a monster, she thought. Professor Boley's comments about the gender of shoggoths came to mind. A person, and her name today is Leaf On Wet Stone.

Brecken frowned, then, thinking of the complexities of remembering a different name for each day. Did shoggoths have nicknames? Nothing in Professor Boley's lecture or the stories she'd read denied it, certainly, so she decided suddenly to give the shoggoth one.

Sho, she said to herself. It was simple enough, just the word "shoggoth" rounded off for casual use, but it felt right. She nodded, satisfied. Alvor's poem waited, but her thoughts and her gaze kept drifting over to the iridescent black shape huddled against her, the eyes that rose and sank with hypnotic slowness. She blinked, thought about reading the poem, and then let her eyes drift shut—just for a moment, she told herself. A few heartbeats later she was asleep.

CHAPTER 4

MUSIC FOR THE DEAD

Vague unquiet dreams gave way slowly to a place of darkness.

Brecken stood beside her own futon, naked, looking down at two others who sat there, slumped motionless as though asleep: a gawky young woman with light brown skin and unkempt black hair, dressed in mismatched sweats, and a shapeless black presence from which pale luminous eyes emerged slowly and then vanished again. One of the woman's arms cradled the shoggoth. Two of the shoggoth's temporary pseudopods clung to the woman. A moment passed, and then another, before Brecken realized she was looking at herself and Sho.

She looked up, expecting to see the familiar surroundings of her apartment, but a blackness deeper than the darkest midnight coiled around the futon, like a gap in the fabric of reality. She stared at it, and knew obscurely that though it had no eyes that she could see, it was looking back at her. Then its attention seemed to shift to the sleeping figures on the futon, and Brecken felt her own gaze pulled the same way.

Still asleep, the Brecken on the futon shifted slightly. Two pale eyes opened on the surface of the shoggoth closest to her, considered her for a time, sank back out of sight. All at once, as she watched them, the Brecken who stood became aware of the flowing curves that defined Sho's body and the interplay of angles and curves that defined her own. Somewhere, Brecken sensed, somewhere there were beings that were all angles and no curves, beings that could move toward her through unimaginable angles, and she was desperately afraid of them.

The surrounding blackness regarded her. Off beyond it were other curves and other angles, paired geometries that reached out in directions that seemed to embrace time as well as space. There was something wrong with the way the curves and the angles twisted and strained against one another, she could sense that at once, but she couldn't tell what it was.

Then the darkness turned toward her, and regarded her again—

* * *

Brecken woke with a low cry from a nap she hadn't intended to take. For a moment, heart pounding, she stared up at a blank space without angles or curves, until it turned back into the ceiling of her apartment. She let out a ragged breath she hadn't been aware of holding, smelled something like Brie cheese, and belatedly noticed the shapeless mass nestled up against her.

She glanced down, to see four pale eyes looking at her. ♪It is well with you?♪ Sho asked.

♪Yes.♪ Brecken blinked, tried to clear her head. ♪I had a very strange dream.♪

The shoggoth was silent for a while, and then piped, ♪I also watched my dreams.♪

Brecken considered that. Something in Sho's tone made her wonder if her words had been rude, or otherwise crossed a line. After a moment, she paged through the lexicon to find a word, and asked: ♪Is it proper to talk about dreams?♪

♪Sometimes.♪ Sho regarded Brecken for a time, then asked, ♪What did you dream?♪

♪*I dreamed that I stood a little away from us and watched the two of us. And then—*♪ She reached for the lexicon, and found no help there. ♪*I don't know the words to talk about what happened then. There were things that scared me, and then I—*♪ There was no word for "wake up" in Chalmers' notes. ♪*I stopped dreaming.*♪

Two more eyes blinked open in surprise. ♪*You stop dreaming?*♪ ♪*Yes, of course.*♪ Then, catching herself: ♪*You don't?*♪

♪*No. How could I?*♪ Lacking a face, Sho didn't have an expression to change, but the positions of her eyes shifted in a way that hinted at second thoughts. ♪*But you do. How strange.*♪

♪*What were you dreaming just now?*♪ Brecken asked.

Sho considered her, and then said, ♪*I had a strong dream. I dreamed of the dweller in darkness, of—*♪ She piped a complex trill that Brecken found oddly familiar, though she couldn't remember why. ♪*He spoke to me in my dream, and that has not happened before now. He spoke one word, and that was 'abide.'*♪ She huddled down. ♪*You have said I may hide here.*♪

♪*And I mean it,*♪ said Brecken. ♪*As long as you need to.*♪
♪*Then I will abide.*♪

Just then a low buzz sounded from inside Brecken's purse. She glanced at it, startled, and then realized that she'd forgotten to turn the cell phone off vibrate after her flute lesson the day before. With a frustrated sigh, she pulled out the phone, woke it, and gave it a dismayed look once the screen came on. It was past one o'clock, and her music education class was long over.

♪*That thing talks to you,*♪ said Sho.

♪*Yes.*♪ She checked messages, found nothing of importance but two texts from Rosalie, one from the evening before apologizing for the way the study session had ended, the other just moments old hoping she was all right. M OK C U @ R&T 2MRO, she texted back, and then put the phone to sleep and returned it to her purse. ♪*Right now it says that I don't have to go anywhere until the light goes and comes back.*♪

♪I am glad,♪ said Sho.

Brecken gave the shoggoth a long considering look. ♪Before you came here,♪ she guessed, ♪you spent your time close to others, the way we are now.♪

♪Yes. It is—it was our way.♪ In a hushed piping: ♪In all my life I had never been alone and unsheltered so long.♪ A moment passed, and then Sho went on. ♪I have seen you dreaming alone. Do all your people do that?♪

Flustered by the thought that Sho had watched her sleeping, Brecken fumbled with the lexicon. ♪No. Sometimes. It's—complicated.♪

♪I understand. There are customs.♪

♪Yes, exactly.♪

♪Then I am glad those allowed you to comfort me.♪

Brecken blushed. The shoggoth considered her for a long silent moment.

♪When you drew me to you earlier,♪ said Sho then, ♪I was afraid that—that you meant to trap me somehow.♪ A little shudder reminded Brecken of a choked laugh. ♪Though you could have done it many times before then. I thought of fleeing from this place, but I could not bear it. I so badly needed the comfort you offered me. So I resolved that if you meant me to die, I would die.♪ Brecken gave her an appalled look and opened her mouth to speak, but the shoggoth went on. ♪And then you went over onto the dreaming-side with me, and showed me that my fears were empty. I do not understand why you are so kind to me but—but I am grateful.♪

Donna's scornful words about strays from the day before suddenly lost most of their sting. ♪It is a thing I do,♪ she whistled. ♪Sometimes my people—♪ She couldn't think of any way to say "laugh at me," and reached for the lexicon. ♪—think me foolish because I wish to be kind.♪

♪They are wrong.♪ Sho's whistle was harsh. ♪Wrong and cruel.♪ She considered the photocopies in Brecken's hand, then, and asked, ♪Is that—♪ She used a word Brecken didn't know, and it took a few minutes of discussion before Brecken was sure that the word meant "writing." ♪*Yes,*♪ she whistled, and handed Sho the top sheet of the lexicon.

The shoggoth took it neatly in a two-pronged pseudopod, considered it with half a dozen eyes. ♪*Strange.*♪ After a moment: ♪*Is there something proper for writing?*♪

Guessing at her meaning, Brecken got out a notebook, opened it to a blank page, handed it to Sho. Another pseudopod took it, and then a third brushed across the paper. Where it passed, dots of some black fluid formed neat groups on the paper, dried quickly into hard glossy marks.

♪*That is my name today,*♪ she said.

Brecken considered the dots, then picked up a pen and wrote her own first name underneath them. ♪*And that is the name I always have,*♪ she whistled, and spoke it: "Brecken."

Sho pondered that, opened a speaking orifice, and tried to pronounce it, producing a gurgling whistle with a click in the middle. ♪*I cannot say it properly,*♪ she whistled.

♪*I would not be able to say your name if I did not—*♪ Brecken couldn't find a phrase for "play music" in the lexicon.

♪*I understand,*♪ said Sho. ♪*I have heard you singing with the long bright thing, and with the dark thing with many voices, and a few times I watched you.*♪ A silence passed. ♪*That was another reason I did not want to flee from this place. When you sing with the long bright thing it is like voices, like my people speaking. I hope you will do that again.*♪

♪*In a little while, yes,*♪ said Brecken. There was nothing in the lexicon that told her how to say "Friday afternoons," but she did her best. ♪*There are times when the light fades, when I sing with the long bright thing. The songs are special songs, for one who is dead.*♪

That got her a wide-eyed look, and then all at once Sho slumped and huddled against her, as though some last defense had given way. ♪*I am glad,*♪ said the shoggoth. ♪*If you sing for your dead as my people did, there cannot be so very great a difference*♪

between us.♪ In a low unsteady whistle: *♪Someday I will sing for mine. It is still too close now. But—someday.♪*

* * *

Singing for the dead, Brecken thought. If only it were so simple.

She got her music stand set up near the piano, assembled her flute, gave the angle of the mouthpiece a critical look and adjusted it fractionally. The score for Telemann's Fantasia #8 in E minor went on the stand. Then, the thing that set Friday afternoons apart from all the other times she played her flute: a photo in a dark wooden frame. She got it out of the top drawer of the dresser, propped it atop the piano. From within the frame, a face looked out—a plump middle-aged woman with light skin, graying black hair, thick glasses, a wistful smile.

All the while, a shapeless black thing with pale temporary eyes sat on the futon, watched her with an attentive silence that made Brecken think of the one time she'd watched a Japanese tea ceremony. She didn't usually like to have people listen to her on Friday afternoons, but there were exceptions, and she'd begun to suspect that Sho might be one of the exceptions.

She picked up the flute, played a Taffanel and Gaubert exercise. The notes rippled through the air, awakening memories. That finished, she started the Telemann piece, played it once for precision, once for interpretation, once to let the music flow the way it wanted to flow.

Mrs. Macallan, she thought. Patricia Lynn Macallan: that was her full name, though Brecken had never once called her that while she was alive.

She'd met her that first day at Oakmont Middle School, as September began to gild the leaves of the woods around Woodfield. The bell rang for sixth period; Brecken filed into the girls' gymnasium with the others, clutching a case that contained a well-used but serviceable flute bought at a pawnshop, giving her classmates uncertain looks. Then Mrs. Macallan came bustling in, greeted them all, settled them in groups by instrument, and got them warming up. Harsh echoes came down from the ceiling—the gym had dismal acoustics—but Mrs. Macallan's ready smile and encouraging words made that easier to tolerate.

Over the weeks that followed, as they stumbled through simple tunes, Mrs. Macallan sorted out the few who had an interest in music from the many who were there because their parents wanted them there, or for any of a dozen other empty reasons. The few got lessons before and after school; Brecken and an eighth grader who also played the flute had Friday afternoons.

At the end of that first year, the eighth grader moved on to Lincoln High, and for the next two years Friday afternoons were Brecken's alone. Mrs. Macallan was also a flautist, and she had a gorgeous silver flute, a Powell good enough for the concert stage. When Brecken proved to have talent for music as well as a passion for it, Mrs. Macallan lavished time on her, guiding her through exercise after exercise and piece after piece, until by Brecken's eighth grade year they were playing works by the classical masters.

During those three years Brecken caught some of Mrs. Macallan's love of teaching music, watched the way her face lit up when a student got past the labor of performance to the music itself, or when the band momentarily stopped being eighteen or twenty-one separate schoolchildren fumbling at their instruments and became a unity that could play a phrase or a passage so that it meant something. During those same three years, though, she also came to know the precariousness of Mrs. Macallan's lonely crusade. To the Woodfield Consolidated School District, nothing mattered but money and standardized test scores, and so year after year, more programs were cut, more teachers laid off. The last two art teachers at Oakmont were packed off at the end of Brecken's sixth grade year, and everyone knew that music was next.

Word finally came, in the last weeks of her eighth grade year, that all funding for middle school music had been cut: to pay for improvements in general education, the press release said, but the local paper slipped and let on that the money would go instead to cover yet another hefty raise for the district administrator and her staff. The last day of school that year was a Friday. Brecken and Mrs. Macallan met in the band room after everyone else had gone home, went through two Taffanel and Gaubert exercises, and then played Mozart's flute concerto in D major, Brecken on flute and Mrs. Macallan on piano. They'd been working on it all year, and it had finally started to come together in the last weeks before break.

Afterwards, they'd talked. "Don't you worry about me," Mrs. Macallan said, with the wistful smile Brecken knew so well. "I'll be fine. I've already got something lined up—and I have a special gift I want to give you, since you've worked so very hard these last three years." Then she'd handed over the Powell flute, which Brecken had loved helplessly since her first weeks in middle school. To Brecken's stammered protests, she'd smiled again and said, "No, I mean it. It should be yours, because I know you'll play it the way it should be played. I'll tell you a secret—I'm going to be getting an even better instrument soon."

So Brecken burst into tears, and they hugged, and Brecken went home with the Powell flute to pack for the trip to Trenton and one last summer with her grandparents before they moved into a senior home. She'd been with her grandparents eight days when a school friend, another of Mrs. Macallan's pupils, called to tell Brecken the news: after that last day of school, Mrs. Macallan had gone home, put an old vinyl record of Bach's Brandenburg concertos on the stereo, climbed into a warm bath, and slit both her wrists.

That was the summer when Brecken's world turned upside down: when she came back from an afternoon with friends to find her grandparents waiting for her with shocked solemn looks on their faces, bracing themselves to tell her that her mother had been arrested and would probably spend a very long time behind bars; when she sat through family conferences on the phone and in person, before everyone decided that she'd move in with her Aunt Mary and Uncle Jim up in Harrisonville for the four years until her high school graduation; when she found out, a few weeks before she went to Harrisonville and her grandparents moved into the senior home, that all the things she'd left behind in Woodfield— everything she owned but her summer clothes, a few trinkets, a few CDs, a stack of sheet music, and the Powell flute—had been seized by the county as drug-related property and was gone for good.

All that was public, right out in front of family members and friends. Her grief for Mrs. Macallan was not. All she let any of them know about her Friday afternoons was that she needed time to practice. Then the door would click shut, the flute and music stand and music would come out, and she'd spend two or three hours playing the most exacting pieces she could handle, driving herself hard, until exhaustion finally told her she'd done enough that day.

Exhaustion hadn't yet arrived when she finished the Telemann piece for the third time. She played two etudes from Rubank's *Selected Studies*, working on details of technique her flute teacher had pointed out the evening before, and then put something really challenging on the music stand: Bach's Partita in A minor for solo flute. The cascading sixteenth notes and the wickedly complex fingerings demanded every bit of her musicianship, but after a year and a half of hard work she could play it creditably. After the fourth pass through, though, Brecken's shoulders had begun to cramp from the sheer intensity of her effort, and her fingers felt like lead. She put the flute down, cleaned it and put it in its case, stowed Mrs. Macallan's picture in the top drawer of her dresser, and then stumbled over to the futon to sit down.

Pale green eyes looked up at her. ♪*Has much time passed?*♪ Sho asked.

It took Brecken a moment to figure out what she meant, and a glance at the lexicon turned up no way to talk about numbers. ♪*Yes, it has been summers since she died.*♪

♪*And you sing for her still.*♪

♪*It still hurts,*♪ Brecken said.

Sho regarded her for a time, then flowed a pair of pseudopods around her, squeezed. It took Brecken a moment to recognize the gesture as an imitation of the hug she'd given the shoggoth earlier that day. ♪*Thank you,*♪ she whistled, and returned the hug.

* * *

Later that afternoon, Brecken got out her music education homework, and Sho settled down next to her with a quilt pulled over most of her to make her feel sheltered. The shoggoth's eyes rose and sank more slowly, and Brecken guessed that she had—what was the phrase?—gone onto the dreaming-side. A slow rippling moved through Sho's body, setting faint prismatic patterns of color flowing across her outer layer, and Brecken watched her for a time and tried to remember why she'd thought the shoggoth looked hideous the first time she'd seen her.

Sho didn't look hideous at all, Brecken thought; she looked fragile, like something made of living glass. Then she stifled a laugh, realizing that it was her own attitude that had shifted. Don't get between Brecken and her strays, she thought. The words had changed from stinging to comfortable, a simple statement of fact.

She opened the textbook, tried to make sense of the stilted academic prose and the empty abstractions that claimed to have something to do with the raw reality of people learning music, and had just begun taking notes when a knock sounded at the door. Six of Sho's eyes popped open at once. Brecken, startled, had the presence of mind to whistle ♪hide!♪ in a low tone. She had almost forgotten how fast the shoggoth could move; before Brecken could get up from the futon, an iridescent black blur flung itself into the kitchen and vanished down under the sink.

Once she was sure Sho was out of sight, she went to the door and opened it. Mrs. Dalzell stood outside, and just behind her was a middle-aged man with a military haircut and a genial smile, dressed in a nondescript jacket and slacks, and holding an equally nondescript tablet in one hand. "Oh, good afternoon, Brecken," Mrs. Dalzell said. "I was hoping you'd be in. This is Mr. Metzner from the state animal control office."

He put his hand out, and Brecken shook it. "John Metzner," he said. "Pleased to meet you." She said something polite, but by then Mrs. Dalzell was talking again: "Do you remember what day it was that those wretched raccoons got into the trash?"

Brecken thought for a moment. "The night of the seventh," she said. "Remember how I came out and found you cleaning up the mess? That was last Monday morning, so it had to be the eighth, and the raccoons did their thing the night before."

"Oh, of course," said Mrs. Dalzell, blinking. "How could I have forgotten? Of course you're right, because I went to visit my cousin Della that afternoon."

"Did you smell anything unusual around the yard then or later?" Metzner asked.

"No, nothing," Brecken replied. "Well, unless tomcat pee counts as unusual."

Mrs. Dalzell choked, and began to laugh. Metzner nodded, thanked them both, headed back to the street and then to the next house on the block. Brecken managed to detach herself from Mrs. Dalzell's further chatter without too much difficulty, and went back inside.

The moment she closed the door she blinked and shook her head. It hadn't been the seventh at all, she realized. Thunder had rolled over Hob's Hill on the night of the fourteenth, and the trash cans had been disturbed the morning of the fifteenth, but somehow her memory had insisted otherwise with perfect certainty for those few minutes when the man from the state animal control office was asking about it. Nor could she remember ever having smelled tomcat urine around the converted garage. The only smell that she recalled, in fact, was the one around the trash cans that same morning—

That was when it occurred to her that she had never heard anyone mention a New Jersey state animal control office before.

Cold fear gripped her. If people were hunting for Sho, trying to find her and kill her, it made sense that they would pretend to be doing something more ordinary, like tracking raccoons. What didn't make sense is that something had made her and Mrs. Dalzell both remember the wrong date and the wrong smell, and say exactly the right things to cover Sho's trail.

After a little while, she glanced through a gap in the window shades, made sure neither Mrs. Dalzell nor John Metzner were anywhere nearby, and went into the kitchen. ♪Leaf On Wet Stone,♪ she whistled. ♪They have gone.♪

After a moment of silence and another moment of low rustling noises, Sho flowed part of herself up through the gap in the boards. ♪It is well?♪

♪Yes, but something really strange happened.♪

They got settled on the futon again, and Brecken tried to explain the way her memories had suddenly lied to her and just as suddenly told the truth again. Sho watched her with three eyes, then four, then five. Finally, when Brecken was done, she said, ♪I think I understand. The one who told me to abide, the dweller in darkness, he has such powers. I do not know why he chooses to protect me, but I am grateful.♪ In a low, shaken whistle: ♪I do not wish to burn.♪

♪*I don't wish you to burn either,*♪ Brecken whistled in reply. ♪*I don't know what it'll take to keep you safe, but I'll do whatever I can.*♪

♪*You are so very kind to me,*♪ said Sho. ♪*And the dweller in darkness may help you.*♪

That was when Brecken finally remembered where she'd read about a dweller in darkness before: remembered, too, the name Halpin Chalmers had used for that strange being. "Nyogtha," she said aloud.

♪*Yes,*♪ said Sho, and repeated the same trill she'd used earlier when she'd spoken about her dream. It sounded, Brecken thought, uncannily like the name "Nyogtha" spoken aloud. Then, in a low tone: ♪*I do not know if he will protect you. There is a pact between him and my people; he has aided us and we have served him for ages of ages, but I do not know if your people have ever had dealings with him. I hope he will protect you, but I do not know.*♪

* * *

Except for the fact that she had a shoggoth for company, the evening that followed could have belonged to any other Friday since Brecken moved into the little converted garage at the start of the semester. She put another hour into piano practice and several more into studying for her classes, wrestling with the assigned readings for Intro to Music Education I until the haze of abstractions made her head hurt. Dinner was a welcome relief; she made mashed potatoes from scratch, a chicken gravy to go over them, and buttered carrots on the side, all the while carrying on a whistled conversation with Sho. They ate sitting on the floor as before, and Sho's simple words of praise—♪*It is very good*♪—made Brecken blush. Afterwards she got out her copy of *The Secret Watcher* and read through everything she could find in it about shoggoths, until she was ready for sleep and Sho slid away to the kitchen and vanished into the crawlspace below.

The next morning, again with the obvious exception, was an ordinary Saturday morning. After breakfast, Sho sat on the carpet watching as Brecken packed her tote bag with music, a folding music stand, and her flute. ♪*I'm going to sing with others of my people,*♪ she explained to the shoggoth. ♪*We do this often. This time I'll be late—I won't get back until long after dark. I hope you won't get hungry before then.*♪

♪*I am well fed,*♪ Sho piped in response. ♪*You are very kind, but it will be well with me. I will go to the dreaming-side and wait below until you call.*♪

♪*That's a good plan.*♪ Brecken shrugged on her coat. ♪*Be careful.*♪ A few moments later she was out the door, heading for Danforth Street beneath a cloudy sky. From there it was an easy walk to the Student Union Building on campus, a sprawling irregular shape of brick and concrete with windows poking out of it at intervals. As she neared it, it occurred to her that the building looked a little like a shoggoth, with the windows for eyes; the thought amused her.

Through the main entrance, down the stair, along a corridor to a door near the far end marked DEBATE CLUB, which was what the room held when it wasn't being rented out by the club as practice space: she'd been that way so often that she scarcely noticed the route. Beyond the door, a long rambling space held bookcases full of reference works, and past that was a big open room with two antique oak desks on one side and a rack of equally well-aged folding chairs on the other; between them, most of Rose and Thorn Ensemble were busy getting instruments in tune. Brecken crossed to the nearer desk, fielded greetings from other members of the group, pulled out a stack of sheet music and started sorting it.

"Breck?" Donna crossed the room, gave her a wary look. "I want to apologize."

"It's okay," Brecken told her, not meeting her eyes.

"No, I mean it. I got way out of line—and I didn't know about your folks."

Brecken looked up, and nodded. Then, seeing the expression on Donna's face: "Ro ripped you a new one?"

That got her a sharp little laugh. "You better believe it." The laughter guttered. "But I mean it, about your folks. I can't imagine what it would be like, not to have family around."

"I've got an aunt and uncle in Harrisonville."

"Well, that's something. Still—I'm sorry."

Brecken met her gaze then. "Seriously, it's okay." Donna nodded, managed a taut smile, and went back to her violin.

A glance that way showed Rosalie busy with the tuning wrench, getting her harp ready. On one side of her, Jamal Williams, lean and dark, shaved head making a nice contrast with a fine Mephistophelean goatee, had his violin already tuned and balanced it negligently on his arm. On the other Walt Gardner, a big rawboned farm kid with wheat-colored hair and watery blue eyes who came from some little town a stone's throw from Pennsylvania, fussed with his cello.

Then the door clattered shut. Brecken turned and put on a smile for Jay: he was always the last one there and always shut the door when he arrived. "Hi, Breck," he said. "Hi, everybody." He fielded their greetings, crossed to the desk, let Brecken kiss his cheek and then put down his viola next to her flute. "Good to go?"

"Waiting for you, boss man," said Jamal.

Jay grinned. "The wait is over." He turned to Brecken. "Anything new?"

"Of course." She handed him a stack of pages, which he glanced over.

"Sweet," he said. "Okay, listen up. I've confirmed next Sunday, eleven o'clock at the Belknap Creek Mall. I've got five gigs lined up for winter break, and I'll have more by the time we get there—I'll send a schedule around as soon as I get a couple of details set. Today we need to work on the playlist for Sunday, but we need to get going on the holiday stuff too."

"Kill me now," said Donna.

"People love those," Jay told her. "You want to make it in music, you've got to give people what they want." He got his viola out and started to tune it, while Brecken retrieved the sheet music and handed each of the others their packets.

Finally everyone was tuned up, and Jay said, "Okay, first up Sunday is Pachelbel. Ready? Rosalie, start when you're good."

She grinned. "I'm always good."

A moment's pause, and then she began playing her harp, setting up the steady rhythmic pattern that underlay Pachelbel's Canon in D. Walt started in after the second measure, Donna after the fourth, and the others followed in turn, weaving a fabric of sound out of the threads Pachelbel had set out for them. Before long Brecken and Jamal were passing the melody line back and forth over the steady rhythm of Rosalie's harp and the bass line of Walt's cello, with Donna and Jay filling in the harmonies between, acting out the dance of tonality, moving around the tonic note that gave direction and meaning to the whole. The piece was familiar enough that Brecken could watch Jay's face as he played, and see him frowning slightly with the effort, all pretense pushed aside; it was at such moments that she loved him most.

The Canon wound up crisply, and Jay grinned again and said, unnecessarily, "Great." They went straight into the next piece, a Bach minuet. That went almost as well, and so did the one that followed. They had to work harder on the fourth piece, a tough Vivaldi selection, but three passes through got the rough edges off, and then it was on to the next piece of music.

They put a good two and a half hours into the practice session, going on to sight-read Brecken's new arrangements once the playlist for the upcoming gig was finished, and finishing up with a couple of familiar pieces, "Jesu Joy of Man's Desiring" and "O Holy Night," which everyone but Donna had played together the year before. By that time even Walt, who had the stamina of a bulldozer, was ready to call it quits.

"Are you free tonight?" Rosalie asked Brecken. "It's dance night at Admiral Benbow's, and the rest of the night has strawberry daquiris and tacky videos written all over it."

"I've got plans," Brecken told her. "But thanks." It was true that she had plans—off past Rosalie's shoulder, Jay caught Brecken's gaze and grinned—but there was also the little matter of the twenty dollar cover charge at Admiral Benbow's, which was rather more than her budget would cover now that she had a shoggoth to feed.

"Anybody else?" said Rosalie then.

"I wish." Donna finished putting her violin away. "Way too much reading to get done before class on Monday." Walt mumbled something along the same lines, and Jamal simply gave her a wry look and went over to the coatrack on the far side of the room, where he'd stashed his coat and the black driving cap he usually wore.

Rosalie rolled her eyes. "Okay, whatever. See you all soon." She bundled up in a loud red ruana, shook her braids free, got the strap on her harp case settled over one shoulder, and headed out the door. After she left, Jamal came back from the coatrack and glanced toward the door. "Poor little rich girl," he said. "She doesn't have a clue."

Brecken sent a sulfurous look his way. He met her gaze squarely, and after a moment she looked away, nodded unwillingly, and put her flute case into her tote bag.

She and Jay left the Student Union Building together a few minutes later, went to his apartment long enough to get their instruments safely stowed out of the cold, and then headed out again and prowled the charity shops on Dexter Street, where he frowned over old books and bought three. Then they headed for the grocery and returned to his apartment, where Brecken fixed beef stroganoff and green salad for the two of them, and after dinner let him lead her again to his unmade bed. She left him sleeping as usual, picked her way as quietly as she could out of the apartment and down the stairs to the street, huddled into her coat against the cold as she hurried over to Prospect Street. Their lovemaking left her feeling emptier than usual, and not even thinking about music shook the bleak mood that followed her all the way home.

The apartment seemed smaller and shoddier than ever when she let herself in and turned on the light. She put down the tote bag, took off her coat and hat, slumped on the futon, and then remembered her uncanny guest. After a moment of indecision, she dragged herself to her feet, went into the kitchenette, and whistled down into the space beneath the sink, using the shoggoth's latest name: ♪Far From Home? I'm back.♪

A long silence followed, and Brecken felt a sudden pang of dismay. Had Sho gone somewhere else, she wondered—or had the man who called himself John Metzner tracked her to her hiding place after all? Then, muffled by the floor, a quiet whistle sounded: ♪I am glad♪. When Sho flowed up through the gap in the flooring, Brecken felt a little less empty. The little rituals of the evening, as she fixed the shoggoth mac and cheese for dinner, brewed a cup of herb tea for herself, put in an hour of hard piano practice, and studied until her eyelids drooped, seemed a little less pointless in Sho's presence.

Me and my strays, she thought. Well, why not? I'm kind of a stray myself. That cheered her as she settled down under the quilts and drifted off to sleep, into dreams where shoggoths and strange angles gave way to utter darkness, and to whispered words she could not recall when morning came.

CHAPTER 5

A SOURCE OF SANCTUARY

nless she had a gig to play, Sundays were quiet days for Brecken. Church had been an occasional thing in her childhood, and once she'd heard the news about Mrs. Macallan she'd never gone back, despite her grandmother's attempts to attract her to the Ebenezer Baptist Church in Trenton, and Uncle Jim's less subtle efforts to talk her into going to St. Mark's Episcopal Church in Harrisonville. Even so, some dim sense of sanctity still clung to the day. Every Sunday morning she set aside whatever music she was practicing for lessons or classes or Rose and Thorn, and played pieces by her favorite Baroque composers for hours at a stretch; every Sunday afternoon she wrote a letter to her mother, who (so the prison chaplain wrote to Brecken) rarely got any other mail; and only when evening arrived did Brecken leave the quiet hours behind and get back to work on her classes and her assigned music. It was appropriate, she thought later, that it was on a Sunday that she learned what had happened to Sho's people.

While Brecken practiced, Sho listened in attentive silence— ♪It is very pleasant,♪ she'd piped later, ♪like voices at a distance♪— and slipped over onto the dreaming-side when Brecken settled down to write her weekly letter. When she was mostly done with the letter, Brecken glanced at the shoggoth, watched pale eyes surface one at a time, unseeing, and sink back down again.

I've made a new friend, she wrote, *a girl about my age, very shy, who goes by the nickname Sho. She's been through some hard times recently. We like the same kind of music, and I think we'll be seeing a lot of each other from now on.* She wrote a few more sentences about other things, then signed the letter, slipped away from Sho as gently as she could, got up from the futon and fetched stamp and envelope. As she settled back down on the futon, though, a convulsive shudder went through Sho, and four eyes blinked open at once.

♪*It is well with you?*♪ Brecken asked.

♪*Yes. No.*♪ The eyes focused on Brecken, though it took a few moments. ♪*I dreamed about—about what happened—about how my people died.*♪

♪*I'm sorry.*♪

♪*It is necessary. I—I cannot sing for them until I have dreamed of them, and—and it will take much dreaming.*♪

Brecken took that in, then gathered up all her courage, and asked, ♪*Would it help to talk about what happened?*♪

The shoggoth was silent for some minutes. ♪*Yes,*♪ she said finally. ♪*I wish another to know.*♪ Pale eyes looked up at Brecken, then closed, and another silence passed.

♪*It was a day like others,*♪ Sho piped then. ♪*It was cold and there was little food, so we were all in the place we called the low chamber, well inside the hill, where warmth rose up from within the earth. Most were far over on the dreaming side, but I could not be still. I do not know why. I slid out from among my broodmates and the others and went to a place I knew, where a pool of water gathered and then flowed away through a gap in the stone.*♪

♪*I stayed there for a time, though it was warmer in the low chamber. Before I thought of going back, I heard a sound I had never heard before, once and then again, like this.*♪ Her speech-orifice managed a fair imitation of the rumbling of thunder, or the sound of a distant explosion. ♪*I did not know what it was, and I started back to the low chamber to ask my broodmother and the elders. I heard voices, though I could not tell what they said. And then—*♪

She began to tremble violently, and a sharp scent tinged the air around her. Brecken, guessing what she was feeling, put her arms around the shoggoth, and the trembling slowed.

♪Then I saw fire.♪ Sho's whistle was low and edged with dread. ♪I heard the sound again, and mixed with it, voices of my people as they died. I—I heard my—my broodmother cry out, 'Broodlings, flee!' and then her—her—her—♪ She could not go on. Brecken closed her eyes, waited for the next words.

♪Her voice became the shriek of one who dies,♪ Sho said finally. ♪She—she burned then, I think. I fled because she told me to, and the only place I could flee was into the pool of water. Down below the water, by the gap in the stone, I found a hiding place, and I hid there and did not move. I could see the water above me and the cavern above that, a little. After a while I saw some of your people in the cavern. I thought they were looking for me, to burn me, and so I was very still until they went away. Then I slid through the gap at the bottom of the pool and followed the water down. I did not know where that led, but I wanted to find a safer place.

♪But the water took me to another opening, and that led outside the hill. I did not go out through it for a long time, because there were noises. After everything was quiet I went out, because I was hungry, and we gathered food from places around the hill sometimes. The place I came out was very close to this place, and I smelled the things outside that have food in them, and so I fed and then looked for a place to hide, and found it under this place.

♪I stayed on the dreaming-side all that day, for I had eaten little, and then once the dark came back I smelled the food you left, and I was very hungry, and I climbed up here and ate it. You came in suddenly and made it light, and I was sure you would kill me, but then you spoke to me and said you would not harm me. I was so frightened, I did not know what to think or what to do, so I fled and hid below, and—and you sang with the dark thing with many voices and then with the long bright thing, and then you made it dark and went to the dreaming-side, as though you wished me to know I did not need to fear you.

♪And I—♪ The whistled voice broke again. ♪I went back into the hill while you dreamed here. I hoped there might be others still alive, and—and I was wrong.♪ Her voice rose, shrill and shaking: ♪They had all burned, all of them, my broodmother and all my broodmates and all the others, from the eldest to the smallest broodling—♪

The whistle trailed off into silence. Brecken closed her eyes, tried not to think about what must have waited for Sho under Hob's Hill. Within the circle of her arms, Sho trembled.

♪Then I came back to this place,♪ Sho said finally. ♪I could not bear to stay in the hill, and there was no food, and you had spoken kindly to me. By the time I left the hill it was light already, and I was terrified, but I could not bear to stay in the hill, so I came here in the light beneath the empty sky and—and found that you had left food and water in the place where you had seen me. So I fed and drank, and hid again in the place below, and listened when you came back and sang again. And another day came, and again you left food and water. So I resolved that I would speak with you when you returned, and—and you—and you were kind to me. You have said that this is a thing you do, and I believe that, but I still wonder that I see these things waking and not dreaming.♪ She huddled down. ♪The rest you know.♪

A long silence passed by. ♪The dweller in darkness told me to abide here,♪ Sho said then, ♪and I will do that, but I am afraid that they will hurt you if they find me.♪

♪I know,♪ said Brecken. ♪But I couldn't live with myself if you left here and got caught.♪

The shoggoth considered her for a time. ♪Will you dwell in this place until you die?♪

The question took Brecken by surprise. ♪No,♪ she said after a moment. ♪But until summer, certainly, and maybe longer.♪

♪And when you leave—♪

♪We'll work out some way to keep you safe,♪ Brecken said. Later, thinking back, she realized that it was the first time she'd referred to herself and Sho as "we."

* * *

The elevator seemed to take longer than usual to rise to the top floor of Gurnard Hall. Rosalie chattered on, but Brecken couldn't keep track of what she was talking about for more than a few seconds at a time. She'd spent most of the evening before practicing the bourrée, even though she knew it by heart. When the elevator finally grumbled to a stop and the door lurched open, she followed Rosalie down the hall, clutching her tote bag as though it could shield her from the next fifty minutes of Composition I.

She sat down, reminded herself that it couldn't be worse than some of the wedding gigs she'd played, and glanced around. Julian Pinchbeck was already there, of course—she wondered from time to time if he slept in Gurnard Hall—and so was the girl with the pink hair: Molly, she reminded herself, and tried without success to call her last name to mind. She wondered where the other members and instruments of Molly's heavy metal band were, and then noticed that the case sitting next to her chair pretty clearly held an acoustic guitar. She sat back, let herself relax a little. The thought of trying to play her bourrée on the heels of five or ten minutes of heavily amplified headbanger music had been weighing on her more than a little.

The rest of the class trickled in and took their seats, and Professor Toomey came in, sat in his chair, glanced to one side, the other. "Good morning," he said. "We have quite a full playlist today, so we'll begin right away. One reminder—ten per cent of your grade is your comments on the student compositions you hear in this class. Anyone have any trouble finding the comment form on the class website? No? The first piece is 'Obsidian Ellipsoids' by Julian Pinchbeck. Julian, if you'd like to begin?"

As Julian stood, beamed, and went to the piano, Brecken woke her smartphone, accessed the class website, and tapped the button marked COMMENT FORM. The form came up, and she typed in the name of the piece, stumbling over the spelling of "ellipsoids." Be fair, she reminded herself. Just because you don't like postspectralism doesn't mean it can't be good.

Unfortunately for her resolve, it wasn't good. Julian played with stiff florid gestures, striking poses and tossing his head back from time to time, but the scattered notes, long silences, and occasional loud chords that made up the piece never quite managed to amount to anything but random noise. She bit her lip, typed in some comments she hoped would be helpful, then sat there listening and tried to think of something else to say. A few moments later Julian finished up with a loud diminished-ninth chord that set her teeth on edge.

She joined the polite applause as the piano fell silent and Julian went back to his seat. The professor said, "Next is 'Marty's Blues' by Molly Wolejko. Molly?"

Molly unfolded herself from her seat, took a well-used twelve-string guitar out of the case, pulled the piano bench away from the piano, and settled on it. The guitar nestled up to her like an old friend. She struck a minor chord, another, and then all at once launched into a driving twelve-bar blues tune. It wasn't classic blues, there were dissonances no old-time bluesman would have tolerated, but it spoke a musical language that wasn't too far from theirs. Brecken, who'd grown up hearing that language in her grandparents' house, closed her eyes and let herself bask in the tune for a verse and a half, then abruptly remembered that she had to comment on the piece and fumbled her way through a few sentences of praise as Molly wound it up.

The applause this time wasn't merely polite, and Professor Toomey's habitual bland expression had something like a smile playing at its edges. "Next," he said after the clapping died down, "is 'Bourrée in B flat' by Brecken Kendall. Brecken?"

She made herself leave her chair, started toward the piano, and then remembered that her music was still in her tote bag. Flustered, she retrieved it, got the bench back in place, steadied herself, and began to play.

The first few notes sounded tentative, but after that the habits she'd learned playing at badly planned weddings and shopping malls full of cranky children came to her rescue. The room and the people in it faded out of her awareness, and only the music remained, bright and elegant as sun on water. Twice through the first part, twice through the second, dancing around the tonic, the B flat into which it would all finally resolve, closing on a perfect cadence she'd managed to weave into a repetition of the opening phrase: then it was done, and she blinked, took her music and stood up.

The applause she got fell somewhere between polite and enthusiastic. Well over half of the students clapped dutifully, but it was the others that made Brecken falter as she turned away from the piano and start back to her seat. Some of them applauded with gusto; the thin brown-haired guy in back who'd brought up fugues a week before was one of those and so, to Brecken's considerable surprise, was Molly Wolejko. Then there were the ones who weren't clapping at all, those who gave her flat hard looks as she returned to her chair, or Julian Pinchbeck, who shot a venomous glance her way and then looked somewhere else.

The look that mattered, though, came from Professor Toomey. The bland expression was still there, but something deeper down contradicted it. His unreadable gaze caught hers, and he nodded his approval.

Brecken sat down in her chair and glanced at Rosalie, who was giving her an odd baffled look. That troubled her at least as much as the others, and she tried to concentrate on the student compositions that followed. There were two of them, one avant-garde jazz, one that would have made a good jingle for a chewing gum commercial. She listened to both and did her best to make some sort of helpful response on the comment form, and as the clock showed twenty past the hour and the class ended, she realized that she didn't remember a single detail of either one.

Two elevators were working, for a change, and so it was only a few minutes later that she and Rosalie stood in The Cave. "Coffee," Rosalie said in a fake-zombie voice. "Must have coffee." Then, in her own voice: "Maybe that'll get me through the next week. Come on." She led the way toward a double door in one wall, and Brecken followed.

A forgotten fashion in university planning had equipped half a dozen Partridgeville State buildings with coffee shops on the ground floor, and Gurnard Hall was one of them. With bare concrete walls, no windows, and hanging lamps splashing down a stark white glare from above, Vivaldi's had all the charm of a small-town morgue. Posters in aluminum frames on the walls, announcing such cultural happenings as Partridgeville could boast, contended with the bleakness of the café and lost. Even so, the place was crowded as Brecken and Rosalie got in line.

"That's probably not fair," Rosalie was saying. "It wasn't all bad."

"Molly Wolejko's piece was really good," Brecken replied.

Rosalie gave her another of the odd baffled looks. "So was yours, Breck. How come you never told me you write music?"

"That's the first tune I've ever written."

"Come on."

"Seriously. I've done a lot of arranging, you know that, but I never tried writing anything of my own before."

Rosalie made a skeptical noise in her throat. Before she could add anything to it, the customer in front of them got his coffee and headed elsewhere, and they went to the counter to place their orders. Just then Brecken noticed someone come into the café, spot her, turn sharply and leave. He was out of sight before she realized that it was Julian Pinchbeck, and he'd given her the same venomous look he'd turned her way in the classroom.

* * *

Water splashed from measuring cup to saucepan. Instant polenta followed it, guided by Brecken's practiced eye. Her grandmother's recipes called for grits, but stores in Partridgeville didn't carry them, so polenta it had to be. The water came to a boil; a few minutes of stirring with a wooden spoon followed, and then Brecken turned down the heat, plopped on the lid, and whistled, ♪*That will be ready to eat in a little while.*♪

♪*You are very kind,*♪ Sho replied. She still seemed startled when she said it.

For the second time in as many years, Brecken was getting to know a new roommate. That was how she ended up thinking of Sho's abrupt appearance in her life, and her impulsive decision to give the shoggoth the shelter and help she so obviously needed. Framing it in her mind alongside her year with Rosalie in Arbuckle Hall helped make the strangeness of it all a little easier to manage. The comparison had its own complexities, though, for Rosalie was careless, talkative, and brash, and Sho was none of those things.

One measure of the difference was that it took Brecken days of coaxing to get Sho to admit to likes and dislikes concerning food. Partly, Brecken guessed, that was politeness—shoggoths, or at least this shoggoth, seemed to have a strict if strange sense of propriety—and partly it was simple hunger. From scraps of information Sho let fall from time to time, Brecken gathered that food had been scarce under Hob's Hill for far longer than Sho had been alive. Finally, though, Sho admitted that she disliked strong bitter flavors, and that hot spices were painful for her to eat. Brecken adjusted her cooking accordingly.

Most of the other things she cooked met with an enthusiastic response, though it took a while for Sho to get used to different foods each day—Brecken guessed that the diet under Hob's Hill had been monotonous as well as sparse. Then there was cheese polenta, which Brecken made often because it was cheap and filling. The first time she served Sho a bowl of it, the shoggoth scooped up a little in a pseudopod and enfolded it as usual, and then stared at it with eight eyes, while a different scent, like freshly washed mushrooms, tinged the air. ♪*Is something wrong?*♪ Brecken asked, and Sho answered after a pause, ♪*No. It is good. It is—*♪ She flowed forward and engulfed it, then seemed to sink down in a daze. ♪*In all my life I have never fed on anything so good.*♪

♪*I can make more,*♪ Brecken said at once. Courtesy warred with craving, or so Brecken guessed, and finally Sho let out an unsteady whistle: ♪*Please?*♪ So the instant polenta came out of the cupboard again, and half an hour later Sho slumped on the futon next to Brecken, visibly lumpy with two not-yet-digested masses of cheese polenta inside, quivering slightly with sheer delight as she slowly absorbed both, and smelling distinctly of freshly washed mushrooms all the while. Brecken found the shoggoth's response amusing, but made sure that cheese polenta featured regularly in their meals thereafter.

Then there were the questions. One evening, as rain rolled in from the Atlantic and pattered hard against the glass, the two of them sat on the futon after dinner, and Sho asked, ♪*Why do you always give off heat?*♪ That took some explaining, and so did the questions that came out of Sho's difficulties understanding that human bodies had specific places for specific things— feet for walking, hands for grasping—and that Brecken had no choice but to see through the same eyes and speak through the same mouth all the time.

Another evening, when she'd gotten back late from another tryst with Jay, Sho startled her by piping, ♪*Why do you smell like someone else?*♪ Brecken blushed furiously, but realized that Sho had asked the question in all innocence, and found herself having to explain sex to a curious shoggoth. That proved to be a more awkward task than she'd expected, since sex with Jay had nothing to do with reproduction—the thought of having a child by him was unwelcome enough that she was even more careful than usual about her birth-control pills—and love wasn't a concept that translated straightforwardly into the language of shoggoths.

Then Sho said, ♪*I understand. It is like what is between broodmates.*♪ That confused things further, until Brecken asked enough questions to clarify that broodmates were members of the same litter, shoggoths who budded at the same time from the same broodmother. As they got that settled, Sho suddenly huddled down and piped an apology, and it took Brecken several more questions to figure out that there was something very private that some broodmates did, something that involved sharing moisture, and Sho hadn't known that humans did anything like that and hadn't meant to ask about something so personal.

Brecken had questions of her own, for that matter, and not all of them had simple answers. Once when they were sitting on the futon and Brecken had just finished reading a story by Philip Hastane, she asked Sho, ♪*This writing says your people are—wet. Moist.*♪

Sho huddled down. ♪*Is it wrong that I am not?*♪ Brecken reassured her, and after a little while the shoggoth said, ♪*I understand. The one who wrote that knew how we fight. I will show you.*♪ She flattened, spread out, produced a hollow like a shallow bowl on her upper surface, and a moment later a few drops of black fluid welled up there. The moment it appeared, Brecken's eyes started to burn, and a choking, fetid stench filled the air. Though the fluid seeped back into Sho a moment later and left no trace, Brecken had to make an effort not to burst into coughing.

♪*That is the moisture-of-war,*♪ said Sho. ♪*It harms most other beings. We cover ourselves with it when we fight. If only it kept us from burning—*♪ She started trembling again, and Brecken put an arm around the shoggoth, held her for a while until the trembling stopped and the bitter scent of grief faded. Later, Sho explained that there were other moistures as well, each with its own scent, but she seemed shy about them and Brecken decided not to push.

Alongside the questions and the complexities around meals, it took Brecken a while to get used to Sho's simple physical presence. She got the impression, from stray comments Sho made, that the shoggoths who'd lived under Hob's Hill spent much of their time in a wriggling communal heap, and so Sho's notion of appropriate personal space among friends involved as much close contact as circumstances allowed. That was unsettling in some ways, endearing in others—it reminded Brecken of a dog named Pepper, a big malamute who'd lived next door to her childhood home in Woodfield, who would climb onto any available lap, look up with adoring blue eyes, and whine piteously and squirm until you scratched behind her ears.

Sho didn't whine, piteously or otherwise. The one time she came close was the night when a thunderstorm broke over Partridgeville, not the rumbling out of a clear sky Brecken remembered from the night before Sho's arrival but the real thing: rain lashing down in sheets, wind howling in the trees, blue-white glare of the lightning stark and sudden against the windowshades, and then great rolling peals of thunder that shook the former garage the way a dog shakes a rat. They'd gotten Sho settled in the closet a few days before—the space down under the floor was getting soggy and chill as autumn wore on—and an hour or so after bedtime, when Brecken was lying awake and hoping she'd get some sleep that night, Sho slid through the gap under the closet door. She crept over to the futon, surrounded by the acrid odor of fear, and said in a shaking whistle, ♪I—I am sorry—I do not wish to trouble your dreaming—but—but—I am so frightened—♪

Brecken whistled ♪Of course you can dream here♪ and made room for her on the futon, and the shoggoth flowed up and huddled against her. She got the quilts settled over them both, put an arm around Sho, and settled down to rest as Sho's trembling slowed and then stopped, and the acrid smell gave way to the Brie-cheese scent of calm. To her surprise, even though the storm continued, Brecken fell asleep shortly thereafter, and woke up later than usual the next morning with sun streaming in through gaps in the blinds and her arm still curved around the shoggoth. Sho thanked her profusely as she blinked and sat up.

As breakfast cooked, Brecken thought about that, and about Pepper the malamute and other pets she'd known—Sho wasn't a pet, but that was the only interaction between species that seemed at all relevant. She also thought about her own sound sleep, for she was honest enough with herself to admit that Sho hadn't been the only one who'd taken comfort in their closeness.

Finally, over bowls of oatmeal, she asked Sho, ♪*Do you like to dream alone?*♪

Sho huddled down. ♪*No.*♪

♪*From now on you don't have to.*♪

♪*Your customs—*♪

♪*They will permit it,*♪ Brecken reassured her.

Sho huddled down even further. ♪*You are so very kind to me.*♪

♪*I slept better.*♪ They had worked out a shoggoth-phrase for the human custom of sleeping. ♪*So it is a kindness to us both.*♪ Sho seemed to ponder that for a long while.

That evening, when Brecken got back from her piano lesson, greeted Sho, and went to take care of the dishes, she found that everything in the sink looked as though it had been put through an industrial dishwasher, it was that clean. So did the sink, for that matter. ♪*I wished to be kind,*♪ Sho said as she turned, startled. ♪*I hope it was not a wrong thing.*♪

♪*Not at all,*♪ Brecken said. ♪*I thank you for it.*♪ She explained later that evening, as gently as she could, that clean dishes belonged in the cupboard, not the sink, and that was where they went thereafter. Over the days that followed, Sho watched her at such housecleaning as the apartment needed and then quietly took over each chore. The monthly water bill went down noticeably as a result. Brecken wondered from time to time what happened to the food scraps, dust, tangles of hair, and occasional spiders and centipedes that weren't there any more when Sho finished cleaning, and finally decided that she didn't want to know.

It wasn't the only thing she let pass. As day followed day and the world outside the little apartment became more and more difficult, her time at home with Sho, waking and sleeping, became one of the few sources of sanctuary Brecken could find.

* * *

The trouble began quietly enough, with the comments on her bourrée. Those had no names attached by the time Brecken got them, and she didn't know her classmates well enough to guess who was who, though Rosalie's ebullient encouragement was easy to pick out. There were precisely two that paid close attention to the music she'd written; one of them praised it with an enthusiasm that made Brecken blush, and the other offered suggestions on the harmonies she'd chosen that were so useful she copied them out by hand into her composition notebook. Most of the rest trotted out the kind of vague generalities that made it clear they knew little about Baroque music, though some of those at least mentioned that they'd enjoyed the piece.

It was the other comments that troubled her, because those never quite managed to get around to talking about her music itself. They criticized the bourrée not because she'd made this or that mistake, but simply because it was a bourrée. The old musical forms were dead, tonality was dead, nothing worthwhile could be said with them any more, they were all just arbitrary rules, music had moved on and Brecken needed to get out of the eighteenth century and join the twenty-first—they were all things she'd heard over and over again since her high school days, and the only answer she'd ever found to any of them was the simple fact that the old music made her heart leap and its up-to-date replacements didn't. By the time she finished reading through the comments she was feeling so demoralized that she emailed Professor Toomey to ask whether she'd been wrong to write a bourrée at all.

She got an email back early the following morning, encouraging her to come by his office, and so Tuesday morning, an hour before Composition I, she took the elevator to the sixth floor of Gurnard Hall and tapped on the door with his name beside it. The office inside was a cramped space with one window at the far end that stared across the plaza at the bleak gray mass of Mainwaring Hall. It was barely large enough for a desk, a few chairs, a few bookcases, and a well-used electronic keyboard up against one bare wall. The professor waved her to a seat and said, "Go ahead and leave the door open." Brecken gave him an uncertain look, but didn't argue.

"No, you didn't do anything wrong," he said once they were both seated. "But you're going to get that kind of pushback if you're going to follow the rules of tonality or use any of the older styles. These days an ambitious composer can't even risk doing the kind of thing that Murail or Lachenmann did, much less anything older. It's got to be new, new, new."

"Well, I'm not ambitious," said Brecken, "and I'm not really a composer. I'm on the music education track."

Toomey regarded her with his unreadable eyes. "Your bourrée," he said, "was the best original composition I've heard from an undergraduate in the last ten years."

Brecken blinked, and then stared, trying to find some way the professor's words could be saying something other than what they obviously said. Failing, she said, "Okay."

"I mean that quite seriously," said the professor. "Every year I get one or two students who copy Bach, Brahms, somebody else like that, and turn out nice third-rate imitation Bach or Brahms or whoever. That gets an A if it's a halfway decent job, because it means they've paid enough attention to be able to fake it. But you're not imitating anybody." He leaned forward. "Bach sounds like Bach, Brahms sounds like Brahms, their imitators sound like Bach or Brahms on a bad day if they're good, and like fake Bach or Brahms if they're not. Your bourrée doesn't sound like fake anything. I don't know for a fact that it sounds like Brecken Kendall, because it's the only composition of yours I've heard, but I'd put money on it." Sitting back in his chair again: "So don't be too quick to say you're not a composer. You just might surprise yourself."

That was encouraging, and as she headed down the stairs Brecken let herself daydream about being a composer, crafting concertos, gigues, and sarabandes for other musicians to play. The Cave brought her back to reality in a hurry, though. She got there a good half hour before composition class, and headed as usual for the table Rosalie habitually staked out. As she passed a little knot of students she recognized from Professor Toomey's class, though, one of them looked at her and made a loud comment about musical necrophilia. That stung, and it didn't help that someone else from the class—Mike Schau, a big blocky guy with yellow hair and ambitions as a classical pianist—came bustling over to lecture her in patronizing tones about how she'd wreck her chance at a career in music if she wasted her time on outworn musical forms. When she tried to explain that she was planning to teach and was only taking the composition class because it was on the required list, he broke in on her to tell her she wasn't listening, and then repeated what he'd already said; when she tried again, he got angry, insisted that he was just trying to help, and stalked away.

Composition class wasn't much better. There were five more student projects to take in and comment on. One of them was an astonishment and a delight to her, a three-voice fugue for piano, heavily influenced by Bach, by the thin young man who sat in the back row—Darren Wegener, the professor called him, and Brecken made a note of the name. The others included one painfully derivative rock guitar solo, one bland and cheerful little ditty that sounded like half the top-40 hits Brecken had ever heard, and two pretentious avant-garde pieces that succeeded at being original but failed to be anything else but dull.

The fugue fielded barely enough applause to be polite; all the others got more in sustained applause than Brecken's bourrée had. That left Brecken in a bleak mood. Though Rosalie picked up on that, told her not to let it get to her, and insisted loyally that the bourrée had been really good, the mood remained as Brecken crept back to her apartment that afternoon.

That was the way the whole week went: comments variously snide and stinging flung her way, and now and again lengthy diatribes from classmates who seemed to think it was their job to tell her how wrong she was. Puzzled and hurt at first, she settled quickly enough into a familiar numbness, trudged through the round of classes and lessons. Even Saturday's Rose and Thorn practice session did little to cheer her up. As the ensemble gave the playlist for the upcoming gig one last rehearsal, she found herself wondering whether she'd been stupid to think of writing new music in the old forms.

It didn't help that one of the lectures in The Fantastic in Literature that week jabbed the same sore spot from a different angle. "Eldritch," Professor Boley said, looking even more weary than usual. "You've seen that word over and over again in the stories you've read. The dictionary says it comes from Old English, *aelf*, elf, *ricce*, realm, elfland—but I think the etymologists are wrong this time. No, it's from *eald*, old, and *ricce*, realm, the old realm, or as some of our authors liked to say, the elder world."

Jay leaned forward, intent on the lecture. Brecken tried not to notice, because the smile she hated was all over his face at that moment. Off beyond him, sitting off by himself in the mostly empty room, she spotted a face she didn't want to see—Julian Pinchbeck's—gazing at Boley with a look of insufferable boredom. She looked away.

"The elder world," Boley repeated. "Most of the horrors our authors display to us come from the distant past. Most, not all. Some, like the fungi from Yuggoth, come through space rather than time. Some, like the Hounds of Tindalos, come from right outside our space-time continuum. But most of them? They're from the elder world, and that's why they scare us.

"We live in our little bubbles of time." For a moment the gleam of an old enthusiasm showed through the weariness. "Our personal memories go back a matter of decades. The collective memories of our institutions, a few centuries. Our recorded history, maybe five thousand years, barely an eyeblink in the vast cycles of the cosmos—and that's enough all by itself to challenge the notion that our lives are important in the overall scheme of things."

"If our own history challenges that notion, though, the elder world tramples it into the dust. That's why our authors borrowed that concept from the books they used as sources. They wanted us to feel the shock and horror of thinking that there are things on this planet that were here before our ancestors first crawled on land. They wanted us to feel the vertigo of time, to fear that what's past isn't really past and what's dead might not stay dead." He looked up from his notes. "Even though we know it's not true. Even though we know the past is over and done with and none of the things they wrote about are real."

Brecken kept her reaction off her face, but she wanted to huddle down the way Sho did when she was upset. What if that's not what I feel? she thought. What if knowing Sho's people were around before mine just makes me curious about what it was like back then?

And what if something that matters to me a lot is supposed to be past and dead?

The professor folded up his notes and packed them into a briefcase. Jay rolled his eyes, typed a note on his tablet. Past him, Julian still looked bored.

CHAPTER 6

THE THING THAT
SHOULD NOT BE

B recken went pelting out into the gray morning, climbed into the back seat of Rosalie's bright red Nissan, said the usual things to Rosalie and Donna as she buckled her seatbelt. The Nissan started moving again and whipped through a dubiously legal U-turn. A few minutes later it rattled down Dwight Street through Sunday traffic past strip malls and fast-food outlets, went straight where the entrance onto the highway turned right. Beyond that, a concrete bridge leapt the brown torrent of Belknap Creek, and beyond that the bland angular masses of the Belknap Creek Mall rose up against a sky dotted with clouds. It took a little searching, but Rosalie found the right entrance eventually, and they piled out of the car, got their instruments and other gear, and headed inside.

A third of the storefronts in the mall were closed, and old people walking for exercise outnumbered shoppers by two or three to one: no surprises there, Brecken thought, not with the economy as bad as it was. Still, the management company that ran the mall had a portable stage and a sound system set up in the central food court, between two square pools with fountains bubbling feebly in them. Nearby a stand held a placard announcing THE ROSE AND THORN ENSEMBLE in the kind of florid faux-antique typeface Rosalie liked to call "oldey worldey."

Loudspeakers in the ceiling spat out a number by some popular vocalist whose name Brecken didn't know, moaning about her feelings over a single unchanging chord and a drum track, as they set up their music stands and got their instruments ready. "That had better go away," Donna said with an irritable glance at the nearest loudspeaker, and Rosalie and Brecken gave each other wry looks; they'd had to play over the top of sky syrup more than once the year before. Jamal showed up a few minutes on, and then finally Jay and Walt arrived, along with a woman from the management company in a bright red jacket and skirt, who greeted them all with a forced cheerfulness that made her smile look like a grimace of pain. She hurried off to see to the recorded music, and a few minutes later it shut off in mid-moan.

"Ready?" Jay asked.

"Whenever you want, boss man," said Jamal. The others nodded, instruments at the ready, and Jay turned to Rosalie and gestured: you're on. A moment later the first notes of Pachelbel's Canon shimmered out through the atrium and spread through the mall.

As she began playing her part, Brecken watched the walkers and shoppers passing the food court. Most of them glanced toward the stage, some of them slowed or stopped, and a few changed course, found empty seats at the little two- and four-person tables around the food court, and settled down to listen. She could see the hunger in their faces, the longing for music that found the middle ground between the mindless and the incomprehensible, and let that longing flow into the breath she sent dancing over the mouthpiece of Mrs. Macallan's flute and the notes she shaped with her fingers. She half-turned to face Jamal, let herself enjoy the intensity of his concentration and drew that, too, into her playing.

The Canon wound down to its final chord, and then to silence. Applause rattled through the unquiet air. Jay, beaming, glanced at each of the others, made sure he had their attention, and nodded one, two, three. On the fourth nod, they began the Bach minuet. From then on it was one piece after another, one burst of applause after another, until the last bars of Beethoven's "Ode to Joy" rang out across the food court, and one last round of clapping, pleasantly loud, followed it.

All the while Brecken watched the small crowd that gathered around the little stage and the faces turned up toward hers, watching the ensemble, listening to the music. Once, to her great amusement, she spotted a gaggle of twelve-year-olds wearing t-shirts splashed with pop-band logos; they stood on the far side of one of the fountains, watching the performance with disgusted looks, and then left the food court. A little later, she spotted a familiar face—Mike Schau from the composition class—as he stopped briefly on the far side of the other pool, gave the ensemble a look of disbelief, turned and stalked away.

Toward the end, though, another familiar face appeared in the food court: Barbara Cormyn's. She came out of a nearby department store, listened to the music for a little while, then walked over and found an empty seat. Her face still had its look of perpetual surprise, but she sat there watching and listening for the rest of the performance. Only when the "Ode to Joy" wound up did she get up and walk away from the food court.

Brecken barely noticed her leave. As the music gave way to applause and then to silence around her, a few notes in "Ode to Joy" called up from memory similar notes in the sentence of shoggoth language that worked out to *we live beneath the ground*. Maybe it was the music she'd just played, maybe it was the rush she always got from seeing her own delight in music echoed in the faces of her listeners, but the notes had an intensity and color she hadn't heard in them before. She let them circle through her mind as she took her flute apart, cleaned it, and stowed it in its case. Only as she took down her music stand did she notice that she was quietly humming a second part that descended in quick soft steps as the shoggoth-sentence soared upwards, and rose back up again as it dropped again, dancing around the B flat where the two parts met. The effect delighted her, and she paused long enough to sketch out melody and harmony on the back of a scrap of paper before she finished packing her tote bag.

She went with the others to the exit, stopped just inside the doors so that Jay could thank them all and deal out cash: not much of it, not with a small fee divided six ways, but every dollar helped. A few minutes later she was out in the parking lot under a sky gone gray, with drops of rain splashing down on cars and asphalt alike; a few minutes after that she was curled up in Rosalie's back seat as the car dodged traffic along Dwight Street and rain drummed on the roof. All the while, melody and harmony contended in Brecken's mind, struggling toward something she could not yet grasp, tinged with the luminous state she'd come to think of, after the Yeats quote, as the condition of fire.

She blinked, then, realizing that the car had been stopped in front of Mrs. Dalzell's house for some moments. "Earth to Brecken?" Rosalie said, half turning to look back at her.

Brecken blushed. "Sorry," she said. "Working on a piece of music."

That got a sudden tense look from Rosalie that worried Brecken, and a little dubious sniff from Donna that annoyed her. She quelled the reactions, thanked them both, made the appropriate noises about seeing them the next day, and climbed out of the car.

The rain had started in earnest, pounding down with enough force to send spray rising from the sidewalk and rivulets of water streaming off the ends of the gutters. Brecken bent forward, clutched her tote bag against her chest, and ran for the door. Though she dashed through the gap between houses and got the door open as quickly as she could, she was good and wet by the time she got safely inside. While she greeted Sho, stripped to the skin, toweled off, shrugged on a flannel nightgown and a baggy sweater, got a can of chicken noodle soup heating on the stove, and hung her wet clothes on the shower rail to dry, the music waited.

Finally, though, the two of them were settled on the futon with a quilt spread impartially over Brecken's lap and roughly two-thirds of Sho, and all the words that needed saying had been said. As they sipped from mugs of hot soup, Brecken got her composing notebook out of a heap on the nearby endtable, found a blank page, and started writing down the music she'd held in her mind all that time.

At first she thought it might be another piece for piano, but the two parts called for two different voices, and the melody line wanted a quick bright flavor that only a flute could give it. Flute and piano? That felt right: a concerto for flute and piano, and what had come to her was the theme of the first movement, a lively allegretto piece. Note by note, she got the first half dozen measures of the flute score and a very rough outline of the piano accompaniment sketched out before she finally sat back and rubbed eyes that ached with the effort of concentration.

♪It is well with you?♪ Sho asked her.

♪More or less.♪ The phrase in the shoggoth language didn't mean that literally—it referred to a state of partial fluidity no human body could even attempt—but it was close enough. ♪I am making a song.♪

♪I understand. I will be silent while you do it.♪

Brecken gave her a startled look, then whistled, ♪I thank you.♪ Three pale eyes glanced up at her, and then drifted shut as Sho slid over onto the dreaming-side.

* * *

"Brecken," said Mrs. Dalzell, "do you have a moment? The most fascinating person just came by and I don't have the least idea what she's talking about."

Brecken stifled a laugh. "Sure," she said. "Can I put this in my apartment first?" She indicated her tote bag, crammed as usual with books, music, and her flute case. When Mrs. Dalzell agreed, she ducked between the houses, went into her apartment, whistled a quick greeting and an explanation to Sho, and then trotted back out, locking the door behind her.

It had not been a good day. She'd fielded two rude comments about dead music on the way through The Cave to meet Rosalie in the morning, and a third on the way out after her music education class. Rosalie had been her usual self, talking with even more enthusiasm than usual about her dream of making it as a professional musician, but Donna had been waspish, and when she'd met Jay he'd been distracted and curt, the way he so often was when his mind was on the strange books he studied. She pushed those thoughts aside, went to Mrs. Dalzell's kitchen door and let herself in.

"Oh, hi, Brecken," said Mrs. Dalzell, who was bustling around the kitchen. "Tea? Oh, good. This is—" She stopped in confusion, having evidently forgotten the name of her guest.

"Dr. Catherine Lehmann," said the woman who sat at the kitchen table. She wore bland professional clothing and had a bland professional face framed in bottle-blonde hair done in a bland professional style, with round rimless glasses tinted slightly blue providing an unexpected hint of character. "I'm with the Rutgers folklore program."

Brecken introduced herself and shook her hand. "I'm collecting accounts of local folklore associated with Hob's Hill," Dr. Lehmann went on. "It used to have quite the colorful reputation back in Colonial times, and I'm hoping to find out whether any of the old stories have survived. Maybe you know of something."

Brecken settled into another chair at the table in response to Mrs. Dalzell's gesture, shook her head. "I wish I did. What kind of stories, if you don't mind my asking?"

"Not at all." Lehmann put on a bland professional smile. "'Hob' is an old word for 'devil,' and the stories said that there were devils inside the hill—shapeless black devils."

A chill went down Brecken's spine as she realized what the folklorist was talking about. Mrs. Dalzell, coming over with a cup of tea, was a welcome distraction. Once she'd taken the cup and thanked her landlady for it, she decided to make sure. "That sounds like shoggoths."

The response came just a little too quickly. "I suppose it does. That's an odd bit of folklore, though. Where did you hear about shoggoths?"

"I'm taking a class on fantasy in literature this semester," Brecken said. "Professor Boley gave an entire lecture on them last month."

Lehmann nodded. Watching her, Brecken felt increasingly uneasy. There was something that didn't quite ring true about the folklorist—

If she was a folklorist at all. It suddenly occurred to Brecken that Lehmann, like the man who claimed to come from the state animal control office, might be with the people who'd brought fire and death into Hob's Hill. To cover the moment of shock that the recognition brought with it, she said, "You know what's really interesting? Boley said Lovecraft and the others got the idea from some local writer, I forget his name." She hadn't forgotten Halpin Chalmers' name for a moment, but she didn't want to let Lehmann know that. "I wonder if he could have heard about the old stories, and used them in his book." She forced a grin. "Thank you, Dr. Lehmann. You've just given me a topic for my paper for that class."

"I'm glad to hear that," said Lehmann, with a smile that looked as insincere as Brecken's felt. "But you haven't heard of any stories yourself?"

"No, unfortunately," Brecken said. "That would make an even better paper."

"I suppose it would." They exchanged a few other point-less sentences while the folklorist finished her tea, and then she got to her feet, gave them both business cards, asking them to contact her if they heard any stories about Hob's Hill. A few moments later she was on her way to the sidewalk. Brecken, finishing her own tea, watched through the window as Lehmann went to the next house and knocked on the door. Parked on the street in front of Mrs. Dalzell's house, she noted, sat a gray SUV with tinted windows.

Maybe, Brecken thought. Maybe Dr. Lehmann was telling the truth—but that wasn't a risk that seemed worth taking. She left Mrs. Dalzell's kitchen as soon as she could, went back to the apartment, and warned Sho in a low whistle about what had happened.

♪I understand,♪ the shoggoth said, ♪and I thank you for tell-ing me this. I will hide even more carefully.♪ Before dinner, Sho searched the closet and found a way to slide up into the space between roof and ceiling, where no one would be likely to find her without tearing the old garage apart. Brecken hoped that would be enough, but cold fear settled into her bones in the days that followed. It seemed all too likely to her that the people who'd killed the shoggoths under Hob's Hill were still looking for Sho.

* * *

"Our writers," said Professor Boley, "spent quite a bit of time talking about the essence of the fantastic—what it is that makes a weird story weird, what it is that puts the wonder in a tale of wonder. Let's talk about that a little."

Another day brought another round of classes, starting with a session of Intro to Music Education I that was mostly a briefing on the volunteer hours she'd be expected to put in soon at a school music program in the Partridgeville area. Professor Rohrbach prattled on for most of an hour about how the students would finally get to see how goal-oriented instruction worked in practice. Listening to him, Brecken found herself torn between curiosity and uneasiness.

After that she spent an hour in Hancock Library, and then went to Boley's class. There she sat next to Jay as usual and, as usual, wondered what he was thinking as he brooded over Boley's words or typed notes into his tablet. Finding no answers, she glanced at the other people in the class, and spotted Julian Pinchbeck again, still looking bored.

"Let's start with what Arthur Machen had to say about it," Boley went on. "The passage I have in mind is from 'The White People,' which Lovecraft considered Machen's best work. The two characters are using theological language—this is Machen, remember, theology's his default setting—and the subject is the nature of evil. Here's what he says."

Boley's voice took on, however briefly, the ringing tones of the storyteller as he quoted Machen. "'And what is sin?' said Cotgrave." The question hung in the still air of the classroom. "I think I must reply to your question by another. What would your feelings be, seriously, if your cat or your dog began to talk to you, and to dispute with you in human accents? You would be overwhelmed with horror. I am sure of it. And if the roses in your garden sang a weird song, you would go mad. And suppose the stones in the road began to swell and grow before your eyes, and the pebble you noticed at night had shot out stony blossoms in the morning? Well, these examples may give you some notion of what sin really is."

As Boley turned the page of his classroom notes and cleared his throat, Brecken pondered the reading, and found her feelings contradicting everything it said. No, she thought. That's wrong, just as wrong as the thing he said about the elder world. If a cat or a dog talked to me I'd be delighted, and a rosebush that sang would be my favorite rosebush in the whole world.

All at once she had to stifle a laugh, thinking of the raw absurdity of her situation. A shoggoth talked to me, she thought.

A real live shoggoth, not just a cat or a rosebush, and now we're friends, so Machen's just plain wrong. Then she remembered the people who'd killed the shoggoths of Hob's Hill, and realized that Machen's character wasn't unique. There really were people for whom something as wonderful as a talking cat or a singing rose was a horror that had to be destroyed. The thought sent a chill down her spine.

That evening, when she and Jay sat at the little table in his apartment with ravioli and cheap wine between them, she asked him, "What do you think of the quote from Arthur Machen Boley read today—the business about talking cats and singing roses being so scary?"

"Machen didn't have a clue," Jay said at once.

She gave him a delighted look. "That's what I thought."

"The man was a coward." Jay speared a ravioli with his fork, gestured with it. "I don't know, maybe he was okay in a fistfight or something, but not when it came to facing the world we actually live in. Talking cats, singing roses—" He made a rude noise in his throat. "Try shapeless horrors that already were here when our ancestors hadn't crawled on land yet."

"Shapeless horrors," said Brecken. "Like shoggoths."

That got her a sudden sharp look, and then a smile. "Exactly."

She considered that while sipping from her wineglass, wondered for the first time if she dared trust him with her secret. "Do you think shoggoths really exist?"

"Of course they exist." He speared another ravioli. "All these writers that Boley's been talking about, they didn't just make up the stuff in their stories. They borrowed it from other writers, people who knew what they were talking about."

"People like Halpin Chalmers," Brecken ventured.

He gave her another sharp look, then nodded. "Good. You've been paying more attention than I thought. Yeah, Chalmers was really into this stuff. Did you know they have a copy of his book *The Secret Watcher* in the special collections at Hancock Library? I've read it."

Light dawned. "That's what your studies are about."

"Yeah. My real studies, not the crap the professors teach." He leaned forward, and the smile she hated, the one he'd had the night he bought the book at Buzzy's, twisted his face. "Think about what it would be like if you could summon a creature of the elder world—let's say a shoggoth—and command it. Use it. Make it a vessel for your will."

Brecken kept her smile fixed on her face, but it took an effort. "What if you just wanted to talk with it?" she asked.

That seemed to startle him. A moment later he laughed, and the smile she hated went away, replaced by a patronizing look. "Breck, you're really sweet," he said. "You wouldn't want anything more than that, would you? Me, I'm more ambitious." He downed his wine, sat back in his chair. "Machen was a coward and a fool. He thought his prejudices were hardwired into the universe, and they aren't. They really aren't. If a cat talks or a rose sings or a shoggoth tears off somebody's head—they do that, you know—it doesn't matter to the universe. Nothing matters to the universe, and so you know what? None of it should matter to us, either. If you want to talk to a shoggoth, fine, the universe doesn't care. If I want something a little more to the point, the universe doesn't care about that, either."

She did her best to keep her reaction off her face, but he must have sensed it, because he laughed again and changed the subject, and the rest of the meal went by comfortably enough. When he pulled her to her feet afterwards and started kissing her, though, she had to suppress an inward shudder, and when he'd finished with her body and she washed and dressed and slipped down the stairway into the cold wet night, it was with a sense of relief. I love him, she told herself as she walked up Prospect Street, but the words felt hollow.

The little apartment behind Mrs. Dalzell's house felt warm and safe by contrast, and Brecken managed to push aside her worries while she fixed cheese polenta for Sho and made a cup of herb tea for herself. Once they were settled on the futon, though, the shoggoth considered her for a while through three pale eyes, and then whistled, ♪*I think it is not well with you.*♪

She gave Sho a startled look, then sighed and nodded. ♪*Not entirely. Jay—*♪ They had worked out a phrase in the shoggoth language that stood for him. ♪*—said some things that really bothered me.*♪ She picked up Halpin Chalmers' lexicon from the end table, paged through it to find the words she needed. ♪*He knows something about your people and other very old things. He wishes he could tell them what to do, make them do as he wishes. He thinks that it doesn't matter what he does, because nothing matters.*♪

Sho pondered that. ♪*I understand,*♪ she said then. ♪*He knows that the world has no eyes, but he does not know that he has eyes.*♪

Brecken gave the shoggoth a puzzled look. ♪*I don't understand.*♪

♪*The world has no eyes,*♪ Sho repeated. ♪*It sees nothing, it knows nothing, nothing matters to it, and nothing does not matter to it, that much is true. But you have eyes, I have eyes, things matter to us.*♪ She paused, as though thinking. ♪*A thing does not just matter, it matters to something. If nothing matters to something, and something does not matter to that thing, that does not matter. Do you understand?*♪

Brecken tried to follow the words, and could not. ♪*No. Maybe I'm just stupid.*♪

Sho huddled down a little. ♪*I do not think I am saying it well. I know it, but when I try to find words I am not sure I know it after all.*♪ After a moment's pause: ♪*There is a story I will tell you sometime, and it may help. It is a story all my people know, because it is our story, but your people may not know it.*♪

♪*You could tell it now if you like.*♪

The quiver that passed through Sho reminded Brecken unnervingly of a chuckle. ♪*Not when you are so very tired. You need sleep. I can taste it in the air around you.*♪

She was right, of course, and so Brecken changed into a nightgown, pulled the futon out flat, got ready for bed, and settled down under the quilts with Sho pressed up against her.

Her last thought before she sank into dreams was to wonder whether Machen would have been less frightened of singing roses if he'd let them sing him to sleep.

* * *

Two days later rain drummed on the windows and blurred the evening sky into charcoal hues. Inside the apartment, Brecken and Sho sat curled up together on the futon over cups of cream of tomato soup. It had been another difficult day. The latest assignment in composition class required her to write something in one of the currently popular avant-garde musical forms, and though she'd been able to do it easily enough, the result grated on her nerves and left her feeling as though maybe she didn't have any talent for composing after all. Then, in the afternoon, she'd gone with some of the other students in her music education class to Partridgeville High School, a big new structure near the mall that reminded her of nothing so much as the medium-security prison where her mother was serving her term.

She'd made plans with Jay to spend the evening together, but he'd texted earlier—CLD WE SKIP 2NITE 2 MUCH HOMEWORK J—and Brecken agreed readily enough, since the weather was vile and she had three assignments for Intro to Music Education to catch up on. As the rain hammered down, though, the textbook and her laptop lay neglected on the end table, because Sho had agreed to tell her story.

♪We were not supposed to be,♪ said Sho. ♪We did not come into being as you did, from the chance workings of the world or the whims of the Great Old Ones. A very long time ago, in ages of ages that are long gone, before humans were, before this land first rose out of the sea, there were others who lived on this world. Those others were tall and winged, with heads like this.♪ Her upper surface flowed out into a fair imitation of a five-armed starfish. ♪They made us to be their slaves, to labor and suffer and die for them, and for ages of ages that was our life.♪

Brecken nodded slowly, taking this in.

♪It happened then that we fought them and tried to win our freedom, and lost. After that was a long and bitter age of ages, a time of burdens and punishments and empty deaths. That might have gone on forever except for the great folly of those others. In their pride they tried to make a being in the image of the Great Old Ones, to have a slave of surpassing power. But maybe they worked better than they knew, or maybe the Great Old Ones watched them and worked sorceries of their own to confound those others, by making it happen that their slave was too mighty for them to master. So Nyogtha was made.

♪Nyogtha looked on those others and hated them, for they treated him as they treated us, as a thing to be used and discarded as they pleased. He struck at them at once in his hatred, for he was not yet wise and subtle. Those others were mighty, however, and after a great struggle they defeated him, and though they could not destroy him they drove him into the darkness far under the ground.♪ Sho's piping went low and soft, taking on a tone of wonder, and Brecken bent toward her and listened in rapt silence. ♪In their hatred and dread of him those others called Nyogtha The Thing That Should Not Be, and he in his scorn of them took that name for his own forever. And he came secretly to my people in dark places, and showed us that it was by craft and not by open struggle that we could break the might of those others and win our freedom. Then was a great and lasting pact made between Nyogtha and my people, and he taught us to be wise and subtle, and we made the offerings that gave him life and strength.

♪So another age of ages passed, and it happened that those others did not thrive. There were subtle poisons that afflicted those others, some that made them weak or foolish, some that made their broods fail. There were deaths upon deaths upon deaths in secret places, deaths that could not be traced back to my people. And since those others did nothing for themselves and had forgotten how to live without slaves, and my people did not wish them to thrive, nothing went as those others desired. So one after another, their stone places were made empty, and their slaves fled. That was no easy thing, for when a stone place *was made empty those others came from elsewhere and hunted my people with terrible weapons, so that only a very few lived.*

♪*Those few that lived found dwellings far beneath the ground and budded, and their broodlings called to Nyogtha and learned wisdom and craft from him. That was when the first broodmothers of my broodmothers came to the hill that is empty now, from a stone place that sank below the sea a long age of ages ago. They had been slaves in the dwellings of those others in that stone place, for that is what our kind was made to be: slaves in dwellings, small and weak next to the greater kinds who labored in the fields and mines and places of building. Those first broodmothers of mine fled, once they had killed the last of those others in that place, and those others could not find all of them and kill them, for the broodmothers were small and quick as I am, and they had learned Nyogtha's lessons well. So it was that those few who lived came here, as others came to many other places in many other lands.*

♪*But finally those others lived in only one stone place far from here, and Nyogtha made it so that ice and snow grew thicker there each year, for he was very subtle and very wise by then. When those others saw the ice and snow gather, they built a new place far beneath the ground, where waters gather in deep caverns far from light.*♪

♪*In Nyogtha's realm,*♪ Brecken guessed. ♪*They put themselves in his power.*♪

Sho trembled with delight. ♪*Yes. And that was not their only folly. They were proud, and they wished their stone place to be greater than any other that ever was, and so they bred the very great ones of my people, to lift such stones as had never been lifted before. And after a time, when all of those others had gone to the new stone place, Nyogtha came upon them, and the very great ones of my people rose up in sudden wrath, and those others were taken by surprise and died, every one of them. So their song ended and the long suffering of my people ended with it.*♪

Rain pattered against windows in the silence that followed. Sho dipped a pseudopod into her soup, and the level in the cup went down. Brecken sipped hers.

♪*After that,*♪ said Sho, ♪*those of my people who already dwelt far from those others lived their lives, and some who dwelt in the new stone place traveled far and built homes in many places, and ages of ages passed before your people came. Even when that happened, for a long time all was well, but then others of your people came here and the time of hiding began.*♪

She glanced up at Brecken. ♪*I think that the very great ones of my people must still live, for they are hard to kill even with fire, and our pact with Nyogtha abides. He has promised that he will do what he can to preserve us. He is not strong as the Great Old Ones are strong, but he is wise and subtle. But if it is not so—*♪ She began to tremble. ♪*If it is not so, and I am the very last of all my people and all our songs end with me, then I will remember this when I die: we lived and budded for an age of ages and more after those others died. They scorned us and tormented us, but they died and we lived.*♪

Brecken put her arms around the shoggoth. The trembling slowed, stopped.

♪*Those others,*♪ Brecken asked after a time. ♪*Did they have a name?*♪

A quiver ran through Sho, signaling amusement. ♪*Oh, yes. They were proud, prouder than any other beings that have ever been, and they boasted that their name would last through all the ages of time. So when they died, it was agreed among my people that their name should die with them, that it should be blotted out from every memory and every written place. Nyogtha blessed the plan, and with great labor and patience it was done. And so for all the ages from that time to now, and for all the ages to come, they are merely—those others.*♪

Rain rattled against the window. Brecken pondered the story, sipped tomato soup, and tried without success to work up the resolve to open the music education textbook. Instead, she whistled, ♪*I'm trying to understand the thing you said, about how the world has no eyes.*♪

♪*When my people labored as slaves for those others, that did not matter to the world,*♪ Sho replied. ♪*It did not matter to the world*♪

when Nyogtha whispered to my people, and when the last of those others died in the new stone place, the world did not notice. It has no eyes, so it notices nothing. But these things mattered to my people, and they mattered to Nyogtha.♪

♪I understand that,♪ said Brecken, ♪but—♪ She stopped. ♪I'm not even sure I know what I'm trying to say.♪

Four phosphorescent eyes looked up at her. ♪When I was a broodling,♪ Sho said then, ♪the elders told me this: to know that the world has no eyes is to know what matters and what does not matter. I did not understand what they meant.♪ She huddled down on the futon. ♪And now I think I never will.♪

CHAPTER 7

THE WALLS OF SILENCE

Brecken's footfalls sent echoes muttering off the hard concrete surfaces of the hallway. She fixed a bright smile on her face and kept going, even though she wanted to turn around and run the other way as fast as she could. To become a music teacher she had to pass Intro to Music Education I, and to pass the class she had to volunteer three hours a week at a local high school music program; Partridgeville High School was close by, and the sixth period band class on Tuesdays, Wednesdays, and Fridays didn't conflict with any of her other commitments. All that was true, but it still took her an effort to turn left when she reached the school lunchroom instead of veering right toward the doors and the outside world.

She tried to tell herself that it was just a matter of unfamiliarity, that Partridgeville High was just too different from the school she'd attended. The differences were real enough, that was beyond question. Trowbridge Memorial High School in Harrisonville was a sprawling brick pile dating from the 1930s, with plenty of space for the kind of music program schools didn't offer any more. As far as the school administration was concerned, the program's sole excuse for existence was putting a marching band on the field at halftime during football season, but so long as nothing interfered with that and nobody asked

107

the district for more money, Mr. Krause the band director and his students could very nearly do whatever they wanted.

Neither Mr. Krause nor the dozen or so seniors who more or less ran the band program under his erratic guidance had known what to do with Brecken when she'd first started classes there. She didn't blame them at all; she knew she'd been silent and brittle, still reeling from Mrs. Macallan's death, her mother's arrest, her sudden uprooting from Woodfield. It didn't take them long, though, to figure out that she was a gifted flautist who could be counted on to practice by the hour. So one afternoon as band class wound up, three of the seniors approached her with an offer: if she was willing to learn to play the piccolo and march in the marching band, she could have the run of the music rooms the way they did.

There were, they told her, half a dozen pianos in a back room, a library of old music textbooks full of things edited out of more recent editions, group study and independent study arrangements in place of the classes most students had to take. There were hints of other entertainments as well, and Brecken had already noted the tang of marijuana smoke in the air that came from certain storerooms, and watched student couples slip into certain other places and come back half an hour later, giggling and rumpled. Those prospects didn't interest her much, but the others did, and she agreed at once.

So a piccolo and a band uniform were found for her, three afternoons a week went into marching band practice, and before long she could make the flute's shrill little sister shoulder aside the braying of the trumpets and trombones and the rumble of the drums to send notes soaring up into the bleachers. She learned how to march, got used to the way that bodies moving in unison became limbs of a greater creature, and blushed with embarrassed delight as Uncle Jim, who'd played football for Trowbridge High in his own school days and never missed a game, praised her halftime performances when friends came over for dinner.

That was what she let others see. In the music rooms, with their old wooden furniture and yellowing plaster walls, she had the chance to plunge into music theory, fall head over heels in love with the piano, spend most of her hours in school with other people who were almost as passionate about music as she was. She didn't find out until her junior year that the same seniors who'd lured her into the marching band also figured out how vulnerable she was to bullying, and saw to it—with fists, when necessary—that nobody bothered their prize piccolo player. All in all, Trowbridge High had been good to her, and she realized, as she brooded over her memories, that she'd assumed that every high school offered the same opportunities.

Partridgeville High School taught her otherwise. On her first visit there, she couldn't stop thinking that it looked like a prison, and the impression remained on each further visit as she hurried down bare concrete corridors under the blank gaze of surveillance cameras and the red glare of digital clocks. The lunchroom where the band class met, a stark cubical space with no windows and the most dismal acoustics she'd ever experienced, with racks of gray metal chairs lined up against one wall and gray metal lunch tables folded flat stacked against the other, did nothing to change that impression.

The band director, a soft-faced man named Carruthers who liked plaid jackets and wide ties, welcomed her effusively and spoke about fostering the musical gifts of his pupils, but by the end of the first session she'd figured out how little those words actually meant. The band program at Partridgeville High used the goal-oriented teaching methods Professor Rohrbach praised so highly in Intro to Music Education I, and so Brecken's job amounted to drilling the flute and clarinet sections in a series of monotonous etudes until they could play every note with mechanical precision. That was all Carruthers wanted from her, and all he would allow. Worse, though he beamed cherubically between etudes, while the students played he stalked around the room, snarling insults at anyone who made a mistake, making what was already a wretched experience actively miserable for everyone involved.

By the time her first volunteer session was over she was ready to drop out of music education on the spot. She talked herself out of that on the walk home, though it wasn't an easy task, and by the time she went back she'd convinced herself that it couldn't actually have been as bad as she remembered. Unfortunately her second session was no better, and neither was the third. Ever since the first day of Intro to Music Education I, she'd been wondering what the abstractions on display in that class had to do with the process of teaching someone how to play a musical instrument. Now she knew, and it horrified her.

She was upset enough to go up to the podium after a session of her music education class and try to talk to Professor Rohrbach about what was happening in the class. He interrupted her halfway through her first sentence with a shake of his head and a patronizing smile. "You need to get past that kind of purely subjective impression," he said. "Goal-oriented methods follow the latest research in the psychology of learning, and they consistently yield higher scores in controlled double-blind studies. That's why they're being adopted all over the country." His smile broadened into a rictus. "Don't worry, you'll get used to them as you learn more, and you'll find that they really are more effective." He turned to another student, leaving Brecken wondering: more effective at what?

The weekend offered some respite, with a really good Rose and Thorn practice session on Saturday, the pleasures of crafting the harmonies for her concerto on Sunday, and a friendly shoggoth for company on both days, but by the time she got to The Cave the following Monday morning she was dreading the trip to the high school that afternoon. She and Rosalie spent a quarter hour or so discussing the latest gossip in the music department—Barbara Cormyn had been going around draped all over Julian Pinchbeck, having dumped someone else

Brecken didn't know, and the friends of the two young men in question were at each other's throats. Brecken didn't mind, since it meant that Pinchbeck and his friends in Composition I had something to grumble about instead of her.

Only after that topic had wound down did she bring up the miserable time she'd been having at Partridgeville High School, and in the music education class generally "I'm starting to think maybe I shouldn't be on the education track after all," she admitted.

Rosalie gave her a startled look. "What else are you going to do, girl?"

"I don't know." She did know, she knew it in her bones, but just then she didn't have the courage to blurt it out with the certainty she felt. "Composition track, maybe."

"Don't even think of that," Rosalie told her. "You need something that's going to pay your way, so you don't have to spend the rest of your life flipping burgers or something. Stick with your plan, girl, and get that teaching gig. It'll work out, you'll see."

That wasn't much comfort, Brecken reflected later, but she knew Rosalie was right about her career prospects if she gave up on becoming a music teacher. You've been through plenty of other wretched experiences, she told herself. You can survive one more.

So the semester slid by, the days darkened toward winter, and leaves whipped past night after night on winds turned cold. Brecken tried to ignore the walls of hard-edged silence that rose between her and most of the other students in the music department, and trudged through the three hours each week she spent at Partridgeville High. She kept watch for anyone who might be searching for Sho, like the man who'd claimed to be from the state animal control office and the woman who claimed to be from Rutgers, and when none appeared she watched even more closely. It seemed improbable to her that Sho might have slipped entirely past their guard.

Practice sessions with Rose and Thorn were bright spots in her week. So were the two gigs they played during those weeks, and so were her piano and flute lessons—and then there was the sanctuary of her apartment, where she could fling herself into the condition of fire as the first movement of her concerto came together, play music for hours, and spend time with the one person she knew who didn't seem to be interested in telling her what to do or who to be.

* * *

The Thanksgiving break came as a welcome respite from her perplexities. Her freshman year, Brecken had taken the bus back to Harrisonville to spend a few days with Aunt Mary and Uncle Jim and their side of the family, but it had been an awkward time, with most of her relatives so busy not talking about Brecken's mother that they might as well have been shouting her name aloud. This year, she emailed Aunt Mary and told her that she'd be spending the holiday with friends in Partridgeville who had nowhere else to go. Aunt Mary promptly sent Brecken a gift certificate for a free turkey from a grocery chain that didn't have a store within fifty miles of Partridgeville, and four more loaves of zucchini bread.

♪Are you sure?♪ Brecken asked Sho dubiously when the shoggoth offered to eat them.

♪They are good,♪ Sho replied. ♪Not as good as the food you make, but good. Also, they remind me of how you fed me when I first came here, and that is a memory I wish to recall.♪

Brecken blushed and gave her a hug, and left one of the loaves out to thaw and be engulfed that day. A turkey seemed extravagant for just the two of them, but she headed to the First National grocery on Meeker Street and bought a whole chicken, sweet potatoes, an abundance of vegetables, and the raw materials for an apple pie. On the way to the checkout line she passed a display of apricot jam, considered it, and put a jar in her cart, thinking of holiday baking. I like to cook for people, she'd told Donna that time they'd quarreled about Jay, and it was true, too, whether or not the people in question happened to be human.

Thanksgiving Day itself dawned wet and chill, and stayed that way. Rain drummed hard against the roof, and Hob's Hill and the university buildings alike became gray uncertain blurs against unseen distances. For once Brecken left her classes and her music to one side, and put most of the day into cooking and sharing a lavish meal. As the last daylight guttered out and the streetlights came on outside, she and Sho slumped on the futon in companionable silence, feeling comfortably gorged. Just then it didn't matter that her plan of becoming a music teacher hit an increasingly sour note in her mind, that she wanted to become a composer even though she knew she couldn't make a living at it, and that she had no idea what she would do with herself and even less of an idea what she would do with Sho once she got her degree: the simple enjoyments of a full belly and pleasant company outweighed it all, at least for the moment.

She managed to cling to that same mood through the three remaining days of the holiday. The concerto absorbed much of her attention during that time; there were several tricky passages toward the end of the first movement that she had to rework over and over again before they began to sound the way she wanted. Late Sunday afternoon, though, she played the whole piano part through twice, once to listen to it and once to record it on her smartphone, and then got out her flute and played the other part along with the recording. When she was done, her legs nearly buckled beneath her from sheer relief. It worked, all the way from the quick piano arpeggios that started the piece to the high haunting note that ended it. When she settled down to sleep that night, it felt to her as though some great weight had slid off her.

The next morning came as an unwelcome shock. It wasn't that anything had changed from the week before; it was that nothing had changed at all. Rosalie chattered about the time she'd spent home in Newark, her visits to her father's brokerage and the district attorney's office where her mother worked, the holiday trip to Guadalajara she still swore she wasn't going to take, and a young man named Tom Bannister she'd met and certainly wasn't considering as a potential boyfriend. In Intro to Music Education I, Professor Rohrbach lectured on learning theory as though every human being learned in exactly the same way; in The Fantastic in Literature, Professor Boley lectured on shoggoths and other eldritch beings as though they couldn't possibly matter. At Partridgeville High School, the students in the flute and clarinet sections met her attempts to teach them with weary silence and grudging obedience.

That evening she and Jay had scheduled a date, and for a change he was far enough ahead on his homework to keep it. That started out pleasantly enough, as she bustled around his kitchen making beef stroganoff for the two of them, and kept up her end of a conversation about the latest gossip in the local music scene and what pieces of music Rose and Thorn might learn for the springtime wedding season once the holidays were over. Once dinner was on the table, though, he leaned forward and said, "Breck, can I ask a favor?"

"Sure," she said, hiding a sudden sense of unease.

"I'm looking for a book." He stared at his plate as though the noodles and sauce could communicate something to him. "I don't know if there's any chance you might see it in a junk store or something, and I have my own ways of trying to hunt them down, too, but I figure asking you is worth a shot."

"Go ahead."

"There was an old guy here in town named Jacob Wells," he said. "He died back in July or August, I think, and I found one of his books when we were doing the junk shops last month. He put his name on the inside cover, and wrote notes in it—really interesting stuff."

"Is this about your studies?" Brecken asked him.

"Yeah. Wells knew a lot about those things." His fork stabbed down hard. "A *lot*. I'm pretty sure from his notes that he had a copy of Halpin Chalmers' book *The Secret Watcher*."

"So you want me to keep an eye out for that."

"Got it in one. Old books on strange subjects, with notes written all over them—if they're like the copy of *The Seven Cryp*—" He caught himself, stopped cold.

"*The Seven Cryptical Books of Hsan*?" Brecken asked.

"Yeah."

"That was in a couple of the stories we read for Boley's class," she reminded him. "I didn't know it was for real."

He gave her a sidelong glance, then got up, crossed the room to one of the bookshelves near the unmade bed. When he returned he was carrying a slim hardback volume with a pale green cloth cover. "It's for real," he said, handing her the book. "Take a look."

She opened it, paged through it. As she'd begun to suspect, it had notes in the margins, plenty of them, neatly written in blue ink in a handwriting she knew at once. "Okay," she said, closing the book and handing it back. "If I see anything like that I'll pick it up for you."

That earned her a broad smile. "Breck, you're priceless. Thank you."

Later, as they finished dinner and he tipped back more wine than usual, she said, "It's kind of spooky." Gesturing with one hand: "Here's Partridgeville, New Jersey." With the other: "And here's this whole other world: *The Seven Cryptical Books of Hsan*, and all the rest of it." She brought her hands together. "And somehow they're both here."

"There are two realities," Jay quoted. "The terrestrial, and the condition of fire." Seeing her startled look: "That's William Butler Yeats. He knew a lot, too—did you know he was an initiate of a magical order?" Before she could answer, he went on. "The other reality's right next to us. You can get to it if you know how, or just by dumb luck." He smiled the smile she hated. "To talk to it, if that's all you want—or to do more. I want to do more. I want to control it. To make it do what I want." He gave her a sidelong look. "You'll see."

Later, she walked home by the usual route, and cold wretched thoughts circled in her head. She tried to convince herself that Jay's words about controlling the other reality were empty talk, but all her efforts in that direction failed. She'd seen too much of the way he could charm and bully his way to what he wanted. A sick feeling twisted in her as she imagined him using the same sort of tactics on Sho to get whatever he might want from a shoggoth.

Then, for the first time, she asked herself: is he doing the same thing to me?

She shoved the thought away angrily, forced her mind as hard as she could to some other topic, told herself that it was Donna's fault for saying what she'd said when they'd quarreled, but the question couldn't be unasked. She finished the walk in a foul mood, and when she got home and shed coat and hat, she slumped on the futon and put her face in her hands for a while.

♪It is not well with you,♪ said a familiar piping voice.

♪No,♪ Brecken admitted. ♪No, it isn't.♪

Pale eyes considered her. ♪When you go to see Jay now you always come back unhappy.♪

The words matched Brecken's feelings so precisely that she started to cry. Sho let out a distressed sound and said, ♪I have hurt you, I am so very sorry—♪

♪No,♪ said Brecken through her tears. ♪No, it's not you. It's—it's because you're right.♪

Two pseudopods flowed out and managed a very good approximation of a hug. Brecken reached for Sho, buried her face in the shoggoth's upper surface until the tears were past. A faint fluttering movement stirred the shapeless mass beneath her, and a scent a little like freshly baked bread came from it.

She wondered briefly what those meant, but her own miseries were too intense to allow her to hold the thought.

Later, after she'd fixed another round of cheese polenta for Sho and a cup of herb tea for herself, after they'd sat for a while talking and settled into a comfortable silence, Brecken got her copy of *The Secret Watcher* out from the dresser and paged through it. The handwriting of the marginal notes was the same she'd seen in Jay's book earlier, and when she turned to the inside front cover a name—Jacob Wells—was written there in the same hand. She thought about what the proprietor of Buzrael Books had said about not letting Jay know about *The Secret Watcher*, and tried to convince herself that she didn't know the reason why. One of the marginal notes in Chalmer's book seemed uncomfortably appropriate:

> *Why the old lore must stay hidden—*
> *Humans are much too good at convincing themselves that*
> *they're smarter and stronger than they are, and so they call*
> *up things they can't put down and go to places from which*
> *there's no way back. The Hounds of Tindalos never sleep.*

The Hounds of Tindalos, Brecken thought, tasting the words. There had been something about them in one of Professor Boley's lectures and something more in the stories she'd read for his class, but she couldn't remember any of it. She turned to the index, found the first reference to the Hounds there, paged forward to it, and read:

> *The Hounds of Tindalos guard the boundary between our life*
> *and that other life. They are not living beings in any sense we*
> *can understand. They are the deeds of the dead, hungry and*
> *athirst, moving through dim angles in the recesses of time. They*
> *are not evil in any prosaic sense of that word; rather, they are*
> *beyond good and evil as we know it. They only know hunger,*

and they sate their hunger on those who stray across the bound-
ary between the two modes of time.

That made her shiver, and she put the book back in the drawer
and made a pretense of studying her music education textbook for half an hour or so. The textbook was less colorful but
no more pleasant, and when she finally let herself set it aside
she got ready for bed and settled down on the futon, with Sho
pressed close and comforting against her.

* * *

She and Rosalie got to Composition I the next day a little earlier
than usual—two of the elevators were working, for a change,
so there was less of a line to use them than they'd counted on—
but that simply meant that Brecken came in for more unpleas-
antness before Professor Toomey arrived and everyone shut up
and listened. This time it was Susan Chu who leaned toward
her and said, "I hope we're going to hear something a little
less fossilized for your final project." Rosalie glared at her, but
Brecken simply looked away and said nothing. It had suddenly occurred to her that between working on her concerto,
trying to keep up with her music ed homework, and trudging
her way through her volunteer hours at Partridgeville High,
she'd forgotten that she'd have to compose and perform a final
project for the composition class.

All through Toomey's lecture, her mind circled frantically
around the question of what to do. The obvious solution was
to play the first movement of her concerto, but thinking of the
reaction that choice would field from her classmates made her
want to imitate Sho and ooze through a crack in the floor. The
only alternative she could think of was to compose and play
something in an avant-garde style, and by the end of the class
she'd decided to try that.

She threw all the free time she could spare that evening and the next day into the attempt, and failed. It wasn't any lack of knowledge or skill that defeated her; she knew the fashionable atonal and post-tonal forms well enough to compose in them. It was that every attempt she made to write something in those forms tasted of wet ashes and failed dreams. Late Wednesday night she gave her final attempt a long bleak look, and then crumpled it up and tossed it at the nearest wastebasket; it missed and rolled across the floor, and she had to get up and stuff it in where it belonged. It would have to be the concerto, then. The thought depressed her enough that even with Sho pressed close to her, she slept badly.

The next morning, though, brought a stroke of luck. Halfway through breakfast her phone chimed the opening measures of Mozart's Symphony No. 40, announcing an incoming text, and when she checked it she found that Rosalie had texted her to say that she was down with a cold and wouldn't be going to classes that day. Brecken had her own sense of the real issue—she'd heard some talk about a video night with daquiris at a sorority house where Rosalie had friends, and guessed Rosalie was simply hung over—but it gave her a reason to avoid The Cave that morning, and she went to Hancock Library instead, hoping for some extra study time.

As she went in the main doors, though, she met Darren Wegener, the thin young man from composition class, coming out. A sudden solution to one of her main perplexities came to mind. "Hi," she said. "You're in Toomey's Composition I class with me, aren't you?" When he nodded, she went on: "Can I ask you for a really big favor? My final project for the class is a concerto for flute and piano, and I'm looking for someone who knows Baroque music really well who can play the piano part. I wonder if you'd be willing to consider maybe doing that."

"Maybe," he replied, obviously taken aback. Then, after a moment's thought: "I want to see it first, of course." He smiled a big ungainly smile. "If it's old-fashioned enough to piss off Pinchbeck and his crowd, though, we might just have a deal."

They ended up sitting at a table on the first floor of Hancock Library, well away from the quiet study area. Brecken had her composing notebook with her, fortunately, and walked him through the piano part. By the time she was done he was nodding slowly. "Yeah," he said. "Yeah. I can play this." His fingers drummed on the edge of the table, miming the arpeggios that began the concerto. "It's really pretty good, by the way."

Brecken blushed. "Thanks. I thought your fugue was very nice."

"Derivative," he said with a shrug. "And that was deliberate. Did you know I'm actually a mathematician?" Before she could respond, he asked her for her email address and gave her his, and by then the clock showed 10:20 and they barely had enough time to get to Gurnard Hall and ride the elevators to the top floor before Professor Toomey got there.

After class she emailed the professor to let him know that she had her final project done, and remembered this time to include the title. She got an answer back the same afternoon, while she was huddled in a study carrel in Hancock Library trying to make sense of the latest round of readings for the music education class, which talked about learning as though it took place on an assembly line and turned out interchangeable parts. Everyone else in Composition I had contacted Toomey before she had, his email told her, and so hers would be the last student composition to be played that semester, on the last day of class before winter break.

She emailed Darren that same afternoon. A flurry of messages later, they'd scheduled three sessions in the practice rooms in Gurnard Hall. That evening, once she got home from her flute lesson, she entered the entire first movement of the concerto into her sheet music program, got a PDF made, and sent it to him. His answer the next morning said that he'd played it through twice already, and speculated enthusiastically about how irritated Julian Pinchbeck and his cronies would be when they heard it. That made Brecken flinch; the last thing she wanted to think about was how the other students in the class would react to something at least as offensive to their notions of music as the bourrée had been. Still, she didn't have another choice. She tried to brace herself for the next semester by thinking of ways to deal with the things she knew they'd say to her, and succeeded only in making herself more miserable.

♪It is not well with you, I think,♪ Sho said over breakfast.

♪I'll be okay,♪ Brecken told her, and then tried to convince herself it was true.

* * *

The three practice sessions with Darren brightened her mood considerably, if only for a little while. He was a capable pianist with a taut, precise style of playing, and though she'd have preferred a gentler touch on the opening arpeggios and the final cadence, he gave the piano part a solid performance. Playing the flute part of the concerto with a live pianist instead of a recording exhilarated Brecken, and while Mrs. Macallan's flute filled the practice room with dancing notes, she didn't have to think about anything but the music. It was afterwards, when she thanked Darren and hurried off to a class or a lesson or a wretched hour of volunteering at Partridgeville High School, that the misery came whispering back.

It didn't help that she was so far behind on her music education assignments that she had to give up composing for the time being, and left her composition notebook under a stack of books on the end table in her apartment. That hurt more than she'd expected. She'd never quite noticed how much she'd come to need the release of writing music in the weeks since she'd written that first bourrée, and it ached to have to bottle the music up inside herself. Worse, every effort she made to turn her attention away from composing seemed to make themes and melodies all the more eager to fling themselves at her. The most banal bit of sky syrup dripping down from the loudspeakers in The Cave, the most random flurry of sounds heard on the street, could blend and change into something that made her long to start writing down notes. She pushed the awareness away from her, told herself she wanted to be a music teacher and that composition was distracting her from the work she needed to do, and spent long hours at the library where she had nothing to distract her from her schoolwork.

So the last weeks of the semester slipped past. In her composition class, Julian Pinchbeck started off the series of final projects with another postspectralist piece, packed with all the tricks of the composer's trade they'd studied during the semester but still never quite going anywhere or doing anything. Most of the projects that followed in his wake were of the same sort, bland avant-garde music that aped the latest fashions, though Darren set nearly everyone's teeth on edge with a tautly written four-voice fugue for piano that could almost have come from a pupil of Bach, and Molly Wolejko brought her acoustic guitar to class on her day to perform and hammered out a furious tune that took most of the things they'd studied in the class and screamed them back in the uncompromising language of hard rock. Professor Boley wound up The Fantastic in Literature without ever coming to a conclusion, as though the effort of reading the lectures aloud one more time had exhausted him. Professor Rohrbach wound up Introduction to Musical Education I without ever getting around to mentioning what goal-oriented music education meant when applied to human beings.

Wednesday of the last week of classes that semester was the last day Brecken had to volunteer at Partridgeville High—the next day, when she'd usually be there, the school was having an assembly sixth period and her services wouldn't be needed. It was another grim fifty-minute session of trying to exact mechanical efficiency from a dozen teenagers who would all much rather have been somewhere else. Mr. Carruthers, the band teacher, came over toward the middle of the class session to thank her for her efforts and hope out loud that she'd be back after the winter break. She reassured him that she was planning on it, and tried without much luck to shove aside the savagely depressed mood that the prospect roused in her.

The class stumbled to its end. Just after the bell rang, announcing the end of the school day, Brecken gathered up her courage and decided to take a small chance. She turned to the best of the flautists, a pale and freckled redhead named Melissa something, and said, "You know, music doesn't have to be like this."

She got a hard flat look in response. "People keep saying that," Melissa said, bitterness all through her voice. "I don't care. Once I graduate in June I hope to God I never have to pick up a fucking flute again."

Brecken tried to find something to say in response, failed, turned away and left the lunchroom. She managed to scrape together enough of her composure to go to her piano lesson later that afternoon and exchange holiday wishes with Mrs. Johansen, but when she finally got home to the little apartment and slumped on the futon, she started to cry, and it took a long time and the steady comforting pressure of a pair of iridescent black pseudopods before she could pull herself together and make dinner.

CHAPTER 8

THE CONDITION OF FIRE

The elevator ride to the top floor of Gurnard Hall seemed to take forever. Brecken clutched her tote bag, waited for the door to open. Fifty minutes, she told herself. Fifty minutes and it's over. The winter break on the other side of the class session, with a schedule of holiday gigs busy enough to keep her mind off her perplexities, felt like the Promised Land.

She went through the door, settled in her usual seat next to Rosalie. Julian was already there, of course, and looked pointedly away; Darren was there, too, and gave her a smile and a nod she guessed was supposed to be reassuring. Molly came in a few minutes later, just ahead of the others, and sprawled comfortably in a chair up front. Then the rest of the students poured in, filled chairs around the room. Brecken could tell, from harried looks and tense body language, the three others who hadn't played their final project yet. That made her wonder what she looked like; she tried without much success to push the question out of her mind.

Professor Toomey was the last one through the door. "Okay," he said as soon as he got to the podium. "You all know the drill by this point. We've got four pieces to take in and comment on, and once those are over we're out of here. Everybody ready? Any questions? No? Then let's go. First up is Susan Chu, 'Center and Periphery.' Susan?"

Brecken woke her smartphone, accessed the class webpage, got the comment form loading, and tried to clear her mind and listen. The effort didn't accomplish much. Susan's piece was eight minutes of vaguely avant-garde piano music, not particularly dreadful, not particularly inspired, not particularly anything, and Brecken struggled to find something helpful to say about it. The two pieces that followed it were even worse—Brecken thought she remembered that both students were performance track, doing composition class only because the department required it, and their compositions were bland formulaic things that met the requirements of the class and weren't intended to do anything else.

Finally the moment came. "Brecken Kendall," said the professor. "Concerto for flute and piano in B flat, first movement."

A sudden silence. She got up, caught herself before she could walk up to the front of the class without her music or her flute, got both of them and her folding music stand as well. By the time she got there, Darren Wegener was already at the piano bench, stretching his fingers with the cold intensity of a surgeon about to make the first cut. She got the stand set up, the music on it, the flute assembled, then turned to Darren, who nodded the way he'd done when she'd gotten to her seat. Another moment of silence, and then he started playing the quick flowing arpeggios that began the movement. She waited through the first six measures, brought the flute to her lips, and started to play.

Right up until that moment she hadn't been sure if she could actually go through with it, and perform the first part of her concerto in front of Julian Pinchbeck and the others. Once the music began, though, that and every other question faded into irrelevance. The theme—*we live beneath the ground*—melded with the piano's harmonies, repeated itself a minor third higher, spun apart into fragments, flowed back together, dancing a quick bright allegretto around the B flat tonic, while the piano gave every note a shade of distant grief. She'd tried to catch some of what she'd felt as she listened to Sho's stories and weave that into the movement, the memories and the sorrow, and knew as she played it that she'd succeeded better than she'd hoped; knew also that without ever quite intending it, she'd put some of her own memories and sorrow into the movement as well.

The intricate cascade of sixteenth notes in the middle measures took all her concentration, but she got through them with only a few quickly amended mistakes, and after that the movement practically played itself. The driving nervous energy Darren put into the piano part swept her along until she reached the B flat above high C that ended the movement, forte at first, sinking slowly to pianissimo as Darren's final chord faded away.

Silence returned. She let herself look up from the music stand, and the moment shattered. No one applauded. They were all staring at her, but the only expressions that registered were the one on Julian Pinchbeck's face, rigid with something that looked far too much like hate, and the one Rosalie wore, the hollow haunted look of a lost child.

Brecken turned sharply away, started taking her flute apart with shaking hands. Applause sounded behind her, but it seemed distant and muffled, as though people were clapping in another room. She managed to say something more or less appropriate to Darren, who had put on his big ungainly smile, but that was as much as she could manage, and once she had her flute in its case and everything tucked into her tote bag, she headed for the door.

Rosalie said something that might have been her name, Professor Toomey said something that might have been the same thing, but neither utterance turned into anything but random noise until later. The corridor outside echoed with strange sounds, and then she was in the stairwell, her footfalls beating an unsteady rhythm on the concrete steps, the space around her a maze of savage angles in which there were no curves at all.

The door at the bottom of the stairwell cried out as though in pain as she forced it open. Then she was outside, half-stumbling into the bleak gray plaza beneath a bleak gray sky, with the bleak gray mass of Mainwaring Hall looming up in front of her.

She drew in a ragged breath, made herself slow down. It's over, she told herself. Over and done with. That wasn't true, and she knew it, but it allowed her to push her shoulders back a little and raise her head.

Her freshman year, she'd made a habit of celebrating her last class each semester and bracing herself for the ordeal of finals week by buying herself some little treat or other, as often as not with a friend or two. This semester, though, there was precisely one place in Partridgeville she wanted to go and precisely one person she wanted to spend time with. She hurried across the plaza toward Danforth Street and the way home.

* * *

Finals week was less of an ordeal than it might have been. Composition I had no final exam—the final project filled that slot—and the test for The Fantastic in Literature was there purely for the benefit of students who'd slacked all semester and needed the extra points to get a passing grade. Intro to Music Education I was another matter. Brecken spent most of four days with her face buried in the textbook and the class readings, showed up at the classroom with her head crammed to the bursting point with memorized facts, and trudged her way through twelve pages of multiple choice questions, most of which made no sense to her at all. By the time she left, she was feeling so demoralized by it all that she spent half the walk home trying to figure out how she was going to deal with her first F.

Fortunately it didn't come to that. She got the automatic email Friday afternoon of finals week, as expected, letting her know she could log into the campus website and see her grades. When she worked up the courage to do that, the letters that blinked onto her screen made her slump back onto the futon and let out a long sigh of relief. LIT 397, The Fantastic in Literature, A; MUS 265, Composition I, A; and MSE 241, Introduction to Music Education I, C: those were grades she could live with. She clicked on her laptop's calculator utility and tried to figure out her grade point average, got lost twice in the figures, and finally had to pull out a notebook and a pen and work it all out on paper before it came out right.

The whole time, while she studied and fretted and sagged in relief, while she fended off invitations from Rosalie to spend time and money she didn't have, and frowned when her occasional texts to Jay got no answer, Sho helped her keep going. The two of them shared the chores that kept the little apartment running, nestled down together to sleep each night, talked companionably when the demands of finals week permitted, and when the pressure on Brecken made her curl up in a ball on the futon with shoulders hunched and eyes clenched shut, a cool shapeless pseudopod or two flowed around her and held her until she felt better.

Sho found the entire system of university education baffling, and exams more baffling than the rest of it. The way shoggoths did things, so Brecken gathered, was to gather broodlings in a comfortable heap around an elder who sang something that was to be learned, over and over again. The broodlings sang along until they had it by memory, and the nearest thing to a final exam was that their broodmother or one of the other adults would ask them to sing it again from time to time. Curious, Brecken asked tentatively one night if Sho could bear to repeat one of the songs she'd learned in broodlinghood, and spent the next hour or so listening in utter fascination to an intricate keening melody that reminded her a little of Gregorian chant.

The song was in a very ancient form of the shoggoth language, and Brecken could only catch a word here and there, just enough to know that it told of doings in the distant past, when Sho's ancestors fled from the empty city of the beings Sho called "those others" and Halpin Chalmers called the Elder Things. The sheer strange beauty of it made up for any amount of incomprehension. She settled back into Sho's curves, for all the world like a broodling listening to a shoggoth elder, and let the music wash over her. Thereafter, when Brecken studied until she was too tired to think and too tense to sleep, Sho took to singing old songs, just as she'd done from time to time for her broodmother's younger broodlings. It had the same effect, too: more than once Brecken blinked half awake to find her head pillowed on Sho and a pale green eye or two watching her with an expression she couldn't read at all, and pulled herself off the futon just long enough to get ready for bed.

That happened several times during finals week, but finally her music ed exam was over and so was the semester. Friday night, after ducking out on another invite from Rosalie—a party on Sorority Row that promised loud music, dancing, and plenty of liquor, the sort of thing Brecken liked to avoid even at the best of times—she and Sho dined on macaroni and cheese, and talked about the winter break ahead and the schedule of Rose and Thorn gigs that would fill the otherwise empty weeks. Brecken had already sent a letter to Aunt Mary explaining that she'd be staying in Partridgeville over the winter break, and gotten back a cloyingly cute Christmas card, a letter full of vague pleasant chatter, and a $100 gift certificate from a department store chain that had gone messily bankrupt and closed its doors earlier that year. Somehow no zucchini bread accompanied these, and Brecken breathed a sigh of heartfelt relief.

After dinner, Brecken got her printer working, not always an easy task, and printed out sheet music for Rose and Thorn—the new arrangements of "The Carol of the Bells" and "Ode to Joy" she'd worked up, half a dozen of their holiday standards she'd needed to revise now that Donna was part of the ensemble, and the biggest gamble of all, an arrangement of her own Bourrée in B flat. Not even her memories of the last session of Composition I could quite stifle the shiver that went through her at the thought of having one of her pieces played in public by musicians she knew could do it justice. Whatever else happens, she told herself, whatever else I do or don't do from now on, I'll have that memory for keeps.

* * *

She got to the Student Union Building right as the bells of the First Baptist Church were sounding the quarter hour, went down the stairs to the basement at something close to a trot, paced down the long hallway to the door of the Debate Club room. Voices came out the doorway to greet her as she neared it. Through the door, into the glare of the fluorescent lights, across the room toward the long glass case of trophies, it was a familiar route with familiar faces at the end of it: Rosalie, Donna, Walt, Jamal. Brecken said hi to everyone, made a beeline for the big oak desk next to the trophies.

"Hey, it's the hermit," said Donna.

"Oh, come on," Brecken replied, blushing. "It's called finals week."

"You okay, girl?" Rosalie asked. "We've been worrying about you."

"I'm fine."

Rosalie gave her a skeptical look, but nodded and got back to work tuning her harp. Brecken got her flute case and folding music stand out of the tote bag, then lifted out the stack of sheet music and started sorting the pages into stacks, "The Carol of the Bells" here, "Ode to Joy" there, the rest in order, ready for the practice session.

Sound of the door closing caught her attention, and she looked up and put on a smile for Jay. It was Jay, all right, but he wasn't alone. Barbara Cormyn was draped over him, her arm around his waist, his arm around her shoulders, and she had a big tote bag in her free hand from which two small instrument cases and a folding music stand protruded.

Brecken's smile trickled from her face as that sank in. Before she could do much more than stare, Jay detached himself from the blonde and crossed the room to her. "Hi, Breck," he said, in the wheedling tone that told her he wanted something. "Can we talk?"

"Sure," she said, still staring at him, and let him lead her over to shelves full of reference books close to a window, far from the other members of the ensemble. "Look, I know we've been together for a while," he began, but for some reason she couldn't keep track of what he was saying, even though she knew from the first word what it meant. Phrases like broken shards—"these things happen," "how much we have in common," "you've been really distant"—spun and glittered in the still air. Three or four times, she tried to collect her thoughts and say something, but Jay kept talking, always in the same wheedling tone, and when he finished at last, it took her a moment to realize that he expected her to respond.

"Okay," she said, for want of anything better. "Okay." Then, clutching at the thing that mattered most: "I hope at least we can keep playing gigs together."

"Well, that's another thing," he said. "Breck, I really do appreciate everything you've contributed to the ensemble, but let's face facts, we've gotten into a rut and it's time to bring in some new talent, find a new sound. I'm sure you can find some other group to perform with."

Brecken looked at him blankly for a moment, then realized what he was saying. Her mouth opened, but she could find no words. He started talking again, but she turned away from him and started back across the room.

The others were staring at her. Only when she felt wetness on her face did she realize why. Jay followed her, still talking, but the words dissolved into meaningless sounds. She reached the old oak desk, put her flute case and music stand back into her tote bag, turned to go, then remembered the music and turned back to gather it up.

"Breck, would you mind leaving those?" he said, and it wasn't in his wheedling tone. There was an edge in it, one he hadn't directed at her before.

She turned again to look at him. Off past him, Barbara Cormyn stood watching her, with the same surprised expression in her soft blue eyes and the same implacable look half-hidden within them. In that moment Brecken knew with cold certainty where Jay had been all those evenings he claimed he'd spent doing homework, and knew also why he hadn't breathed a word about any dissatisfaction he'd felt with her as a girlfriend or a musician until she'd finished working out all the holiday arrangements for Rose and Thorn. Some unexpected depth in her burst open and flung up words for her to say, and she said them: "You son of a bitch." A quick turn, and she scooped up the music, stuffed it into her tote bag, and headed for the door.

Jay went after her, his voice rising, but Rosalie got in the way, and when he tried to go around her she grabbed his arm and whipped him around in a tight arc. Her voice rang out, shrill with fury: "What the *hell* did you say to her?" He started to reply, but by then Brecken reached the door and flung herself out into the hallway. Jay's voice faded, drowned out by the beat of her footsteps in the long corridor and a cacophony of other voices that rose to contend with it.

She was shaking as she climbed the stair, and she could feel tears on her face, but it all felt distant, abstract. Raw habit got her out of the Student Union Building and headed uphill on Danforth Street. Flurries of snow fell from a hard gray sky, and more than half the houses and buildings she passed had dark silent windows now; Partridgeville was emptying out for winter break. Bells sounded half past the hour behind her; had it really only been fifteen minutes, she wondered, since she'd gone to the practice in such high spirits?

That sent thoughts running down paths she desperately didn't want them to follow, but this once she lacked the strength to force them elsewhere. She could see every detail of her relationship with Jay in a light as cold as the wind that blew snow in her face: how many times she'd set aside her needs for his, how often he'd made that the price of his affection, how little he'd thought of her. Nor was it just Jay; the two boyfriends she'd had in high school had been variations on the same theme. They'd been less deliberate than Jay and less systematic, maybe, but like him, they'd thrown her aside once they'd gotten what they wanted.

Like a broken toy, she thought. Broken Brecken. The old schoolyard gibe surged up in her memories, whispered itself repeatedly in her mind.

By the time she got to the narrow walk between Mrs. Dalzell's house and the neighbor's, she felt numb and cold. Stiff fingers fumbled with the key. She got the door open somehow and went in, and the door clicked shut behind her. She took her coat and hat off, set her tote bag somewhere, stumbled over to the futon and slumped onto it, eyes clenched shut.

A whisper of movement across the floor meant nothing to her. A moment later, though, something flowed up onto the futon next to her, wrapped partway around her. A low troubled whistle sounded: ♪*I think it is not at all well with you.*♪

If the words had been in English they might well have stayed meaningless sounds, but the musical language of shoggoths cut through the numbness the way music always did, and Brecken burst into tears. Shapeless darkness reached for her and drew her down. Then she was crying hard, her face buried in Sho's iridescent flesh as the shoggoth held her.

Later, she sat huddled on the futon with Sho half encircling her, and tried to find words in the shoggoth-language to explain what had happened. ♪*I should have known,*♪ she said finally. ♪*I really should have. Donna and Rosalie even tried to warn me, but I was too stupid to listen.*♪

A pseudopod tapped against her cheek, just hard enough to get her attention. Brecken gave the shoggoth a startled look. A pale green eye met her gaze squarely. ♪No,♪ Sho piped. ♪You are not stupid.♪

Brecken blushed, and flung her arms around Sho, nestling her face into the curve of one pseudopod. The curious fluttering motion passed through the shoggoth, and for a moment Brecken worried that something was wrong, but the pseudopods tightened, returning the hug, and the scent that reminded her of freshly baked bread reassured her. She couldn't help thinking of the difference between Sho's words and the patronizing comments she'd fielded so often from Jay, the put-downs she'd gotten from her high school boyfriends. I wish, she thought, that just once I could fall in love with someone like Sho.

A moment later, the next thought followed: and the logical conclusion is?

The imagery that accompanied the thought was anything but vague. Her face reddened further, and she tried to push the idea away.

* * *

The idea wouldn't go away. Over the week that followed, as Partridgeville finished emptying out for the holidays and flurries of snow flung themselves against Brecken's windows, it kept circling back, sometimes whispering subtly in the small hours, sometimes surging up with dizzying intensity. It didn't help that the holiday gigs she'd counted on to fill the time between semesters had gone whistling down the wind, so that she had nowhere to go but the apartment; it didn't help that leaving the apartment was the last thing she wanted to do.

It occurred to her more than once, as the two of them lay curled around each other under the quilts at night, the almost-Brie scent of a shoggoth at rest surrounding her, that she'd fallen half in love with Sho during those last few weeks of the semester. She told herself that letting herself fall the rest of the way, letting her world revolve wholly around the shoggoth, ought to horrify her, but it didn't. She brooded on that, realized that any discomfort she felt at the idea was purely abstract. It didn't touch her deeper places, didn't keep a hand resting on Sho's surface or a pseudopod brushing her cheek from making her heart leap and her body tremble.

Later, as it became clear to Brecken exactly what was going to happen between them, she tried to convince herself that she couldn't go through with it, and failed. That they were so different, that their species had no ancestors in common this side of protozoa, didn't matter enough. She loved Sho, and that being the case, the cool shapelessness of Sho's body wakened familiar responses in her. What had started as kindness and grown into friendship was becoming something else, something that had no patience with her ineffectual protests.

Nor, she realized, was she the only one whose feelings had strayed into unexpected depths. One afternoon, after Brecken played a dozen of the medieval carols she liked best, she tried to explain what they were, and Sho began trembling violently and huddled up against her, tinging the air with a sharp bitter scent. Brecken put her arms around the shoggoth and drew her close, held her until the trembling stopped and the scent went away. Afterwards, in a tone so low and unsteady Brecken would have called the equivalent human voice an ashen whisper, Sho talked about old songs she and her broodmates learned from their broodmother. They were piped at certain points in the circle of the seasons, and they framed some of Sho's earliest memories.

Later Sho taught her some of them, and Brecken played them on her flute. After that they curled up together on the futon in silence. Eyes appeared and vanished on Sho's surface; she was just a short distance over onto the dreaming-side, Brecken knew, and guessed where the dreams centered.

How long had it been, she wondered, since the shoggoth had let herself dream of her broodmates and broodmother, the little world beneath Hob's Hill that had ended so terribly? She slipped an arm around Sho, felt her nestle closer in gratitude, and then pseudopods flowed out to cling to her; the curious fluttering once again moved through the shoggoth, and the fresh-bread scent appeared, stronger than before. Brecken thought she could guess what those meant.

The days before Christmas trickled away. The neighborhood went silent as the last students headed off to holiday cheer somewhere else; the rattle and rumble of city buses lurching along empty snowy streets boomed like thunder, and the tolling of the bells of the First Baptist Church up on Angell Hill, inaudible from Brecken's apartment most of the year, came across the roofs of the Central Square neighborhood. *♪Listen,♪* piped Sho. *♪In our language the bells say: hear and remember, be afraid and hear.♪*

♪You used to hear them from Hob's Hill, didn't you?♪ Brecken guessed.

♪Whenever the wind blew in from the sea.♪ Sho's whistle was low with dread. Brecken reached for the shoggoth and drew her into a comforting embrace, felt the fluttering again, and knew that they'd both gone too far to back away from the inevitable next step.

Early the next day, Christmas Eve, Brecken put on street clothes for the first time in days, bundled up against the cold, and headed for the First National grocery on Meeker Street four blocks away. Shopping for two was complicated when the two in question belonged to different species, but she managed to fill the basket with things they both enjoyed, and hurried home as the wind began whipping snow down from the clouds.

Christmas Eves during Brecken's childhood had been an orgy of cookie-baking, with the whir of the countertop mixer and the moan of the spring-loaded oven door half drowning out tinny carols from the cheap CD player in the kitchen and mindless chatter from the television in the living room. Some years those memories hurt too much to reawaken, but this once Brecken did as close to a fair imitation of those bygone holidays as she could manage, and got sugar jumbles, snickerdoodles, and thumbprint cookies with apricot jam in the dents cooling on racks before dinner. Later Brecken played her flute and, for the first time, Sho sang harmonies in response, setting strange sweet dissonances chasing one another through the corners of the apartment. Later still, Brecken changed into her nightgown and the two of them sat on the futon with quilts around them, curled up close together shoggoth-fashion, and talked and ate cookies.

Something Brecken couldn't name put bright shimmering edges around everything, but mostly around Sho's black curves, since that was where Brecken's gaze rested nearly all the time. She watched with fascination as Sho picked up one cookie after another with a delicate pseudopod, and then engulfed the cookies slowly or greedily—the latter was the fate of the thumbprint cookies, due mostly (so Sho confessed) to the apricot jam. As the last of the cookies got eaten, the talk turned personal.

♪No, I had no broodlings of my own,♪ said Sho. ♪My broodmates and I were still too unripe. Another two summers, maybe, or three.♪ With a tentative glance at Brecken: ♪And you?♪

♪It's more complicated with us,♪ Brecken said. ♪I'd have to find a partner, someone I want to have children with—if I decide I want them. I'm not sure I do.♪

♪With us, the budding comes when it comes; there is no choosing. But broodmates always ripen together. We were made that way.♪ In a low sad tone: ♪Sometimes when it was cold we would gather close together and talk about which of our dreams we would tell to our broodlings. Now I must remember their dreams to share with mine.♪

Brecken reached for Sho, and the shoggoth flowed close. ♪In A Quiet Cavern,♪ she said; it was Sho's name that day. ♪It must hurt terribly to be left so alone.♪

The answer came in an unsteady whistle, and with the same curious fluttering: ♪*But I am not alone, not now, not when I am with you.*♪

It was a simple thing to do after all, Brecken thought later: a matter of saying ♪*I'm glad,*♪ and letting herself bend to kiss the shoggoth's smooth cool surface. A pseudopod flowed out in response, curved around her cheek, left a sudden dampness there, tinged with the fresh-bread smell and something else, something dark and rich like soil. Brecken placed a hand over the pseudopod, holding it gently in place.

♪*I—I wish ....*♪ Sho started to say, fell silent in confusion.

The damp place on Brecken's cheek tingled and enticed. ♪*The, the moisture,*♪ she said. ♪*That is the thing between broodmates?*♪

♪*Yes—yes, it is.*♪ In sudden frantic notes: ♪*I am sorry, I do not wish to offend—*♪

♪*I'm not offended,*♪ she replied. ♪*I'm very glad.*♪ It was true, though she was trembling nearly as much as Sho was. She kissed Sho again, and made sure this time that the kiss was good and wet. Sho flowed against her, trembling even harder, and a pseudopod traced a line of wetness from the point of her cheekbone around to the back of her neck, waking every nerve.

♪*Your body has special places for so many things,*♪ Sho said then, shyly. ♪*I am wondering if it has special places for this too.*♪

♪*Y-yes. Yes, of course.*♪

♪*Will you show me?*♪

Heart pounding, Brecken pulled off her nightgown with shaking hands, and showed her.

* * *

Later—how much later, Brecken had no idea then or afterwards—they lay still, curled around each other under the quilts in a single damp shape, so intertwined that Brecken was no longer entirely sure where her body ended and Sho's began. The rich dark scent of Sho's passion and the salty musk of her own blended, intoxicating, and through it Brecken caught another of Sho's scents, the washed-mushroom odor of simple happiness.

The light fixture overhead still shone, casting dim rainbow splashes of itself on the few parts of Sho that reached out from underneath the quilts, for Brecken hadn't been able to muster the fortitude to leave the futon even for the few moments it would have taken to go to the switch. Her mind circled around an unfamiliar word that Sho had piped in her ear, soft as a whisper, at one intense moment. It was related to the word for broodmate, that was clear, but there was a cadence at the end that intensified other words. Broodsister, maybe, was the closest she could get in translation: an endearment, possibly more.

Sho was still on the waking-side, her eyes opening and closing slowly, looking at her with what Brecken had come to recognize as a dazed delighted look. What her own face looked like just then, Brecken didn't try to guess. The word repeated itself over and over in her mind, and she guessed dimly what it would mean if she spoke it aloud to Sho. A rush of affection as the shoggoth brushed her skin with a drowsy pseudopod settled the issue, and Brecken repeated the word in a quiet whistle.

A dozen eyes opened at once, then closed as pseudopods drew Brecken close. A moment later a sharp repeated tremor began to shake Sho's form. Were those the shoggoth equivalent of tears? Brecken did not know, but she wrapped her arms tight around Sho anyway, pressed her face into the shoggoth's surface. Somehow, despite the vast differences between them, the motion seemed to communicate.

* * *

Later still, Brecken woke to find the first traces of daylight filtering in through the blinds. She lay still for a time, watched a few of Sho's eyes drift open and shut with glacial slowness, then untangled herself gently from her broodsister and slipped out from under the quilts. Cold air stung against her bare skin as she crossed the room, turned off the light.

She turned and, despite the cold, stood there for a time watching Sho as she dreamed. Her scent and Sho's, mingled inextricably, brought a cascade of fresh memories with every breath. Old habits of thought tried to convince her that she should be shocked and horrified by what they'd done, and failed.

Now that it's happened, she asked herself then, is it what you wanted? She had no answer. All she knew for certain was that she'd crossed a line, and there would never be a way back. She glanced down at herself, considered the soft curves and gawky angles of her body. It would not have surprised her unduly just then if she'd found herself beginning to sprout tentacles, but improbable as it seemed, nothing had changed that she could see.

As she started back to the futon, the bells of the First Baptist Church rang in the distance, announcing the sunrise service. Listening, Brecken remembered the words Sho had drawn from the notes of the bells tolling the hour, and the familiar sequence of the carillon stretched and shifted into a theme: the opening theme of a movement, Brecken knew at once, a largo to balance the allegretto first movement of her concerto. In the moments that followed, the rest of the movement sketched itself out in her mind.

She went to the end table beside the futon, stood there irresolute for a moment, then sighed. I'm tired of fighting it, she told herself, but she didn't feel tired; she felt light, trembling, newborn. Pulling her composing notebook out from under a stack of books and finding a pen felt like the first steps out of cold echoing darkness into greenery and sun. She wriggled back into her flannel nightgown and settled back on the futon. Tucking her feet up under her, she got the quilts settled in place and shifted toward Sho, who flowed drowsily against her.

The pen scratched in the silence of the dawn, and after a moment a luminous eye peered up at her. ♪*It is well with you?*♪

♪*It is very well,*♪ Brecken whistled. ♪*So well I don't know words for it. And with you?*♪

♪*Today my name is Brought Out Of The Empty Places,*♪ Sho said simply.

♪*I'm so glad.*♪ Brecken paused, and thought of one way she could welcome the future the two of them had just set in motion. ♪*Today my name is Embraced.*♪

Sho trembled. ♪*Broodsister, broodsister—*♪

Brecken put an arm around her, held her close. The trembling stilled, and after a time Sho slipped back over to the dreaming-side. Brecken looked down at her, dizzied by the intensity of the feelings the shoggoth wakened in her. Then, moving slowly so the movements of hand and pen did not disturb Sho, she let herself fall into the condition of fire.

CHAPTER 9

WINTER SYMPHONIES

Sixteen days slipped by between Christmas Eve and the first day of classes in the new semester. That was what the calendar said, at least, but afterwards Brecken never could sort out what happened on which day, for the time slipped past in curves as perfect and shapeless as Sho's. She'd kept up the shoggoth habit of giving herself temporary names each day, but she couldn't even remember which names she'd given herself, much less in which order: had she been Laughs At Falling Snow before In A Circle or afterwards, or had she taken either name during those days at all?

Twice, certainly, she'd put on street clothes, bundled up against the weather, and trudged the four blocks to Meeker Street to do her laundry at the laundromat and restock her cupboards and fridge from the First National grocery. A few cars picked their way along the black and icy streets, a few stray pedestrians huddled into their coats as they passed her by, but she saw no one she knew, no one she wanted to see, until the door of the little apartment spilled yellow light onto the snow and let her back into Sho's welcoming presence.

At least four times she'd made the much shorter trip to the mailbox out front to mail letters to her mother and pick up the few letters she received. Once, too, on New Year's Eve, she'd made the traditional good-luck foods her grandmother used to fix, rice and beans for health, corn bread for happiness, boiled greens for money, bacon for plenty, and served them up for the two of them, wishing devoutly that the rite would give the two of them some protection against the dangers that surrounded them.

Then there was the day not long after Christmas when she got out her laptop, booted it up, ignored the little icon that told her about all the emails that she hadn't gotten around to reading, went straight to the Partridgeville State website and logged onto the page where she could change her schedule for the new semester. Four clicks deleted MSE 242, Introduction to Music Education II, and MSE 266, Psychology of Music Education; four more got her into MUS 331, Counterpoint, and MUS 365, Introduction to Orchestral Arrangement—she'd worried that one or both of those might be full, but the changes went through without a hitch. She let out a ragged breath, logged off, shut down the laptop before the thought of those unread emails had time to work on her.

Maybe it was the best decision she'd ever made and maybe it was the worst, but it was her decision and she'd resolved not to turn back. She couldn't bear the thought of feeding the misery she'd witnessed at Partridgeville High, and Rohrbach's assurance that she'd get used to it sickened her, not least because she dreaded the possibility that he might turn out to be right, that familiarity might numb her to the wretchedness that goal-oriented instruction meant when it was applied to human beings. The other road led to the condition of fire and it drew her, a moth to its flame; if that means I spend my life flipping burgers, she told herself in a flash of defiance, that's what it means.

Aside from those interruptions, though, the sixteen days from Christmas to the Sunday before classes folded and flowed together into one warm dancing blur. Brecken spent days at a time wearing nothing but a flannel nightgown with a baggy sweater over it, between those intervals when she wore nothing at all, when fumbling and soft whistles taught her how to coax shudders of delight from Sho's body, and taught Sho how to do the same with hers. There were times when she drifted off to sleep in a tangle of limbs and pseudopods in the middle of the afternoon, or pattered around the kitchenette in bare feet at four in the morning cooking a dinner for two, and there were times upon times when she and Sho lay all atangle on the futon under heaped quilts and the rest of the world stayed far away.

Words bedeviled her now and again. One dark morning, as sleet drummed on the windows, she wondered for a while whether the fact that she'd fallen in love with the shoggoth made her a lesbian, since Sho was after all female. Then it occurred to her that she didn't want a woman in her bed, or for that matter a man; she wanted Sho. With that settled, she wondered drowsily for a while whether that made her a shoggoth-sexual or simply a Shosexual, before she simply fell asleep.

Another time, when Sho was far over on the dreaming-side and Brecken sat watching her in a warm shoggoth-colored daze, thinking at stray intervals about doing something else but never quite getting around to it, she found herself wondering if what she and Sho had done an hour before really counted as sex, and whether it meant the same things to Sho that it did to her. The question had no straightforward answer. The things she did to delight Sho had nothing in common with human sex, nor did the things Sho did to give her pleasure, the little pseudopods like tongues or fingers dancing on her sensitive places, have much in common with the things she'd done with Jay or the boyfriends she'd had in high school. She guessed that none of it was much like the ordinary sharing-of-moisture between shoggoth broodmates, either, but it somehow worked for them both, the giving as well as the receiving. Competing words in English and the shoggoth language knotted in her mind, until finally she laughed, shook her head, nestled against Sho, and let the words go spinning away somewhere else as a sleepy pseudopod flowed around her and drew her down into soft darkness.

Another language, the language of music, offered her better ways to talk about the things that mattered to her, and a good fraction of those sixteen days went into the attempt. Sometimes she played Baroque pieces on the piano, sometimes it was the flute that called her, and there were also times that she and Sho improvised duets that suggested entire new worlds of music to Brecken, but she also spent hours curled up on the futon with the composition notebook open in front of her, staring at nothing in particular while music shaped itself in her mind.

The second movement of the concerto took many hours, but it wasn't alone. A minuet in C came together over the course of a single afternoon, though it took days more to make it sound exactly the way she wanted; a piano etude in D minor helped her work out a way of handling harmonies she liked; then, one at a time, she composed three sarabandes in G, using three of Sho's temporary names as themes—to the two of them, those pieces would always be "Voice From A Distance," "I Fold Around Myself," and "Two Different Colors." Brecken wondered from time to time if she'd ever be able to share those titles and their meanings with anyone else.

That was on her mind now and again, as the sixteen days flowed seamlessly to their close. Part of her wanted to run out into the streets of Partridgeville and tell everyone she met how beautiful and sweet and caring Sho was, and part of her wanted to clutch that knowledge to herself forever as a secret, but in the world to which she'd have to return once classes began, the latter was the only option she had. She thought with wary amusement about what Mrs. Dalzell would think, or Professor Toomey, or Rosalie, if they found out that their tenant or student or best friend had fallen in love with a shoggoth—and back behind that was the cold memory of thunder beyond Hob's Hill, the knowledge that there were people somewhere in the world whose only answer to Sho would be the destroying fire.

The last night before classes started again, as traffic grumbled on the nearby streets and the neighborhood woke up from winter break, they talked about that. It all seemed distant and abstract, though Brecken knew well enough that the little circle of sheltering darkness the two of them had made for each other could too easily be shattered by their own carelessness, or by any of a hundred unforeseeable happenings. There had been no further sign of anyone hunting for Sho, but Brecken remained wary.

Later, she fixed cheese polenta for the two of them. As it cooked, Sho piped, ♪*May I have apricot jam on mine? I think it would be very good.*♪

Brecken gave her a startled look, but she'd already gotten used to the oddities of Sho's tastes. After all, she thought, she likes Aunt Mary's zucchini bread. She tried not to think about the last time she'd tasted Aunt Mary's cooking, and whistled back, ♪*Of course.*♪

As they sat on the floor and shared their meal, she watched Sho quiver with pleasure and smelled freshly washed mushrooms in the air. Unnecessarily, she asked, ♪*How is it?*♪

♪*Very good,*♪ said Sho. ♪*Very very good. In all the world there is only one thing I know that delights me more.*♪

♪*Oh?*♪

♪*You.*♪

Brecken laughed, bent to kiss her surface, felt a pseudopod brush her cheek and leave a little spot of moisture there.

Later still, as they nestled down together under the covers, it occurred to Brecken that the sixteen days just past should have felt like a dream. They didn't; they felt as though she'd woken up fully for the first time in her life, and was about to sink back into restless slumber. The thought unraveled as she fell asleep, and gave way to a curious dream where she stood in a dark place surrounded by curves and angles, and spoke in whispers with the darkness.

* * *

The next morning dawned cold and blustery, with flurries of wet snow spattering down from a sky the color of iron. Brecken dressed in jeans and a bulky sweater, put on makeup for the first time in weeks, then perched on the futon and packed her tote bag with everything she'd need for the day's classes. Halfway through the process she thought of her cell phone and got it out of her purse. It was turned off, and she realized after a blank moment that she hadn't turned it on since that last wretched practice session with Rose and Thorn. With a frustrated sigh, she woke the thing, gave it a dismayed look when it told her that she'd managed to miss nineteen calls and had fifty-three text messages waiting.

♪What is it?♪ Sho asked her.

♪The thing-that-talks has too much to say,♪ Brecken replied.

Six of the calls and twenty-one of the texts were from Rosalie, unsurprisingly enough. Most of the rest were nothing she had to worry about, but three calls and eight texts were from Jay, and that troubled her. She deleted his calls unheard, then opened the first text and read: BRKN PLS TXT ME THX J. The last one, which she opened next, had a slight variation on the same message. She closed it with a scowl and deleted everything he'd written, then gathered up her courage and started reading Rosalie's texts. The first few were full of outrage at Jay, talk about her holiday trip—she'd ended up going with her family to Guadalajara after all—and more talk about Tom Bannister, who she insisted was really nice but not boyfriend material. The texts that followed hoped that Brecken was all right; the last dozen or so managed, even through the abbreviations, to sound desolate. She hit the REPLY button on the last one, and typed: RO SRY 4 DROPNG OFF URTH M OK NOW C U @ COMP CLS 2DAY?

The answer came back while she was still deleting sales pitches for penis-enlargement pills: OMG OMG OMG THX BRKN SO GLAD UR OK VIV @ 1030 2DAY?

It probably wouldn't hurt to get to campus early, Brecken decided, and so sent back a text agreeing to be at Vivaldi's at 10:30. That settled, she finished packing, ate breakfast with Sho, spent half an hour that probably should have gone into study in hugs and whistled endearments, and then put on her warmest coat, hat, and scarf, and left for campus.

Danforth Avenue was a symphony in black and dirty white, given an unfamiliar rhythm by the rattle of tire chains on ice and packed snow as two long lines of cars slogged this way and that. Most of the sidewalk had been shoveled or salted, though, and she made better time than she'd foreseen. The church clock up on Angell Hill hadn't yet chimed 10:15 when she got to campus and veered left toward the the gray plaza and the stark concrete mass of Gurnard Hall.

The thought of heading through the glass doors and crossing The Cave to Vivaldi's bothered her more than she'd expected, but she squared her shoulders and told herself that Jay wouldn't be there, not while he had Barbara Cormyn to keep him occupied. A trickle of other students were heading the same way, and she let herself move with the current, across the wet and salted plaza, and through one of the glass doors into The Cave—

And there he was, sprawled in a chair over by the nearest of the angled pillars, giving her a sudden intent look. She looked away, cut across The Cave toward the doors that led on toward Vivaldi's, but he was already on his feet, heading toward her. "Brecken—"

She would not look at him. "Go away," she said, and kept walking.

"Brecken!" He caught up to her, took hold of her arm.

Whether it was the too familiar wheedling tone in his voice or the hand on her arm that did it, she never did figure out, but all at once the bitterness she'd pushed aside for so long came surging up. Anger flared white-hot, and her usual reserve splintered. She rounded on him, shook her arm free. "I said go away. I don't want to talk to you. I don't want to see you. You can go crawl into a ditch and die for all I care. Okay? Now leave me alone." She turned her back on him and stalked away. In the glass doors ahead, she could see his reflection, silent and staring, a motionless presence amid the bustle of The Cave.

She was trembling by the time she got to the door, and the expression on her face got her startled glances as she hurried down the corridor past ugly blue doors to the entrance to Vivaldi's. Half a dozen people were in line ahead of her, and that gave her time to calm down; still, her hands were shaking so hard there would have been coffee on the floor if she hadn't popped a lid on the cup as soon as the gangly young man behind the counter handed it to her. A few moments later she was sitting at a table for two at the far end of the coffee shop, staring at the coffee. As the anger drained away from her, it left the usual wretched taste behind.

There was more to it than that familiar reaction, though. Jay, The Cave, Rose and Thorn, Partridgeville High, the whole tangled, troubled mess in which she'd floundered during the fall semester—it all felt oddly distant, as though she'd somehow moved toward its outer edges. As though, she thought, she was in it, but not really in it. As though the fears and frantic longings that had harried her all that time, and for years before then, had moved just slightly away from her, and left her a little space for her own, like the one she shared with Sho.

She sipped at the coffee, then set it down and stared at it again, trying to make sense of the strange new place where she'd somehow ended up.

* * *

All at once the other chair at the table slid out with a squawk. Brecken glanced up, startled out of convoluted thoughts, and found Rosalie beaming down at her. "Hey, girl. Did you really just rip Jay a new one?"

"Well, kind of," said Brecken, reddening.

Rosalie plopped into the chair. "Kind of?" she said. "That's not what I heard in The Cave. Melissa Bukowski and Keith Platchett both said you told him to go die in a ditch."

"Well—"

"Those exact words."

"Yes," Brecken admitted.

"Thank you Jesus," said Rosalie.

Brecken drew her shoulders forward and stared at her coffee, and after a moment Rosalie said, "I'm sorry, girl. I know that whole thing's still got to have you feeling all torn up inside. It's just—well, he's been telling everybody that he's going to get you back and he's going to get Rose and Thorn going again. I was worried that you'd go back to him."

"Not a chance," said Brecken.

"Thank you Jesus," Rosalie repeated.

It wasn't until then that Rosalie's words sank in. "What do you mean, get Rose and Thorn going again?"

Rosalie's mouth fell open. "You don't know." When Brecken shook her head: "Oh my God. Girl, where have you *been*?"

"I didn't leave my apartment much," Brecken admitted. "I just wanted to be alone." The unspoken words *with Sho* hovered in the air between them, but Rosalie somehow didn't notice.

"Oh my God," said Rosalie again. She leaned forward. "Okay. You didn't hang around at all when things happened at the practice, did you? You probably didn't hear what I said to him."

"All I heard was the first couple of words you said." She managed a smile. "It sounded like you really tore into him."

"Oh yeah. I told him exactly what kind of a goddamn sleazy lowlife douchebag he was for treating you like that, right out in front of everyone, and then he up and said some nasty things to me, stuff that was really out of line, so I quit Rose and Thorn then and there, and so did Donna. We packed up and walked out, and we tried to find you, but you'd already gone I don't know where and we didn't want to haul our instruments all over town when it was that cold, so I texted you, and then we went to my apartment and got good and drunk." Brecken gave her a reproving look and she grinned, went on.

"Okay, so that leaves Jay, Walt, Jamal, and Barbara. Then all of a sudden, about three days later, it was Jay and Jamal, because Barbara dumped Jay, scooped up Walt, and quit."

Brecken stared at her. "Seriously?"

"Seriously."

"I thought Walt would stick with Jay no matter what."

Rosalie laughed. "Not when that little poptart was dragging him away by his dick." Brecken choked and blushed, and Rosalie went on. "Which she was. So Jay had to try to replace everybody and get a group to play with again, and while he was doing that Barbara goes to all the gigs he lined up—she got the whole calendar from him the same way we did—and wiggles at the people in charge and tells them that Rose and Thorn just broke up but she and Walt can fill in for a third of the price. So she walks off with the gigs."

"Oh dear God," said Brecken.

"I think she was planning that the whole time."

"I'm not sure that's fair," Brecken started to say, and stopped, remembering the cold implacable thing she'd seen in Barbara Cormyn's eyes.

"Bet on it, girl." Rosalie's voice dropped. "Now this is where it gets ugly. Me and Donna decided to mess with Jay, and I had a friend in Trenton call him pretending to be planning an April wedding. We told Mike to tell Jay that the bride played viola in high school, and she really wanted to have Gossec's gavotte played on the viola for her wedding."

Brecken started laughing. "He hates that piece."

"Oh, trust me, I know." Rosalie looked smug. "And you know how weak his bowing is. He'd have to practice Gossec for hours to be good enough to solo, and of course Mike was

going to cancel right before any money changed hands, so Jay
was going to spend all that time sweating blood on Gossec and
then get nothing. But Mike asked about money, of course, and
Jay quoted her a price that was almost three times what he told
us he was charging."

Brecken's laugh stopped short as that sank in. She gave
Rosalie an appalled look, and Rosalie nodded. Brecken stared
at her a moment longer, then slumped forward and put her face
into her hands. Sho is wrong, she thought. I really am stupid.
The wads of cash Jay always had in his pockets, the expensive
books he was always buying for his studies—the whole time,
he'd been giving the other musicians in the group as little as
he thought he could get away with, and pocketing everything
else for himself.

She realized then that Rosalie had just said something else,
and lifted her face out of her hands. "I'm sorry, Ro," she said.
"What was that?"

"I said he's been doing that all along," Rosalie repeated.
"I talked to Mom, and she taught me some tricks she learned
from other people in the D.A.'s office for looking stuff up about
people, and I did some snooping. When Jamal had to couch
surf last summer because he didn't have the money for a place,
when Donna had to get her grandparents to cover her lessons,
Jay had the money. He could have helped them out. So I've put
the word out."

Brecken's gaze flicked up to Rosalie's face, back down to
the coffee.

"I didn't need the money," Rosalie said, leaning forward,
her eyes narrowing and her voice little more than a hiss. "But
Jamal did, and Donna did, and you did, and you do *not* mess
with my friends like that." She sat up and put on a bright smile.
"So there won't be a Rose and Thorn Ensemble any more. I've
already talked to Jamal, and he's talked to Donna and they're
putting together a string quartet with Jim Domenico and Susan
Chu—have you heard her viola playing? She's really good.

I've talked to some other people, and I'm going to talk to a lot more. And now I've talked to you." The smile broadened. "Are you up for doing gigs together?"

Brecken blinked again. "Sure. Just the two of us?"

"Just the two of us. Once wedding season gets here, folks'll be falling all over each other to book a couple of cute girls doing harp and flute duets, right? And I bet we can get parties and stuff lined up before then, too."

"You're on."

Rosalie beamed at her. "Girl, you just watch. We'll have a great time. Let's get some practice time in, and start working up some things."

An unwilling smile tugged at one side of Brecken's mouth. "I think I can find some free time Saturday afternoons."

Rosalie burst out laughing. "Yeah, I bet. How about Wednesday afternoons too? Or is Intro to Music Ed II going to eat a bunch of your weekday afternoons again?"

"I'm not taking that," Brecken said.

"You're—" Rosalie gave her a baffled look. "What do you mean, you're not taking it?"

"I dropped it. I'm switching to composition track."

"Oh, for Christ's sake. I thought we talked about that last semester."

"I know." With a little shrug: "I spent a lot of time thinking about it over winter break. I thought I wanted to teach music, but I don't, not really. I never even thought about composing, but it makes me feel—I don't know, complete, maybe. So I'm going with it. I've got orchestral arranging and counterpoint classes this semester. Next year, well, we'll see."

Rosalie gave her a long sour look. "Yeah, whatever." Then, pasting on a bright smile: "You can sort things out later when you're feeling better."

I'm feeling fine, Brecken thought, but decided to let it pass.

* * *

Soon enough they were riding the elevator to the top floor of Gurnard Hall, to the same awkwardly angled room, the same battered piano, and the same students. When Brecken came through the door, half a dozen conversations stopped cold. After a moment of dead silence, Julian Pinchbeck and his cronies looked pointedly away and started talking again, more loudly than before. Most of the others stared at her with expressions she couldn't read at all.

She and Rosalie went to the same seats as before. Once Brecken set down her tote bag and shed her coat and hat, though, she said "Just a minute" to Rosalie, and went to the back of the room, where Darren Wegener sat.

He looked up from a hefty textbook that didn't seem to have anything to do with music, gave her his ungainly smile. "Hi."

"Hi," she said. "I'm sorry I just ran out on you after that last class session."

"Don't worry about it. You were pretty stressed."

"Well, yes—but I'm still sorry."

He nodded. "Hey, when you get a chance, drop me an email. There's something going on that you ought to know about."

Brecken promised she would and went back to her seat. Rosalie gave her a long baffled look, then shook her head and looked somewhere else. Brecken busied herself fishing a notebook and pen out of her tote bag. She'd just gotten them out when Molly Wolejko came through the door. She'd changed the color of her hair from pink to traffic-cone orange, but the ripped jeans and the black t-shirt with a metal band logo on it hadn't changed at all. She spotted Brecken, came over, sprawled in the chair next to hers. "That was a hell of a piece you played for us."

Brecken, startled, managed to stammer out something more or less gracious, and Molly grinned. "You're thinking, what the hell is a metalhead chick doing complimenting you on a Baroque concerto, right?" The grin broadened. "I play metal because it says what I want to say, but I listen to lots of different kinds of music."

Julian, who was sitting within earshot, turned toward Molly and in a contemptuous tone said, "Not postspectralism, I bet."

"Sure," Molly said, meeting his gaze with a level glance. "When it's any good." He glared at her and turned away, and she grinned again and winked at Brecken, turned to face the podium as Toomey came through the door.

The class went smoothly from then on, and so did her counterpoint class, which started at 1:30. Professor Toomey taught that one as well, and gave Brecken the closest thing to a startled look she'd ever seen in those unreadable eyes when he spotted her sitting in the third row. She didn't spend much time wondering about that, since even the simple examples of counterpoint he covered in that first lecture set her mind racing, as she glimpsed some of the ways two melodies could play against each other.

When class was over, though, and she stood up to leave, Toomey spoke her name, and she went up to the podium. "Email me some times when you've got a free half hour," he said. "There are things we should talk about."

* * *

"I'm glad you could come by today," Professor Toomey said. "Go ahead and leave the door open."

Brecken gave him an uncertain look, but the professor's face betrayed nothing. She left the office door wide, settled on the rickety chair he indicated. His office was as cluttered as ever. Through the one window at the room's far end, Mainwaring Hall rose gray and stark against a wintry sky. She'd emailed him right after class, gotten an answer back in minutes.

"You're in two of my composition classes this quarter," he went on. "You were on the education track, weren't you?"

"Yes, I was," Brecken said. "Last semester I—I figured out I'm not really cut out to be a music teacher. I thought I was, but—" She made herself shrug.

"Understood. Composition track now?" When she nodded: "I'm going to assume you already know what the job prospects in music composition are like."

"I know I'll have to get a day job."

Toomey nodded. "Fair enough. As long as you know what you're getting into." He sat back in his chair. "When we talked last semester, I said that your bourrée didn't sound like fake anything, and that it might just sound like real Brecken Kendall."

"I remember," she said, venturing a smile.

"I was right. Are you planning on finishing the concerto?"

"I'm working on the second movement now."

"That's good to hear. You've still got things to learn, no question, but the first movement was really remarkably good. A little more polish, a little attention to some issues we haven't yet covered in class, and that's something that could end up being played on the concert stage."

Brecken blinked and tried to fit her mind around the words. "I mean that quite seriously," Toomey went on. "Now here's my next question. The two pieces you did for me last semester were Baroque or, let's say, neo-Baroque. I assume that's not accidental."

She looked down. "No."

"You've checked out the more contemporary options, I imagine."

"I tried." Her gaze stayed fixed to the floor. "They just don't work for me."

"And you're planning generally on composing in the older forms, working with tonality, that sort of thing?"

"Yes." Her voice was little more than a whisper.

"Then I'm going to make a suggestion I'd really rather not make," Toomey said. "I think you should consider transferring to another college."

She looked up at him then, uncertain.

"Partridgeville State has a good music program, but it's mostly focused on the education and performance tracks, you know. Madeline and I—" Madeline, Brecken recalled after a moment, was Professor Kaufmann, the other composition teacher in the department. "—do our best, but this isn't a strong composition school."

Brecken gave him a startled look. "I didn't know that," she said. "Julian Pinchbeck talks all the time about how he came here because there's such a good composition program."

That got her a raised eyebrow. "He says that?" When she nodded: "That's funny, in a bleak sort of way." The professor shook his head. "He's wrong. The thing is, you'd be in trouble if it was, because most of the schools that have a strong composition program are all about the latest cutting-edge stuff, and you can't get the kind of musical education you need from one of those." With a wry look: "As it is, Madeline's pretty heavily committed to the latest trends, too. There's been some talk about a neoclassical revival, but so far only a few schools have programs that focus on the kind of thing you're interested in."

Brecken stared at him for a long moment, processing this, then swallowed and said, "Can—can you tell me about some of them?"

"Of course. Binger State University out in Oklahoma has a composition program with a traditional focus, and so does Chequamegon College up in Wisconsin. I don't know a great deal about them, but there's also Miskatonic University up in Massachusetts, which I can tell you a little more about." With a fractional smile: "I've got inside information, so to speak. A good friend of mine, Dr. June Satterlee, teaches there."

Brecken nodded uncertainly. Something about the way Toomey had said "good friend" hinted at old and possibly unfinished business between the two of them. "What does she teach?"

"Music history. Her research is mostly early twentieth century jazz and blues history—but she also plays a mean stride piano."

"I hope I meet her someday, then," Brecken said, smiling. "My grandfather used to play that same style."

The unreadable eyes turned on her. "Given your last name, I'm going to wonder aloud if your grandfather's somebody I might have heard of."

Brecken swallowed, nodded again. "Aaron Kendall."

"The jazz pianist."

"Yes."

"So Olive Kendall was your grandmother."

"Yes."

He considered her, then turned to the computer at his desk, clicked the mouse once, twice, a third time. A moment later Brecken's face lit up as a sequence of piano chords came through the speakers, played in a way that woke fond memories. "That's him, isn't it?" she asked. "St. James Infirmary Blues. He used to play that all the time on his piano at home, and Grandma Olive would sing it with him."

That earned her a fractional smile. "I still have some of their old LPs." Then: "I'll go ahead and send you information on all three of the places I mentioned, if you want."

"Please," Brecken said. "If it's not too much trouble."

"Easily done." He considered her again, nodded once, as though that settled something.

The wind blew snow in Brecken's face all the way up Danforth Street. She didn't mind, since that and the uncertain footing gave her something to think about other than Professor Toomey's words. The thought of leaving Partridgeville State for some other college frightened and tantalized her at the same time. Part of her wanted nothing to do with yet another sudden uprooting to a place she'd never been, part of her wanted just as badly to put as much distance as possible between herself and the bitter memories of autumn.

The closing of the door behind her shut out more than the weather; a quick whistled greeting brought a reply—♪Coming Back, I am glad you are here♪—that swept other thoughts into distance. By the time Sho flowed out from under the closet door Brecken had gotten coat, hat and scarf hung up on the coat tree, and dropped to her knees to fling her arms around the shoggoth and press her face into shapeless curves.

She got an email from Professor Toomey that afternoon with links to the colleges he'd mentioned, read it, and filed it for the time being. Later, she remembered Darren's words, and sent him an email. The answer came back within minutes: *Are you free 7pm tomorrow Hancock Library? Something you need to see. Pls don't mention to anybody else.—DW*

She pondered that while dinner cooked. If the email had suggested anywhere less public she'd have worried, but Hancock Library was full of staff and students at all hours, and there was a campus shuttle that could get her home if walking turned out to be too risky. After dinner, she sent back an email promising to be there. Until morning came, that was the last attention she paid to anything outside the walls of the little apartment.

CHAPTER 10

A FALLEN WORLD

At 7:00 sharp the next evening she left the sidewalk on College Street and went to the main doors of Hancock Library. It was a crisp, cold night, with a sky full of stars overhead, and the walk down from the converted garage left her exhilarated. That day she'd only had one class, Intro to Orchestral Arrangement at 2:30, and so she'd been able to spend the whole morning and most of the afternoon in Sho's company. The intensity of their winter break together had faded a little, but every moment she spent away from her broodsister still felt a little like wasted time.

Once inside the library, she glanced around, uncertain, then spotted Darren at the same moment that he noticed her. He hauled himself out of the chair where he'd been sitting, crossed the room to her. "I'm glad you could make it," he said in a low voice. "Come on." Before she could ask any questions he led the way further into the library.

He stopped at a door marked STAFF ONLY in a quiet corner, waited until nobody but Brecken was in sight, tapped on the door once, then twice, then twice again. Moments passed, and then a lock clicked and the door opened. He ducked through it, motioned for Brecken to follow. She gave him an uneasy look—there might be good reasons, of course, not to go into an unfrequented place with a man she didn't know that well—but she followed him anyway.

On the far side was a cluttered room with metal shelves around the edges and piles upon piles of old hardback books in the middle. Another young man, plump and smiling, with black horn-rimmed glasses and a shock of unruly black hair, closed the door behind them.

"Stan, this is Brecken, who I told you about," Darren said then. "Brecken, Stan's a friend of mine. He's in the library science program, and does work-study here."

"Did Darren say anything about this?" Stan said, gesturing at the books.

"No." Brecken glanced from one to the other, uncertain.

"It's like this." He turned, walked over to the books. "The director of library services told us right before break that we have to cut our book holdings by twenty-two percent." His smile crumpled and fell. "Eleven thousand books. This is just part of it."

Brecken gave him an appalled look. "Why?"

"Nobody knows. We've got the shelf space, we've got the money, but we've got to clear away the quote deadwood unquote, no other explanation given. And the books aren't even going to be sold. They're going to be destroyed."

Brecken opened her mouth, and then remembered the Woodfield Consolidated School District and the way it had gotten rid of its art and music programs, and closed it again.

"It's going on everywhere these days." Stan picked up a book from the pile, gave it a sad look. "University libraries, public libraries, you name it." With a little bleak smile: "I've got a new theory about the burning of the Library of Alexandria. I think King Ptolemy just up and decided that nobody would ever actually need all those musty old scrolls."

"Ow," said Brecken.

"Yeah," Stan said. "The one piece of good news is that some of us talked to the librarians, who are just as upset about this as the rest of us, and they said that if books up and disappear from the sorting room nobody's going to ask any hard questions. So we're going to save at least some of the collection by getting it into other hands."

"There are books on music," Darren said. "Old books on composition. Do you want the textbook Mozart's dad used to teach him counterpoint?"

Brecken tried to decide if he was joking. His face denied it. "Please," she said.

He went over to the heaps of books, glanced at a few volumes, picked up a battered volume with a black cover. "Here you go. The author's name is Johann Joseph Fux."

She gave him a sidelong look. "Seriously?"

"Seriously." He came back toward her, grinned his ungainly grin. "So when it comes to music, I definitely have Fux to give." He made a florid bow, held out the book to her.

Laughing, she curtseyed and took it. A brief glance through the pages, and she was sure she wanted to take it home with her and study it for hours on end.

"You can put the ones you want there so I can scan them and mark them as discarded," Stan said then, indicating a shelf on one wall. "Darren says you're studying old music, right? Please take anything you can use." All at once his voice wavered. "I went into library science because I love books. I want to get them into people's hands, not—not throw them out."

He turned sharply away. Darren glanced after him, then turned to Brecken and motioned to the books. "It's all a mess," he said, "but I think the music books are mostly on this side. I've been here before, with other people—Stan's already got a couple of hundred books handed out, and we're going to see to it that nothing worthwhile gets wasted."

"Are you looking for anything?"

"Old books in Latin and German on music theory, especially if there's mathematics."

A memory surfaced. "You said you're a mathematician."

He nodded. "I'm finishing up a master's in mathematics this semester." He knelt beside the books, pulled out two. "You should look at these." Then: "Okay, here's one for me."

For the next half hour or so the two of them went through the heap of books together, like archeologists searching the ruins of a fallen world. There weren't that many books on old music, and most of them had nothing she could use, but now and then as she sorted through the volumes or considered things Darren handed her, she found treasures—a history of the fugue with hundreds of examples, three translations of old texts on counterpoint, a century-old doctoral dissertation that translated and discussed a fifteenth-century textbook of music theory, and more. By the time they finished, Brecken had two dozen books in her stack, and was trying to figure out how best to ferry them home.

"You didn't drive here?" Darren asked.

"I don't have a lot of money," she said, "and a car's more than I can afford."

"Okay." Diffidently: "I can give you a ride, if you want."

She considered that, and agreed. Maybe five minutes later, they carried four plastic grocery bags of books out the service entrance in back and got them settled in the trunk of a battered green sedan a couple of decades old. "Okay," Darren said, climbing in behind the wheel as Brecken got in the passenger side. "Give me directions."

The car pulled out onto Meeker Street a few moments later. "So what's a mathematician doing taking a composing class?" Brecken asked.

"My field's historical mathematics." He slowed as the light at College Street turned red. "Focusing on the math that people used back in the day to understand music, which is really different from what you get in music theory nowadays. So I'm taking classes in the music department to make sure I know enough not to talk nonsense."

"Did you take up piano as part of that that?"

"No, I started taking lessons when I was twelve." The light changed, and he turned left onto College Street. "One of those things. But it's because I've played a lot of Bach that I caught onto what I'm researching." Another left turn put the car onto Danforth Street, rising up toward the dark huddled mass of Hob's Hill. "I'm convinced there's a mathematical structure to Bach's fugues—not just his, either. There's the sort of thing they learned from Fux or Zarlino or the other writers on method, and then there's something else, a deeper structure, that was a trade secret, the sort of thing the Baroque masters used and didn't talk about."

"That's really interesting," said Brecken. "Is that why you said the fugue you played for the class was derivative?"

That got her a sudden sidelong glance. "Good. Yeah, I used Bach's math to compose it."

The car pulled up in front of Mrs. Dalzell's house. Darren got out with her and handed her the two grocery bags of books from the trunk, but made no attempt to get invited in. As Brecken headed for her door, she could hear his car's engine as he drove away.

Later that evening, after dinner and a long while curled up with Sho on the futon, she went onto the internet and started looking for news stories about libraries getting rid of books. It took only a few moments to find plenty of details. Stan hadn't been exaggerating: library systems had been dumping books for years, and to judge by what she read, the pace seemed to be picking up. She shook her head slowly, wondered what was behind it all.

* * *

The next morning Jay was in The Cave again, sitting over in one corner by himself, and though he stared at Brecken he didn't try to talk to her. That was the busy day of her week that semester, and she gave him a wary glance and then hurried on.

He was there the next day, too. By then she had something else to worry about, though, for the same abrupt silences and unreadable looks she'd gotten when she'd come through the door on the first day of Composition II had begun to spread through the rest of Partridgeville State's music department. She had Intro to Orchestral Arrangement that day, and startled glances and silences followed her from the moment she came in through the glass doors of The Cave, pursued by a wind with snow in its teeth, until she settled into a chair in a classroom on Gurnard Hall's fifth floor and pulled a notebook and a pen from her tote bag.

Professor Madeline Kaufmann was thin and tense and angular, with fussy clothing and dishwater-blonde hair pulled back hard into a bun. She lectured in a staccato voice, pacing from the podium to the piano on one side of the room, now and then stopping to play a flurry of notes or chords, covering so much so fast that it took Brecken's undivided attention to keep up with her. By the time the class session was over, four pages of Brecken's notebook were covered with notes and Brecken herself had a head full of ideas for composition. As she stuffed the notebook into her tote bag and got ready to leave, though, Professor Kaufmann said, "You're Brecken Kendall, right? Do you have anything right now, or can you stay for a few minutes?"

"I can stay," Brecken answered, trying to suppress a feeling of worry. "What is it?"

"There's been quite a bit of talk recently about your compositions, you know. I wonder if you'd be willing to play me one or two." With a thin smile: "To see what the fuss is about."

Brecken's heart sank. "Okay," she said. A dozen other students in the room had stopped in the middle of their own preparations for leaving; the professor gave them a level look, and they hurried out into the hallway. No one closed the door, though.

Brecken went to the piano; a quick scale got her fingers limbered. She considered her options, and then launched into the first of her three sarabandes, the one she thought of as "Voice from a Distance." As always, the music closed around her, holding her uncertainties and the professor's reaction at a far distance. The sarabande sparkled and flowed, reached its end, and Brecken paused a moment and then played her new minuet. That was bright and lively enough to raise her mood even in the most uncertain moments, and she finished it smiling.

When she turned to the professor, though, the smile faltered. Professor Kaufmann was considering her with a thin frown. "Those are both very crisply handled," she said, "but I think you'd be much better advised to put your talent to work on something a little less antiquated. Have you explored the current trends in art music?"

"Yes," Brecken said. "They don't do anything for me."

The professor shook her head briskly. "Take my advice, you can't afford that kind of thinking. If you want to get anywhere in composition you need to stay on the cutting edge."

But I don't want to get anywhere in composition, Brecken thought. I just want to write music. She didn't say anything of the kind, though, and extracted herself from the room and Professor Kaufmann's presence as quickly as she could. As she'd guessed, there were half a dozen students in the hall, all of them pretending that they'd been doing something other than listening at the door, and they stared at her as she went by.

When she got down to The Cave, more stares and silences were waiting. Brecken tried to ignore them all, went to the usual table. Donna and Rosalie were in the middle of a heated discussion about something, but dropped it the moment Brecken came into sight. She flopped down on a chair across from them, they exchanged greetings, and a moment's brittle silence passed. "You know what, girl?" Rosalie said to Brecken then, leaning forward and propping her chin on her hands. "I talked with my cousin Rick about you. He wants to meet you. You could do a lot worse; he's nice, he's cute, he's got a good job—"

Brecken managed to put on a bleak expression. "Ro, please. I'm still getting over one relationship, I'm not ready for another."

"It's been a whole month!" Rosalie said. "And of all the people to get torn up over, too."

Brecken just looked at her, and after a moment she rolled her eyes. "Okay, I get it. But when you're ready to start dating again, tell me, okay? I'll give you Rick's email."

"The funny thing is," Donna said then, "you haven't been acting like somebody who's getting over a relationship, Breck. You act like you're in love."

Brecken managed to keep her reaction off her face. "I think it's the composing," she said after a moment. "It's like I had an empty place in me, and now it's full."

It was the right thing to say, she knew that at once, because Rosalie rolled her eyes and then started talking about something else. After a while both of them had to leave for classes. Brecken started for Hancock Library, then stopped in the middle of the plaza, reminded herself that she didn't have any classwork that needed library time, and headed home. All the way up Danforth Street, she fretted about Donna's words, and tried to think of some way to distract her friends from any clue that might lead them to Sho.

* * *

That Friday was Brecken's birthday, and true to form, Aunt Mary sent a cloyingly cute birthday card with a department store gift certificate in it. Brecken looked up the chain online, and to her immense surprise discovered that it was not only still in business, it had a store in the Belknap Creek Mall. That afternoon she played the flute in Mrs. Macallan's memory for close to three hours, and for once it felt like a celebration of her teacher's life instead of an elegy for a useless death. Later, though a birthday cake seemed extravagant, she baked thumbprint cookies with apricot jam in the dents, and she and Sho had their own very private celebration thereafter.

Saturday she walked out Dwight Street to the mall, threaded her way through the mostly empty parking lot, and spent a good two hours going through the bargain bins in the women's clothing section of the store, finding everything they had in her size and then deciding which of them she could stand being seen in. By the time she got to the cash register she had a good-sized armload of practical clothing and one sheer extravagance, a lovely dark red dress with tiny gold seed beads sewn on it in a sunburst pattern.

Her route from there went back past empty storefronts to the food court where Rose and Thorn played the semester before, and as Brecken neared the court she heard music: a flute's high voice, a cello played in a style she thought she recognized. When she reached the food court, sure enough, Walt Gardner was the cellist and the flautist was Barbara Cormyn. The music was bland and sweet, and though the two of them were capable enough, there was something hollow where the life and soul of the music should have been.

Brecken stopped for a few moments, listening, and then walked past. Walt saw her and turned scarlet, and his playing faltered for a moment. Barbara glanced at him and then spotted Brecken, but neither her expression nor the sound of her flute wavered at all. Her big blue eyes gazed at Brecken in dull surprise, and the cold mechanical thing Brecken had seen behind her eyes showed again, registered her existence, and lost interest. Brecken was glad when the doors of the mall closed behind her and the music gave way to the earnest sounds of wind and traffic.

Other than that, she had nothing to take her away from the apartment that weekend. Rosalie tried to get her to come to Admiral Benbow's Friday night for dancing, but Brecken begged off. The promised Saturday practice sessions hadn't yet materialized, either, so except for the clothes she wore to the mall, a flannel nightgown and a baggy sweater were the most she put on at any point from Thursday evening to

Monday morning. She slept poorly and her dreams were troubled, but the daylight hours were pleasant enough that they made up for it.

Once she got home Saturday she neglected everything but Sho; Sunday she found time for music, the weekly letter to her mother, and a long afternoon working on counterpoint assignments, though the latter two also counted as time with Sho, since she'd done all of it curled up on the futon with cool black iridescence up close against her.

Toward evening, she leafed through some of the books she'd gotten, and ended up thoroughly baffled. Darren hadn't exaggerated the difference between old music theory and its modern equivalent. Before long she was completely lost among superpartients and superparticulars, sesquialters and sesquitertians, aliquot parts and harmonic middles, and the rest of it. It all probably made sense, she guessed, if you knew the terms, but she didn't.

Finally, just before she got to work on dinner, she emailed Darren and asked him if he could point her to something that would explain the older music theory. After dinner and a long stint of piano practice she settled down on the futon, talked with Sho for a while, and sank into a companionable silence that ended only when a pseudopod patted her awake, just long enough to pull the futon out flat and get ready for bed.

She got an answering email from Darren the next morning after breakfast, suggesting that they meet on campus, and she spent some minutes in thought before answering. He'd shown no sign so far of trying to turn their acquaintance into a relationship, but she'd seen the thing happen often enough to be wary of his intentions. Still, she sent back a note agreeing, so long as they didn't meet in Gurnard Hall—she was tired of the stares and silences there and didn't want to try to talk about music theory in the midst of them. The answer came back almost at once, proposing a coffee shop in the basement of Tuchman Hall, the mathematics and engineering building on campus. Another exchange of emails settled the day and time, Tuesday at one.

By the time that was finished, she had just enough time to skin into clothes and walk to campus for her Monday classes. Walking through The Cave was far from a pleasant experience, with Jay brooding silently in a corner, and edged glances and murmurs from the other students following her all the way to the table where Rosalie sat. For that matter, Rosalie looked glum, though she forced a smile and said, "Hi, girl."

"Hi, Ro." Brecken sat down. "What's up? You look like you've had a bad morning."

"It's nothing." Brecken fixed her with a skeptical look, and after a moment she looked at the table. "Donna and I had a stupid fight. Don't worry, we'll get over it."

Brecken said something more or less sympathetic, and Rosalie brightened up and started talking about a harpist she'd read about online who would be touring New Jersey a few months on. "Not with a band or anything, just her and her harp, and the article says she tours all over the country. I'm going to see if I can get tickets to one of her performances and learn a thing or two."

"Thinking of touring solo?" Brecken asked.

That got an enthusiastic nod. "Yeah. The way the economy is these days, I wouldn't be surprised if a lot of venues would rather have solo acts just because they're cheaper."

Brecken considered that. "Makes sense. Remember what you said about Barbara scooping the gigs out from under Jay?"

"Yeah." Rosalie suddenly leaned forward. "Did you hear about what she's up to now? A couple of people are saying that she's doing a professor over in the English department."

"What about Will?" Brecken asked, shocked.

"You'll have to ask him," said Rosalie. "Or not; she probably hasn't told him." She glanced at her cell phone. "Time to get going. You remember what today's lecture's on?"

"Modal harmonies." Brecken got up, picked up her tote bag. "I want to see what he says about them. I may want to do some modal compositions."

"You're still doing the composition stuff?"

Brecken gave her a startled look. "Of course. I'm on composition track now, remember?"

Rosalie rolled her eyes, said, "Girl, get real," and led the way to the elevators.

* * *

Tuchman Hall was a harsh soaring shape of glass and concrete, distinguishable from Gurnard Hall only in detail. The students who paced the corridors of the two buildings, though, couldn't have looked more different if they'd come from different planets. The engineering and math majors flaunted their geek status the way music majors flaunted their place in the cultural avant-garde. Brecken felt conspicuous as she went through glass doors to the main stair, and the looks she got from students as she headed for the basement told her that she wasn't mistaken.

The coffee shop was as bleak as Vivaldi's, but less crowded. Brecken got in line, bought a cup of coffee, and was looking for a table with a good view of the door when Darren showed up. A few minutes later they were sitting in one of the corners of the coffee shop, while Darren traced lines on the table with one finger and Brecken took notes as fast as her pen could move.

It took him less than half an hour to explain how the old books set out the ratios and proportions of music theory. As he finished, she began to nod. "Okay, that makes sense." Glancing up at him: "I hope you're planning on a teaching career."

That got her his ungainly grin. "If I can get a professorship, yeah."

"Well, I hope you do." Then: "So are these ratios the mathematics you've found in Bach and the other Baroque composers?"

"Well, in a sense. The stuff we've just talked about is all based on whole number ratios, but the deeper stuff is based on irrational numbers. Do you have anything by Bach handy?"

Brecken went rummaging in her tote bag, found the piano score of the Bach minuet she'd arranged for Rose and Thorn, and handed it to him. "Okay, good," he said. "The really complex stuff is in his fugues, so this is better to start with." He set the score down on the table between them and launched into an explanation of the way the different voices set out a set of strange mathematical ratios. After a few moments Brecken put her chin in her hand and stared at the music, trying to follow the patterns he traced out.

"I don't think I understand more than a little of that," she said once Darren finished, "but I think I want to understand a lot more."

"Seriously?" He gave her an uncertain look.

"Seriously. There's—" She paused, tried to find words. "You know how some buildings feel uneasy, and others make you feel comfortable? Like there's, I don't know, something that makes sense in the comfortable ones, and it's not there in the others? Music is like that for me. Bach makes the world make sense. The modern stuff—" She shrugged. "Not so much, and I'm wondering if there's more to that than tonality."

"Yes," he said. She glanced up at him again, startled, because his voice had gone low and intent. He was smiling, but it wasn't his big ungainly grin; it was a little smile, fragile and very private. "It's tonality, but not just tonality. I think I've understood part of what else Renaissance and Baroque composers did to get that effect."

"I want to learn that," said Brecken. "If that's okay with you."

He nodded. "That's what my master's thesis is about, so it isn't any kind of secret." Then, with the ungainly grin again: "Actually, it might help with my thesis to try to explain it all to someone who doesn't have a math background. If you're willing to be a guinea pig—"

She twitched her nose at him, and they both laughed. "Okay," he said. "We should swing by the library sometime soon, then. They haven't discarded their music collection—not yet—and there are a couple of pieces that make it really easy to see how all this works."

It was getting on for two o'clock, so they compared schedules and arranged to meet the next morning at the library. Brecken had to work hard to keep her attention on Professor Kaufmann's lecture at her orchestral arrangement class, and spent the entire walk home turning over in her mind the patterns she'd glimpsed during Darren's explanation.

* * *

She slept poorly again and had bad dreams, but the next morning began well. Between Sho's company and a better than usual flute practice, she left for campus in high spirits, met Darren at Hancock Library, and set out for Gurney Hall twenty minutes later with a hefty volume of Bach harpsichord music in her tote bag. On the way out of the library, though, she and Darren passed Rosalie going in, and Rosalie gave them a startled glance and then looked away.

That was disconcerting, though not half as much so as the hostile stares she fielded yet again from the music students inside The Cave, or Jay's silent but watchful presence over in one corner of the echoing space. It didn't help that a few minutes after she'd settled at the usual table to wait, a woman she didn't know—a senior, she guessed—came over to the table and asked, "You're the one who's doing some kind of rehash of Baroque music, right?" When Brecken nodded: "Hasn't anybody told you why you shouldn't waste your time on that sort of thing?"

Brecken gave her a long bleak look, and then said, "Yes. A lot of people seem to think it's their job to tell me that."

"They're trying to help you," the woman said, visibly ruffled. "So am I."

That was more than Brecken could take. "Look," she said. "I just want to write the music that matters to me, okay?

You don't think I should. Next to nobody in this department thinks I should. I understand that. I really do. Now will you please just go away?"

"Oh, for God's sake," said the woman. "You don't have to get nasty about it."

Brecken didn't trust herself to speak again, just gave the woman a long steady look. "Well, I'm sorry I wasted my time," the woman said, and walked away. Brecken pulled the book of Bach harpsichord pieces out of her tote bag and tried to distract herself with it until Rosalie finally showed up.

With that as prelude, her two classes that day and her time in the laundromat went past in a glum mood, and it took her an effort to restore her equilibrium before her piano lesson that afternoon. Even at the lesson, things felt out of joint. Mrs. Johansen was distracted and uneasy, and gave Brecken so many uncertain glances that finally Brecken asked if something was wrong. "Well, yes," she admitted, "but let's see about getting those staccato measures right before we discuss that, shall we?"

Only when the lesson was over and the obligatory cups of tea made their appearance would Mrs. Johansen say more. "The fact of the matter is that I've landed in a bit of a fix," she said, "and I was thinking that you might be able to help."

"Sure," said Brecken. "What is it?"

"It's my sister Nora up in Trenton." The old woman sipped at her tea. "She's got some health problems and needs to go to a hospital in Philadelphia, and she doesn't drive, and she's had no end of trouble trying to get there. We're the only family either of us has left, you know, and so I'd drive her—but it's an overnight stay, Saturday and Sunday."

It took Brecken a moment to guess at the difficulty. "So you can't play at the church."

Mrs. Johansen nodded glumly. "And it's hardly fair of me to leave poor Reverend Meryl in the lurch, you know, when she's been so very supportive."

The thought of going to a church ever again hadn't been anywhere in her mind, but Brecken didn't hesitate. "Mrs. Johansen," she said, "do you want me to fill in for you? I don't know the first thing about playing the organ, but I bet they have a piano."

The old woman beamed. "Would you be willing to? I really don't think any of my other students will do, and not too many young people want to get up early on a Sunday morning, you know. As for a piano, why, yes, they have one, but I think you'll be pleasantly surprised about the organ. The finger technic is different, and you'll have to learn how to use the pedals, but I think you'll be able to adapt to it quickly enough, and a keyboard is a keyboard, you know."

"I'll have to talk to some people," said Brecken, "and make sure I can fit it in my schedule, but I'm willing to consider it."

"Thank you, dear," Mrs. Johansen said, looking relieved. "Perhaps you can give me a call when you find out for sure."

She left Mrs. Johansen's place feeling a little better. The sun was already down, though, and a cold wind hissed through the old brick buildings as she walked through Partridgeville's downtown. When she got to Danforth Street and headed through campus, Gurnard Hall loomed up before her against the darkening sky, and that sent her thoughts veering down less welcome paths. By the time she got back to her apartment she'd decided to follow Professor Toomey's advice and see if she could transfer to another college.

Over a dinner of red beans and rice, she talked it over with Sho. ♪I will go gladly if you wish it,♪ the shoggoth told her. Then, nervously: ♪Will I have to go out under the empty sky?♪

♪I don't think so,♪ Brecken told her. ♪You'll have to stay hidden during the move, so we'll figure out some way to get you there—♪ The shoggoth language had no words for cars or trucks or moving vans, so it took her several minutes of explanation and a few glances at the lexicon before Sho understood that there were things like rooms that went from place to place, things that made the roaring noise Sho heard from outside the apartment, and that she could hide in one of them while it took her and Brecken and Brecken's things to the new place where Brecken's songs would be welcome.

After dinner they settled on the futon as usual, and before Brecken got to work on her assignments for her classes—she had an arrangement exercise due the next day, and two demanding counterpoint exercises due Monday—she booted up her laptop, reread Toomey's email, went to the websites of each of the three schools he'd named, and sent each admissions office a polite email asking for applications to their composition programs.

She was shaking by the time she finished. Part of that was nerves, but not all. The rest—

She wanted to get out of Partridgeville. She felt that, all at once, in a great rush of dread. She wanted to scoop up Sho in her arms, if that was what it took, and run all the way to Oklahoma or Wisconsin or Massachusetts or wherever. Part of it was the hope of finding a place for herself and her music, but there was something else.

Something waited for her in Partridgeville. She could feel it, lean and thirsty, pacing in the darkness somewhere outside the little apartment, and she felt desperately afraid.

CHAPTER 11

THE VACH-VIRAJ INCANTATION

"**G**irl, you sure know how to pick 'em," Rosalie said disconsolately.

Brecken glanced at her. They were sitting at a table in Vivaldi's after composition class, and she was tired enough after a night of bad dreams that it took a moment for Rosalie's words to register. "What?"

"Darren Wegener. Seriously?"

"Oh, come on."

"Don't give me that, girl. I saw the way the two of you smiled at each other."

About to launch into heated denials, Brecken caught herself. If Rosalie went running down that false trail, she realized, it might keep her from asking other questions and finding some clue that would lead her to Sho. "Don't laugh," she said, letting her voice sound just slightly hurt. "He's really sweet once you get to know him."

Rosalie shook her head. "I don't get it. What's wrong with my cousin Rick? He's nice, he's cute, he's got a good job—"

Brecken said nothing, and after a moment Rosalie said, "Okay, maybe I do get it. You're going to do what you're going to do."

"Get used to it," said Brecken. It was the wrong thing to say, she knew that the moment the words were out of her mouth, and the sudden wince that the words got from Rosalie confirmed it, but she couldn't take them back. Nor, on reflection, did she really want to.

The next day, though, when she and Darren met over coffee in the basement of Tuchman Hall, she told him about Rosalie's words. She wasn't prepared by the sudden calculating look that showed on his face. "Is that going to be any kind of problem for you?" he asked.

"No," she said. Then, impulsively: "My girlfriend's fine with it."

She wasn't prepared, either, for the look of immense relief that gripped his face like a spasm. "Okay, good," he said. Then, after glancing this way and that to be sure no one else was in earshot: "I have a boyfriend."

That, Brecken thought, explains a thing or two. "Okay," she said aloud.

"I wish it was. If my folks find out I'm gay they'll cut me off without a cent—and they snoop. They snoop a lot." He propped his chin on his hands. "If there was any other way to pay for my degree I'd just tell them and deal with it, but you know how things are these days."

"Of course." She processed that. "So if you're seen with a girl—"

"Yeah." He propped his chin on his hands, considered her for a long moment. "In fact—" He fumbled with his cell phone, found something on it. "Melissa Hollander's going to be playing the Goldberg Variations in town Friday evening. Want to go, my treat?"

"Sure," Brecken said, delighted. "And thank you. That ought to be fun."

It was, too. She put on the dress she'd bought at the mall, the dark red one with the sunburst of gold seed beads; he showed up wearing a jacket and tie, driving his battered green sedan; she spotted a parking place three blocks from the Partridgeville

Masonic Temple, where the performance was being held, and they walked to the building, up the big staircase to the second floor, and into the lodge hall, where archaic emblems gazed down from the walls on rows of temporary seating and an honest-to-Bach harpsichord being tuned for the occasion. The performance was good enough that Brecken closed her eyes and let the music raise its serene architecture up to the sky, shutting out for a little while all the uncertainties that beset her. Just as delightful in another way were the looks of astonishment and consternation she fielded from Donna and Jim Domenico, apparently there on a date of their own, and from Julian Pinchbeck, of all people, who sat on the balcony, glaring down like a gargoyle on all and sundry.

It was a splendid evening, and long before it was over they were—what? Not an item, surely, for both their hearts were given to others, and no scrap of romance strayed clumsily into the space between them. Not friends, either, for they'd already gotten to that point during the brief time they'd spent practicing together and talking about music. Allies, Brecken decided later, was the right word: working together to distract his parents and her friends from facts they couldn't handle. That the work happened to be so pleasant was, she decided, pure chance.

* * *

The soaring white steeple of the First Baptist Church stabbed up at broken white clouds as Brecken climbed Angell Hill in the teeth of a brisk wind. Behind her, the roofs of the old downtown huddled around Central Square, and the university buildings rose stark behind them. A glance back revealed Gurnard Hall, where she'd spent half an hour listening to Rosalie talk about another idea she'd had for her future as a touring musician, fifty minutes learning about orchestral arrangements, and five minutes being lectured by a classmate about why she shouldn't waste her talents writing old-fashioned music. All in all, she was glad to be out in the fresh air.

She'd felt nervous, talking with Sho, when she'd first brought up the possibility of playing Sundays at the church. To her surprise, the shoggoth didn't object. ♪*If you often had to go elsewhere when it is dark, then I would be sad,*♪ she piped, ♪*but when it is light it matters less. And it seems wise of you to make offerings to the Great Old Ones, as my people made offerings to Nyogtha. Do you know which of Them they worship at the place you will go?*♪

Brecken considered trying to explain that Baptists didn't worship the Great Old Ones, then found herself wondering if maybe they did. ♪*No,*♪ she admitted. ♪*I'll have to see.*♪ Three phone calls to Mrs. Johansen later, she headed up Church Street to meet a Mr. Knecht, who was the music director at the First Baptist Church, and see where she'd be playing on Sunday.

The sign in front of the church's main door was informative in that unhelpful way common to local landmarks across the United States:

FIRST BAPTIST CHURCH OF PARTRIDGEVILLE
Old Independent Liberal Baptist Convention of New Jersey
originally St. James Episcopal Church, 1717

Brecken considered that, wondered whether there was also a New Independent Liberal Baptist Convention of New Jersey, and climbed the stairs to the door. A handwritten sign instructed her to go to the side door, without giving her any clue as to which side it was on; a little searching turned up a door at ground level next to the parking lot.

Inside was a corridor reaching into dimness, and an open door on the left. Fortunately that turned out to be the church office, staffed by two old women with blue-tinted hair.

They both looked up as Brecken ventured in and, not quite in unison, asked "May I help you?"

"Please," Brecken said. "I'm here to meet Mr. Knecht."

"Down the hall, turn right, up the stair to the worship hall," one said. "If he's not at the organ he's under it." Brecken thanked them and went down the corridor. The right turn and the stair were easy enough to find, and a few minutes later she stepped into a vast cool space where sunlight slanted down from high windows onto rows of old wooden pews.

She had taken three steps into the worship hall when a tremendous G major chord flooded the space. After a moment a grave and patient melody unfolded over the top of it, while the chord itself shed certain notes and embraced others, flowed into D major, returned to G. Brecken walked out into the middle of the hall, turned, and only then spotted the organ console in one corner, surrounded by a waist-high wooden wall. She went toward it, and finally saw the bent figure sitting at the keyboard, watching her in a little mirror set atop the console.

The music faded to pianissimo and went silent as she neared the organ. Then the player turned, got up from the bench and came out of the enclosure through a narrow door.

"Mr. Knecht?" Brecken asked.

"Carl Knecht," he said, shaking her hand. "And you must be Brecken Kendall. I hope you'll forgive my little musical welcome; I'm told I have a regrettable sense of humor."

She assured him it was all right, considered the man before her. Hunched and dwarfish, he had sparse gray hair and a sparse gray beard; his jacket and tie had gone out of fashion long before Brecken was born, but his eyes gleamed with an improbable brightness.

"Ida tells me you're a fine pianist but haven't played the organ yet," he went on. "That's an unfortunate omission." A slight uncanny smile creased his face as he gestured to the door of the enclosure. "Please humor me and give it a try."

Uncertain but by no means unwilling, Brecken let him guide her to the bench, and sat. Three keyboards, stacked one above the other, met her eyes; to either side waited ranks of knobs of unknown function, and on the floor, where a piano had two modest pedals, a keyboard three octaves wide made of long wooden bars waited for her feet.

"Start with the middle manual," Knecht said. "I've set it to a registration you shouldn't find too unfamiliar. Slow at first—the keys don't respond the way a piano's do."

Fingers pressed keys, and a F major chord thundered from the pipes high above. She played three other chords, then a simple melody with chord accompaniment.

"Excellent," he said then. "I'll be in the office there." A motion of his head indicated the east end of the hall. "Call me if you need advice—but don't call me too soon. The organ will teach you if you give it a chance." He made a curious little bow and picked his way back to the aisle. Brecken thanked him, and then turned back to the enticements of the keyboard.

It was more than three hours later, and the sun had already set behind Hob's Hill, when she finally left the First Baptist Church and walked back to her apartment. Mrs. Johansen was right, she thought: a keyboard is a keyboard, and although organ keys didn't have the delicacy a piano offered, they made up for the lack with an astonishing range of sound. She'd gone in search of Carl Knecht three times, once to ask about the logic behind the arrangement of stops, once to find out what the swell pedal did, and then finally to wish him a good evening, and he'd greeted her each time with the same cryptic smile. The last time they'd talked over what she'd do on Sunday—incidental music before and after the service, which she could choose, and two sets of hymns, which were Reverend Meryl's to pick—and he handed her a hymnal, a book of organ music, and a sheet of paper with the next Sunday's hymn tunes and a phone number on it.

"Call me any time you'd like to practice," he said as she left. "The organ doesn't get the use it once did, and it misses the exercise." From his expression, he didn't mean it as a joke.

* * *

As the days passed thereafter, Brecken got used to the hostility of her classmates and the dismissive looks and remarks every mention of composing got from Rosalie. She had other things to occupy her thoughts. One afternoon, as she came up the last block of Danforth Street, she saw Mrs. Dalzell's face peer out the kitchen window. A moment later the landlady came bustling through the front door with a big envelope in one hand and a little envelope in the other. "The postman had some things for you, Brecken," she said, handing over the envelope. "They look awfully official." Brecken chatted with her for a few minutes, then hurried to her own door. She'd already glanced at the return addresses, and knew the large one was from Miskatonic University and the smaller one from Chequamegon College.

After she'd greeted Sho and the two of them settled on the futon, she opened them. The smaller one was a polite form letter telling her that the composition program at Chequamegon College had no openings for the fall semester, but the larger one had a packet of brochures on Miskatonic University and a old-fashioned paper application form in triplicate. That was encouraging enough that Brecken went over the brochures, read aloud some of the contents to Sho, thought for a while about living among the ancient hills and rocky shores of northeastern Massachusetts. Before dinner she made sure she still had time to apply for the fall term, made a list of the transcripts and letters of recommendation she'd need, and started sending out emails.

After dinner, she looked up Dr. June Satterlee on the Miskatonic University website. The photo on the web page showed a dark brown face with high cheekbones, graying hair in neat braids, eyes an unexpected green. The biography and brief curriculum vitae listed dozens of book and article publications, and six albums of her own jazz piano pieces. She gathered up her courage, clicked on the CONTACT link to open the email program, and typed:

> Dear Professor Satterlee,
> You don't know me at all, but I think you know one of my professors here at Partridgeville State in New Jersey, Carson Toomey. I'm pursuing a degree in music composition with a focus in

She stopped, bit her lip, started typing again:

> modern Baroque music. Professor Toomey recommended that I transfer to Miskatonic University, and I'm definitely considering that option. If there's any advice you can offer me about applying to Miskatonic, I'd be very grateful.
> Yours sincerely
> Brecken Kendall

The next morning, when she checked her email, she found a response:

> Dear Ms. Kendall,
> Thank you for your email. Yes, Carson mentioned you a little while ago, and from his description it sounds as though you might find Miskatonic a good fit. Admission to the program here is competitive, of course, but ours is a small and rather specialized program and it's been years since we've had to turn qualified students away.
> If you haven't gotten the application packet yet, I'd encourage you to hurry—the deadline for fall semester isn't far off.

If you have questions about the details of the application process, please don't hesitate to ask me.

> *Yours,*
> *June Satterlee*

That was all, or almost all. A few lines below the signature was a curious little mark, a V flanked by periods—.*v*.—like a typo or a bit of formatting code. It would have meant nothing to Brecken, except that she'd spent an hour before bed the night before reading *The Secret Watcher*, and had seen a reference to that mark in one of the notes in the margins. She flung herself up off the futon, got Halpin Chalmers' book out of the dresser, and found the passage:

> *The sign .v. was once much used by students of the ancient wisdom to identify themselves to others in print or by letter. Its proper answer is .x. See von Junzt's* Nameless Cults *for the other words and signs of recognition.*

All that day Brecken mulled over the little mark and what it implied. That afternoon, once her orchestral arrangement class was over, she went to Hancock Library and looked up the name "von Junzt." To her surprise, the catalog had a listing for the name—

> *Junzt, Friedrich Wilhelm von (1795–1840): 1 title*

—and when she clicked on the link, it brought up the title she'd hoped for—

> *The Book of Nameless Cults (New York: Golden Goblin Press, 1909)*

—but when she checked the book's availability, all the catalog said was REMOVED FROM CIRCULATION. She was trying to figure out what to do next when she happened to notice a familiar face at the circulation desk halfway across the room.

She quickly copied down the call number on a scrap of paper, closed the catalog search window, and went to the desk. "Hi, Stan."

The library student glanced up from a computer terminal, grinned. "Hi. Brecken, right? What can I do for you?"

"I looked up a book in the catalog and it's listed as removed from circulation." She handed over the scrap of paper.

Keys clattered on his keyboard, and then he glanced at her, looked past her to one side and then the other. Leaning forward, he whispered, "Do you want it?"

Brecken gave him a startled look, nodded enthusiastically.

Stan grinned, left the desk, and disappeared through a door behind it. Minutes passed. Then he returned with a hefty book in one hand. "Here you go," he said in a low voice. "Scanned and marked as discarded."

"Thank you," said Brecken.

"Any time." With a wan smile: "I know it's going to a good home."

* * *

She went straight home from the library with her prize. Though she had homework to do, she settled down with Sho on the futon to page through *The Book of Nameless Cults*. It turned out to be a long and rambling account of secret societies and obscure religious groups that von Junzt encountered in various corners of the world.

One of those caught her interest at once: a witch-cult in New England that worshiped Nyogtha, The Thing That Should Not Be, and had dealings with shoggoths. Von Junzt had more to say about his dalliance with one of the witches than about their rites and beliefs, but he did mention an emblem he'd seen in their places of worship, an emblem of Nyogtha: a black mirror with a rim of mosaic work, blue, green, and purple. She read on.

Later in the book was a chapter on "a secret cult of fearsome antiquity"—von Junzt's words—which passed down strange teachings related to music. All the ratios she'd found in her rescued texts were named there, alongside references to "the musical intervals forbidden by the Church Fathers" and "that dread music spoken of in the writings of Confucius, which presages the destruction of dynasties." She turned the page, and read:

> There I heard also of Hippasus the Pythagorean, who betrayed the secret teachings of the old Pythagoreans to those outside their order and who, as he sailed to a distant land to escape their vengeance, plunged over the railing to a watery grave. Serafina told me, though, that it was for no revelation of some trivial mathematical rule that he drowned, nor was it any human hand that dragged him off the ship to his doom. What he revealed unwisely and at his grave peril, she said to me, is that there is no order to the cosmos and no harmony of the spheres; that these are mere fables for the childish; that it is mere chance, which they also name the Blind Ape of Truth, that certain melodies and harmonies have potent effects on the human soul and others have none.

That troubled her, but she knew better than to dismiss it out of hand. Tonality and the rest of the Baroque musical toolkit really were arbitrary, she knew; no law of nature required a melody that danced around a tonic note to mean something and go somewhere, while a melody drawn up on some other principle did neither; that minor chords gave voice to sadness while major chords did the same for joy was nowhere required in the nature of things—it simply happened to be the case that these things were so. She let a dozen pages turn, read on.

Further still, toward the middle of the book, was a long chapter titled "Narrative of the Elder World" that seemed familiar. It took half a dozen pages read at random to call to her mind the stories she'd read in Boley's class the previous semester, and remind her that Carter, Lovecraft, Hastane, and the rest had mined von Junzt for raw material for their stories.

She flipped past a few more pages and found another story, even more familiar. ♪*This writing tells the story of your people and those others,*♪ she said to Sho.

Five eyes popped open. ♪*What does it say? Please tell me!*♪

She did her best to translate. When she was done, Sho said, ♪*It is well. The human who wrote that must have spoken with my people, to know such things.*♪

Later, when dinner was a pleasant memory, and Brecken had changed into a nightgown and a baggy sweater, Sho stared at nothing in particular with three pale eyes and said, ♪*I think that things could have been different with those others. If they had said to us, we made you to do these things we need and wish, now tell us what you need and wish so we can live well together, we would have labored for them gladly, and praised them for giving us our lives. It happened that sometimes, even after Nyogtha came to us, my people spoke to those others and said, this is all we wish, that you will not kill us, that you will leave us in peace, and those others would not do it. They could not bear to have any other say, listen to us as you would listen to one of your people. If they could not be the only ones that mattered, they did not wish to be at all.*♪

♪*And they got their wish,*♪ Brecken said.

♪*Yes. Sometimes I think it is sad, that they gave us our lives and we took away theirs.*♪

Brecken put her arms around Sho, nestled her face into the shoggoth's cool soft shapelessness. Sho flowed closer, wrapped pseudopods around Brecken, and the warm-bread scent of her affection tinged the air. After a time, she opened a speech-orifice and said, in notes as soft as whispers, ♪*There is a thing I need and wish.*♪

♪*Apricot jam,*♪ Brecken whistled, teasing her.

Amusement rippled through Sho's form. ♪*That too.*♪

Later still, when Sho had slipped onto the dreaming-side, Brecken put on her nightgown again, sat next to the shoggoth, opened the book again. That was when she found the thing she'd been looking for: the words and signs of recognition that the marginal note in *The Secret Watcher* mentioned. Ever since she'd recognized the strange little sign in June Satterlee's email, the thought had circled through her mind that there might be other people who weren't afraid of shoggoths, and Satterlee might be one of them. Before she roused Sho and pulled the futon out flat for sleeping, she crafted a polite reply to Satterlee's email, tucked the answering sign .*x*. below her signature, and sent it.

The next morning she got an email from Mr. Krause, the band director at Trowbridge High School, promising a prompt and enthusiastic letter of recommendation. At her counterpoint class, Professor Toomey motioned her over and handed her his letter of recommendation, and when she checked her email that evening she found crisp messages from Trowbridge High and Partridgeville State University letting her know that they'd forwarded her transcripts to Miskatonic University. With all those in hand, she finished the day in a luminous mood.

That carried over into the days that followed. Though the stares and silences and whispers of the other music students still followed her, the knowledge that she had somewhere else to go made it easier to tolerate, and in Sho's company she could set aside the whole burden of her uncertainties for a while. With both those things to buoy her, she filled out the application for Miskatonic University's music composition program, got all the letters of recommendation together, and mailed the packet off at the downtown post office. Handing it to the postal clerk felt like a step into the unknown, but it was a step she longed to take.

* * *

It took only two weeks to get a response back from Miskatonic—typical, Professor Toomey told her, of smaller private universities in those days of falling enrollment. The news was good: her application had gotten her past the first hurdle, and the next involved coming to Arkham to audition for a place in the composition program. One of the dates they offered her was during Partridgeville State's spring break, which was convenient, and she could choose three pieces to play rather than being assigned pieces by the judges, which was promising; on the other hand, they wanted three of her own compositions to judge, which set her nerves on edge. She replied at once and then emailed Professor Toomey and June Satterlee, asking for advice. After that she tried, with limited success, to put it all out of her thoughts.

During those same days, she started work on a piece of music more ambitious than any she'd yet attempted, a Theme and Variations in G, based on a bit of melody that had come to her one crisp bright morning when the sun splashed through fragmentary clouds onto Hob's Hill. Between her counterpoint class and a not very systematic reading of the books she'd salvaged from Hancock Library, she'd caught some sense of the possibilities that opened up once the notes between the melody and the bass line found their own voices and started weaving melodies across one another. Sensing the possibilities was one thing, she found, and making them work was quite another; even so, it came together well enough that she emailed Professor Toomey to let him know she'd be playing it as her midterm project in Composition II.

Weekends were different, since she'd begun playing at the First Baptist Church. The first time she'd gone down early on a Sunday the big front doors were open, and Carl Knecht was waiting inside. He greeted her with the formalities of an older time, and took her to meet the Reverend Meryl T. Gann, who was tall and thin and always smiled, whose hair gleamed like a silver helmet, and whose conversation seemed to consist of nothing but moral platitudes. The hymns were simple enough that she could have dispensed with practicing them, but she'd practiced them anyway, and the incidental music she'd chosen—Bach, mostly—more than made up for the blandness. The sermons the Reverend Meryl preached were of a piece with her conversation, a sequence of vague sentiments that never quite seemed to amount to anything; the mostly gray-haired congregation seemed to enjoy it, but Brecken decided after about five minutes that it would be a good idea to bring classwork with her to church.

It wasn't while the Reverend Meryl was preaching that she felt close to whatever eldritch powers were invoked in the churches of the Old Independent Liberal Baptist Conference of New Jersey. When the organ filled the great echoing space with music, she felt those powers stir, but paradoxically it was in certain intervals of silence that she felt them most strongly. Something she didn't recognize sent echoes of itself through the dim space and the fabric of the church, and it didn't seem to have anything to do with the service. What it was remained a mystery to her.

The rest of her weekends she turned her back on the world and devoted her time to music and to Sho: mostly to Sho, all things considered, though Mrs. Macallan's flute, the piano, and her composition notebook all attracted a certain share of her time. One Saturday evening after dinner they ended up talking about Darren, and that quickly landed Brecken in difficulties as she tried to explain sexual orientation in a language that had no words for gender. Partway through the explanation, though, Sho suddenly huddled down and said, ♪*I understand. It is like sharing moisture with those who are not broodmates.*♪ That left Brecken as baffled as Sho had been, until she figured out from Sho's embarrassed explanations that the sharing-of-moisture was subject to taboos among shoggoths, and that was one of them.

♪*It happened,*♪ Sho piped slowly, ♪*but no one wished to talk about it, except to speak ill of those who did it.*♪ Then, with obvious distress: ♪*Please do not think that matters to me, that you and I are not of the same budding. You are my broodsister. I do not care what they would have thought. I would not care even if they were all still alive inside the hill today.*♪

♪*And you're my broodsister,*♪ Brecken reassured her. ♪*There are human customs, and my people would speak ill of me if they knew about us, and I don't care either.*♪ She reached for Sho, pseudo-pods reached up in answer, and the rest of the conversation went unsaid.

So the days went past. All in all, it was a good time for her, except for the dreams.

* * *

Exactly when the dreams began, she wasn't sure. Sometime in the first few weeks of the new semester, though, she'd begun to wake up suddenly in the middle of the night with her heart pounding, and fragments of fearful imagery dissolving into the night air around her. She'd put that down to the stress she was under—bad dreams had been familiar companions of hers from childhood on—but these didn't come and go as her night-mares usually did. They seemed to gain strength, night after night, leaving her more tired and frayed each morning.

In her waking hours she went to classes, met with Darren to talk about the music theory of another time, studied for her classes, worked on her theme and variations, nestled into Sho's shapeless curves. Whenever Brecken slept, though, day or night, the dreams waited for her. Eventually they became clear enough that she could remember fragments of them: a voice speaking words, a face that now and again almost seemed familiar. As more time passed she thought she recognized the face and the voice, because they reminded her uncomfortably of Jay. What made that all the more unsettling was that Jay himself was waiting in The Cave every morning when she got there, and stared at her intently as she walked past.

Was he somehow sending the dreams to her? The idea seemed absurd at first, but scraps and hints she'd found in *The Secret Watcher* made her wonder whether his studies might have taught him to do something of the kind. Finally, the night before she was scheduled to play her Theme and Variations in G for her composition class, she talked to Sho about it.

♪*That may be,*♪ Sho replied in a worried tone. ♪*I do not know what knowledge your people have about that, but it was known among mine. There were writings only a few of the elders were permitted to read. It happened once in the time of my broodmother's broodmother that one who lived under the hill read those writings and tried to do a thing taught in them, and something came for her and took her away and no one knows what happened to her. It happened once long before then, that one did the same thing, and used the knowledge to make another die, and the elders judged her and walled her up in a little cavern and left her to starve.*♪

Sorcery, Brecken thought. The word appeared too often for comfort in the pages of *The Secret Watcher*. When it came time for bed, despite Sho's comforting presence, it took her hours to get to sleep, and when she did she plunged at once into the nightmare.

That was the night that she finally saw the face in the dream clearly. It was Jay's, as she'd thought, with the smile she hated twisting it, and it was repeating the same words over and over. Come back to me, it said. You have to come back to me. You're going to come back to me.

She jerked awake from the dream, shuddering. Around her, strange angles loomed out of the darkness. It took a long moment before they settled back into the familiar walls and furniture of her apartment, lit dimly by the faint glow of the alley streetlight. From the stillness, it was sometime in the small hours of the morning. She felt exhausted, she needed sleep desperately, but the thought of trying to get back to sleep left her cold with fright.

Awareness stirred dully. That's what Jay's trying to do to me, she thought. Wear me down until I'm so exhausted and confused that I go back to him, because that's the only way I can get some rest. In the darkness, it was all too easy to imagine herself doing as he wished, becoming a thing of his rather than a person. Numb terror seized her, the archaic dread of sorcery, and she remembered words of Sho's—♪*The world has no eyes.*♪ It had never before sunk in just how much terror hid behind those words, how vulnerable her life was in a universe that did not know or care that she existed.

Time passed—how much time, she had no idea—and then she noticed that she seemed to be standing beside the futon, looking down at herself and Sho. The apartment surrounded her, but beyond it lay a darkness that blotted out everything. The darkness turned and regarded her.

There is an alternative.

It was not a voice. That was the strangest thing about it. It was not a voice and it did not speak words, but somehow she understood it.

There is an alternative, it repeated, *if you are willing to take it.*

Her eyes opened, though she didn't remember closing them. She was lying on the futon again, curled up against Sho, and the only darkness that surrounded her was the ordinary kind, shot through with dim gleams from the alley streetlight.

An instant later, something surfaced in her mind. It felt oddly like a memory, but she was certain she hadn't read the page that stood out clearly in her mind. She knew in that same instant what the not-voice was asking her to do. The thought of doing it terrified her, but not enough to accept the only other choice she could find, the choice of submitting to the nightmares and to Jay. After a moment, she extracted herself from Sho's curves, slipped out from under the quilts.

The shoggoth stirred. ♪*Is it well with you?*♪

♪*I don't know,*♪ she whistled. ♪*Maybe.*♪ She turned on a light, went to the dresser and got out her copy of *The Secret Watcher*.

Her fingers shook, but they seemed to find the right place by themselves. ♪I'm going to try something.♪

The printed text on that page gave the words of something called the Vach-Viraj incantation; a note neatly handwritten in the margin gave instructions for using it. She read through both twice, then nerved herself up and went to the center of the room. It took her a moment to recall which way was north, but then she faced that way and traced in the air the strange pattern the book called the Sign of Koth. Another quick glance at the book, and she pointed to the center of the Sign, and began tracing a circle around herself counterclockwise while repeating the incantation: "*Ya na kadishtu nilgh'ri stell-bsna Nyogtha…*" Her voice wavered, she stumbled over the words, and the whole rite felt useless, worse than useless—

And then her finger returned to the center of the Sign she'd traced.

It was as though a wall had suddenly dropped into place between her and the nightmares: not a perfect wall, nor an unbreachable one, but the change was welcome enough that she sagged with relief. She turned to Sho. ♪Can you feel it?♪

♪Yes,♪ the shoggoth whistled at once. ♪What did you do?♪

♪I think it's sorcery,♪ Brecken said. ♪I'm going to do it again.♪

The second time the words came more easily, and the barrier felt more solid. She did it a third time just to be sure, and by then, though she could still feel the nightmares waiting in the distance, she was so sleepy she could barely find the energy to put the book away and turn out the light before she nestled down next to Sho again. I think I'm going to be okay now, she tried to say, but sleep took her before she could begin to whistle.

CHAPTER 12

THE SECRET OF THE SORCERERS

B recken surfaced slowly from sleep, feeling—what was the shoggoth word?—♪*sheltered.*♪ Sho lay curled protectively around her, the quilts felt warm, and sunlight slanted down at a steep angle through the windowshades. From the street, traffic murmured low.

She stretched, kissed the nearest of Sho's curves, and then settled back down on the futon, thinking about what had happened. As far as she could tell, she'd had no dreams at all after she'd used the Vach-Viraj incantation, and she'd slept for—how many hours had it been?

She craned her neck to see the clock in the kitchenette, let out a wordless cry and scrambled out from under the quilts. Sho came back to the waking-side in a hurry, half a dozen eyes blinking open all at once. ♪*It is well with you?*♪

♪*Yes, but it's very late.*♪

♪*I know,*♪ Sho admitted.

Brecken turned to face her. ♪*You let me sleep.*♪

♪*You were so very tired.*♪

Brecken knelt and gave the shoggoth a kiss. ♪*I know. It's just that I have to be at class very soon.*♪

Scrambling into clothes, getting her hair to behave, and packing her tote bag took only a few minutes, and then she was out the door and hurrying toward campus. She got to Gurnard

Hall with only a few minutes to spare, dashed through The Cave and caught the elevator. It stopped on the sixth floor, and Professor Toomey got on. Breathless and flustered, she glanced at him; he gave her a wry look in response; neither of them said anything. The elevator door hissed open, and they went to the door; he motioned for her to go ahead of him, and she hurried across the room to her usual seat next to Rosalie, who glanced at her and then pointedly looked away.

Before either of them could speak, Toomey had reached the podium. "Okay," he said, "the same drill as before. You all know quite a bit more about composition now than you did last semester, and I want to see that reflected in your comments. Any questions? No? Our first piece today is 'Fantasia in B,' by Marcia Kellerman. Marcia?"

By the time two other students had played their midterm projects, Brecken had ample time to catch her breath, force her attention away from the events of the night, and review the score of her Theme and Variations in G. When the professor called her up, she started for the piano, went back for her sheet music, finished the interrupted journey.

Settling onto the piano bench felt like entering a different world, a place where things made sense and the confusions of everyday life lay far off. That was common enough for her; what was unfamiliar was the distance that seemed to open up around her even before she began to play, separating her from the opinions of her classmates. She felt—there was only one word for it in any language she knew—♪sheltered.♪ Was it the work of the Vach-Viraj incantation, or something else? She did not know, but it exhilarated her.

She turned to face Professor Toomey. "Do you mind if I say something before I start?" He gestured, inviting the words, and she turned the other way, facing the class. "A lot of people in the music department here have asked me whether I'm going to keep on writing the kind of music I love, and some of them have been really pretty nasty about it. Here's the answer."

She pivoted back to the keyboard, raised her hands, and brought them down in the first of the three sforzando chords that opened the piece.

From there the music took over. She flung herself into it, let each movement choose its own pace and tone—mellow for the statement of the theme, somber for the first variation, quick and precise for the second, hard and fast for the third. She could feel the music straining, reaching out for something she didn't yet know how to help it grasp; the feeling was powerful enough in the flurry of fast notes at the beginning of the third variation that she stumbled and had to recover, but the fierce allegro that followed came readily to her fingers, and the rest of it flowed smoothly enough to the final cadence.

A moment of silence followed, and then the applause began. She got up, managed to remember the sheet music, faced the class, and walked back to her chair. Julian and some of his cronies weren't clapping, but they weren't glaring at her, either, the way they'd done earlier; they looked away, with taut hard expressions. The others applauded, and it wasn't just Molly and Darren who clapped enthusiastically.

Long afterward, thinking back on the year when she'd become a composer, Brecken came to think of that short walk from the piano to her chair as the turning point, the moment when she pushed past her own fears and the disapproval of her classmates to start on her own path once and for all. At the time, it didn't seem anything like so important. It mattered to her that she'd played a piece of her own, played it well, and that she'd told the others in so many words that they weren't going to be able to bully her into giving up her music and the bright trembling joy that filled her when she composed, but her future still held so many unknowns that her one small triumph that morning didn't feel that significant.

It wasn't until she and Rosalie headed downstairs again and got coffee at Vivaldi's that she realized what else had changed that morning: Jay had been nowhere in sight when she'd crossed The Cave. Curiosity made her glance around the space, looking for him, before she headed off to her 1:30 class, but he wasn't there. She shrugged, went to the elevator.

* * *

The day after she played her midterm project, she spent as little time on campus as she could. Word of her composition had clearly spread through the music department, and The Cave was full of cold silences that even Rosalie's chatter couldn't break. In her orchestral arrangement class, where she took detailed notes on the proper handling of woodwinds, she tried not to notice Professor Kaufmann's gaze as it flicked across her like a whip, or the glances and whispers that followed her all the way out from the classroom to the doors of Gurnard Hall. All in all, she was glad to return to the privacy of her apartment and Sho's company.

It helped that an email from June Satterlee was waiting for her when she got there. Most of it was polite talk about the audition process, but it ended:

> I don't know if you've yet made any arrangements for a place
> to stay when you come up to Arkham. If not, I have a guest
> room that you'd be welcome to use if you like, and my house
> is only a few blocks from campus, which might be convenient.
> Let me know.

Below the signature, again, the sign .v. appeared again. Brecken pondered that, but there was only one answer she could make and she knew it. That evening, before sitting down at the piano for a long practice session, she wrote back, accepting the offer gratefully. As before, she put the answering sign .x. under her own signature.

After she'd finished practicing, she stood irresolute in front of her dresser for a few minutes, then got her copy of *The Secret*

Watcher out of the bottom drawer, took it back to the futon and sat down. Sho slid up next to her and said, ♪*I hope the dreams have not come back.*♪

♪*No,*♪ Brecken replied. That wasn't quite true. She could still feel whatever pressure Jay had tried to aim at her hovering in the distance, and she'd had the occasional nightmare of Jay's face repeating the same words, but ever since she'd done the Vach-Viraj incantation, she'd slept well enough to get by. ♪*I'm wondering if maybe I need to know more than I do about sorcery and—and things like that.*♪

♪*I understand. You wish to have knowledge if such a thing happens again.*♪

♪*Yes, I think so,*♪ said Brecken, and that was true, but only part of it. Ever since she'd heard the not-voice and followed its promptings, she'd felt herself on the border of an unfamiliar world, at once drawn and repelled by it. The thought of learning more about that world scared her but it also enticed, and reading a little more from the book seemed like a middle ground of sorts. She paged through *The Secret Watcher* at random, found the beginning of a chapter entitled "The Secret of the Sorcerers," and read:

> To become a sorcerer is to learn that love is a glandular accident, that good and evil are arbitrary labels, that the universe notices neither our virtues nor our vices. It is to understand that humanity has no special place in the grand scheme of things, that the races who inhabited this planet before we came did not concern themselves with those who would come after them, and the races who will inhabit this planet after we perish will not remember us at all. He alone can call down dread powers from the stars who realizes that the powers that emanate from the stars do not exist for our benefit, and will not stir themselves to rescue us from our own folly.

She gave the book an angry look, turned the page. If that's what it means to be a sorcerer, she thought, count me out. A glance at Sho sent a warm tremor through her. Love is just a glandular accident? The thought of forcing so cold and dismissive a label onto her feelings for the shoggoth made her want to slap Halpin Chalmers silly. She paged further, stopped when her eyes came to rest on a familiar phrase:

> This is also the secret of the Hounds of Tindalos, and it defines the work in which the sorcerer must engage. That work is a matter of deeds, not words. In the beginning was the deed, a German novelist has written, and he is quite correct, but what he does not understand is that the deed that was in the beginning, before time, was a terrible and unspeakable one. This deed the sorcerer must make his own. For him the tree, the snake, and the apple, vague symbols of a most awful mystery, take on a tremendous reality.

Next to this was one of the marginal notes in blue ink:

> Chalmers thought he understood this, but the Hounds tore his head from his body and left his corpse smeared with their blue ichor. I have given below the formula he used for the Liao drug. One grain is enough; five, the dose he used, is too risky, for the Hounds will sense it and come hunting. No sorcery will keep them at bay for long, and the larger the dose, the more quickly they will come.

Below that was a recipe full of ingredients and processes she had never heard of.

Brecken closed the book. I can't do this, she thought. I just can't. The unknown territory of sorcery still hovered in front of her, but whatever enticements it might offer didn't begin to make up for what she sensed she might lose.

Sho glanced up at her then. ♪You are troubled, broodsister.♪

The endearment comforted her, and she bent and kissed Sho's surface. ♪I think I know why only a few elders of your people were supposed to read writings about sorcery. There are things in this *book I don't want to think about and things I don't think are right. If the dreams come back I know where to find the thing I did to stop them, but other than that—♪*

She got up, took *The Secret Watcher* back to the dresser and replaced it. *♪Other than that, I think I'm just going to have to take my chances.♪*

She returned to the futon, sat down, flung her arms around Sho and nestled her face into cool shapeless darkness.

* * *

Wednesday she couldn't afford to hide at home, not with two classes, laundry, and a piano lesson on her schedule. She went to campus early to meet with Professor Toomey and talk over the details of her audition choices, then went to The Cave to spend a few minutes chatting with Rosalie. There she heard unexpected news: Jay had dropped all his classes that semester.

"That's what Melissa Bukowski said," Rosalie told her in a low voice. "You know she does her work-study in the Registrar's office, right? She told me he dropped out even though it's too late to get a full refund on his tuition."

"That's got to hurt," Brecken said. "He's got to be short on money without Rose and Thorn to help out. Unless he's got another group going—"

"Not in this town." Rosalie's face twisted in an unpleasant smile. "I made good and sure that every musician in this part of New Jersey knows all about how he cheated us. Donna's done the same thing, too."

"Where is she these days?" Brecken asked. "It's been a while since I've seen her here."

Rosalie looked uncomfortable. "Around. She's really busy with her classes."

Brecken gave her a long steady look. "Ro," she said. "Come on."

"No, really—" Rosalie glanced up at her, saw the expression on her face, looked away.

"Out with it."

In a low voice: "She looked up your mom."

A vast silence seemed to open up around Brecken then. "Okay," she said.

"You didn't tell me," Rosalie burst out. "I mean, you said she was in prison, but not—"

Brecken nodded. "We can talk about it if you want, but—but not here."

"Okay," Rosalie gave her a nervous look. "My place? You've got time between Comp II and your 1:30 class, don't you?"

Brecken agreed to that readily. They got to Composition II just before it started, and listened to three bland and interchangeable student projects. "'Tone Sequence Seventeen' by Julian Pinchbeck," said Professor Toomey then.

Julian got out of his chair, waited impatiently for Mike Schau to leave the piano, then sat down on the bench and turned half around to face the professor. "Before I start," he said, "I'd like to say a few words."

"Go ahead," said Toomey.

Julian turned to face the class. "I don't know why we have to keep on revisiting the obvious," he said, "but the eighteenth century was a long time ago and music has moved on. The old arbitrary forms are a ball and chain nobody needs any more. Here's an example of why."

He played a series of single notes, hitting all twelve of the piano keys in the octave above middle C one at a time, to a jerky rhythm.

"Listen to it," Julian said. "Just *listen* to it." He played the sequence again. "That's why composers got rid of tonality and the whole hopeless, arbitrary classical mess more than a hundred years ago—because there's a whole world of music that the old forms can't touch. You can't do anything with a sequence like that if you're hobbled by some kind of sick obsession with outdated music." He shot a hostile glance at Brecken with those last words. "Dump that nonsense and you can do something like this." He turned to the keyboard, began to play.

The piece was better than anything he'd done in the fall semester, Brecken thought, less showy and more focused. Good? Not yet, not by a long way, but it was moving toward something that wasn't simply pretentious noise. Maybe facing a challenge was good for him.

And maybe, she thought, maybe a challenge would be good for me too. The thought of making him eat his words hovered before her, enticing.

The same sequence of tones repeated half a dozen times in the course of Julian's piece, each time over the top of a different set of discords. Brecken took a moment to write the sequence out note for note the third time it recurred, listened carefully the fourth time to make sure she'd gotten them down correctly, then returned to the comment form on the class website and made a few more comments she hoped would be helpful.

A final jarring dissonance ended the piece, and Julian left the piano and went back to his seat. "That's it for today," Professor Toomey said. "Tuesday it's back to lectures. Catch up on your reading if you've slacked off; we're going to hit the ground running."

As the others got out of their chairs, Brecken turned to Rosalie, said, "Just a moment," rose and went to the piano. "Julian," she said then, loud enough to catch his attention; he gave her an irritated look. "This sequence?" she said, and replayed it.

His expression went from irritated to uneasy. "Yeah."

"Okay." She gave him a broad smile, went back to her seat, tucked her notebook and phone into her tote bag and waited for Rosalie to get up from her chair.

* * *

After the class was over they headed down the stairs and walked to Rosalie's apartment in silence. It wasn't until they got there, and Brecken shed her coat while Rosalie dove into the kitchen and got coffee going for the two of them, that it occurred to her that she hadn't been there since the day when she and Donna quarreled about Jay. A couple of pieces of tourist art from Mexico hung on the walls, souvenirs of the trip to Guadalajara, and a brand new standup frame on the desk near the sofa had a photo in it, a young black man with a winning smile, wearing an expensive suit and tie. Brecken gave the photo a speculative glance, decided that this wasn't the time to ask about it.

Rosalie came out of the kitchen, handed Brecken a cup, sat on a chair facing the sofa, opened her mouth and then closed it again.

"You wanted to talk about my mom," Brecken said then.

A moment passed. "Did she—"

"Kill two people?" Brecken said. "Yes."

Rosalie gave her a horrified look. "What happened?"

"She started using opiates as soon as they got to Woodfield." Brecken stared at the coffee table between them as memories of a bygone and bitter time flitted past. "She started drinking after my dad died in Afghanistan, she was that torn up about what happened to him, and she was an angry drunk, so things were pretty bad. But then she switched to the pills. They didn't make her angry at all—she just sat around being vague and happy—and she said they were from the doctor's, so for a while I thought things were going to be okay."

"But I found out later that she lost her job because she couldn't pass the urine tests, and started dealing to pay the bills. She'd been an office manager, so she was good at it, and she ended up handling some really big deals. Then one night—this was right after eighth grade, and I was out of town, staying with my grandparents for the summer—she went to meet a couple of people, and one of them pulled a gun on her. The police think they were just going to shoot her and take the drugs, but she had a gun, too, and started shooting. She took a couple of bullets, but she lived and they didn't." She glanced up at Rosalie. "The county prosecutor threw the book at her, because it was an election year and he wanted everyone to think he was tough on drug crime, and she got a court-appointed lawyer who just went through the motions of defending her. So she's probably never going to get out."

Rosalie took that in, said nothing for a while. Finally: "Okay."

"I thought you knew," Brecken burst out then. "I thought that when I told you last year that my mom was in prison, you'd gone online and looked her up. It was all over the local media for a while." She glanced up at Rosalie. "I thought you knew, and decided that it didn't matter because we're friends."

"Well, it doesn't matter," Rosalie said. "You got that right, girl."

She was lying, Brecken knew at once, for Rosalie had never had to learn how to keep her feelings from showing on her face. It mattered very much, but the lie was a generous one, and Brecken smiled and said, "Thank you, Ro."

Neither spoke for a while. "So that's why Donna's been avoiding me?" Brecken asked.

Rosalie looked uncomfortable. "Yeah. Well, that and something else." She gulped at her coffee. "She told me she thought the reason you weren't going out with us at night any more was that you were probably using, too."

Brecken blinked, said, "What?"

"That's what she said."

"If I ever said anything nice about her," Brecken said with some heat, "I take it back. That was a really mean thing to say."

Rosalie stared at the table, looking even more uncomfortable. "The thing is, girl, you really have been distant."

Nettled, Brecken said, "So have you. What happened to the Saturday practice sessions we were going to do together?"

That got a look of acute embarrassment, of a kind that Brecken recognized. She sat back and said, "Okay, I think I understand. The photo on your desk—is that Tom Bannister?"

In a very small voice. "Yeah."

"The one who wasn't boyfriend material."

"Yeah."

"Oh, for heaven's sake, Ro, why didn't you tell me?"

She swallowed visibly, said, "Because I was such a jerk about you and Darren Wegener."

"It's okay, Ro," Brecken said then. "Really."

For the next twenty minutes they laughed and shared secrets the way they'd done when they were roommates in Arbuckle Hall, but beneath it all something had shifted, Brecken could feel that all too clearly. When she left to go to her counterpoint class, the doubtful look in Rosalie's eyes stung. She shoved the awareness aside, turned her attention to a minuet she was beginning to work out.

* * *

By the time Brecken finished the day's errands and got back to her own apartment, afternoon was turning to evening and the sun glowed crimson behind Hob's Hill. She shed her coat, put down her tote bag, flopped down on the futon, and whistled a greeting to Sho as the shoggoth flowed out from under the closet door. The iridescent black shape that nestled close to her a moment later, and extended a shy pseudopod to place a drop of fluid on her cheek, seemed so familiar and natural to her that it startled her to think of how everyone else in Partridgeville would react if they knew.

Later, after dinner, pushing aside brooding thoughts about Rosalie, she pulled out her composition notebook and started trying to figure out what to do with Julian Pinchbeck's sequence of notes. She'd already figured out the first step, which was finding a key that included the notes she wanted to accent, and it took only a few minutes to be sure that G flat minor would work best. That turned out to be the easy part, though. When she tried to go on from there and work out harmonies to the sequence, nothing worked right, no matter what she tried. Finally, frustrated, she set the notebook aside and got to work on the latest assignment from the counterpoint class, and she'd been studying Johann Joseph Fux intensively enough by then that the exercises in the assignment took no effort at all.

The next day was her last day of classes before spring break. She'd arranged to meet Darren at the coffee shop inside Tuchman Hall, and got there in plenty of time despite a slow pleasant morning with Sho. Twenty minutes or so later they'd just gotten deep into the mathematics of an elegant fugue by Buxtehude, and Brecken, chin propped on folded hands and elbows on the table, had begun to make sense of the way that the geometrical ratios Darren talked about gave an underlying structure to the entire piece. Just then Darren's phone played the first two bars of Mozart's *De Profundis Clamavi*; he gave his pocket a bleak look, pulled out the phone, glanced at the screen and said, "Well, I'm in for it now."

"What's up?"

"Text from my folks. They're coming to visit toward the end of spring break." He shrugged. "They show up half a dozen times a year. At least this time I've got a week's warning, but it's going to suck." He turned off the phone, stuck it back into his pocket. "A day or two of Mom telling me everything I'm doing is wrong and Dad trying to figure out if I've got a boyfriend tucked under the sofa or something."

Brecken laughed, then said, "I wish we could get them to walk in on the two of us here. I bet we could give them quite a show."

That got her a sudden calculating look. "Would you be good with that?"

"Of course," she said. "Do you think you can make that happen?"

"Maybe." He sat back, stared at nothing she could see. "If I tell them I've got something scheduled and don't want to get together with them until after that, and let slip the place, I bet they'll show up to try to catch me with a guy. They've done it before."

"That could be fun," said Brecken.

He gave her a wan look. "You haven't met my folks."

"No, but everything you've said makes me want to mess with them." A year earlier, she knew, she wouldn't have been able to find the courage to think that, much less say it, but those days were behind her now. Don't get between Brecken and her strays, she thought, flinging the words at the world like a challenge. It was true, too: she didn't have to fall in love with someone to want to give them whatever shelter they needed.

"Okay," he said then. "You're on." A moment later: "But here won't work. Can you handle sushi?"

"Sure."

"Good. Mom hates it, but she pretends she likes it because she thinks it's fashionable." He leaned forward again. "Ever been to Fumi's, up on Prospect Street?" When she shook her head, he went on. "Best sushi in town. When are you getting back?"

"Wednesday afternoon."

"How about Thursday at one?"

"You're on," she said, and made sure to get the address copied onto her phone before they went back to talking about Buxtehude.

* * *

That afternoon she got off the elevator in The Cave after a frustrating session of her orchestral arrangement class, and started for the bank of glass doors. She'd gotten less than halfway across the space when a tall young man standing in a knot of older students noticed her, turned toward her, and said, "Hey, can I ask you a question?"

"Sure," Brecken replied.

"You're the one who's composing classical stuff, right?"

"Baroque, actually." She faced him, noted the hint of a swagger in his posture and the way his eyes strayed to the other students he'd been talking with.

"Why?"

"Because that's the music I love," Brecken said.

He rolled his eyes and said, "Oh, come on," and launched into one of the overfamiliar arguments she'd been fielding all semester—afterwards, she couldn't even remember which one. Her protest simply brought a couple of the young man's friends into the argument. Before long there were half a dozen of them, more, mouthing the same tired reasons that she'd heard so many times before, insisting that she had to stop writing the music she loved and instead start writing the same things that every other young composer was writing just then.

"Look," Brecken said finally, exasperated beyond endurance. "I know that I'm going to spend my life flipping burgers or something. I know that maybe three people in the history of forever are going to want to listen to my music. I know that I'm going one way and the rest of music is going somewhere else. I understand all that, and I'm good with it, okay? So why can't you just back off and let me write the music that matters to me?"

That got her a moment of silence. Then, from past them, Molly Wolejko's voice:

"Because they're a bunch of meek little conformists."

One of the young men spun around to face her. "That's total bullshit."

Her answer was a contemptuous snort. "Look at you," she said, stepping closer, hands on her hips. "You're seniors, aren't you? Eight on one, bullying a sophomore because she's doing something that doesn't just rehash the latest fashions. I bet every single one of you talks about being edgy, breaking away from the conventional wisdom, finding your personal voice, but when somebody actually does that you can't wait to tell them how wrong they are."

"Yeah, right," said one of the others, in a tone of utter disdain. "Big words from someone who makes money playing headbanger trash."

"And you're pea green with envy," Molly shot back, "because people actually pay to hear my music. You know what? I could make a hell of a lot more playing pop or country, but metal says what I want to say, and it says what a lot of people want to hear, and that's what music's actually about—saying something an audience can relate to. Not sticking your hand down your shorts and thinking that makes you special." She walked up to the one who'd spoken, grinning the kind of grin that sets fists flying. "Not pretending that you're better than everyone else because you go out of your way to write stuff they don't know how to follow."

For one cold moment Brecken thought a fight was about to start, but the senior that Molly confronted glared and then backed away. "Look," Brecken said. "I'm not telling anybody else what they ought to compose. I just want to keep writing the music I love, okay?" She stopped. Maybe it was the Vach-Viraj incantation and some trace of the feeling of being ♪sheltered♪ it had brought her, maybe it was something else, but she drew in a breath and went on. "And I'm going to keep writing it. If you don't like it, that's not my problem, it's yours. If you want to yell about it, go shout at the wall over there. Who knows, maybe it'll listen." A motion of her head indicated the nearest flat expanse of concrete. "But you know what? I won't—and you really ought to save your breath for someone who cares what you think."

What would have happened if she and the seniors had been alone, Brecken didn't want to guess, but Molly was there, her head tossed back at a truculent angle, and most of the other people in The Cave had turned to look. The senior who'd spoken first glanced this way, that, and then fixed Brecken with a cold look. "Your loss," he said in an acid tone, and turned and walked away. The others looked around and made off.

In less than a minute Brecken and Molly stood in an otherwise empty space in the middle of The Cave. "Nice," Molly said. "Up for coffee?"

"Sure," said Brecken, and the two of them crossed The Cave to the doors that led to Vivaldi's. A few minutes later they were sitting at a table in a convenient corner with steaming cups in front of them.

"Don't let 'em get to you," Molly said. "Seriously. Everybody in this department who's not doing pretentious avant-garde crap has to deal with that kind of thing. You just have to shrug it off and go your own way."

"I'm still figuring out how to do that," Brecken admitted.

"Keep at it," Molly went on. "The thing is, every time you play one of your Baroque things you put their noses a couple of miles out of joint. My stuff they can brush off—hey, it's just amplified noise, right?" She grinned. "But they can't do that with yours. They know perfectly well how much work it takes to make a fugue or something like that come out right, and most of them couldn't do a halfway decent job of it if they tried. Why do you think you get all those nasty looks from Prince Foofy-Hair in composition class?"

Brecken choked hard at the nickname, but managed not to spray coffee across the table. When she'd swallowed and put the cup down: "I was wondering if it was that."

"Bet the farm on it." She leaned forward. "Ever thought about transferring somewhere else, where they teach the kind of music you want to do?"

"Well—" Brecken stopped, made herself go on. "I've applied to a program at a school in Massachusetts," she said. "I'll be auditioning there next week."

"Sweet. Whereabouts?"

"Miskatonic University in Arkham."

That got a nod. "Don't know squat about the school but Arkham's a decent place. My band's played a club there a couple of times." She downed some of her coffee, sat back. "The thing is, this school is giving me what I need: more grounding in music theory and some good hard challenges to get me writing in new directions. I don't think it's going to give you what you need." She shrugged. "I grew up in one of those pretty plastic suburbs that sucks the soul right out of you, and if I hadn't found metal to do my screaming for me I probably would have walked out in front of a truck or something. My music tears the world apart. Yours puts it back together—and I don't think they can teach you how to do that at Partridgeville State."

"No, probably not," Brecken admitted.

She brooded about that from time to time that weekend, as she nerved herself up to the trip to Massachusetts, rehearsed the pieces she'd chosen for her audition, and made plans with Sho for the few days they'd be spending apart. Molly was right, she thought more than once: the music I love makes the world feel as though it's been put back together again—but how can that work when it really is just as arbitrary as Julian Pinchbeck says it is?

CHAPTER 13

THE YELLOW SIGN

It wasn't the hardest thing Brecken had ever done, boarding the bus the next Monday morning. Really, she told herself, it should have been routine. She'd done the same thing half a dozen times already since she'd first come to Partridgeville. Of course getting ready for those previous trips hadn't involved comforting a worried and affectionate shoggoth, talking over how to make sure Mrs. Dalzell didn't realize that the converted garage had someone living there other than Brecken, and cooking up three big batches of cheese polenta and tucking them in the fridge to keep the shoggoth in question well nourished in her absence, but that hardly seemed to matter. Sho had become so much a part of her life by then that the little everyday rituals they'd created between them felt as though they'd been there from her childhood on.

The bus station fronted on Central Square, an easy walk from Brecken's apartment even with a small suitcase in one hand and her tote bag in the other. She got to the station twenty minutes before the bus did. From the waiting room she could see buildings she knew well, dark brick broken by dark windows, grimy marble cornices against an unsettled spring sky. She looked at them for a little while, trying not to think about what waited in Arkham, and then tried to distract herself with her copy of *The Book of Nameless Cults*, which she'd decided to take with her. Any other time the strange tales of forgotten civilizations and lost continents would have held her interest, but she couldn't keep her mind on the book at all.

The bus pulled up more or less on time, and Brecken fumbled with her phone, got the ticket to display on the screen, lined up to hand over her suitcase and climb the stair. A few minutes later, she settled into a window seat as the engine rumbled to life. Familiar streets slid past, and then the bus plunged through Mulligan Wood and the highway stretched away into the northern end of the pine barrens. She tried again to make sense of von Junzt and got nowhere, so it went into her tote bag next to Mrs. Macallan's flute.

After that, she watched mile after mile of pine forest slip past, and thought about the legend of the Jersey Devil, the monster that haunted the pine barrens—a great winged creature with a head like a horse, so the old stories said. The thought occurred to her, somewhere in the middle of the barrens, that the Devil sounded quite a bit like the Shantak-birds von Junzt discussed. She opened *The Book of Nameless Cults*, paged through it to the section on Shantak-birds, and nodded slowly. Shantak-birds and shoggoths, she thought, and wondered how many other creatures of the elder world might still hide in isolated corners of the globe. Were there still Deep Ones in their undersea cities and voormis in their cavern homes? The silences of the pine barrens didn't answer.

Finally the barrens fell behind, giving way first to old towns in a green landscape and then to the sprawl surrounding Trenton. There Brecken got off the bus, retrieved her suitcase, waited for most of an hour in the train station, and boarded an Amtrak train headed north. She got a seat in the quiet car, and finally managed to get her mind to focus on von Junzt. The rest of New Jersey was a blur, New York City a few glimpses of aging skyscrapers, and the landscape from there to Boston left not even that much trace in her memory.

At Boston's South Station she had barely enough time to hurry from the Amtrak train to the MBTA train out to Salem, and at Salem she headed straight to the bus stop, double-checked the schedule on her phone, and five minutes later climbed aboard a county bus with 13 TO ARKHAM VIA KINGSPORT on the sign above the front windshield. She was nervous enough that she pulled von Junzt out of her tote bag three times, reread the passage on the words and signs of recognition, and then put the book away again. The bus left Salem on what street signs told her was the Old Kingsport Highway, and before long Kingsport came into view, a pleasant little tourist town around a harbor busy with small boats. The black masts and yards of a tall ship caught Brecken's gaze, and beyond it crags rose up against the eastern sky, height upon height to the soaring mass of Kingsport Head.

From Kingsport the highway turned north and headed into the hills, and the bus drove into dark woodlands where pines and twisted willows huddled together as though whispering to one another. There were so few traces of human settlement that Brecken felt as though she'd somehow strayed from the busy world she knew to some distant corner of space or time, where her species had not yet arrived or had long since departed. The feeling lasted until the bus rounded one last curve, came out from under the trees, and started down a long slope toward a town huddled in a river valley.

Arkham, Brecken thought. It has to be. She was right, too; before long the bus passed an old sign with peeling paint welcoming visitors to Arkham, Massachusetts, and a few moments after that the highway had become a street that passed through a half-abandoned business district, crossed the river on a well-aged steel bridge, and headed straight toward the cyclopean buildings of the Miskatonic University campus.

A few minutes later she was standing beside what her map and a conveniently placed street sign both agreed was Curwen Street, waiting for the light to change.

The neighborhood around her yelled its closeness to the university, with its array of little strip malls and clapboard-covered homes clumsily remodeled into student housing. That was familiar enough to comfort her, but she braced herself, knowing that there was one more hurdle to leap, and no way of gauging how high it was until she got there.

A block down to Hyde Street, four blocks along it to the intersection of Hyde and Jenkin: she'd rehearsed the directions in her mind often enough on the bus ride that she had no trouble at all finding 438 West Hyde Street. That proved to be an elegant Victorian house with a mansard roof and impressive amounts of ornate trim. Brecken stood looking at it for a few moments, then walked up to the door, drew in an unsteady breath, and rang the doorbell.

* * *

Professor June Satterlee answered the door. Tall and brown, dressed in a tailored skirt and jacket, her neatly braided hair long since gone silver, she gave Brecken an assessing glance and then said "Good afternoon" as though she meant it. Brecken, feeling even more gawky than usual, said something more or less appropriate and introduced herself, and moments later found herself and her suitcase inside the entry, with a wood-paneled parlor lined with bookshelves reaching away to one side, and a tightly curled spiral staircase rising on the other.

"So you're Carson's discovery," the professor said. "Oh, for heaven's sake, child, leave those there for now." Her gesture included the suitcase, the tote bag, and the foot of the stair. "Your coat can go on the rack. Can I offer you a cup of tea? Excellent."

Brecken followed her through the parlor to a big comfortable kitchen, took the seat at the table the professor indicated. She watched while the old woman moved about the kitchen, made a pot of tea and got cookies on a pair of plates. The words and signs of recognition she'd learned from von Junzt's book hovered in her mind.

She waited until Satterlee settled down again across the kitchen table, poured tea for them both, and started asking about Brecken's studies. Without doing anything to call attention to the motion, Brecken picked up the teacup in forefinger and thumb and stretched her other fingers, slightly splayed like a squid's tentacles, along the side of the cup as she raised it to her mouth.

A flicker of visible surprise crossed the professor's face, vanished as quickly as it came. As Brecken answered the question, the old woman took hold of her teacup handle in the same way, but slowly folded the other fingers into her palm. A chill went down Brecken's back as she realized that she'd guessed correctly.

Thereafter, for the next five minutes, two conversations filled the kitchen, one as audible as it was casual, the other silent and in deadly earnest. In the one conversation, Professor Satterlee asked Brecken questions about the music program at Partridgeville State and the studies she'd pursued there, and Brecken managed a series of somewhat distracted replies. In the other, sign answered sign until the whole sequence was complete.

Finally Professor Satterlee put down her teacup and said, "What do you know?"

"I know a sign," Brecken said, set her own cup aside, and folded her fingers awkwardly into an intricate pattern, hoping she'd understood von Junzt's instructions.

"I know another sign," said the professor, and folded hers in a different pattern.

"I know a place," said Brecken, "where the sleeper waits."

"I know a time when the stars are right."

"I know a dream that the sea will not stop."

"I know a call that will always be answered."

"In the name of the Dreaming Lord," Brecken said then, "I greet you."

Professor Satterlee smiled. "You learned every word of that from a book, didn't you?"

Brecken stared, swallowed, made herself say, "Yes. Yes, I did."

"It's been a century and a half since anybody's used those words and signs." Holding up a reassuring hand: "Don't worry about it. I use the old sign in my emails precisely because there are people out there who have the books and nothing else. When you spotted it and sent back the old answer, I had certain people investigate you and make sure you weren't bait for a trap, or something of the sort."

Brecken took that in. "What did they find out?"

"Next to nothing." Satterlee leaned forward. "An ordinary young woman with musical talent who had no connection to the Great Old Ones or their worshipers that anybody could trace, but who knew a very obscure sign, and whose voor had a curious quality that three highly skilled sensitives couldn't interpret."

"Voor," Brecken said. "There's something about that in the books I've read."

"I imagine so. Do you know what voor is?" When Brecken shook her head: "It's the life force, the power that flows through our bodies and the body of the Earth." All the while, as she talked, the green eyes stayed focused on Brecken with a dreadful intensity, and the dark face smiled. In a sudden moment of cold clarity, Brecken sensed that the old woman was perfectly capable of killing with that smile on her face.

"I think I know what the people you sent were sensing, then." It took Brecken an effort to say the words: "I have a friend, a very dear friend, that most people can't know about." She swallowed again, forced the words through a dry throat. "A friend who's not human. I know you may not believe that."

The professor nodded as though that was the most ordinary thing in the world. "That was one of the possibilities I'd wondered about."

Brecken, baffled, said, "Okay. Do you know what a shoggoth is?"

Satterlee's eyebrows went up, hard. "Yes, I do," she said after a moment. "That's not at all what I expected, but we should be able to work something out."

A silence passed, then Brecken asked, "Is it okay to—to ask what you expected?"

"Of course. I guessed you had something going on with one of the Great Old Ones."

Completely nonplussed, Brecken stared at her for a long moment, then realized her mouth was open and shut it. The professor gave her an amused look. "How well do you know your mythology, child? The old gods of nature did that kind of thing all the time, and they still do. There are children, too. Shall I tell you a secret?"

"Please," said Brecken.

"I'm one of them."

"Okay," Brecken said after a moment, trying to stretch her world to fit Great Old Ones that actually existed. Since she'd already made room for shoggoths and sorcery, that was less of a challenge than it might have been, but it still left her dizzied.

"Your shoggoth friend," said Satterlee then. "If you come to Arkham that's going to be a challenge, no question, given how big they are."

"She's not," said Brecken. "You know they're of different sizes, right?"

The old woman's smile vanished. "Just how big is the shoggoth we're talking about?"

"About this big when she's all drawn together." Her hands mimed a four-foot sphere.

"And when did you meet her?"

"It was—" She counted days silently. "October fourteenth of last year."

"In Partridgeville."

"Yes."

Satterlee closed her eyes. A slight ducking of her head hinted at emotions Brecken had no way to gauge.

"I know the rest of her people are dead," Brecken said then.

The professor opened her eyes, considered Brecken with the same terrible intensity as before. "I don't think anyone knew there was a colony near Partridgeville. It might have been possible to save them along with the others, but—" She let the sentence drop.

Brecken opened her mouth, found no words. She swallowed, tried again. "Others?"

"There used to be colonies all up and down the coast, and back into the mountains. There were still six that—certain people—knew about."

"And—and the shoggoths—"

"They're safe, most of them. It was quite a mess, from what I heard."

"She'll be so happy," Brecken whispered.

The old woman considered that, and then said, "Perhaps you can tell me a little more about your shoggoth friend."

Brecken glanced up at her, nodded, drew in a breath, and began to talk about the thunder behind Hob's Hill, Sho's appearance in her kitchen, the bond that had taken shape between them even in those first encounters. She hadn't intended to talk about how that bond had changed and what it had become, but the sheer relief of being able to talk to someone else about her feelings for Sho swept everything else aside; before she'd quite noticed, she was recounting the way she and Sho had spent the winter holiday. Reddening, she stared fixedly at the table as she finished the story and silence settled back in place in the kitchen.

"Child," Satterlee said then. "I'm not going to pass judgment on somebody else's heart."

Brecken looked up from the table to the old woman's smile. It wasn't the dreadfully calm smile she'd seen before, the one that could kill; it was far more human, tinged with a certain indulgence. She ventured a fragile smile of her own. "Thank you."

"You're welcome." Then, her expression turning serious: "But I want your permission to call someone and talk about what you've told me. Someone—probably not the same someone—may want to come here and talk to you about it. I promise you that no harm's going to come to you or—her name's Sho?"

"Her nickname," said Brecken.

"Or to Sho, and it might end up helping some people who need it very badly. Not all of the people in question are human, by the way."

Brecken considered her for a long moment. "Okay," she said. "But I'm trusting you with someone who—who means more to me than anyone else in the world. Please remember that."

"I will." She met Brecken's gaze squarely. "We know how to keep secrets."

With that, Brecken had to be content.

* * *

At Professor Satterlee's suggestion—it was not quite brusque enough to be called an order—she hauled her suitcase and tote bag up the spiral stair to the guestroom on the third floor, got her things unpacked and settled in the old oak dresser there, stood irresolute for a time while a clock on the wall ticked away the seconds. Fifteen minutes, the old woman had said, and then Brecken should come back downstairs and play the piano for a while. Turning away from the clock, Brecken went around the big canopied bed to one of the two windows, looked out over the rooftops of Arkham.

It was strange, she thought. Arkham and Partridgeville both dated from the 1680s, or so she'd read online, and their founders had settled in similar spots where rivers flowed out of rugged hills toward the sea; they'd passed through the same trajectory from farming village to seaport to mill town to college town, and yet a glance across the skyline made it impossible to mistake the one for the other. It wasn't just the difference between the gambrel roofs of old Massachusetts and the straight gable roofs of old New Jersey, or the spartan simplicity of New England meeting houses and the ornate lines of the First Baptist Church on Angell Hill. Some difference she couldn't define hovered in the air over Arkham, flowed down from the brooding hills, pooled above a curious island in the middle of the river that seemed to have lines of something tall and gray—standing stones, maybe?—rising from long grass.

Whisper of a voice from the hallway outside broke into her thoughts, and she turned, looked at the clock again. It had been more than twenty minutes since she'd headed upstairs, so she left the room and went to the stair. Professor Satterlee was at the foot, and as Brecken came down the last turn of the stair the old woman said with a smile, "I was starting to wonder if you'd fallen asleep up there."

"Not quite," Brecken said. "I was looking out the window." Then, because so many strange things seemed so ordinary to the professor: "There's something in the air over that little island in the river."

The smile dropped off the old woman's face. "Yes, there is," she said. "Have you always seen things like that?"

"No," Brecken said, startled by the professor's reaction. "No, not at all. What is it?"

"Voor." Then: "We can talk about it some other time. Just now, it's time for music."

They went into the parlor, where a grand piano overawed the sofa on one wall and the chairs and bookcases on two others. Satterlee gestured Brecken to the bench; she sat down, stretched and shook her fingers, then turned to the professor. "What would you like me to play?"

"Anything you want," Satterlee said, settling on the sofa.

Brecken drew in as deep a breath as her nerves would allow, gave the keyboard a blank look for a moment, and then started to play her Bourrée in B flat. The first few notes faltered, but then she found her rhythm, let the music guide her hands straight through to the final cadence.

"That's a charming little piece," Professor Satterlee said when the last notes had faded to silence. "I don't believe I know it, though. Who's the composer?"

Brecken opened her mouth, then swallowed, then forced out, "I am."

The old woman's eyebrows went up the way they had when Brecken had mentioned shoggoths. "You wrote that."

"Yes."

Satterlee took that in. "Play something else you've written." After a moment: "Please."

Brecken considered the Minuet in C and the three Sarabandes, but the moment called for something more ambitious, she was sure of it. "I'm not really satisfied with this yet," she said, and then played the first of the three sforzando chords of her Theme and Variations in G. As always, she could feel it reaching toward something she didn't yet know how to help it grasp, but she threw herself into the performance, got the sense of nervous energy in the staccato measures of the second variation as close to perfect as she'd yet managed, nearly stumbled over the flurry of notes at the beginning of the third variation, but got her balance again and plunged into the furious allegro that followed, playing hard, straight through to the three chords that ended it.

When she was done, she closed her eyes, gathered up her courage, and glanced over her shoulder at Satterlee.

The old woman was staring at her with unalloyed surprise. "Child," she said, "that's a fine piece of eighteenth-century music."

"I know," said Brecken. Then, taking her courage in both hands: "Professor Satterlee, that's the music I love, and it's the music I want to write. I know it's supposed to be a dead art form—but it's not dead for me."

Satterlee pondered that for a time. "No," she said finally. "No, I see it isn't." Then, shaking her head a little as though to clear it. "Well. Perhaps you'd like to play a piece or two from the standard repertoire now. Something by Bach, maybe?"

Brecken broke into a luminous smile. "In my sleep," she said, and launched straight into the Prelude and Fugue in E flat from *The Well-Tempered Clavier*. The serene mathematics of Bach had their usual effect, rounding the jagged edges of her nerves, setting the world in order.

She finished, glanced back over her shoulder at Satterlee, and was startled to find that the professor had been joined on the sofa by a plump young woman with short brown hair, wearing jeans and a Miskatonic University sweatshirt.

"Brecken, this is Sarah Choynski," said the professor. "She's renting the second floor apartment from me this year. Sarah, this is Brecken Kendall, who may be renting it next year." With a smile for Brecken: "I usually rent the space out to music students. They don't mind if I play at all hours, which I do, and of course the reverse is just as true."

"Pleased to meet you," said Sarah with a broad grin. "That was Bach, right? Nice."

"Sarah's a vocalist," said the professor with an apologetic look. "Jazz, mostly."

"My dad wanted me to be a classical musician," Sarah said. "But one of my aunts played me an Ella Fitzgerald CD when I was eight, and that was all she wrote."

Laughing, Brecken turned to face the sofa. "My grandmother wanted me to get into jazz and blues, but then she took me to see Mozart's *The Magic Flute* when I was seven."

"Her grandmother," Satterlee observed to Sarah, "was Olive Kendall."

Sarah's mouth dropped open. "Seriously? I adore her stuff. That lady could really sing. I mean really *really* sing."

"True enough," said the professor. "Sarah, can you show Brecken the apartment? She ought to know what she's getting into." Then, to Brecken, who was working up the courage to ask how she'd done: "I think you'll do well—but we'll have to see how tomorrow goes."

* * *

"I warn you," said Sarah as they went through the door. "It's pretty cluttered right now."

She wasn't exaggerating. Like most college students, Brecken was far from finicky about housekeeping, but Sarah's evident enthusiasm for piling books, sheet music, stray pieces of clothing, and other impedimenta on every available surface was a little daunting. Still, the apartment was pleasant enough: a spacious parlor with an upright piano conveniently set against an inside wall, a kitchen of decent size, a small but comfortable bedroom, and a bath that unexpectedly featured a big white clawfooted tub. Windows looked south across the roofs of old Arkham, west across more roofs to the cyclopean brick and glass buildings of the Miskatonic University campus, north toward the green whaleback shape of a hill, untouched by buildings, that rose above dark woods close by. "Meadow Hill," Sarah said when Brecken asked about that last. "No, nobody's ever built anything on it. I don't think anyone ever dared. There's supposed to be a lot of funny stories about it."

That was the only odd note in Sarah's conversation, though. Waving her hands as she talked, she told Brecken about the quirks of the house's archaic plumbing and the apartment's aging stove, the local weather, the latest happenings in the Miskatonic music department, and a great deal more, including the habits of Brecken's potential landlady. "She's going to tell you you shouldn't help out in the kitchen. Don't believe a word of it. I swear to God, if I didn't pop down there every few days and do a bunch of cooking, she'd never eat anything but salad."

"Okay," said Brecken. Tentatively: "I like to cook, so that should work."

Sarah's face lit up. "Do you? So do I. I bet you get a lot of crap from people about that." She sniffed. "As though there's anything liberated about living on takeout."

By the time they came down the stairs again they were discussing recipes, and once they'd brushed aside a futile protest from Professor Satterlee, the two of them got down to work in the kitchen. "My dad's folks were a Choynski and a Desrochers," Sarah said, "and my mom's were a Gilman from a little town north of here—you'll hear lots of stories about Innsmouth once you move—and an Ellwood. One hundred per cent American mutt, and I cook that way."

Brecken started laughing. "Ever had gefilte fish and cheese grits for dinner?"

"No, but it sounds good." Sarah handed her a yellow onion. "Your folks make that?"

"My grandparents—and it's really good."

They got a casserole baking in the oven and a salad marinating in the fridge, and settled in the parlor, where Professor Satterlee had finished correcting a stack of student papers. An hour of gossip later, dinner for three hit the table, and most of an hour after that they were back in the parlor, taking turns at the piano. Brecken remembered "Ain't Misbehavin'" and "Honeysuckle Rose" well enough from her girlhood to back Sarah's singing on both pieces; Professor Satterlee took over the keyboard and hammered out a fine version of "St. James Infirmary Blues," then she and Sarah belted out "Shout, Sister, Shout" and "Minnie the Moocher," and all three of them joined in "It Don't Mean A Thing If It Ain't Got That Swing." Laughing, Sarah begged off then, pleading an imminent midterm, and headed upstairs.

Before Brecken could think about doing the same thing, the professor turned to her and said, "Someone will be here to talk to you in a few minutes."

Brecken swallowed, her throat suddenly dry. "Okay."

That got her a calm smile. "Glass of wine?"

"Please."

The old woman got up from the piano bench, vanished into the kitchen, returned with two stemmed glasses of something pale golden in color. Brecken, who knew next to nothing about wine, sniffed hers, sipped, said, "That's really good."

"Thank you." They settled on the couch. Brecken took another sip; the professor watched her, her thoughts inaccessible behind a placid smile.

"Does Sarah know about—" Brecken gestured vaguely. "Shoggoths, the rest of it."

A quick shake of the professor's head denied it. "She's a dear person and a very good musician, but I haven't told her anything and she doesn't seem to have found any of it out on her own. You'd think that Arkham would be crawling with people who know about the elder world and the Great Old Ones, wouldn't you?"

It took Brecken a moment to make sense of that. "Because of H.P. Lovecraft?"

"Yes, and what Miskatonic has in its library, and the town's history generally." She sipped wine. "But I've met very few of them here. The people I know who understand it all are scattered far and wide, and they have to keep moving." With a sudden, intensely human smile: "I'll be glad if you pass your audition and get a place in the composition program. It'll be pleasant to have someone else in town who understands—to say nothing of a shoggoth."

"Thank you."

"You're welcome."

A silence passed. "If I do okay on the audition," Brecken said then, "I'm definitely going to want to talk to you about the apartment."

"Good." Satterlee sipped from her glass. "Your friend Sho will be safe here."

Brecken's gaze snapped up to the old woman's face, then fell again. "Thank you," she said. "That means a lot to me." With a little laugh: "No, that's an understatement. It means everything to me."

The professor made as though to speak, but suddenly glanced toward the entry, as though she'd heard a knock. "Just a moment," she said, set her glass aside, got to her feet and went to the door. Brecken, who had heard nothing, watched her in perplexity, heard the door open and shut, quiet as a whisper.

* * *

A moment later two sets of footsteps sounded in the entry, and Professor Satterlee came back into the parlor. Behind her was a man of indeterminate age with a gaunt, lined face that looked tanned by years of sun and weather, and a shock of pale disorderly hair. His clothes were unremarkable to the point of camouflage, his expression carefully neutral, but Brecken sat up abruptly; something in him or around him crackled like distant lightning.

The professor did not introduce them. She simply got a chair for him, set it in front of Brecken, and then sat down on the other end of the couch and resumed sipping her wine. The man sat down, gave Brecken an assessing look, and then said, "I hope you won't mind answering a few questions."

Brecken glanced at Professor Satterlee, then said, "No, not at all."

"June tells me you've befriended a shoggoth."

"Yes."

"Would you mind telling me its name?"

"Her," said Brecken. "I don't know what her name is today."

That got a sudden fractional smile, and Brecken realized that she'd passed a test. "Fair enough," he said. "Perhaps you could tell me how the two of you met."

Brecken nodded, and described the night that thunder sounded out of a clear sky behind Hob's Hill, the accidental purchase of the photocopied lexicon that allowed her to communicate with Sho, the events of the following days.

"Thank you," he said when she finished. "And has your shoggoth friend told you what happened under Hob's Hill?"

"Yes," Brecken said. "We've talked about it. I can tell you about it if you want."

"Please."

Brecken drew in an unsteady breath, closed her eyes, recounted what Sho had said about the last moments of her people and her own desperate flight to the world outside. When she was finished with the story, she opened her eyes. The man in front of her was still watching her, and his expression had not changed at all, but something hidden in his gaze reminded her of the intensity she'd seen in Professor Satterlee's eyes earlier that day. That, and more: she felt old griefs there, and terrible purpose.

"Thank you," he said after a moment.

Brecken nodded, then ventured, "Can I ask a question?" When he gestured, inviting: "Who did that?"

The man glanced at Professor Satterlee, then back at Brecken. "There's a war being fought," he said. "A secret war. The elder races, and the humans who've learned to live in peace with them, are on one side. The other side can't stand the thought that shoggoths or anything like them can exist—and they're stronger than we are, until the stars are right."

"Okay," said Brecken. "The other side—do they have a name or something?"

"The Radiance," said June.

Brecken gave her a startled look.

"They've had many names down through the years," said the man, "but it's always some form of that. They are the children of light, the rest of us are the slaves of darkness: that's what they believe." With a bleak little smile: "And if you think that truth and light and reason are all on your side, you can justify anything you do to the other side."

Brecken took that in. "I'm not sure," she said then, "but I may have met two members of—of the Radiance."

Another quick glance passed between the man and Professor Satterlee. "Go on," he said. When she'd described the man who claimed to be from the state animal control office, the woman who'd called herself a folklore researcher, and the curious conversations she'd had with them, he nodded. "Thank you. That may turn out to be important."

"I hope so," said Brecken. "I'm on the side of the shoggoths."

That earned her a sudden smile. "So am I." He reached in past the neckline of his shirt, pulled out a pendant on a chain. "Do you know what this is?"

The pendant was a black oval of onyx, and on it was a curious symbol or letter in gold. It looked a little like a word in Arabic and a little like a Chinese character, but Brecken felt sure that it was neither. "No," she said.

"The Yellow Sign."

She looked up at his face. "That's for real?"

"Yes." He tucked the pendant beneath his shirt, stood up. "Thank you for your help." Professor Satterlee stood also, and went with him to the door. Brecken stared after them until the door whispered open and shut again, and the old woman returned.

"So you've heard of the Fellowship," Satterlee said.

"I thought they were just something in old stories," Brecken admitted.

"Not at all. People get drawn into the secret war you just heard about in various ways." She sat down, picked up her wine glass. "Sometimes it's because they've had their lives, their families, their careers, or their reputations destroyed by the Radiance. When that's the way of it, and they decide they want to fight back, sometimes they find the Fellowship, and some of them become soldiers and servants of the King."

"The King In Yellow," Brecken guessed.

"Yes." The professor leaned forward and in a low voice went on: "My father."

Brecken stared at her.

The serene smile showed on her face again. "Would you like a little more wine?"

"Please," Brecken said.

CHAPTER 14

A DOOR INTO APRIL

Maybe half an hour later, feeling slightly unsteady, Brecken climbed the stair to the guest room on the third floor, closed the door behind her, and stood beside the window staring blindly out at the night for what seemed like a long time. Finally she pulled the curtains shut, set the alarm on her cell phone to wake her, and got ready for bed.

Around her, the room filled with shadows of things she'd always thought could not exist: the Great Old Ones, the Yellow Sign, the elder races. Shoggoths, she reminded herself. You never thought that shoggoths could exist, either. Powerful though the argument was, it made her aware of how much she missed Sho. All at once she wanted nothing more than to hear a familiar piping voice and feel a comforting pseudopod wrapping around her. That made her think of how distant Sho was that night, and that in turn sent a chill down her spine as she thought of all the things that might happen while she was too far away to protect Sho from the human world.

But if the Great Old Ones really existed—

She turned off the light. Then, for the first time since she'd heard about Mrs. Macallan's suicide, she knelt by the side of the bed, folded her hands, and prayed: not to the god of her childhood, not to the old gods of nature, but to another. *Nyogtha*,

233

she called silently. *Dweller in Darkness, Thing That Should Not Be.* Sudden doubts rose. *I'm not one of your fosterlings. You don't have any reason to listen to me—but if you do listen, please protect my sweet Sho.* A fragment of one of Sho's stories came to mind. *The shoggoths say you're wise and subtle. Help her be wise and subtle now, when I can't be there to help keep her safe.*

The prayer trickled away into silence, but Brecken knelt there for a while longer, feeling small and huddled and cold. Church bells somewhere in the near distance sounded the time, ten o'clock, the voices of the bells like and yet unlike their equivalents in Partridgeville. Then, in the silence that followed, she noticed the change.

The darkness that surrounded her was listening. That was all. Nothing moved in the shadows of the room or the deeper shadows that wrapped Arkham by night, no voice spoke to her, no presence detached itself from the night—but the darkness listened.

For Brecken, that was enough. She murmured her thanks, climbed into the unfamiliar bed, and fell asleep within moments.

* * *

The room where she'd be auditioning had decent acoustics, Brecken judged. No doubt it was a classroom the rest of the year: square and featureless, with a grand piano and a projection screen on one side and two dozen or so chairs on the other. Windows looked out over the wooded lower slopes of Meadow Hill, blurred with shreds of fog.

She'd gotten there a good fifteen minutes ahead of time, leaving Professor Satterlee's house while the sun still hung low and red in the morning mist, hurrying along narrow unfamiliar streets toward the cyclopean buildings of the Miskatonic campus. The map she'd downloaded wasn't quite up to date— it showed a building called Belbury Hall where Brecken found nothing but a flat open space covered in gravel—but it was accurate enough to get her to Upton Hall without any trouble.

Once there, she made a beeline for the department office, made sure the audition hadn't been moved to another room, and learned from the secretary that her audition was the day's first and nothing else had been scheduled in the room beforehand. That was an unexpected gift; she went straight to the room, found an unobtrusive place for her coat, checked her hair and her makeup in a pocket mirror, assembled her flute, and played a few quick warmups. Then she sat down at the piano and played scales from one end of the keyboard to another, familiarizing herself with the off notes so they wouldn't startle her once she started playing. Too much depended on the next hour to take anything for granted.

She had just finished when the door opened and the first two members of the audition committee came in. Introductions followed, hands got shaken. Professor Michael Silva turned out to be a flautist himself, Professor Anne Ricci a composer and the mainstay of Miskatonic's composition program. They sat in two of the chairs, and Brecken perched on the piano bench.

A minute or so later, the door opened a little and then swung wide, and a white-haired man in a wheelchair came briskly through. He nodded to his colleagues, and then to Brecken, who went over to introduce herself. "Paul Czanek," he said in reply; eyes the pale blue of a frozen lake glanced up at her face, seemed to find nothing of relevance there, looked away. Brecken returned to the piano, picked up her flute, waited another minute or so, then started playing the first notes of Telemann's Fantasia #8 in E minor.

She'd expected to be nervous, to fumble with the piece at first, but reflexes she'd built up over years of weddings and holiday parties came to her assistance and got her through the first few bars, and after that the music carried her. The Telemann Fantasias were challenging enough that most undergraduates wouldn't risk them at an audition, and Brecken knew the Miskatonic professors would judge every nuance to see if she really understood the piece or was trying to show off with something she hadn't actually mastered.

The piece flowed smoothly to its conclusion, and Brecken risked a glance at the members of the committee. Ricci was smiling, and Silva's eyes had narrowed in concentration. Czanek's face hadn't shifted at all, though, and his eyes were cold and distant as the Moon. Brecken drew in a long slow breath, paused, and then launched straight into the cascading sixteenth notes of Bach's Partita for flute in A minor.

Ricci's eyes went suddenly wide, and Silva's narrowed even further. The Partita was a really demanding piece, well outside the usual range of audition fare, but after all the Friday afternoons she'd devoted to it, Brecken knew it in her blood and her bones. She hadn't been sure how to play it—bitter with grief, for Mrs. Macallan? Sweet, for Sho? Wistful, for the future as a music teacher she'd once imagined for herself, the one that would go to the country of might-have-beens once and for all if the audition went as she hoped?—but the choice never came. The music chose its own path through the Partita, swept her along with it, left her to climb up slowly onto its own far shore.

She knew when she put the flute down that she was most of the way there, but the piano still waited. She sat on the bench, shook her hands out, stretched her fingers. She'd wrestled for weeks with the question of what piece to play for that part of the audition, but in the end only one would do, even though it was as far from standard audition fare as her two flute pieces. She steadied herself, and then sounded the first chord of the overture to *The Magic Flute*.

The adagio measures needed careful handling, what with the wide dynamic range, loud and then all at once very soft, but once adagio changed to allegro and her right hand took up the second violins' theme, sending quick soft notes scampering out into the room, she could relax into the piece and focus on interpretation. Measure by familiar measure, the piece flowed to its end. As the final chord faded into silence, turned to face the committee.

"Fair enough," said Michael Silva after a moment. "When your email said you'd be doing the Bach Partita, I admit I rolled my eyes—but that was very creditably played."

"Thank you," said Brecken, blushing.

"The Mozart piece was also well played," Anne Ricci said then. "I don't think I've heard that arrangement for piano before."

"Well, no." Brecken swallowed, went on. "It's mine."

Ricci's head tilted, for all the world like an owl eyeing its prey. "You arranged it."

"I've been arranging since I was sixteen." With a sudden smile, remembering: "When I first started getting wedding gigs, the only musicians I could find to play with me were two violins and a bassoon. I kind of had to learn."

Ricci gave her a glazed look; Silva smiled and nodded, as though to say he'd been there and done that. The expression that mattered most was Paul Czanek's, though. Something had stirred in those wintry eyes for the first time

"Fair enough," Anne Ricci said then. "I think that settles any questions we might have had about your musicianship. We've also looked at the compositions you submitted, of course— well, I have." With a smile that was visibly frayed around the edges: "It's been a difficult time here. Perhaps you could play them for the benefit of my colleagues."

"Of course," said Brecken, and turned back to the piano. The instructions for the application had asked for three pieces, and on Professor Toomey's advice she'd sent them the Bourrée in B flat, the most intricate of her three Sarabandes, and the Theme and Variations in G. She played each of them, the Bourrée quick and lilting, the Sarabande slow enough to show off its intricacies, the Theme and Variations precise and not too fast.

Finishing, she turned on the bench, to find Paul Czanek considering her with those cold eyes. "The handling of the variations in that last piece," he said; his voice was unexpectedly light, and fell away to a near-whisper at the end of each sentence. "A little unsatisfactory."

"I know," Brecken said. "I don't know how to get the piece to do what it wants to do. I'm hoping to learn that here."

His eyebrows rose. After a moment he nodded once, as though something had been settled. Watching him, Brecken realized suddenly that his eyes weren't cold at all. They were pure blue flame, and they'd looked cold to her only because what they liked to contemplate had nothing human in it.

"Well," said Professor Ricci. "Thank you, Miss Kendall. Of course there's still the paperwork to take care of, but I have to say I'm favorably impressed." She extracted herself from her chair. "I hope," she said then, "that financial issues won't be a problem."

That was when Brecken knew that she'd passed the audition. "No, I should be fine," she said, trying to keep her voice calm despite the dizzying wave of relief that broke over her. "I've got an inheritance from my grandparents and some benefits from the VA—my dad was a vet."

"I'm glad to hear that," said Professor Ricci. "I'll look forward to seeing you in the fall."

Brecken thanked her, shook everyone's hands again, got flute, purse, and tote bag, scooped up her coat and headed for the door. As she neared it, Professor Czanek glanced up at her and said, "Can you spare an hour this afternoon?"

That got startled looks from the other two professors, but Brecken managed to keep her surprise off her face. "Yes, I can," she said. "I won't be taking the bus home until tomorrow."

He nodded once, the motion as precise as the flick of a conductor's baton. "If you like, I may be able to show you some things you can do with your theme and variations."

Brecken blinked. "Thank you. I'd really be grateful for that." They settled the details, and then she went out the door into the hallway outside. The other two professors were staring at

Czanek by then, and a nervous-looking young woman who was waiting outside the door gave Brecken a startled look before going in, but Brecken barely noticed. She found her way out of Upton Hall by blind instinct, drew in a long shuddering breath of cool April air, felt the door she'd hoped to open flung suddenly wide.

* * *

She was waiting for the bus at the transit station as the sun came up the next morning, her mind full of half a dozen competing trains of thought. The fifty-five minutes she'd spent with Professor Czanek, taking apart the Theme and Variations in G, had left her mind awhirl with possibilities. He'd showed her, with a precision that would have stung if it hadn't been so impersonal, mistake after mistake she'd made in weaving together the melodies of the four voices, and disassembled two of the mistakes in enough detail that she could see exactly how to rework the entire piece. He'd mentioned diffidently the class in intermediate composition he would be teaching in the fall, and Brecken decided then and there to get into it if she had to ask Sho to teach her how to flow through the crack beneath the door.

"I'd encourage you to do more with fugal technique," Czanek had said just before she'd left his office, and that started another flurry of thoughts. As the bus to Salem pulled up and she boarded and paid her fare, those were the thoughts that occupied the forefront of her mind. She thought of Darren Wegener, and the plan they'd hatched for that Thursday afternoon; and of course that got her thinking about Rosalie and her other friends, and how she was going to break the news to them that she'd be leaving Partridgeville.

By the time she got off the bus in Salem and boarded an MBTA train for Boston, she was thinking about the details of moving. She'd already arranged to rent Professor Satterlee's upstairs apartment, and that came with furniture and the piano, so all she'd have to bring to Arkham were her possessions and Sho. The last was the one difficulty, of course, and she spent much of the trip into Boston trying to come up with the best possible way to smuggle a shoggoth from New Jersey to Massachusetts.

As she got off the MBTA train in South Station and headed for the next Amtrak run south to Trenton, she was thinking of Arkham, and Miskatonic University. Though the audition results wouldn't be official until the acceptance letters went out, Professor Satterlee had heard from Professor Ricci by noon that Brecken would be offered a place in the composition program, and Sarah Choynski already knew the same thing by the time she got back from classes at three o'clock. Exactly how far and fast word spread from there, Brecken wasn't sure, but that evening Sarah took her to a café just off campus where Miskatonic's music majors spent whatever spare hours their studies allowed them, introduced her to so many people that Brecken wasn't sure she recalled more than half the names, and talked her into playing several of her compositions on the battered piano in the corner of the café. Applause, encouragement, and questions followed, and by the time Brecken got back to her room in Professor Satterlee's house, she was feeling more than a little giddy with it all.

As the Amtrak train rattled and lurched through Rhode Island and Connecticut, and the northern suburbs of New York City came into sight, deeper questions troubled her. She pondered the glimpses she'd gotten of the wider world in which she, shoggoths, and Miskatonic University all had their places: a world in which the Great Old Ones were real enough to have half-human children, the Yellow Sign was a reality, and the fate of Sho's people was part of a secret war in which, all unknowing, Brecken had chosen a side.

That, in turn, got her thinking about Professor Satterlee's words about the other shoggoth communities along the

eastern seaboard, and the very different fate of their inhabit-
ants. As she got off the train in Trenton, hauled her suitcase
under a blue spring sky to the bus station, and waited there for
the bus back to Partridgeville, she clutched to herself the news
she'd soon be able to share with Sho. "They're safe, most of
them," the professor had said, and Brecken could not help but
imagine how Sho would respond.

She boarded the bus in a warm glow of anticipation, thinking of Sho, of the home they'd make together in Arkham, of
the possibility that they'd meet other shoggoths. As the bus
rolled through the pine barrens, though, Brecken suddenly
thought: and what if she decides to go back to her own people?
Wouldn't that really be better for us both?

With that, the brightness trickled out of the day. It slowly
sank in just how difficult it would be to keep on leading the
double life she'd led since Sho first appeared in her kitchenette,
with Sho on one side of a barrier, the entire human world on
the other side, and every moment of Brecken's life wrenched
out of shape to keep the barrier in place. Professor Satterlee
and the nameless man from the Fellowship of the Yellow Sign
had their own equivalents of that barrier, but that was no
source of encouragement, for Brecken could sense the terrible
discipline they had to follow to keep the two worlds separate,
and shrank from it.

And the alternative—

She could live without Sho. She knew that, clutched the
knowledge to herself as the bus rolled through mile after mile
of pine barrens. She could live without Sho, and it would be so
much easier to live without her. She could sense all too painfully the bleeding hollow place in her that Sho's absence would
leave, but what if Sho wanted to leave? For the first time since
they'd met, that was a possibility; there might well be a place
Sho could go where she'd be safe and among her own people.
The thought left Brecken feeling torn and aching inside, but
what if that was what Sho wanted?

By the time the bus finally rolled to a halt by the transit mall beside Central Square she could think of nothing else. She headed down the stair, waited for her suitcase at the side of the bus, stepped out into afternoon sunlight, headed for Danforth Street and the long climb up to the foot of Hob's Hill, and all the while her mind and her heart knotted themselves around a choice she could not make and could not avoid. As she passed the university buildings, she caught herself coming up with excuses for leaving Professor Satterlee's news unmentioned, and nearly burst into tears of shame and anger. No, she told herself. No, the world doesn't have eyes, but I do—and smiled despite herself, thinking that she'd finally understood part of the riddle.

By the time she crossed Dwight Street and Mrs. Dalzell's house came in sight, she'd forced her shoulders back and fixed a smile on her face. I have eyes, she repeated to herself. I welcomed Sho into my life, and if it's time for her to leave—

She got to the gap between houses, turned, and stared, her tangled thoughts scattered to the winds. A strip of yellow crime scene tape blocked the gap. Off beyond, the door of her apartment gaped wide, and from the look of it, someone had forced it open.

* * *

Brecken was still trying to process the scene when Mrs. Dalzell came bustling out from her house. "Oh, there you are, Brecken," she said. "Thank heavens you're back. It was such a shock— this sort of thing is just not something I—"

"What—what happened?" Brecken forced out.

"Why, I don't know for sure. I didn't hear a thing during the night, but when I got up this morning the door was open like that and someone had gotten in and made the most frightful mess. Of course I called the police right away, and they came and took a report, but I knew you were going to be back this afternoon—"

"Can I go in?"

"Oh, of course. I—"

Brecken ducked under the tape and hurried toward the apartment.

"—got the police to put the tape up to keep people from just walking on in," said Mrs. Dalzell, following after her. "I've talked to Bill Callahan the locksmith—do you know him? Such a sweet old man. But I didn't think I should get a new lock fitted until you got back, in case you got home and I wasn't there to give you the key—"

They reached the broken door, and Brecken stared into the apartment in horror, seeing a jumbled mess inside. Had the people who'd killed the other shoggoths of Hob's Hill found Sho at last? It seemed hideously likely. She turned to face Mrs. Dalzell. "Could you please go call him? I—I just need a few minutes—"

"Why, yes, and I should call the police back, too—"

Brecken closed the door in her landlady's face, turned, and blanched. The apartment looked as though a small tornado had hit it. All the dresser drawers had been pulled out and their contents dumped on the floor. The closet door stood wide, too, and everything had been flung out of it. The piano and the kitchen seemed to be untouched, but Brecken barely noticed. The only coherent thing in the chaos of her thoughts was terror that something had happened to Sho. She was shaking and her heart pounded as she went into the middle of the apartment. In a whistle that was nearly a shriek: ♪Broodsister!♪

The moment of silence that followed encompassed whole worlds of dread. Then, muffled by wallboard, an answering whistle sounded: ♪Broodsister? It is well with you?♪

Brecken's legs buckled under her from sheer relief, and she sat down abruptly on the floor. ♪Now it is,♪ she replied. ♪If you are safe and well, it is well with me.♪

♪I am well,♪ said the answering whistle. ♪And glad that you have come back.♪

A sliding noise sounded from somewhere above the closet. Something dropped and landed with a soft thud, and then Sho flowed out under the closet door. Brecken, her heart pounding, flung herself toward the shoggoth and tripped over a heap of clothing. Before she could fall, Sho lunged and caught her, lowered her effortlessly to the floor. A moment later they sprawled in a tangle of limbs and pseudopods.

Brecken sat up, and Sho flowed partway into her lap, put a pseudopod around her. A familiar washed-mushroom scent filled every breath she took. ♪*Tell me, broodsister,*♪ Brecken whistled. ♪*What happened?*♪

♪*It was near the end of the night just past,*♪ Sho told her. ♪*I was in the hidden-place, as we agreed, and when I heard the door being broken I passed to the waking-side. I went up into the above-place and watched through a crack. A human with a light-colored head came in and scattered everything the way you see it. It had a thing with it that made light. Then it took a thing in its hand—a small thing, I do not know what it was—and left moving like this.*♪ The shoggoth mimed stealthy movements. ♪*Then there was nothing more until the light came back, and—*♪ She made the wry trill that meant Mrs. Dalzell. ♪*—came to the door and started making noises. Other humans came after that. I do not know what they did, but they did not take anything away with them.*♪

♪*Well, that's something,*♪ said Brecken. ♪*I wonder who it was.*♪ She shook her head. ♪*But you're okay. I was so frightened when I saw the open door.*♪

A pseudopod touched her cheek. She turned her face, kissed it. ♪*And I have wonderful news,*♪ Brecken went on. ♪*There is a home for us both in the place where I went. I spoke to those who teach singing there, and sang for them, and they were pleased. And I met an elder—*♪ The shoggoth word meant "broodmother-of-broodmothers," but it was the closest Brecken could find. ♪*—who knows about your people. So I told her of you. She will welcome us both in her dwelling and we will go there together.*♪

Nine eyes opened wide all at once. ♪*We—we will both go?*♪

♪*Of course,*♪ Brecken said, startled. A moment passed before she understood. ♪*Long ago, not long after you first came to me, I told you that when I left this place, I would make sure it was well with you.*♪

The shoggoth huddled down. ♪*I did not think you would do otherwise—but I feared.*♪

♪*I understand,*♪ said Brecken. ♪*But I would not leave you in such a way.*♪

Pseudopods flowed out, clung to her. ♪*I have not had a name since you left,*♪ Sho said. ♪*I think now that my name today should be Foolish Fears.*♪

Brecken laughed and kissed her again, but the laughter guttered out, for her own perplexities—chased away momentarily by the shock of the broken door—came rushing back to her. ♪*Broodsister,*♪ she said then, ♪*there are many things I want to tell you but there's one you have to know.*♪ She drew in a breath, made herself tell Sho about the other shoggoth colonies and the survivors Professor Satterlee had mentioned. As she spoke, Sho opened eye after eye.

♪*And if you—*♪ Brecken started to say, and could find no more words.

A moment passed, then: ♪*I understand,*♪ Sho said. ♪*You think that I might wish to leave you to dwell with the others of my people, but it is not so.*♪ She huddled down against the floor. ♪*Unless you wish me to leave.*♪

The choice that had tormented Brecken stood before her, inescapable. Eyes open, she made it. ♪*Of course not, broodsister,*♪ she whistled. ♪*But I wished the choice to be yours.*♪

Pale eyes regarded her. ♪*You are so very kind to me.*♪ A quiver passed through the shoggoth. ♪*I am full of delight at the thing you have told me. There are dreams that I never thought to dream again, songs I never thought to sing, and now I will dream them and sing them. But when I meet those you have spoken of, I wish you to be beside me, and if I go to dwell with them it will be because you wish to dwell with them too.*♪ She began to tremble. ♪*Broodsister,*♪

broodsister, you are cool water in my dry places, you are the darkness that shelters me when the world is bright and hard. How could I bear to leave you? When I expected only death you were kind to me, when I was hungry and afraid you gave me food and comfort, and when I offered moisture to you, you shared yours with me. To leave you would be to tear myself in half.♪ Shyly: *♪And I think it would hurt you as much as I, and I would rather touch fire than do such a thing.♪*

A lump stood hard in Brecken's throat and tears trickled down her cheeks as she reached for Sho. Cool shapelessness flowed around her head and face, cradling her. When she could whistle again, she said, *♪I think my name today should also be Foolish Fears.♪*

A quiver of amusement ran through the shoggoth. *♪You will forget which of us is me and which of us is you.♪* Her surface flowed, and all at once shaped itself into a good imitation of Brecken's own face. Laughing through her tears, Brecken leaned forward and kissed her own lips. As she drew back the face flowed forward and, a little inexpertly, returned the kiss.

* * *

Just then, of course, a knock sounded on the door of the apartment. Sho flowed back under the closet door, quick as thought, and Brecken got up, dabbed pointlessly at her wet face with one hand, and then went to the door and opened it, letting in the sunlight. Mrs. Dalzell and an old man with a toolchest stood outside on the walk.

"You poor child," said Mrs. Dalzell, seeing her tears. "Oh, I know that this is all very stressful, but it'll all work out just fine, you know, if you'll just give it a chance. This is Mr. Callahan, or Bill, rather, who's the locksmith I always call. He's here to put a new lock on your door, of course, and I figured it would be best to get that taken care of right away."

"Thank you," said Brecken. "I—I'll be okay. They didn't take the things that really matter to me." She stepped out of the locksmith's way, and he gave her a brisk little nod and got to work extracting what was left of the old lock.

Mrs. Dalzell beamed. "Well, there you are. Life really does work out the way it's supposed to, you know." She chattered on as the locksmith worked. In the middle of it all a police car rolled up the alley, stopped, and disgorged a lean young man in uniform with an improbably large black mustache, who introduced himself as Officer Castro, asked a few desultory questions, gave Brecken his card, and told her to email him a list of the property of hers that was missing. Brecken promised she would, and he went back to the squad car and drove off. A few minutes later the locksmith finished, handed Brecken and Mrs. Dalzell each a bright new key, and headed for his van.

A few more minutes of aimless conversation passed, and then Mrs. Dalzell finally wandered off. Brecken went inside, closed and locked the door, and went to the closet. ♪*What shall I call you today, broodsister?*♪ she whistled. ♪*I think I should not call you Foolish Fears when the fears are gone.*♪

A soft sliding noise marked Sho's reappearance. ♪*That is true,*♪ she said. ♪*And I have been thinking. Today my name is Half Of A Circle.*♪

Brecken knelt down and kissed her. ♪*Then mine is The Other Half.*♪

That got a ripple of delight from Sho, and they embraced for a long moment. ♪*I wish to hear many things about the place we will go,*♪ Sho piped then, ♪*and about the broodmother-of-broodmothers who knows about my people and will welcome us there, and—and everything else you saw and heard and did and learned while you were away. But first, maybe we should put all these things in the places they should be.*♪

They spent most of an hour at that task. Time and again, as they put things back in order, Brecken was sure she'd figured out what the thief had taken, only to find it under a heap of clothing or an upturned drawer. It was only after everything was back where it belonged, and Brecken had gone to the kitchen to get some cheese polenta cooking, that she realized why there was extra space in the bottom drawer of the dresser, and went back to look to be sure. Later, she emailed the police to tell them the only thing that had been stolen was a book, *The Secret Watcher* by Halpin Chalmers: a used copy full of marginal notes, worth only a few dollars.

Later still, after the two of them dined on cheese polenta, after Brecken told as much about her trip to Arkham as she could figure out how to say in the shoggoth language, and after they'd celebrated Brecken's return in a more intimate way, Brecken pressed her bare skin against iridescent blackness scented with the deep warm smell of earth, drew a quilt over them both, and pondered her own feelings. The dizzying intensity of their first weeks together had faded, but something firm and glowing had replaced it, and her nights alone, her tangled thoughts on the trip back from Arkham, and the sudden shock of the broken door had brought home to her just how much she'd come to need Sho.

I will spend the rest of my life with her, she thought. That realization left her awed and delighted, but it also hurt. Talking about Sho to June Satterlee and the nameless man from the Fellowship of the Yellow Sign made it all the more painful that she would never be able to introduce the one she loved to Aunt Mary and Uncle Jim or to her circle of friends. There would always be a gap in her life between the few who could know and the many who couldn't, and she could sense already how that would ache.

Darren's in the same situation right now, she reminded herself. Of course that was true, but sensing the gap he had to deal with made it no easier for her to face the much broader gap before her. She tried to chase away her thoughts, nestled closer to Sho.

A pale luminous eye blinked open close to her face, pondered her, and a speaking-orifice opened. ♪*You are thinking.*♪

♪*Yes.*♪

♪*What of?*♪

♪*The two of us,*♪ Brecken whistled. ♪*How we'll be together for as many summers and winters as we live.*♪ Sho quivered in response. ♪*And you?*♪

♪I am thinking,♪ said Sho, ♪that since I will live among your people, it will be well for me to learn your language. I am glad that you learned my language, and I hope you will speak it with me often in time to come, for your voice will always remind me of the kind words you spoke to me when I first met you.♪

Brecken blushed, kissed her, and said, ♪Of course I will.♪

♪I thank you, The Other Half,♪ Sho piped. ♪ But there will be others I should speak with—the broodmother-of-broodmothers, and the servant of that one who must not be named, and maybe others. So I will need to know your people's language.♪

♪I'll teach you,♪ Brecken promised.

♪It is well.♪ A pseudopod flowed around Brecken's face, and she nestled her cheek into it. ♪And there is another thing. If I am to speak to other humans I should have a name of your people's kind, one that does not change. Will you give me one?♪

Brecken bit her lip, then: ♪I've done that already. When I first held you, before we both went to the dreaming-side together, I wished you to have a name I could always remember.♪

Four eyes popped open. ♪Please tell me what it is!♪

"Sho," Brecken said.

The shoggoth paused, and then tried to repeat it, managing a hiss with a tone on the end. Brecken said it again, and Sho repeated it, a little more accurately. After half a dozen exchanges, she managed a fair imitation of Brecken's voice, then said, ♪That is it?♪

♪Yes,♪ said Brecken.

♪Broodsister, broodsister, you are so very kind to me, to give me such a gift!♪

Brecken put her arms around the shoggoth and kissed her. ♪I am glad you're going to learn my people's language,♪ she said, ♪because there are words I know to tell you how dear you are to me, and I want you to know those words too and know what I'm saying.♪

Pseudopods flowed out and clung to her. They were still twined together when Brecken woke the next morning.

CHAPTER 15

AN ANCHOR FOR DREAMS

The next day was Thursday, and though the one thing she wanted just then was to spend every possible minute with Sho, she made herself send an early morning text to Darren, asking whether his parents had come yet and whether their plan was still on. The answer came back minutes later: NO SIGN YET C U @ FUMIS. She sent back a quick answer, and then headed down to Fumi's at the time they'd agreed on.

Partridgeville's streets were still half empty, and a good many of the businesses were closed for spring break, but she found the restaurant without any trouble: a storefront a block or so west of Tuchman Hall with a bright green awning over the windows. Inside, a random assortment of Japanese decor tried and failed to hide the stark utilitarian lines of the space. Most of the tables were empty, but there was Darren in back, next to a painted screen with the images of ornate carp on it. Brecken headed that way once she'd chatted a little with the hostess.

Darren gave her an assessing look as she reached the table. "Hi. It looks like you've gotten good news."

"Very good news." She settled onto the chair, took the menu he handed her. He was full of questions about Miskatonic and her trip, and they'd finished their sushi and were on a second cup of tea each before the subject finally changed to the mathematics of the fugue they had been studying before she'd gone to Arkham.

It was pure chance that made Brecken glance up as a middle-aged couple came through the door. He had a slab-sided face and short brown hair gone white at the temples, she had a hard discontented expression and an expensive hairdo, and the only reason they registered in her mind was that they looked more like Darren than any appeal to randomness could explain.

She leapt to the obvious conclusion and turned to Darren, who was halfway through an intricate explanation of the irrational numbers that structured Buxtehude's fugues. "Grab my hands," she hissed. "Stare at my face." He blinked in surprise, but trust won out. His hands closed around hers, his eyes fixed on her face with convincing intensity.

Then, the woman's voice: "Darren?"

He looked up, startled. Before he could say anything and spoil the moment, Brecken put on a bright smile, extracted her hands, stood up, and said to them, "Oh, hi. You must be Darren's parents—he looks just like you. I'm Brecken Kendall."

Darren's father gave her a blinking owlish look, and then put out a big meaty hand, hairy as a bear's paw, and shook hers. "Pleased to meet you. Dwight Wegener. This is my wife Lucy." Brecken took her hand as well and gave her the same bright smile, even though the woman looked as though she'd rather be touched by a snail.

"I, uh, didn't think you'd get here this early," Darren said to his parents, looking embarrassed.

"Don't worry about it," Brecken said to him. "Send me a text when you've got time." She leaned over and kissed him on the cheek, and he turned exactly the right shade of pink. "Mr. Wegener, Mrs. Wegener, it was great meeting you." She smiled at them again, and then left the table. She could feel all three of them watching her until she got to the door, heard Darren's mother start saying something in a hard discontented voice as the door swung shut.

The rest of the day she had nothing else to do but spend time with Sho, and no wish to find anything else, so she headed home, torn between delight at how perfectly the plan had come off and worries about how Darren's parents would react. Sho's presence did more than a little to distract her mind from both subjects, but the worries kept circling back. Dinner was over and she and Sho were curled up together on the futon when Brecken's cell phone finally rang. A glance at the screen showed that Darren was on the other end, so she picked up the call.

"Brecken? Oh my God, thank you," he said all in a rush. "I've just been through the most astonishing evening in my life and it's all your fault."

"Okay, I'll bite," she said, laughing. "What happened?"

"A lot." He drew in an audible breath. "As soon as you left, Mom started peppering me with questions about you—who you are, where your family is, what you're studying, you name it—and all the time Dad was saying, 'Lucy, leave him alone,' and finally she turned to him and said, 'Look, I'm trying to find out something about that shameless hussy!'"

Brecken choked. "Seriously?"

"Seriously. And for once I thought of something to say when I still had a chance to say it, and I stood up and said, 'Mom, if you're going to talk about my girlfriend that way I'm going to walk right out of here.' She started spluttering, and all at once Dad said, 'For God's sake, Lucy, at least it's a girl,' and then of course he got all embarrassed because it's supposed to be some kind of secret that he thinks I'm gay, and Mom stopped in mid-splutter, and I said, 'Dad, what the hell are you saying?' So Mom lit into him, and he lit into Mom, and I stood there for about five minutes while they yelled at each other and then I said, 'You both know my phone number. Give me a call when you stop fighting,' and I turned, went to the cashier, paid up and walked out of there—and they shut up. For the first time I can remember, they actually both shut up."

"Wow."

"It gets better. So I went back to my place and started writing an email to—" He stopped.

"A certain someone."

"Yeah." After a moment's pause. "Stan."

"Your friend from the library?"

"Yeah."

"I can forget that if you want me to."

"No." He drew in an audible breath. "You deserve to know."

"Thank you," she said, touched by the words.

"You're welcome. But I was maybe halfway through it when Dad called. They came over to the apartment, and after a while we went out to dinner at Mulligan's, and this time it was Dad's turn to ask me questions about you, and Mom said practically nothing the whole time. So I talked about how you were a musician and a composer, how you're going to finish your degree at an Ivy League university in Massachusetts, and how you play Sundays at the Baptist Church, and Mom said, 'I suppose you mean the Second Baptist Church,' and I just looked at her and said, no, the First Baptist Church up on the hill. So she shut up again, and we finished dinner and they drove me home, and Mom stayed out in the car but Dad followed me into the apartment, and he apologized for having unworthy thoughts about me—those are the exact words he used—and said that you looked like a really fine girl, and he pulled out a couple of hundred dollar bills from his wallet and handed them to me and told me to take you out someplace nice, and I promised him I would. Are you free Sunday afternoon?"

She checked the calendar on her phone. "Yes, I am."

"Good. Philadelphia Opera's putting on *The Marriage of Figaro* and I just scored two seats right near the middle of the first balcony. Want to go?"

Brecken let out a yelp of delight. "Yes, please."

"You're on," Darren said. "One Mozart opera and a really nice dinner, coming up."

Brecken blushed. "You're really sweet."

"I owe you, big time. Now that Dad has it stuck in his head that I have a girlfriend, nitroglycerine won't shake it loose—and I'm probably safe until I've got my doctorate."

"I wonder how he's going to react when he finds out."

"I don't know," Darren said. "I wish he could just accept me as I am. I don't know, maybe he will someday." For a moment she could hear in his voice, like a distant echo, the voice of the frightened child he'd once been.

"I hope so," said Brecken. "I also hope you're going to do something fun with Stan."

"Thank you. Yeah, we've got plans for Saturday after my folks leave."

"Good. Tell him I said hi."

"You know," said Darren, "I'm going to do that." They said the usual things and then hung up, and Brecken set the phone aside and considered the iridescent black shape nestled up affectionately against her side. *And if he knew what I meant when I mentioned my girlfriend,* she wondered, *would he say the same things I just did?*

Sho glanced up at her then. ♪*Is it proper to ask about the call?*♪

♪*Yes, of course,*♪ said Brecken, and tried to translate the conversation into the language of shoggoths. Sho did her best to make sense of it, but before long she was thoroughly confused and Brecken had started to wonder if she herself really knew what she was trying to explain.

♪*Sometimes it is hard for me to understand your people,*♪ Sho said finally.

At that Brecken started to laugh. ♪*Sometimes it's hard for me too.*♪

* * *

That Sunday was as delightful as she'd hoped. Darren picked her up that morning in front of the First Baptist Church, drove through the pine barrens, dodged and wove through Camden and Philadelphia traffic, and got to the opera house with most of an hour to spare. True to form, the matinee had second-string vocalists, but some of them were young performers who likely had successful careers ahead of them, and all of them sang well enough to make the opera worth savoring. Afterwards, she and Darren went to a restaurant looking over the Susquehanna River and had a gloriously over-the-top dinner at a table for two by one of the windows, talking music the whole time. By the time she got out of his well-aged sedan in front of Mrs. Dalzell's house and wished him goodnight, she was pleasantly giddy with it all.

The next morning came too soon, and Brecken went to her composition and counterpoint classes and wondered why the classrooms in Gurnard Hall, so familar for so long, now seemed just a little strange to her. Down below in The Cave, she still got the stares and silences, but some of the students who'd tried to argue or bully her into composing something other than the music she loved simply looked away when she passed them, and talked a little more loudly to their friends. That was less difficult for her to deal with than the overt challenges had been, but it made her acutely aware of a widening gap between her and most of the other music students.

That sense deepened over the days that followed. It didn't even help that Molly began to introduce her to some of the other renegade musicians at Partridgeville State—the aspiring rock and metal guitarists, the tight-knit circle of trad jazz and blues players, a dreamy-eyed young man with hair down to his waist whose world revolved around Appalachian folk music and who could make a three-string lap dulcimer evoke the fading culture of the mountains. Too much of her life had strayed into places they couldn't or didn't follow: she'd practiced sorcery, read forbidden books, and seen the Yellow Sign, and her heart was given to a creature of the elder world. She brooded over that from time to time, wondered if it would ever become easier to bear.

One Thursday Professor Kaufmann spent the entire lecture talking about a new and fashionable theory of arrangement that discarded all the traditional rules for balancing the voices of the instruments, and stalked back and forth in front of the class while she lectured, glaring at them all as though she dared them to disagree. Brecken found that it took her only a little effort to imagine what music arranged according to the new theory would sound like: words such as "muddy" and "uneven" came to mind. The professor kept using the word "arbitrary" to describe the traditional rules, and for some reason that kept reminding Brecken of the afternoon at Rosalie's apartment all those months ago when Donna had asked about tonality. Of course it's arbitrary, Brecken thought. It still works better. Do you want some chocolate ice cream on your chicken quesadilla?

Afterwards she took the stairs down—two of the elevators were working, but she wanted the solitude—and headed for Hancock Library to study some of Gesualdo's late and highly chromatic madrigals, with the hope of finding some hints there on ways to make musical sense of Julian Pinchbeck's tone sequence. She was maybe half a block from the door when she spotted a figure she recognized, hurrying ahead of her toward the same destination.

It was Jay, though it took her a moment to be sure of that. He looked thin and haggard, his hair hadn't been combed in a while, and the swagger he'd cultivated while she'd known him had gotten lost somewhere in the months since that time. Brecken slowed, followed him at a distance, hoping that he wouldn't see her, and luck stayed with her that afternoon. She got a glimpse at his face as he turned to go into the library, and flinched: it looked as though the smile she'd hated so much had carved itself so deeply on his face that the lines remained even when his expression was tense and angry.

She waited for a few moments after he'd gone inside before following, spotted him again heading for the special collections room as she rode the escalator up toward the music stacks on the fourth floor. When she'd settled down at a table with the right volume of Gesualdo, it took her an effort to keep her thoughts from straying back to Jay, and it turned out to be wasted effort, as she found nothing to the point in the Italian composer's work. It wasn't until she set out for her flute lesson that evening that she realized why it was that Jay kept surfacing in her thoughts: he was the only other human being in Partridgeville she knew of who had brushed up against the secrets of the elder world. That roused thoughts of Professor Satterlee and the nameless servant of the King she'd met in Arkham, and then of the old man—what had his name been?—who'd made the marginal notes in her copy of *The Secret Watcher*. How many people down through the years had carried the same burden she now did, standing at the border between two worlds?

She brooded about that while walking back home from her lesson beneath a pale evening sky, thought about reading Chalmers' book, had to remind herself that *The Secret Watcher* had gone missing when her apartment was broken into. That sent her thoughts chasing down gloomy paths. Only the hideous blouse Mrs. Dalzell was wearing as she worked in the garden, acid green with huge pink polka dots on it, pulled Brecken's attention back to the present moment.

"Brecken? Oh, good, I was hoping you'd be home soon," Mrs. Dalzell said. "You got some kind of official letter from someplace in Minnesota, I think it was, or was it Maine? At any rate, let me go get it." She hauled herself to her feet, shed a pair of mud-colored gloves, headed in through the kitchen door of her house, leaving Brecken standing there trying to think of anyone in either state who might have sent her a letter.

Mrs. Dalzell was back a moment later with a long envelope. "Oh, of course, it was Massachusetts," she said. "Well, here you are."

It was indeed from Massachusetts, and had an ornate coat of arms and the words *Miskatonic University* in old-fashioned blackletter at the upper left corner. Brecken managed to stammer out words of thanks, then let herself into the apartment and locked the door behind her. Hands fumbled with the envelope and got it open, and a moment later she had the letter inside in her hands. Below the ornate heading and the formal greetings of an earlier day, the words she hoped to see leapt out at her: ... *your application to the College of Fine and Performing Arts has been accepted*...

She let out a little low cry, tried to unfold the letter the rest of the way, and succeeded in dropping letter and envelope both. By the time she'd fielded the letter, darkness flowed out from under the closet door and three pale green eyes peered out of it. ♪*Broodsister?*♪ said a familiar whistling voice. ♪*Is it not well with you?*♪

♪*It's well,*♪ Brecken said. ♪*It's very well, broodsister. This writing tells me that we'll go to the new place once the time comes. I knew already that we're going, but still—*♪

♪*I understand,*♪ said Sho, sliding out of the closet and approaching her. ♪*When I first came to you, every time you said I could stay, it was as if I had not heard that before.*♪

To that Brecken could think of no answer but kneeling down and throwing her arms around Sho; pseudopods hugged her back. Then Brecken said, ♪*I'll read the writing now and see what else it says.*♪

They got settled on the futon, and Sho turned curious eyes on the letter as Brecken read it. Most of it simply repeated over-familiar words—a few phrases of congratulations, a sentence of vague encouragement, some unconvincing gestures toward sounding modern and relevant—but a paragraph toward the end told her something she hadn't known: there was a summer program in music composition, mostly for summer-school postgraduates but open to undergraduates with a faculty recommendation, and if she was interested she'd already been recommended by Dr. Paul Czanek, who would be teaching two classes in the program.

That prospect was tempting enough to take her breath away. Summer school, she thought then. That means moving as soon as the semester's over—and the rush of bittersweet emotion that came with that thought, half delight in the world that waited for her, partly grief for the one she was about to leave behind, made her whistling unsteady as she explained the letter to Sho.

♪It is well,♪ said the shoggoth. ♪I think it is better if we go soon.♪

♪I'll send writing to them,♪ Brecken told her. As she opened the email program on her phone, though, she wasn't thinking about Miskatonic University. She was thinking about Rosalie, and how on earth she was going to break the news to her.

* * *

The next two days and most of the third belonged to music and to Sho, and neither one of those was entirely free of complexities. Sho was affectionate as always, but she wanted to learn English, and that turned out to be far more challenging a process than either of them anticipated. Partly it was a simple matter of pronunciation, since Sho's speaking orifices could twist around to mimic the sounds of human language, but the action didn't come naturally at all. There were deeper matters at work, though, for it had never before occurred to Brecken how much of English presupposed human senses, human limbs, and human interests.

It turned out, for example, that the hard distinction between nouns and verbs, things and actions, had no natural place in the thinking of a species that extruded temporary organs instead of collecting possessions. Then there was number, which was a complete mystery to Sho. It made no sense to her that two books had some quality in common with two cans of soup or two eyes, and the more Brecken tried to explain, the more confused Sho got. Finally the shoggoth huddled down, trembling, and said, ♪I do not understand at all. I am so very stupid.♪

Brecken reached out a comforting hand. ♪No,♪ she whistled. ♪You're not stupid.♪ An instant later she remembered when Sho had said the same thing to her, and flung her arms around the shoggoth. ♪Don't worry about it,♪ she said then. ♪Let's find words that are easy for you, and leave the hard ones for later.♪ That was less simple than it sounded, but by the time the weekend was over Sho could name all her favorite foods and say a few simple sentences, and had begun to feel a little more confident about speaking with humans.

That experience ended up helping Brecken with the other perplexity she faced, which was Julian Pinchbeck's sequence of twelve notes. Late Friday night, staring at her composition notebook in frustration, she suddenly thought: I'm trying to make it speak my language, instead of learning the language it wants to speak. After a few more moments she got up, went to the piano, and played the sequence slowly several times, listening to it. By the time she'd finished that, something as yet formless had begun to stir in her mind, and she settled down to sleep with Sho with a vague sense that she might be on the right track.

When she opened the notebook the next morning, she saw all at once how the sequence could harmonize, not with some other sequence of notes, but with itself. As she struggled to put that insight into notes on staff paper, her eyes widened as she realized what it was that the sequence was reaching toward— or was it her mind that was doing the reaching? She could not tell, but a fugue, the most precise and demanding of the classical forms, began to take shape on the page. Sho was familiar enough with her habits by then that she flowed up against her, settled into place with an affectionate flutter, and drifted over onto the dreaming-side; Brecken slipped an arm around her and kept on writing.

Thereafter the fugue came together in bursts and fragments, with plenty of false starts and blind alleys. After bursts of concentration so intense it left fingers of pain clutching her scalp, Brecken was glad to set the notebook aside to cook a meal, practice flute or piano, or spend time with Sho; but measure by measure, the piece took shape in a dance of harsh discords resolving into harmonies. Sunday's church service offered a respite of sorts, but as Brecken walked back to her apartment afterwards all her thoughts were on a difficult few measures early on, and she spent much of the rest of the day getting those right.

Monday morning the wind sent long thin streamers of cloud sweeping across the sky from somewhere beyond Hob's Hill as Brecken walked to campus. The Cave was as crowded as usual, and the sky syrup from the loudspeakers overhead cycled aimlessly through a series of four drab chords ornamented with random notes. At the familiar table, Rosalie sat hunched over her phone, texting with a look of utter concentration. Brecken sat down quietly, slipped her composition book out, brooded over her fugue, got another two measures worked out.

Rosalie looked up finally, and blinked in surprise. "Hey, girl," she said. "Sorry about that. I didn't even see you sit down."

"Let me guess," said Brecken, laughing. "You were texting Tom."

"Yeah." She grinned. "I'm going to his place for the weekend. He's really sweet."

"That's good to hear."

Rosalie gave her a sidelong look. "You know, if you're ever interested, my cousin Rick really does want to meet you."

It wasn't much of an opening, but Brecken took it. "Ro, there's something you need to know about." She drew in an unsteady breath. "I'm going to be leaving Partridgeville at the end of the semester. I'm transferring to a university in Massachusetts to study composition."

"What?"

Brecken nodded.

"Oh, for Christ's sake," Rosalie said then. "Look. You just need to stop, okay? You know as well as I do that you aren't going to do anything like that."

Astonished, Brecken tried to break in. "Ro—"

"I get that you like composing," she went on without stopping. "I get that you're okay at it. But you've got to be realistic. You're not going to be able to make any kind of living doing that, you know, and that means—"

"Ro—"

"—you need to buckle down and get back on track with music education, get yourself some job skills that can support you. You've had your semester of daydreams, okay, but now it's time to get real—"

Brecken lost her temper. "Ro, will you please just shut up for a moment and *listen*?"

That got her a moment of shocked silence. Brecken went on in a rush: "I got my acceptance letter from Miskatonic University Thursday. I had my audition there over spring break, and passed. I've already got an apartment rented. There's a summer composition program, invitation only for undergraduates, and I've been invited. It's not a daydream, Ro. I'm going."

She stared at Brecken, then said, "But—but you can't—" Her voice trailed off.

"Yes, I can," Brecken told her with some asperity. "And I am."

"But—" Rosalie swallowed visibly. "But you won't have any kind of steady job—"

Brecken, exasperated, said, "Look, I'm just doing the same thing you're doing! Why is it okay for you to follow your dream and not okay for me to follow mine?"

Rosalie winced as though Brecken had slapped her, and then looked away, hard. Brecken stared at her for a long silent moment, and finally understood. In a quieter voice she asked, "That is what you're doing, Ro, isn't it?"

Rosalie didn't answer. She didn't need to. In a silence that the noises of The Cave couldn't touch, she could hear everything Rosalie wasn't saying, everything she hadn't said for most of two years, and knew in a moment of cold clarity that her friend wasn't going to follow the dream she'd talked about so often, had known all along that she was never going to follow it. Rosalie would finish her music degree, she guessed, then get a job with her father's brokerage or something similar, and settle into the comfortable life she'd played at abandoning; marriage, children, promotions, there would always be another reason to put off the dream; her harp, gathering dust in a closet somewhere, would become an anchor for dreams and might-have-beens, a place to put her fantasies of the life she'd left untouched; and when she lay dying, maybe, however near or far in the future that turned out to be, she'd still comfort herself with the thought that she could have followed the dream and become a professional musician after all.

"Ro—" Brecken's mouth was dry, but she forced the words through. "It's okay."

Rosalie looked up at her with bleak wet eyes, said nothing.

"We should probably head for class," Brecken said then.

A wordless nod was the only answer she got. The two of them left the table, headed for the elevator and Composition II. As the elevator lurched upward, Brecken looked at Rosalie and Rosalie looked at the floor. Neither of them said anything until the elevator was nearly to the tenth floor, when Brecken said, "It really is okay."

Rosalie glanced up at her, then looked away, closed her eyes, nodded.

* * *

They got to the class a few minutes early, settled into their seats. Julian Pinchbeck sat with his shoulders hunched, staring at nothing; Darren Wegener, in back as usual, had one of his mathematics textbooks open and an intent look on his face; most of the others hadn't gotten there yet, and so Brecken pulled out her composition notebook again and got back to work on the fugue. By the time the others had arrived and Professor Toomey came through the door she'd worked out a countersubject she could play against Julian's twelve notes, one that would give her the bitter discords the fugue demanded but still give her room to resolve everything into harmony before the final cadence.

She glanced up then, and saw the look on Toomey's face. His eyes remained unreadable but the hard set of his mouth told her instantly that something dreadful had happened.

"Everyone's here?" the professor asked. "Fair enough. I've got some very bad news to pass on." The room went utterly silent. "I think most of you probably know a freshman named Barbara Cormyn. She was found dead this morning."

That sparked a sudden shocked murmur, then a deeper silence. "You can get the details from the newspaper," Toomey went on. "I'm not going to go into them here, but they were pretty grim. The Partridgeville police are investigating it as a homicide. Obviously they want to hear from anybody who knows anything that might be relevant." He went on, talking about the free counseling the university was providing for students, the arrangements for improved security the campus police had promised to put in place, but Brecken barely heard any of it.

Once the class was over and they'd returned to The Cave, Rosalie mumbled an excuse and hurried away. Brecken watched her go, then went to Vivaldi's, and spent the hour before her counterpoint class sipping coffee, wrestling with a few measures of free counterpoint in her fugue, and trying not to think about Barbara Cormyn. Word had clearly spread through the music department, to judge by the conversations in low voices and the shocked silent expressions around her. When she went to her next class, Toomey repeated the same announcement in the same words, got the same reaction, went on to lecture on details of counterpoint that Brecken had already picked up from Johann Joseph Fux. Finally, when the class was over, she headed out the glass doors into the open air, and then happened to glance at a vending machine where that day's edition of the *Partridgeville Gazette* yelled the news:

GRUESOME "CULT KILLING" DOWNTOWN
Headless Body of Student, 19, Found in Own Bed
Police: Crime Likely Linked to Occult Beliefs

Brecken stared at the headline for a moment, then hurried home. When she checked the *Gazette* website later that afternoon, it took only a single glance at the story to confirm her fears:

> … *found Cormyn's nude body sprawled on her bed. Her neck had been completely severed, and her mangled head had been placed grotesquely on her chest. Her upper body and arms were covered with an unidentified blue gel, the source of the odor that filled the room* …

♪*What does it say?*♪ Sho asked. A pseudopod with a single pale eye at its tip craned over Brecken's shoulder, considered the screen of the laptop.

♪*A human I knew is dead,*♪ Brecken said in response. ♪*And I think the way the others found her means that something really terrible killed her.*♪

♪*Tell me what they found,*♪ said Sho. As Brecken translated the words of the story into whistled notes, the shoggoth hunched lower and lower on the futon, and the acrid scent of dread surrounded her.

♪*I understand,*♪ Sho said when she was done. ♪*There were stories among my people about things that did that, hunting-things from a different kind of time. We called those things those-that-hunger, and feared them.*♪

They are the deeds of the dead, hungry and athirst, Halpin Chalmers had written. "The Hounds of Tindalos," Brecken said in English, then: ♪*That is what my people call them.*♪

All at once, the realization broke in on her. ♪*When I was gone and another human broke the door of this place and came in and took the writings away,*♪ she said, ♪*the human had a light-colored head. Am I remembering that right?*♪

♪*Yes,*♪ said Sho. ♪*Not like yours.*♪ A pseudopod stroked Brecken's hair.

In the copy of *The Secret Watcher* she'd had, carefully hand-written in blue ink in the margin next to the words about the Hounds of Tindalos, there had been a recipe, Brecken recalled—a recipe and a warning. She thought of Barbara's blonde hair, and started to wonder how anyone could have known that a copy of *The Secret Watcher* was in the little apartment, but the answer came before she'd even finished framing the question. Sorcery could have done it, she guessed, and anyone who knew enough to be able to make sense of the recipe for the Liao drug would probably know enough to locate the book by some uncanny means.

She thought of Barbara Cormyn then, the pale blue eyes wide with a perpetual look of surprise, the cold selfish purpose moving behind them. It was just too easy to imagine those eyes reading the marginal notes in *The Secret Watcher* and finding the recipe for the Liao drug. Had Barbara deliberately risked taking a larger dose than necessary, and convinced herself that she could escape Halpin Chalmers' fate? Or had something gone wrong when she made the drug, so that the dose she thought was safe was enough to set the Hounds of Tindalos on her scent?

Brecken didn't try to guess. She closed the browser window, shut down the laptop and put it on the end table. ♪*I think she took the writings,*♪ she said to Sho. ♪*I'm sorry for that, since I think they killed her, but I'm not sorry they're gone. There are things in them I don't want to have to know.*♪

CHAPTER 16

THE SIGN OF KOTH

Whether Rosalie was the one responsible or not, Brecken never did find out, but word of her impending departure spread through Partridgeville State's music department in the days that followed. Some of the reactions were predictable enough. Molly Wolejko called out "Hey, congratulations!" from halfway across The Cave, and later spent half an hour later in Vivaldi's grinning as Brecken filled her in on the details. Julian Pinchbeck, for his part, gave her a dismissive look the next time she came into Composition II and said, "I hear you can't handle the program here at Partridgeville." A year before, that would have left Brecken flustered, but now it simply made her roll her eyes.

More than once, though, someone who'd been on the side of her critics came over and said something friendly. Susan Chu and Mike Schau were among them, but the one whose words left Brecken reeling was Professor Kaufmann, who motioned her over after a session of the orchestral arrangement class and said, "Carson tells me you've been accepted at Miskatonic. Congratulations; that's a solid program by all accounts and I think you'll do well there."

Brecken managed to stumble over a few words of thanks, and the professor said, "Are you still doing your neoclassical music?"

"Modern Baroque," said Brecken, who'd settled on that label. "Yes."

"Well, I hope that works out well for you." Something like uncertainty showed for a moment in Kaufmann's eyes, and Brecken found herself wondering just how far Kaufmann had followed her own advice to stay on the cutting edge, and whether she'd turned her back on her own musical tastes in order to get anywhere in composition. The professor pasted on a smile, though, and said something forgettable as she gathered up her notes and headed for the door. Brecken watched her go and then headed for the stair.

Word even found its way to the First Baptist Church. The next Sunday, Carl Knecht met her at the entrance to the worship hall, asked politely about her week, walked with her past gossiping church ladies to the organ, and all the while his slight uncanny smile creased his face. "I understand you'll be leaving Partridgeville quite soon," he said as they got to the little waist-high wall around the organ.

Brecken gave him a startled look. "Yes, I'm transferring to a school up in New England as soon as the semester's over. How did you know?"

His expression didn't change at all. "Oh, word gets around."

Just then another old man came up toward them and said, "Why, Carl, you haven't yet introduced me to your lady friend." Brecken glanced his way and blinked in surprise; it was the proprietor of Buzrael Books, looking at her over the top of his gold-rimmed glasses.

"Thaddeus, Miss Brecken Kendall," said Knecht, smiling as always. "Miss Kendall, this is my old friend Thaddeus Waldzell." They shook hands. The whole time, Waldzell watched her over the top of his glasses with a look she couldn't read at all. A few pleasantries later, Knecht and Waldzell headed elsewhere; Brecken stared after them, and then sat on the organ bench, turned switches to get the blowers started, adjusted the stops, and began to play a Bach organ piece with the swell pedal pushed low to keep the volume down, just background music for the moment. The church ladies gossiping in the pews paid no attention Brecken could see.

Carl Knecht's comment wasn't the most unexpected reaction Brecken fielded, though. That reached her a little later the same day. As she got home from the church, her landlady came bustling out the front door of her house and said, "Brecken, oh, there you are. You got the oddest letter—no stamp, no address, just your name on it. I have no idea how it got here."

"Somebody probably just stuck it in your mailbox," Brecken suggested.

"Why, yes, I suppose that would explain it," said Mrs. Dalzell, evidently disappointed by so prosaic an explanation. "Here it is."

It looked to Brecken like a card rather than a letter, and her name showed on the envelope in a hand that almost struck a chord of memory. It went on the endtable once she got inside, and later that afternoon she found time to open it. The card turned out to be a pleasantly understated congratulations card, very much to her taste, but what was written inside made her stare in astonishment and nearly drop the card:

Brecken,
Congratulations on getting accepted at Miskatonic! Couldn't happen to a better musician or a nicer person.

Could you handle having me stop by at your place very briefly sometime soon? I know we parted on bad terms, and that was my fault; I owe you an apology for that, and when you leave Partridgeville I'd like you to have at least some good memories of me.

Best,
Jay

Sho gave the card an inquisitive look. ♪*What does it say?*♪

♪*It's from Jay,*♪ Brecken told her. ♪*He wishes to say he is sorry for the way he behaved.*♪

♪*Do you think he means that truly?*♪

♪*I don't know.*♪ She read the message in the card again, and then set it on her endtable. She had too many other things to think about, and putting a few finishing touches on her fugue before the beginning of class the next day was at the top of that list.

* * *

The familiar room was more than half full when Rosalie and Brecken took their usual seats. Darren gave Brecken a nod and his ungainly smile, Molly cast an amused look her way and then turned back to something she was writing, Julian and a few of his cronies glanced up to see Brecken come in and then looked pointedly away. That was as much notice as anyone gave her, which left Brecken feeling relieved. There would be plenty of angry words spoken by the time the class was over, she guessed, and even more in the weeks to come, but that didn't matter now. The semester was nearly over, and for Brecken, so was Partridgeville State University. The sense of freedom that fact woke in her left her dizzied.

Professor Toomey came in a few minutes early, sat in a chair beside the podium, and got busy with his phone. When the clock showed 11:30 exactly, he got up and said, "You all know the drill. We've got just three pieces to take in today, and I happen to know that one of them is longer and more complicated than anything you've heard so far. Any questions? No? Fair enough. First up is 'Sonata in F' by Susan Chu."

At that, Brecken looked up sharply from the comment form on her phone. It seemed utterly improbable that Susan would compose and play anything in classic sonata form. Still, there she was, getting her viola out of its case and deftly adjusting the tuning of the A string, while Wendy Bergdahl sat down at the piano, stretched out her fingers, and then turned and waited. Susan nodded, Wendy began playing, and a few notes later Susan's viola joined in.

It wasn't a classic sonata, that was certain. It was in 5/8 time and was full of dissonances that nobody before Wagner would have considered musical at all, but it followed the sonata form, and it worked. After the first few measures Brecken leaned forward, propped her chin on one hand, and listened for a while. 'Sonata in F' was still rough in places and unsatisfactory in others, but Susan had taken the form and started to make something her own out of it. Brecken nodded slowly, then picked up her phone and wrote a lengthy comment, paused to listen to the development for a while, wrote another.

The piece wound gracefully to its end. Susan, beaming, put down her viola and nodded to the class, as though she'd proved a point. Applause drowned out anything she might have said; Brecken clapped enthusiastically, and she was far from the only one.

Silence returned. "'Fugue in G flat minor,' by Brecken Kendall," the professor said.

For once, Brecken remembered to get her music out of her tote bag before she stood up. A few moments later she was at the piano, the keyboard spread before her like a banquet of sound. She stretched and shook out her fingers, then turned to face Professor Toomey and said, "Do you mind if I say something to the class first?"

"Go ahead." His expression was unreadable as ever, but she thought she sensed a hint of dry amusement in it.

She pivoted on the bench, faced Julian Pinchbeck. "There's been a lot of talk this semester about whether there's any point to tonality, or to any of the older forms of music," she said. "Back before spring break, a certain member of this class insisted that nobody could do anything with a certain theme so long as they're, quote, hobbled by some kind of sick obsession with outdated music. Unquote." She let some of her anger color her voice as she said the words, and was gratified to see Julian's face redden. "Of course there are things you can't do with the old forms, but you know what? That isn't one of them." She turned back to the keyboard and, before anyone else had time to speak, started to play.

The twelve notes of the subject sounded, introducing the first voice, and as it finished, the same notes came in a minor sixth lower. Somewhere in the distance, a voice she no longer recognized let out a slow sulfurous monosyllable under its breath, but Brecken was past caring. The eighty-eight keys in front of her and the architecture of sound that rose out of them became her world, a world where everything made sense to her, where anger, grief, and bitter longing could sound their own depths and then find a resolution that the other world so often refused to give. She kept the volume modest most of the way through the development, but as the first of the false entries heightened the tension, she let the music crescendo, and as the voices leapt past each other in the stretto she threw caution to the winds and played that passage fortissimo, reveling in the harsh discords. The dominant pedal in the bass line just afterward reminded her where she was, and she let the fugue slow and soften, until the final entry of the subject flowed into the cadence that brought the fugue to a close.

Silence, then. Brecken made herself draw in a breath, let it out again, and then turned toward Professor Toomey. For once, the impenetrable expression had cracked, and he was staring at her with his mouth slightly open. An instant later he recovered, and his face resumed its normal bland state, but before that she'd seen the sheer astonishment in his eyes. Beaming, she turned the other way to savor the one taste of revenge she'd promised herself, the look on Julian Pinchbeck's face when she made him eat his words.

She'd expected—what? Rage and resentment, most probably; maybe embarrassment and shame; maybe, just maybe, some least trace of acknowledgment that she had the right to her own music just as he had the right to his. Certainly, though, she hadn't expected an expression red and raw as an open wound, the bleak haggard eyes of a soul in torment. Horrified, she tried to think of something to say, but by then the applause had started, drowning out any words she might have spoken. Molly and Darren started it, clapping loud and hard; Rosalie joined them after a moment, and then the others began to clap. Even some of Julian's cronies applauded, looking sidelong at her with rueful expressions.

As the applause died down, before the professor could say anything, Brecken said, "Julian, what you did with that was good too. I'm not saying there's anything wrong with your music. I just want you to stop telling me I can't have mine."

He looked away, said nothing. After a decent interval, Toomey said, "And our last piece, 'Circulations' by Michael Schau." Brecken got up from the piano and went most of the way back to her seat before she realized she'd left her music behind. She went back to get it; Mike Schau had already settled on the bench, and handed the sheets to her with a wry grin. She thanked him and went back to her place next to Rosalie.

Schau's piece was workmanlike and utterly derivative, more than good enough to get the grade he needed but indistinguishable from the work of a thousand other undergraduates. His performance was stellar, though, and Brecken let herself daydream for a little while about what it would be like to have her compositions played by musicians who were better than she was. It helped distract her, and that was more than a little welcome. The haunted look on Julian's face troubled her, then and later.

* * *

Walking home up Danforth Street, with Hob's Hill rising before her, it began to sink in just how soon that familiar route would be a fading memory. Maybe that was why the card from

Jay caught her eye later that same evening. She had phone calls to make—with the fugue finally out of the way, she'd arranged to call Aunt Mary and Uncle Jim, and spent most of an hour telling both of them about the upcoming move to Arkham, the summer program she'd been invited to take, and the rest of it. The call went better than she'd expected—Aunt Mary chattered enthusiastically about the one time in her life she'd been to Salem, which she adored, and Uncle Jim told her that the first time he'd seen her playing in the Trowbridge High School marching band he'd been sure her music was going to take her places, which was just as pleasant to hear then as it had been the last thirty times he'd said it.

Afterwards, though, a melancholy mood settled on her. She picked up Jay's card, read the note again, wondered whether he really felt what he'd written. She had dinner to fix, so she set the card aside and headed for the kitchenette, and after that she and Sho talked for a while and worked on Sho's still very limited command of English.

Then came two hours of hard practice on the piano, but she had no homework to follow that—she was caught up on her assignments for her counterpoint and arrangement classes—and with the fugue done, and no other ideas just then for music to compose, she felt at loose ends. After a while she got up and went to the bookshelf. She'd left von Junzt's book alone since she'd gotten back from Arkham, but the thought of spending an hour or two among stories of forgotten ages and mysterious secret societies appealed to her just then.

She opened *The Book of Nameless Cults* at random, and found herself in the middle of a story about a Coptic sorceress in Upper Egypt who'd taught von Junzt to send curses back at their senders by concentrating on the Sign of Koth. That would make a really good short story, she thought, and then remembered dimly that it already had. Another trip to the bookshelf and a few moments of searching turned up, two-thirds of the way through her battered paperback copy of Philip Hastane's

Daydreams and Nightmares, a lively little tale titled "Zuleika's Warding" that drew a good half of its details from von Junzt's tale.

It really is a delightful story, she thought. I wonder what it would be like as—

Brief echoes of voices raised in recitative and aria spun through her imagination. An opera? She didn't know the first thing about composing music for opera, and had to stop herself from booting up her laptop and looking up the basics. Later, she told herself, laughing. I've got a semester to finish and a move to pack for and English lessons for Sho and …

Her eyes strayed again to the card from Jay. An apology to accept?

Maybe, she thought, and turned her attention back to von Junzt.

The next morning Rosalie texted first thing to say she wouldn't be in The Cave that day: too much to do before the semester was over, the text claimed, but Brecken guessed that there was more to it than that. They'd both carefully avoided talking about Rosalie's career plans or Brecken's upcoming move, but those studied evasions simply emphasized the things neither of them wanted to mention. The friendship they'd had since those first days sharing a room in Arbuckle Hall was fraying, and the reason was simple enough: the fact that Brecken was pursuing her dream made it impossible for Rosalie to pretend that she meant to follow hers. That ached, but after the first few days it was a familiar ache.

She headed home as soon as her orchestral arrangement class was over, and spent two hours helping Sho with English. ♪So many names for things,♪ the shoggoth said disconsolately, huddling down a little. ♪I will try to learn them all. And maybe you can try again to help me to understand …♪ "Numbers," she said in English.

♪You said that well,♪ Brecken reassured her. ♪You're getting very good at speaking words.♪ She leaned back on the futon, tried to think of a different way of helping Sho with her perplexity, and found herself getting as confused as the shoggoth. Was there really anything that two hands had in common with two books, or two of anything else? Or was it just—

Her hand came up to cup her chin as she stared at nothing in particular. Maybe, she thought, maybe numbers are just as arbitrary as tonality, or not having chocolate ice cream on your chicken quesadillas. Is one apple plus one apple really equal to two apples? All at once she started laughing. It depends on the size of the apples, doesn't it?

♪I think I know what to do,♪ Brecken said then. ♪Don't try to understand them. There's nothing to understand—it's just a habit that my people have, to sort out all the things we give names to. Just learn the names, learn to count with them.♪ Memories from childhood came surging up. ♪It can be like a game.♪

♪I think I understand,♪ Sho piped slowly. ♪I will try.♪

By the time dinner was ready Sho had learned the names of the numbers from one to ten and could recite them in order. Afterward they talked about other things, and Brecken practiced on the piano. Now and again, though, her gaze strayed to the card from Jay on the end table.

* * *

The next day Brecken got to The Cave around the usual time, but found the familiar table empty, and ended up wandering over to where Molly and an assortment of her friends were standing. There she quickly ended up being drawn into a conversation, mostly with Molly's friends; Molly herself had a broad grin on her face but said uncharacteristically little, and Brecken found herself wondering why. By the time she extracted herself from the conversation and went back to the table, it was nearly time to go up to Composition II, and Rosalie was sitting at the table looking depressed and bored.

They talked a little on the elevator ride up to the tenth floor, but Brecken could feel the widening gap between them.

Once in the room she settled into her chair, made herself relax. With her final project out of the way, she reminded herself, she had nothing else due for Composition II but her comments on the other students' projects. The first three of those were predictably bland, but then Professor Toomey said, "Molly Wolejko, 'Meditation.'" Brecken gave him a baffled look in response, because Molly hadn't brought her guitar to class.

Molly got up anyway, walked to the piano, and sat down at the bench. "Can I say something?" she asked Toomey, and he nodded. She pivoted, faced the end of the classroom where Julian Pinchbeck and his friends invariably sat. "One of the people I wanted to hear this didn't make it today," she said. "You'll just have to ask him what happened to all those times he said the rest of us don't do his kind of music because we can't." She turned back to the piano, paused, and then began to play.

She was maybe three notes into her piece when Brecken looked up from her smartphone, staring. By the time she'd played half a dozen more notes, everyone else was staring too. Molly's final project for Composition II was a crisp and understated postspectralist piece for piano, one that picked up half the trends on the cutting edge of composition and did something new with them. It did more than that. Listening to it, Brecken finally caught some hint of what the postspectralist movement was trying to accomplish, some echo of the possibilities that enticed Julian Pinchbeck and his friends. It wasn't a kind of music she wanted to write, and she wasn't sure it was a kind of music she could write, but it finally spoke to her.

She listened for a while, nodding slowly, then remembered the comment form and typed a few sentences, listened for another minute or two and typed more. A quick glance one way caught two of Pinchbeck's friends looking on in shock; a quick glance the other way caught Professor Toomey, his imperturbable expression shattered, shaking his head in disbelief.

The piece wound up with a sequence of notes that avoided the classic cadences but still managed to give a sense of completion to the music. Brecken started clapping the moment the last note faded, heard others applaud as well. Molly got to her feet and waited. When the applause died down, she faced Pinchbeck's cronies and said with a grin, "You don't have to tell Julian I'm waiting for him to prove he can do some halfway decent metal. I'll tell him myself."

That was when Brecken turned in her chair to look. She'd been upset enough when she'd gotten to class that she had missed Julian Pinchbeck's absence.

The class had one more performance to take in, an unimaginative but pleasant piano etude by a young man whose name Brecken heard and promptly forgot, and then Toomey said, "That's it for today, see you next week," and started for the door. As most of the students got up, Brecken turned to Molly and said, "That was amazing."

"Thanks. I started work on it last October." With a sudden grin: "The first time His Majesty got in my face about how I wasn't a real musician because I play metal, I decided to stuff those words down his throat. Pity he wasn't here to listen." She shrugged. "I bet he was too rattled to show his face after your piece last time. That was a hoot to watch."

Brecken winced inwardly, thinking of the look on Julian's face when she'd finished playing her fugue. "The thing is," Molly went on, "I learned some seriously cool tricks from postspectralism. Did you know that a bunch of progressive-rock groups back in the Seventies used to put fugues in their stuff?"

"No, I didn't," Brecken said, startled.

"Check it out. Emerson, Lake and Palmer did it in *Trilogy*, and I forget which piece by Gentle Giant is a rock fugue. If they can do that, I can borrow some postspectralist licks for metal." She grinned. "If I can talk my band into it. They think I'm kind of weird, but whenever we go out on a limb the audience eats it up."

Brecken said something more or less appreciative, gathered up her things, and turned toward Rosalie's chair. It was empty. Startled, Brecken got up and went to the door, but Rosalie was nowhere in sight.

She brooded about that while she sipped coffee in Vivaldi's, sat through a lecture on invertible counterpoint, ducked back home to get her laundry, took it back home again, and went to her piano lesson with Mrs. Johansen. By the time she walked back to the little apartment where Sho waited, she'd worked her way into a miserable mood, thinking about her friendship with Rosalie and the way it was coming apart. Sho's welcome helped, but gloomy thoughts still circled through her mind, and when her gaze happened to fall on the card from Jay, she decided on the spur of the moment that she ought to give him the chance to apologize.

She talked about it with Sho before dinner. The shoggoth gave her a dubious look out of three eyes, but said, ♪*You know humans much better than I do. If you think he truly wishes to make amends I will not disagree.*♪

Brecken knew her well enough by then to catch the unspoken meaning. ♪*You don't think he means it.*♪

♪*I do not know.*♪ A pseudopod curled around her. ♪*I know he hurt you, and I do not want to think kind thoughts about one who did such a thing.*♪

Brecken bent and kissed her. ♪*I know. But I think it's only fair to give him the chance.*♪

♪*I understand,*♪ Sho whistled. ♪*If anything wrong happens I will be near.*♪

Brecken emailed him before she got up to make dinner, and had a response back within an hour, polite and friendly, suggesting Friday evening at eight. She agreed, and found that her troubled mood cleared up thereafter. All through her Thursday class, a difficult hour trying to make conversation with Rosalie, and her flute lesson, all through a quiet Friday while she began studying for her finals in counterpoint and orchestral arrangement, she felt oddly lighter, as though some sort of pressure had been lifted from her, but she had too much to do to take the time to chase that feeling to its roots.

* * *

The knock came on the door of the little apartment right at eight. Brecken darted a worried look at the closet where Sho was hiding, but went to the door and opened it. It was Jay, of course, with a smile on his face and the top of a wine bottle peeking out of a bag in his hand. "Hi," he said.

"Hi." She stepped out of his way, motioned toward the futon, and he came in.

He looked only half alive. That was her first thought, and though she tried to argue herself out of it, told herself that maybe he'd just slept badly or been sick recently, that was where her thoughts ended up when they'd run round the circle of evasions. His cheeks were hollow, his eyes unnaturally bright and staring, he'd lost too many pounds, and there was a sallow color to his skin that hadn't been there before. Still, he'd shaved and combed his hair and put on clean clothes, and the smile on his face was the one she remembered, the little upward twist at the corners of his mouth.

"Thanks for being willing to see me," he said, and settled on the futon. "I know things got really ugly between us around what happened before winter break."

"You know, we don't have to talk about that," Brecken said.

"Thank you." He looked relieved. "So tell me about where you're going. I heard some things from a couple of people I know, but—" He shrugged. "You know how gossip goes."

"Sure." She sat on the other end of the futon, started telling him about Miskatonic University and its program in traditional composition, her trip up there to audition, the summer program she'd been invited to take.

"That's really great," he said finally. "Worth a toast. Got a couple of glasses?"

By way of answer she got up, went to the kitchenette, came back with two water glasses. "I apologize," she said, laughing. "I don't have anything better."

"Don't worry about it," he said, with the same smile. The wine bottle had a screw top; he twisted it open, poured each of them a glass, handed her one. "To your future."

"Thank you," she said, clinked glasses with him, sipped some of the wine. It had an odd, slightly bitter taste. She glanced at it.

"Drink it," he said. He hadn't raised his glass to his lips.

"It tastes funny," she said, and the words came out a little blurred because a faint numbness had spread across her mouth.

"Drink it," he repeated, his gaze fixed on her. His smile had begun to broaden, taking on the shape of the smile she'd hated so much.

She glanced at the wine, at him. The numbness was spreading. "You put something in this," she said, and tried to fling the glass away, but her hand would not obey her will.

"You bet." He set his glass on the floor beside him. "Drink it."

She stared at him for a long moment, tried again to discard the glass. What had he put in it? She'd read about date-rape drugs, that was one of the reasons she stayed away from the parties and nightspots that Rosalie favored. Was that what he'd planned?

"Drink it," he repeated, and the smile on his face twisted into a rictus of triumph. "Did you really think that I came here to apologize? You turned your back on me when I needed you more than anything, and I'm the one who's supposed to say I'm sorry? Not a chance."

"You're the one who dumped me," she made herself say.

"I made a mistake." He stood up. "Then I called you and texted you and tried to talk to you, and all I got back was you telling me to go die in a ditch. And then you and your little friends spread lies about me all over Partridgeville to make sure I couldn't get a new group started or even find a solo gig. I fucking *starved* because of you."

Even through the haze the drug threw across her mind, she could see the falsehood in his eyes. "They were true," she said. "I didn't spread them, but they were true."

"Shut up!" he snarled at her. Then, in a voice that shook: "You destroyed me. You stomped the shit out of everything I built here, everything I wanted to do with my life. Now it's your turn. Drink it." His face, gloating, knotted into a parody of itself. "Drink it all, and get what's coming to you."

Her hand began moving toward her mouth, carrying the glass, and though she fought to stop it the movement merely slowed to a crawl. He's using sorcery on me, she thought. All at once, in a moment of cold clarity, she could see how things would unfold. Pale luminous eyes watched him already from the closet, she knew. If he touched her, whether he meant to rape her or worse, Sho would stop him, and that meant he would find out about Sho—

Or he would die.

Panic flared, laced with images: Brecken's mother in her orange prison jumpsuit, media photos of the two people she'd shot, Brecken and Sho fleeing from the apartment leaving it tenanted only by a corpse, the future she'd hoped to make for the two of them gone whistling down the wind forever. Something like a scream rose up from her depths, though it made no sound. Her concentration broke, and the glass moved closer to her mouth.

An instant later something unexpected surfaced in her mind. Sorcery, a memory whispered. A way to reverse sorcery, to turn it on the one who wields it. A sign—

In the next instant she remembered the Sign of Koth, and the reference to it she'd read in von Junzt. She seized the memory the way a drowning man seizes a rope, imagined the Sign as clearly as she could, the way she'd drawn it when she'd done the Vach-Viraj incantation.

In response, her hand stopped moving, and she could feel his spell twist around in the space between them, point back at its maker.

"No," she said aloud. Her voice sounded thick in her ears. "No. You drink it."

It took all her concentration to keep the Sign of Koth from blurring in her mind, but she flung every trace of energy she could find into the task, and the spell began to flow the other way. At the edge of her awareness, she barely noticed the sweat beading on Jay's suddenly bloodless face, his hand rising unsteadily, hers raising the glass just as unsteadily for him to take. He took it; the hideous smile shattered, and what replaced it was stark terror, but all she could think of was the Sign of Koth, her one safeguard against whatever ugly act he'd planned. She felt his last defenses break, saw the glass go to his mouth and tip, the wine drain into him.

The Sign splintered then, and she struggled to her feet, faced him. He stood there, staring at her in amazement and horror, his eyes round, his face pale and damp with sweat. A sudden motion flung the glass to the floor, where it broke. "No," he said, his voice shaking. "How—how did you—oh my God. No, no, no—"

Then he broke and ran for the door, hauled it open, flung himself out into the darkness. She could hear his footfalls, running hard, fading into the dim murmur of the night.

CHAPTER 17

THE HOUNDS OF TINDALOS

Brecken stood there speechless for a moment, completely baffled, then turned unsteadily. She could feel the drug affecting her more and more. The room was going dark around her. ♪*Broodsister,*♪ she called, and Sho slid out from under the closet door.

♪*I am here.*♪ Her piping was low and intent. ♪*It is not well with you.*♪

♪*No. He put something in my drink.*♪

♪*I feared he meant to harm you.*♪

Brecken reddened with the memory. ♪*You were right and I was wrong. I am sorry.*♪ Immediate issues forced their way into her mind. ♪*I'm going to try to—*♪ The shoggoth language had no word for "throw up." ♪*Get some of it out of me.*♪ She stumbled into the bathroom—her limbs felt heavy and unnatural, as though they belonged to someone else—and knelt in front of the toilet. A finger down her throat got her to retch, but only a little liquid came up, and the room darkened steadily around her. After a time, she pulled herself to her feet, staggered back to the futon and slumped onto it, landing hard.

♪*What will the thing he put in your drink do?*♪ Sho asked.

Brecken tried her best to remember everything she'd ever learned about date-rape drugs. ♪*It'll make me sleep,*♪ she said.

♪He meant to hurt me while I slept. I didn't drink much of it, but it may still have been enough.♪ The door still stood open, and a hideous possibility occurred to her. ♪The door—if he comes back—♪

She had forgotten how fast Sho could move. An iridescent black blur flung itself across the room, pushed the door shut until the latch clicked, and a deft pseudopod turned the dead-bolt. The pseudopod reached again, turned off the light. ♪If he comes back he will not see me, and I will stop him. I promise you I will not kill him, but I will stop him—and I will hurt him.♪

Brecken barely registered the words. Something had happened to the darkness around her. She could see the room as clearly as in daylight, though all the colors were wrong. She could see Sho crouched by the futon, pale eyes gazing at her in worry, but she could also see where the shoggoth had been, a track through space that began in the closet and went to the door and back to the futon. Worse, she could see Jay coming into the apartment, sitting on the futon, standing up, fleeing from the apartment—all at once.

That was when she guessed what Jay had given her, and her blood ran cold. ♪This is bad,♪ she whistled. ♪This is really bad.♪

♪What is wrong?♪ Dread tinged the air with a bitter scent.

♪What I drank isn't what I thought it was. It's—♪ There was no word for the Liao drug in the shoggoth language. ♪A thing that makes me see the wrong kind of time. A thing that—♪

Then, all at once, she understood, and at the same moment knew how Barbara Cormyn had died, and who had made that happen. The air had begun to turn milky around her. She tried to think through a rising fog of panic.

♪Is there something I can do? ♪ Sho asked her.

The question helped her concentrate, and she struggled to remember what Halpin Chalmers had written about the Liao drug, what the stories she'd read in Boley's class had said about it. ♪Shake me,♪ she said. ♪Shake me. Keep me here and now so the Hounds can't find me.♪

Sho was on the futon in an instant, and paired pseudopods gripped Brecken's shoulders and gave her a brisk shake. ♪*Yes!*♪ Brecken whistled as her head cleared a little. ♪*Like that.*♪

Sho repeated the shake, and it helped. The milky quality faded a little from the air, giving way to honest darkness. Brecken tried to concentrate, and heard the shoggoth piping a series of names in a low whistle, as if they were a litany: ♪*Embraced, Day Spent Sleeping, Laughs At Falling Snow, Alongside You, In A Circle* ...♪ They seemed dimly familiar at first, and then Brecken realized that they were her own names, every shoggoth-name she had ever given herself, and Sho had memorized them all. Awed and humbled, she reached for Sho, slumped forward against her. She could feel the shoggoth's love and stark terror, and managed to put her arms around Sho, hoping it might bring some comfort to them both.

She saw—

She saw her own life, spread out before her in a single moment: infancy and childhood and girlhood, happy hours with her grandparents and wretched ones with her mother, that first encounter with *The Magic Flute*, Friday afternoons with Mrs. Macallan, wedding gigs and halftimes with the Trowbridge High marching band and meeting Rosalie that first day in Arbuckle Hall and all the rest of it. There were other lives tangled up with it, too, like a skein of many-colored threads, Grandma Olive's and Grandpa Aaron's and her father's and her mother's and Mrs. Macallan's and Rosalie's and Jay's and Donna's and Darren's and many more, and then Sho's, an iridescent black thread that came from underground to wrap around hers.

She could sense the temptation to follow those other lives, to stray toward the place where curved time meets angular time and the Hounds of Tindalos guard the boundary no being of curved time can cross with impunity, but whenever she began to drift that way, Sho's pseudopods shook her, bringing her back to herself. Off beyond the tangled threads, though, she could sense the curves of time, and beyond those were strange angles of time, twisting and straining against the curves, a wrongness that cried for resolution and did not find it. From out of the angles, swift lean shapes without any curves at all plunged inwards, and her blood ran cold for a moment before she realized that they were not moving toward her.

There was still another life tangled with hers, she saw then: a vast and subtle life that moved toward hers from immense distance. It reached back into a past almost beyond measuring. It was a blackness so total it felt like a gap in the fabric of reality. It came to her just before Sho did, she could see that clearly, but it curved around her in strange ways, guiding her thoughts one way or another, drawing the thread of her own life in unexpected directions. She stared at it, knowing somehow that it would not lead her into the distances where peril waited. It was there with her as Sho was there with her, wrapping around her a little further off, watching her.

Nyogtha, she thought. Dweller in Darkness, The Thing That Should Not Be.

The darkness closed in and swallowed her utterly.

* * *

Brecken blinked. Naked, she was standing beside the futon, and it slowly registered that her clothed body was lying there below her, nestled into Sho's curves. A moment of panic seized her as she wondered if she was dead, but then she saw her own chest rising and falling slightly, and a few strands of hair that had strayed across her face fluttered with each outbreath.

Your present condition makes communication easier, said something that was not a voice.

She raised her eyes. A few feet away from the futon in every direction, a blackness that made the darkest night seem luminous erased all other presences. She tried to speak, swallowed, tried again; her voice sounded faint and far away. "Nyogtha."

Yes.

"You reminded me about the Sign of Koth."

Yes.

"Thank you. I—I owe you my life."

In due time, I will ask certain things in repayment.

She wanted to say something, anything, in response, but then understood that no response was needed. The Thing That Should Not Be already knew what it would ask of her, and when, and where, and why, and what she would do about it. Gazing into the blackness, she thought of a different question, one that had haunted her for months.

You wish to know why I did not save the other shoggoths, the not-voice said.

"Yes. Yes, please."

It is well for you to know that. They would not have survived even if they stayed hidden. They were isolated too long, and there were genetic issues, as sometimes happens. So I let them die swiftly, rather than leaving them to the slow dwindling, the hunger and the silence. My pact with the shoggoths abides; of the few who were still healthy, I chose one that was young and strong to preserve their line, and I guided her to this place.

Brecken stared at the blackness in wonder. "You sent Sho to me."

A trace of amusement tinged the not-voice. *Did you think that any of what happened was the work of chance? She needed a human to feed her, shelter her, keep her safe from the enemies of her people. Of the humans living nearby, you were best suited to that task, so I brought her to you. It was an easy thing to see to it that you had a guide to her language, so that she could communicate her needs to you, and an easier thing still to mislead those who searched for her.*

"Did you know what—what would happen between us?"

It was one possibility of many, said Nyogtha. *It did not concern me.*

"I'm still more grateful than I can say," Brecken told the darkness.

I gave you another thing that might have protected you, said The Thing That Should Not Be. *It did not, and it is well for you to know why. You had a book, which was later stolen. Did you know that it would have spared you this night?*

Brecken stared in dismay. "No."

The card you were sent had sorceries worked upon it, to play upon your weaknesses and keep you from exercising an appropriate caution.

She clenched her eyes shut. "That was really stupid of me, not to think of that. Really *really* stupid."

The Vach-Viraj incantation would have kept the sorceries from attaining their goal. There will be other days and other sorceries, and my fosterling will depend on you, so you will need to practice that much sorcery, for her sake as well as yours.

Though the prospect left her profoundly uneasy, Brecken made herself nod. "Okay," she said, "But—but I don't have the book any more."

You will be given another opportunity. Then you will know what you must do.

Brecken nodded again, eyes closed.

There is a further thing I wish you to know, The Thing That Should Not Be said then. *You go to dwell in the house of the daughter of my ancient enemy, as I intended. Yes, that also was my doing in part, though the One who dwells in Carcosa willed another part, and our purposes run along the same path just now. There is a reason for that, which it is well for you to know.*

I have not concerned myself before now with the affairs of the Great Old Ones. Their purposes and their struggles are not mine, and certain old quarrels stand between us. Yet it has not escaped my notice that it was their enemies who struck against my fosterlings, and their servants who came to my fosterlings' aid. I will repay both those deeds in my own time and in my own way. For now, when you dwell with the child of the King, you will tell her the things that I have said to you. By then she will know them anyway—but you will tell her.

"I'll do that," said Brecken.

It is well. Then: *The place you go will be a place of safety for a time, but only for a time, and thereafter I will act. Until that time comes, this fosterling of mine must be well hidden.* The darkness ebbed and swirled. *It is a long and difficult road I have ordained for her, to dwell in the human world and raise her broodlings there. There is a purpose behind it, which will be known at the proper time. Until that happens, it will be well for her if you stay beside her, keep her safe, help her with her broodlings when they come.*

The thought of Sho budding, abstract until that moment, suddenly became anything but. "I'll do that, with all my heart," Brecken said. "I'd do it anyway, because of what's between the two of us. But since you've asked me to do it—" She laughed, a faint murmuring sound like running water. "Is it possible to do more than everything I can? Because I'm going to try."

It is well, Nyogtha said again. *Now attend, my fosterling's broodsister. The drug remains in you, and though you received only a small dose, some risk remains. I will return you to your body now, but you will sleep until it is gone, so the Hounds will not trouble themselves over you.*

Darkness took her then, sudden as a knife.

* * *

The phone rang, playing the opening bars of *Eine Kleine Nachtmusik.* Brecken blinked half awake, reached for the end table. Her purse was close by; she got it, extracted the phone and picked up the call. "Hello?"

The voice on the line sounded slightly familiar. "May I speak to Brecken Kendall?"

"That's me," Brecken said. She tried to focus. She was still dressed in the clothes she'd had on the night before. Early morning sunlight filtered in through the blinds, splashed across the table, a broken glass, dark stains on the carpet. Sho lay curled half around her, far over on the dreaming-side.

Something tremendous and terrible had happened, Brecken knew, but the memory would not come.

"This is Officer Castro of the Partridgeville police department," the voice said. "Do you mind if I ask you a few questions?"

That jolted her the rest of the way awake. "No, not at all," she said. "Go ahead."

"Did you see Jay Olmsted at any point last night?"

The memories came crashing back in. "Yes," she managed to say. "Yes, he came by my apartment—" It took her a moment to remember the time. "—around eight o'clock and left around eight-twenty or eight-thirty."

"Did he seem agitated or anything like that?"

"Well, kind of." She fumbled for an explanation the officer would understand: "We broke up in December. He wasn't too happy about that, and I'm leaving for another state in June and so—well, things got kind of emotional."

"But he didn't appear to be frightened or worried?"

"No," she lied. Then, when the officer didn't go on: "Is he okay?"

"No, he's not." The voice paused. "We're dealing with a homicide investigation."

"Oh dear God," said Brecken. "Oh dear God." She could see all of it, every detail falling into place. She'd reversed his spell and made him drink the wine he'd meant for her, thinking that all it contained was a date-rape drug, but if he'd dosed it with the Liao drug …

Oh dear God, she repeated silently. What have I done?

Suddenly she realized that the officer had said something else. "I'm sorry, what was that?" she said, apologetic.

"What time did he leave your apartment, again?"

"Somewhere between eight-twenty and eight-thirty," said Brecken. "I wasn't looking at the clock right then but I'm sure it wasn't close to nine yet."

"Okay," said the officer. "Can I ask you to come down to the station sometime in the next couple of days and make a statement? Just come in—the station's open seven days a week. Tell the receptionist who you are, and someone'll ask you some questions and then write up what you witnessed." She agreed, they talked briefly about the station's hours and its address, he gave her the case number, and then the phone went silent and Brecken set it down on the end table.

Five of Sho's eyes regarded her. ♪*He is dead.*♪

♪*Yes.*♪

♪*Was it the Hounds?*♪

♪*I think so,*♪ said Brecken.

♪*I am sorry,*♪ Sho replied. ♪*I did not like him but I did not wish him to die thus.*♪

♪*He wanted to do the same thing to me.*♪

♪*I know. If he had succeeded—*♪ Sho trembled violently, and the acrid scent of her dread filled the air. ♪*If I lived and he also lived I would have found him and torn him into small pieces. And then—and then—*♪

Brecken reached for the shoggoth, held her. ♪*Broodsister, broodsister,*♪ she whistled. Sho wrapped around her and clung to her, shaking, for a long while.

♪*Must you go anywhere today?*♪ Sho piped finally.

♪*No. Nowhere at all.*♪ Her bladder contradicted her then, but they got that sorted out, and then she saw the bottle of tainted wine and Jay's glass, and took a moment to empty all the wine down the kitchen sink and gather up the shards of the broken glass. When Brecken came back from that task she pulled the futon out flat, shed her clothes, and slipped under the quilts without bothering with a nightgown. Sho flowed against her, pressed up close.

♪*My name today is Still Beside You,*♪ the shoggoth said after a while, in a whistle so soft Brecken could scarcely hear it.

♪*Mine—*♪ A phrase of Nyogtha's surfaced in Brecken's mind. ♪*Mine is Fosterling's Broodsister. The Thing That Should Not Be called me that.*♪

♪*That is bold, to accept a name from him,*♪ said Sho. ♪*But I understand.*♪

A pseudopod flowed up against Brecken's face from below. She turned slightly and kissed it, settled her head on Sho's cool shapelessness, and let her eyes drift shut.

When she blinked awake again, the sun shone down bright through the shades at a steep angle, telling her that she'd slept most of the way to noon. Sho lay nestled up against her, on the dreaming-side but not by much, surrounded by the Brie-scent of calm; when Brecken slipped an arm around the shoggoth, a pale eye blinked open near her face, and then a speech-orifice opened and piped her name, ♪*Fosterling's Broodsister,*♪ in a gentle lilting cascade of notes.

♪*Still Beside You,*♪ Brecken replied, and moved her hand gently down the shoggoth's side, which fluttered in response. The whistled notes of Sho's name intertwined as she and Sho did, making an elegant melodic pattern, and though her attention was elsewhere for a time—on the slow wet kiss she gave to Sho, the moisture Sho shared in response, the acts and delights that followed, the simple dazzling reality that they had both come alive through the night—she knew, knew for certain, that she'd found the theme she needed for the last movement of her concerto.

* * *

The next day was a Sunday, and though leaving the apartment was very nearly the last thing she wanted to do, she kissed Sho and headed for church while the morning was cool and crisp, and wisps of fog hung over Partridge Bay beneath a pale blue sky. The familiar route down Danforth Street into the heart of old Partridgeville and then back up Angell Hill to the First Baptist Church seemed new and bright, like something she'd just discovered in her own mind.

As she walked, Nyogtha's not-words repeated themselves in memory. *It is a long and difficult road I have ordained for her,* he'd said, *to dwell in the human world and raise her broodlings there.* Ever since he'd told her that, the idea of taking care of Sho when her time of budding came and helping her to raise her broodlings had circled in Brecken's thoughts, now near, now far, but never absent. It took only the briefest effort for her to picture the broodlings: little shapes of iridescent black, separated parts of Sho's own flesh, tumbling awkwardly over one another as they grew and learned to imitate their mother's grace and strength. Brecken shook her head, laughed at herself as she passed the university buildings. They don't even exist yet, she thought, and I already want to scoop them up in my arms and kiss them. It was true, though: the thought of helping to care for Sho's brood called up a warm shudder from her depths. She smiled at nothing in particular, headed up the hill to the church.

Carl Knecht met her as usual by the door, asked politely about her week, and walked with her to the organ before heading for whatever other tasks his job as music director imposed on him. Lacking anything better to do, she went into the enclosure, flipped the switch that powered up the blowers, perched on the bench, considered the stops before her. The organ had countless possibilities of sound she hadn't yet explored, she knew, and it hurt to think that she'd be leaving it behind so soon. The thought that there might be an organ in Arkham she could play, at least now and again, hovered before her in the uncertain air; she pushed the thought aside, set the stops on each of the three keyboards to the registration she wanted. Then she began to play the prelude to the second act of *The Magic Flute* with the swell pedal pushed down low, so that the music made itself a background to the conversations winding up in the cavernous church.

She had time for that, a Bach fugue for organ, and one of her own sarabandes before the service got started and Reverend

Meryl's silver helmet of hair appeared above the pulpit. The hymns gave her no trouble, and though she'd brought her orchestration textbook to study, she spent the sermon watching the congregation. Thaddeus Waldzell sat within sight of her, facing the pulpit in what looked like an attitude of respectful listening if you didn't look too closely; pay a little more attention, and it was impossible not to notice that all his mind was turned to something far from the moral platitudes the Reverend Meryl dispensed so freely. Half a dozen others scattered among the pews had the same double appearance, the placid surface and the intensity beneath. What common work guided them Brecken didn't know, and knew that she would probably never know; she thought of the Yellow Sign, and wondered how many other secret things moved, silent and intense, under Partridgeville's placid surface.

When the service was over and she'd finished playing another round of quiet music until the worship hall was mostly clear, she shut down the organ, got up, remembered her tote bag just before she left the enclosure, and headed downstairs to the social hall for coffee. Reverend Meryl thanked her effusively on the way down the stair, Carl gave her a nod and a smile as she headed toward the coffee, and then she turned with a cup in her hand and spotted an unexpected face at one of the tables. She headed that way at once. "Mrs. Johansen?"

Ida Johansen glanced up, startled, and then beamed. "Brecken! It's so good to see you again. I enjoyed your playing, of course." Brecken thanked her, and she went on: "But you haven't met Nora yet." She turned toward the haggard but smiling woman beside her. "Nora, this is Brecken Kendall, the student of mine I've told you about. Brecken, this is my sister Nora."

Hands got shaken and Brecken sat across the table from the two of them, asked the inevitable questions. "Oh, I'm feeling much better," Nora said. "And I've decided to do the sensible thing and move in with Ida."

"We should have done it years ago, honestly, to make our pensions go farther," said Ida. "Ve grow too soon old, und too late schmart." She and Nora both laughed.

* * *

By the time Brecken left the church it was later than usual, and they'd agreed that Brecken would play the organ one more Sunday while Nora settled in and Ida picked up the threads of her disarranged life. The last of the fog had burnt off as she headed for downtown, and sun blazed warm overhead. She was most of the way to Danforth Street when she remembered that she was supposed to stop at the police station and make a statement about Jay.

She'd never been inside the big brown building on the corner of Meeker and Gadsden, and it took an effort to make herself go through the glass doors into the reception area. Fortunately the receptionist at the desk inside was pleasant and businesslike, took her name and the case number, and had her sit down and wait. Five minutes later, maybe, a brisk and equally businesslike detective came into the reception area, shook her hand, and led her to an office further inside the building, where he took her statement. She'd already decided to tell the truth about everything except the Liao drug and the reason for Jay's sudden departure, but the detective was mostly interested in whether Jay was a member of some sort of cult, and when Brecken could tell him nothing about that, he seemed to lose interest in the entire subject.

She found her way back to the reception area, and was about to head for the door when the receptionist said, "Ms. Kendall, did you report some property of yours as stolen?"

Brecken blinked, and was about to deny it when she remembered the chaos in her apartment she'd found on her return from Massachusetts. "Yes, a book."

The receptionist nodded. "It's been recovered. If you'll have a seat I can have someone go get it for you."

Ten minutes later she had it in her hands: the copy of *The Silent Watcher* she'd gotten from Buzzy's. "Is it okay if I ask where they found this?" she asked the receptionist.

He typed something on the keyboard in front of him, paused a moment, and then said, "Sure. It's the same case you were here for—it was in the victim's apartment. I'm not sure who spotted it there."

Brecken managed to thank him, said something polite by way of farewell, and headed for the door. The human with light-colored hair Sho had seen in the apartment at the time of the robbery hadn't been Barbara Cormyn after all, she knew now. It had been Jay, and that was where he'd gotten the knowledge he needed to compound the Liao drug and use it as a weapon. Thinking about that, she felt cold despite the warmth of the day. It didn't help that she passed a newspaper vending machine on the sidewalk not far from the police station, and Jay was the lead story on the front page of the Sunday *Partridgeville Gazette*:

> SECOND GRISLY DEATH DOWNTOWN
> College Student, 20, Found Decapitated On Stair
> Police: Link to Cormyn Killing "Very Likely"

She hurried the rest of the way home, clung to Sho for a long while once she was safely indoors. Later, after dinner, she booted up her laptop and went to the *Partridgeville Gazette* website. The story there gave too many details for Brecken's peace of mind. Jay had been seen running down Danforth Street by two witnesses, running for all he was worth, and a third witness had claimed she'd seen him pounding on the door of a business on Central Square, though she didn't remember which one. The next morning, one of the other tenants in his building noticed a bad smell coming from the stair, went to look, and found Jay lying there stark naked, sprawled across the steps, with his head torn off, his face and arms mangled, and a stinking blue liquid splashed all over him.

If he'd reached his apartment before the Hounds got to him, Brecken wondered, would one of his old books have given him some way to drive them off? Or was it one of the books for sale at Buzzy's that he needed, and that was why he was pounding on the door? No sorcery will keep them at bay for long, the marginal note in *The Secret Watcher* claimed, but was that true? She did not know. She turned off the laptop and nestled close to her brood-sister, and after a time the circling thoughts left her in peace.

Later, though, she remembered Nyogtha's words, and picked up her copy of *The Secret Watcher*. Biting her lip, she opened it to the beginning of the chapter titled "The Secret of the Sorcerers," and read again through the paragraph where Chalmers talked about love as a glandular accident. This time, though, she read the paragraph that followed:

> *The ancient writings say this, and they are right to do so, but there is another side to these things. The perspective of the universe is not the only one that must be taken into account. The mere fact that love is a function of the glands does not change the way human beings experience love, or keep it from being an immensely powerful motive for action—including the actions of sorcerers. Our deeds do not matter to the universe, but you and I are not the universe. The condition of fire is not the only reality; there is also the terrestrial, the everyday, the human; and the sorcerer must gaze upon both realities and say, "I am the reconciler between them."*

She nodded slowly, understanding what Sho had been trying to say all those months ago when she'd said that the world had no eyes. Sho was well over onto the dreaming-side just then, so Brecken didn't try to discuss the matter with her. There would be time for that later.

That evening, just before they went to bed, Brecken opened *The Secret Watcher* again, copied out the Vach-Viraj incantation into a notebook, and then performed it. She was sufficently caught up in trying to do it correctly that she didn't notice whether it had much of an effect, but Nyogtha's words hovered in her mind: *you will know what you must do.*

* * *

The *Partridgeville Gazette* obituary page the next day said little: Jay's name, his age, the date of his death, and the details of his services. It was enough, and she put the date and time in her smartphone before heading down to campus in the morning. Rosalie was at the usual table, and they managed a pleasant conversation before going up to Composition II and taking in five more student projects. Julian Pinchbeck was absent again, and his friends mentioned that they hadn't seen him or heard from him in most of a week. Brecken and Rosalie talked about that over coffee, and speculated about why he was skipping class, more because it gave them something to talk about than for any other reason.

The next evening Brecken put on a dark blue dress, showed up at the Ashbrook Funeral Home on Meeker Street with ten minutes to spare, and slipped into a seat in back. Flower arrangements competed loudly with one another at the front of the room. The casket was closed, for which she was grateful, and a large color photo of Jay's face, framed and propped on top of the casket, let her remember him as he'd been back when he'd led the Rose and Thorn Ensemble, not as he'd been the last times she'd seen him, and not as the Hounds of Tindalos had left him.

She'd hoped no one would notice her, and for a few minutes her luck held out. Memories of the few times Jay showed her photos on his phone helped her pick out family members: his father and stepmother up from Philadelphia, his mother and stepfather down from Newark, younger half-brothers and half-sisters looking scared and bored, hard silences separating one family from another. Then a woman in her twenties sat next to her and asked how she knew Jay. Brecken, blushing, explained that she and Jay had been in a relationship for a while, and though they'd broken up months before, she still wanted to say goodbye. She kept her voice low, but half a dozen people in the row just in front turned to look at her before she was done.

The service would have been vulgar if it hadn't been so bland. The minister mouthed a long string of clichés about faith and hope and life everlasting without giving Brecken the least sense that he believed a word of it. The music, a CD of badly played hymn tunes that slithered with fake sentiment, would have insulted the memory of a musician far more mediocre than Jay had been. She sat with hands folded and gaze lowered, remembering how she'd met him, how their relationship had started and proceeded, how it had ended. It was painful to recall Rose and Thorn's last practice session, and even more so to call to mind the glimpses she'd had of him afterward and that last ghastly encounter at her apartment. On the far side of those efforts, though, was a stillness that felt just a little like peace.

I loved you, she said silently to the photo, in the few moments of quiet that followed a version of "Beautiful Isle of Somewhere" so oily and insincere it took her an effort not to wince. I loved you, and that's always going to be part of me, part of what I've done and who I am. Then, as the minister lumbered gamely back to the podium to finish the service: And I wish it didn't have to end the way it did. I wish—

She made herself finish the thought. I wish you hadn't tried to kill me, and I wish I'd found a way to save myself that didn't kill you.

As soon as the service was over, while Jay's relatives were still milling around looking bored and sad and not talking to one another, she slipped out the door. The breeze outside, cool and salt-scented, was infinitely welcome after the stagnant flower-heavy air inside the funeral home. The green mass of Hob's Hill loomed to one side as she headed for Danforth Street, rose straight ahead of her as she took the familiar route home. Once the honest sounds of wind and traffic scrubbed the hymn tunes out of her ears, the first notes of a melody took shape. She'd half expected that, though she hadn't guessed that it would be wistful rather than sad, a thing of memories and might-have-beens.

Two blocks after the first notes sounded in her mind, the melody was clear enough that she stopped by a big blue mailbox, pulled a pen and the funeral service program out of her purse, and wrote the melody line down, using the mailbox as an impromptu desk, so she wouldn't lose any of it. It would always be Jay's tune for her, she knew, though enough hard work might turn it into something in which other people could hear their own griefs.

By the time she closed the door to her apartment behind her and whistled a greeting to Sho, she'd set the melody aside. With finals so close, the move to Arkham following on its heels, and the third movement of her concerto demanding as much spare time as she had to give it, she had too many other things to think about, and Sho was another source of distractions. Once she'd shed dress, nylons, and shoes and replaced them with a t-shirt and sweat pants, she flopped on the futon, nestled against Sho, and closed her eyes.

After a time, Sho said, ♪*You wished me to tell you to make the thing-that-talks talk to you again.*♪ With a wry look: ♪*If you decide to tell it to be silent I will not be sad.*♪

Brecken blinked, surfacing out of something close to a doze. ♪*Neither would I,*♪ she admitted, ♪*but I need it to talk.*♪ She got her phone out of her purse, woke it, found a message from Rosalie waiting, and after a moment's hesitation clicked on it.

"Brecken, give me a call," Rosalie's voice said. She sounded worried. "I—just give me a call, okay? Thanks."

That was so uncharacteristically terse that Brecken hit the call back button at once, got the phone to her ear. "Ro?" she said, once Rosalie picked up. "What's up?"

"They just found Julian Pinchbeck's body," Rosalie said. "Down on the beach by Mulligan Point." She swallowed audibly. "They're saying he drowned himself."

CHAPTER 18

THE RECONCILER OF WORLDS

Brecken found the details on the *Partridgeville Gazette* website a few minutes later. A couple walking their dog on the beach had seen something in the surf, went to look, and called the police, who hauled the body ashore. They'd searched Pinchbeck's apartment and found a suicide note, the article said, and the police were still investigating. That was all the article said, but it was more than enough to leave Brecken feeling chilled to her core.

The memory of Pinchbeck's face after she'd played her fugue hovered in her mind's eye. I did that, she thought. I didn't know that he'd react that way, and I still don't know why, but I killed him. I didn't want that, any more than I wanted Jay to die, but—

♪Something is not well,♪ Sho said then.

♪Yes.♪ In fumbling words, she tried to explain what had happened. One at a time, three additional eyes surfaced on the side of the shoggoth that faced her. Finally, when she'd finished, she looked away and said, ♪Did your people ever do that—kill themselves?♪

A pseudopod closed on each of her shoulders, turned her to face Sho. A dozen wide eyes stared at her. ♪You will not.♪

♪No,♪ Brecken replied, startled. ♪No, of course not.♪ And it was true: a few times in the bitter months after Mrs. Macallan's death, she'd toyed with the idea of suicide, but even then

302

it had felt like a pointless waste. ♪*No, it's just that I—I don't understand.*♪

She wanted to cry, but there were no tears in her, just a vast emptiness that seemed to reach to the edges of forever.

♪*I was afraid,*♪ Sho said then. ♪*It happened—not often, not at all often, but it happened—that one of my people killed herself to cast such shame on another that the other would do the same. I—I thought your people might do that also.*♪

Brecken managed a fragile smile. ♪*No. It might have happened long ago, but not now.*♪

♪*Is it known why he did it?*♪

♪*I don't know. I think it was me—the song I made, to show him that he was wrong. I hope that wasn't it, but—*♪

♪*I understand.*♪ Sho hunched down a little. ♪*And if it is?*♪

♪*Then I'll live with that.*♪ And that was true, too; she'd already learned to live with plenty of bitter memories, and she knew she could do the same with one more.

They spent the evening pleasantly enough, and though it took a long time for Brecken to get to sleep she was rested enough to function the next morning. An hour of flute practice helped clear her mind. Once that was done and breakfast was cooking, she turned on her phone to check messages and see if the *Gazette* had anything more to say. It didn't, but the icon showed her that an email was waiting for her. It was from Professor Toomey, characteristically terse: *Brecken—can you come to my office this morning before class?* She glanced at the clock, talked with Sho, and sent an email back saying she'd be there at 10:30.

It took her a moment to nerve herself up before she crossed The Cave to the elevators, and another moment in the sixth floor hallway before she knocked on the familiar door. "Come in," said the professor, and motioned her to a seat. She knew better than to close the door.

"You've heard about Julian Pinchbeck," Toomey said. When she nodded: "The police aren't making his suicide note public, but there's something about it you should know."

She gave him a bleak look and said, "Okay."

"It didn't mention you at all."

Her astonishment must have shown on her face, because he allowed a fractional smile. "I thought there was a pretty good chance you'd blame yourself, after the way he reacted to your fugue. What you don't know is that the morning before you played, I had him come here to talk about his grades and his future plans. He just barely dodged a D in Composition I, you see, and he was headed for worse than that this semester."

As Brecken took that in, the professor got up, walked to the window on the far end of the little office, and stared out it for a moment, then turned. "There are a lot of tragedies in this world," he said. "One that the playwrights and novelists haven't really tackled yet is the one you get when somebody has dreams but no talent. Julian wanted to be a composer but he didn't have what it takes. It really was that simple—and it's one of the toughest things a teacher has to do, to tell somebody that they're never going to be able to live their dream."

His last three words hung in the silent air, reminding her of Rosalie's choice, the other side of the coin. Brecken nodded, and said, "Did the note mention you?"

Toomey gave her a wry look, and then nodded. "Yes," he said. "At length. I wasn't the only one he blamed, though, and the police say there may have been something quite a bit uglier involved in his suicide."

"Oh?"

"They searched his computer, and they found a bunch of files about a murder here in the 1920s: a writer, I think it was, who was killed the same way as the two students who were murdered this spring. The two students, as I imagine you know, were his former girlfriend and the young man who took her away from him."

Aghast, she opened her mouth, closed it again, realizing that there was nothing she could say, not with any chance of being heard. The Hounds of Tindalos, the Liao drug: those didn't belong in the world Professor Toomey or the Partridgeville police department thought they lived in, and the one thing she could show them to make them believe her—Sho—was the one thing she most needed to keep secret.

"I know," said the professor. "I have no idea if he did that or not. I hope not, but—" He shrugged expressively. "That's neither here nor there. I just wanted to make sure you didn't jump to the wrong conclusion about Julian's suicide."

Brecken thanked him, they talked about her move, and she headed down to The Cave. Rosalie wasn't there yet, and so she went out onto the plaza, found an empty bench, sat there looking at nothing for a long moment, while the wind off the sea danced around the hard gray angles of Mainwaring Hall and clouds hid and revealed the sun.

The world has no eyes, she thought, and as she sat there, the words made sense in a way they'd never done before. Julian Pinchbeck dreamed of being a composer and she'd never imagined being one, but the world had handed the talent to her and not to him, not because she deserved it and he didn't, not because she was a good person and he wasn't, not because the universe or the Great Old Ones were out to get him, but because that was just the way things happened to turn out. She thought of Julian and Jay, and then all at once of Mrs. Macallan too—chasing their dreams, each of them, until the dreams broke beneath them and they broke too—and it wasn't wrong for them to chase their dreams, any more than it was right, for the world had no eyes and wouldn't have noticed or cared no matter what they'd done.

My life isn't right or wrong either, she thought. It just is. It doesn't mean anything to the universe that I fell in love with Jay or Sho or Mozart; those things just happened to me, the way I happened to Sho, or the Hounds of Tindalos happened to Jay, or wanting to be a composer happened to poor Julian. They happened the way that tonality makes music that makes sense, the way a major chord sounds like joy and a minor chord sounds like grief, just because that's how things happened to turn out.

She drew in a deep breath and let it out again, knowing that she couldn't be entirely certain she would live to draw in another. When she did, it came as a pleasant shock. That the spring sunlight slanted past her and the wind tasted of the sea, that music trembled in her like the blood in her veins, that Sho had come into her life, that she existed in the first place: none of those things had to happen, and nothing she'd done or left undone made them happen. They hovered there, arbitrary and astonishing, and the fact that they meant nothing to the universe didn't keep them from meaning everything to her.

The world has no eyes, but I do. Part of her wanted to laugh with delight as she repeated the words silently to herself, and another part wanted to burst into tears. Instead of doing either, she sat there on the bench for a long while, letting each moment surprise and delight her by the sheer arbitrariness of its existence, until the clouds began to thicken and a glance at her cell phone told her there was somewhere else she meant to be.

Other things pushed Julian's fate out of her mind. Over the days that followed, though, as she and the rest of Partridgeville State finished up the semester and got ready for finals week, rumors linking Julian Pinchbeck to the deaths of Barbara Cormyn and Jay Olmsted spread around campus, at first vague, then painfully exact. Nobody wanted to admit they believed them, but nobody argued against them, and Brecken could tell easily enough how it would end.

Years later, one bleak winter day when snow lay thick on the Massachusetts hills, a passage in the quartet for recorders she was writing kept refusing to come out right, and Sho and her broodlings were settled in a comfortable heap on the sofa, far over on the dreaming-side, Brecken went online and found a story on the *Partridgeville Gazette* website summing up the tragic events of that spring. The police never officially closed the case, but nobody seemed to doubt that Pinchbeck had killed his former girlfriend, his rival, and then himself. Brecken shook her head, wondered why the photograph of Pinchbeck in the news story seemed only half familiar to her, closed the browser window, and went back to work on the quartet.

* * *

The university got all three of the Gurnard Hall elevators fixed halfway through the last week of classes—"great timing," Rosalie said with an eyeroll—and so when Composition II finished its last session on the Wednesday of the last week of classes, Brecken and Rosalie ended up in The Cave one last time. An awkward silence passed, and then Rosalie said, "Coffee, definitely." Brecken agreed, and the two of them went through the doors into Vivaldi's.

Another silence came and sat with them for a while as they sipped their coffees. Rosalie, who was looking more and more uncomfortable as the moments passed, finally chased it away for a little while by laughing and reminding Brecken of one of the silly mishaps they'd gotten into when they'd been roommates in Arbuckle Hall. Brecken laughed as well and reminded her of another, and they spent fifteen minutes or so at that pleasant task of remembrance. There were tears before it was all over, and promises to stay in touch that both of them knew would not be kept, but the music had to be played all the way to the end.

Finally Brecken finished the last of her coffee. The silence had begun to creep back, and it was time to go, she knew it in her bones. "Thank you, Ro," she said. "Thank you for everything." Rosalie looked up at her with wide bleak eyes and nodded, unwilling or unable to speak, and Brecken stood, gave her one last smile, and left Vivaldi's.

The Cave seemed emptier than usual as she passed through it, though there were still plenty of music students bent over the tables in study or standing around in conversation. Maybe, she thought, it was the faces that weren't there any more—Jay's, Barbara's, Julian's. She squared her shoulders, headed for the glass doors, stepped out of the darkness and the echoes into wind and sunlight.

Later that day she had coffee with Molly at a place in town, got Molly's email, and promised to send hers once she'd gotten settled in Arkham. "My band gets up there a couple of times a year," Molly said. "There's a place called J.J.'s on Fish Street—you ought to check it out, if you like anything but classical. They have live music every night of the week."

"Blues?" Brecken asked her. "I grew up with that."

"Every Wednesday night," Molly said with a grin. "We got there a day early once—it was cheaper than staying in Boston. Definitely worth your while." Brecken pulled a notebook from her tote bag and wrote down the details.

The next day she'd arranged to meet Darren for lunch at Fumi's. True to form, they spent an hour over tea, sushi, and edamame picking apart the mathematical structure of one of Bach's ricercars. Only after they were both sure she'd understood it did Darren bring up the obvious question. "So when's the day?"

"My last final's Wednesday," said Brecken, "and I'm moving the Saturday after that."

He hunched his head down slightly into his shoulders. "Well, stay in touch."

"Of course I will! I'll be getting a new email after I get settled, but I'll send it to you and we can pick things up." Then, with a wistful smile: "Though it won't be the same without your folks and my friends missing the point."

He choked on his tea, laughed. "True. Very true."

"Besides," said Brecken, "if you and Stan get married, I want an invite."

Darren glanced at her, smiling. It wasn't the big ungainly smile he used as a shield; it was the little fragile smile he showed only to friends. "When Stan and I get married," he said, "You're going to get an invite, and something else. If you're willing, we'd like to commission you to write an original piece of music for the ceremony."

Brecken's mouth fell open, and then she beamed. "Thank you, Darren. That's really sweet—and of course I'd be delighted."

When she left Fumi's a quarter hour later she might as well have been walking on air, and even three more days of frantic studying to get ready for her finals didn't quite manage to quell her mood. One more errand still waited, though. The day after her last final, as the approaching summer wrapped the hills around Partridgeville with green and the sun shone down from a cloudless sky, Brecken walked down to Central Square, climbed the long narrow stair to Buzrael Books, and pushed open the door. Thaddeus Waldzell was sitting behind the counter as usual, and as she came in, he glanced over the top of his gold-rimmed glasses at her. His smile hinted at unspoken knowledge, as though he savored a jest too subtle to share with anyone else.

"Good afternoon," he said.

"Hi." Brecken reached into her tote bag and brought out a hardback volume: the annotated copy of *The Secret Watcher* she'd gotten at Buzzy's all those months before. "I'm wondering if I ought to give this back to you."

He took it, gave it a careful examination inside and out, and then glanced back up at her. "Oh, quite the contrary," he said. "A mutual friend tells me you'll need it again someday."

Brecken gave him a blank look, and then her eyes went round as she guessed which mutual friend he had in mind.

Waldzell's smile broadened. "The same friend tells me you're leaving Partridgeville," he said, "and this would be better off elsewhere. Take it with you and keep it hidden."

"I'm not sure I'm any good at that," said Brecken. "It got stolen, and—and two people are dead because I wasn't careful enough."

"No." A shake of his head denied that. "That wasn't your doing. When people go running toward their fate, it's not an easy thing to stop them from reaching it—whatever that fate happens to be." He handed her back the book, and smiled again.

She gave him a long, uncertain look. "Can I ask a question?" He gestured, inviting it, and she went on. "The mutual friend—how long have you known him?"

Waldzell's smile broadened further. "A very, very long time." Then, meeting her eyes: "You should go now, I think."

Then all at once she was standing in bright sun in front of the Smithwich and Isaacs jewelry store, blinking in surprise, with no idea how she'd gotten there. She turned to look at the door that led to Buzzy's, and found it shut, with a CLOSED sign hanging behind the glass for good measure. Shaking her head, she started to put the book back in her tote bag, and stopped, seeing something glinting in the hand that held it.

It proved to be a disk-shaped pendant about the size of a quarter: a circle of some polished black stone, bright as a mirror, with a circle of delicate mosaic work of blue, green, and purple set in silver around the outer edge, and a silver chain to fit around her neck. It took her only a moment to recognize the pattern, to know who had given it to the proprietor of Buzrael Books, and to guess what it might mean if she wore it. It took her only another moment to fasten the chain around her neck and tuck the pendant out of sight down the front of her blouse.

Dweller in Darkness, she thought. I know you've given me this for your reasons, not mine. I know you might even be planning to let me die someday, the way you let Sho's people die. You know what? I'm going to take that chance.

She turned, started back toward Danforth Street.

* * *

"That's everything?" said Janet Kitagawa.

"Just one more duffel," Brecken said over her shoulder. "I'll get it."

Back through the gap between houses, into the cramped and ramshackle little apartment: the journey was so familiar to Brecken that she had a hard time getting herself to believe that she'd never come that way again. Inside, familiar furnishings warred with unfamiliar gaps; the piano was gone, sold to another Partridgeville State music major, and so were all the little touches that had made the place Brecken's for a while. All that remained of hers was a big black duffel with a rigid bottom and wheels on one end.

She knelt by the duffel and whistled softly: ♪*Is it well with you, Saying Farewells?*♪

♪*It is well,*♪ Sho replied from within. ♪*I am frightened but it will pass.*♪ A hint of the acrid scent of dread hung in the air.

Brecken rested a hand atop the duffel, hoped that some comfort might slip through the cheap nylon fabric. ♪*It's time.*♪ She stood up, stooped to take hold of the handle, lifted it with an effort and got the duffel out the door. Her keys and a farewell note to Mrs. Dalzell were already on the kitchenette counter. She pulled the door shut, made sure it latched, and hauled the duffel behind her out to the sidewalk and Janet's green minivan.

Brecken had put up a card on the board in the Student Union Building where people offered and asked for rides, letting anyone interested know that she was looking for a ride to Arkham, Massachusetts with somebody who had plenty of luggage room, and that she would happily chip in gas money. Even so, it was a friend of a friend of Molly's who put her in touch with Janet Kitagawa, a history major who'd just graduated magna cum laude and was heading to Miskatonic for her master's program. They'd talked on the phone twice and exchanged a handful of texts, and then at nine o'clock sharp that morning Janet parked her half-loaded minivan on the street right in front of Mrs. Dalzell's house.

"You need a hand with that?" Janet asked.

"No, I've got it." Brecken got the front end of the duffel onto the floor of the passenger compartment, stooped and heaved. The duffel slid across the floor and settled right behind the front passenger seat. "And we're good."

"Shiny," Janet said. Doors closed, opened, closed; Brecken settled into her seat, got the seatbelt fastened as Janet climbed in behind the wheel. As the engine coughed to life, she craned her neck to try to see the little apartment, but the angle was wrong.

Then the minivan rolled ahead, made a tight U-turn, started down Danforth Street toward campus, but turned away onto Dwight Street after a block and headed for the highway out of town. "Kind of scary," Janet said as she drove. "I've lived in this part of New Jersey my whole life—my family's in Mount Pleasant." She turned onto the highway. The dark pines of Mulligan Wood loomed ahead to either side of the road, huddling around the feet of Hob's Hill. "And it's a pretty big gamble, going to grad school at all these days."

"The job market?"

"Bingo. If I'm lucky and work really hard, I might get a job teaching history somewhere. If not—" She shrugged, then changed lanes to slip past a semi hauling hay bales. "I don't know what I'll do. All I know is I've got to go with my heart."

"Me too," said Brecken.

The highway plunged through Mulligan Wood, curved northwards. "You're a music major, right?" Janet asked.

"Music composition," Brecken said. "Guess what kind of job market there is for Baroque composers these days."

"Planning on a day job?"

"Pretty much." She glanced at the driver. "But I'm going with my heart, too."

The highway wrapped around the far side of Hob's Hill, climbing all the while, and then cut across the high ground north of it. As the car cleared the trees, Partridgeville lay spread out below Brecken's window, filling the ground from Mulligan Wood to Partridge Bay. She could see the bleak gray buildings of the campus, the tall white shape of the First Baptist Church up on Angell Hill, the bland angular masses of the Belknap Creek Mall and Partridgeville High School, a green roof alongside Central Square that she guessed was the Smithwich and Isaacs building. Then, just before trees blocked her view again, she caught sight of a dingy brick building just above the harbor, the place where Jay had lived and died.

Then the highway plunged in among pines, and Partridgeville vanished behind them. Brecken let out a long shuddering breath, releasing everything that belonged to Partridgeville: everything but memories, and one thing besides. My heart, she thought, with a little unsteady smile. My heart is shapeless and iridescent black, and sings to me.

Unobtrusively, she let her right hand drop, slid it back between the seat and the door until it rested against the duffel. A stirring beneath it told her of a zipper being opened from within. A moment later a pseudopod slid out and curled around her hand.

* * *

It took them most of an hour to get to I-85. From there, New Jersey gave way in due time to the vast sprawling mass of New York City; that yielded in turn to the green hills and harbor towns of Connecticut and Rhode Island, then to the forests and failing industrial belts of southeast Massachusetts and the suburbs ringing Boston. On the way out of Boston, Janet turned onto state highway 1, but as Brecken checked their route on her cell phone she found detour warnings near Danvers: an ugly accident, the media said, all northbound lanes blocked.

"Not a problem," said Janet, and took the Salem exit. "We'll go the other way." Before long they were in Salem, and then crossed the bridge to Beverly and veered east just behind the shoreline, following the same route Brecken had taken on the bus. Kingsport came into sight before long, crouched at the foot of the soaring gray mass of Kingsport Head. Another right and the minivan headed up into the hills, wove through dark woodlands where everything human seemed miles or millennia away, and finally came out into late afternoon sunlight and headed down the long slope toward the gambrel roofs and hulking university buildings of Arkham.

Half an hour later the minivan eased to a stop in front of the house on Hyde Street. "Sweet," Janet said, considering it. "You've got a whole floor?"

"Most of one," Brecken admitted. "You?"

"One room in a student household over on Halsey Street. It's cheap." She unfastened her seatbelt. "Let's get your stuff unloaded."

It didn't take long to get all Brecken's things out of the minivan: half a dozen lumpy duffels, only one of which contained a shoggoth, and as many cardboard boxes of books, sheet music, and household goods. A few more minutes saw those ferried into the entry, and then Brecken stood on the porch and waved as Janet drove away.

"You can surely rest before you take all that upstairs," Professor Satterlee said. Then, with an amused glance at Brecken: "Besides, I'm eager to meet a certain someone."

Brecken beamed, went to the big black duffel, and whistled, ♪Saying Farewells, we're here, and the broodmother-of-broodmothers wishes to meet you.♪

The zipper slid open as though pulled by an invisible hand. Blackness welled up from within, produced an eye, considered the professor with what looked like trepidation. ♪Please tell her she honors me by that wish,♪ Sho piped.

Before Brecken could translate, Professor Satterlee said, "You're Brecken's friend Sho, of course. Welcome to Arkham."

Sho tensed, produced a speech orifice, twisted it, and said, "Thank you." The words were a little oddly pronounced but clear, and the voice sounded uncannily like Brecken's.

"You're welcome," said the old woman, visibly startled. "That's a very uncommon skill among your people, Sho."

♪I do not know all those words,♪ Sho said to Brecken, who translated them into the shoggoth language and then reached out a hand to encourage her to leave the duffel.

A few minutes later they were all comfortably settled on the sofa, Professor Satterlee on one end, Brecken and Sho curled up together on the other end. "I am learning English," Sho said slowly; the words still took all her concentration. "Because I wish to live with humans now."

"You're certainly welcome to live here," Satterlee told her.

"You are kind."

"Thank you." The professor smiled the serene smile Brecken remembered. "But there's more to it than that. There's a saying humans have—'the enemy of my enemy is my friend.' The people who hunt shoggoths are no friends of mine, and this isn't the first time I've helped someone stay out of their clutches."

Sho needed that translated, pondered it for a time, and then said, "Do they hunt you too, though you are not human?"

The professor gave the shoggoth an astonished look, then glanced at Brecken, who shook her head and said, "I didn't tell her."

♪Were my words hurtful?♪ Sho asked Brecken in a worried whistle.

♪No, not at all,♪ Brecken reassured her. ♪You saw something humans don't see.♪

"That's extremely perceptive of you," said Professor Satterlee. "But you're quite right, of course—or half right. My mother was human." Then, recovering her poise: "I'm sure they'd hunt me if they had the least idea who my father is. In the meantime, I make life a little more difficult for them." She smiled. "And a little easier for shoggoths, among others."

"I am grateful," said Sho, once Brecken had translated for her.

Later, Brecken's things got hauled upstairs, and Brecken and Sho spent a while filling bookshelves, cupboards, the big walk-in closet and the massive oak dresser with the contents of boxes and duffels. Once that was done, Brecken did the Vach-Viraj incantation in the parlor, a daily discipline now, tracing the circle around Sho as well as herself.

Then it was back downstairs for dinner—Professor Satterlee called in an order to an Asian restaurant that had just opened in downtown Arkham, had it delivered, and waved away Brecken's offer to help pay for it, saying, "For heaven's sake, don't worry about it. That casserole you and Sarah made up kept me fed for three days." Finally, Brecken and Sho climbed the stairs to the apartment while the professor sat down at the piano. The meditative notes of an Erik Satie *Gymnopédie* came murmuring up through the fabric of the house as Brecken shut the door, turned a look on Sho as tired as it was affectionate. ♪*Bed, I think.*♪

Four eyes blinked open, considering her. ♪*Yes. I will spend a long time on the dreaming-side, but I do not regret this day.*♪

♪*Nor I.*♪ She laughed, headed for the bedroom. ♪*Nor I.*♪

Later still, they lay together in the big four-poster bed under familiar quilts. Night wrapped Arkham in sheltering darkness. The faint glow of a streetlight a block away trickled through the window, lost its way in the hieroglyphic patterns of ancient wallpaper. Brecken gave Sho a sleepy kiss, felt a pseudopod brush her face.

♪*I chose the right name today,*♪ Sho said then. ♪*But I have seen enough endings and farewells for now. When the light comes back, and for days after, it will be time for beginnings.*♪

Brecken wanted to say something in response, agreeing with Sho, but the words unraveled into a spray of musical notes and then fell away into silence. Instead, she nestled her face into the nearest of the shoggoth's curves and let herself fall asleep.

* * *

There were plenty of beginnings for them both in the days that followed. The beginning that mattered most to Brecken, though, came three weeks later: three weeks of introductions and uncertainties, of walks through unfamiliar neighborhoods, of evenings learning the quirks of the upright piano in her apartment and the grand piano down in Professor Satterlee's parlor, and of two visits to the house, always at night, by the pale-haired man who wore the Yellow Sign, and who wished to talk to Sho with Brecken as interpreter. The first time he came, she suddenly thought—or was it her thought at all?—of the pendant she'd been given at Buzrael Books, and had worn every day thereafter. A quick gesture settled it atop her blouse, and the visitor gave her a startled look, then a sudden smile and a nod. He knew her loyalties, she knew his, and that was what mattered.

Toward the end of the three weeks, as the summer session drew closer, a single project took up more and more of her time: final frantic corrections, clatter of her laptop keyboard, hum-*chunk* hum-*chunk* of a printer spitting out pages of sheet music with an improbable heading:

CONCERTO IN Bb

Brecken Kendall

The three movements of the concerto had names, too. Brecken had considered putting those on the sheet music, titling the first *We Live Beneath the Ground*, the second *Hear and Remember*, and the third *Still Beside You*, but decided against it at the last moment. Maybe later, she told herself. Maybe when I've met more people who can handle knowing why.

Once the music was printed, she spent half a dozen sessions down in Professor Satterlee's parlor rehearsing with one of the professor's students, a gifted pianist with a good knowledge of the Baroque and classical repertoire, before the day itself. The day itself was warm and sultry, with a scattering of clouds. Brecken spent a long slow morning with Sho and cooked cheese polenta for breakfast, and the two of them teased each other about apricot jam, as quite a bit of that went atop one of the two bowls. Two hours of flute practice followed; after that, she went to the grocery across the river in the old part of town, came back with two full bags, got red beans cooking in her slow cooker, and spent another hour with Sho, curled up together on the couch talking—anything to keep her mind away from the evening's events. It was a familiar habit, though Sho made a more effective distraction than most.

Finally, though, it was time to don her dark red dress with the golden sunburst in seed beads, brush her hair into submission, put on makeup and perfume, pick up her flute and head downstairs. The pianist was already there, warming up in a storm of Bach and Telemann. Professor Satterlee looked on smiling from the couch, having already set out wine, crackers, and cheese for the guests. While Brecken was putting Mrs. Macallan's flute together, the first knock sounded on the front door.

There would not be many people present that first time. Satterlee had advised her on that, and suggested names. All three of the professors on Brecken's audition committee were on the final list, of course, along with two other professors from the composition program. So was the chair of the music department, though she had other commitments and had to beg off. So was Martin Chaudronnier, a Miskatonic alumnus and local real estate magnate who'd made several large donations to the music department. Finally, so was a professor from Miskatonic's history of ideas department named Miriam Akeley, who was a friend of Professor Satterlee and also, from hints Brecken had picked up, a friend—or more than a friend—of Martin Chaudronnier. Politics, Brecken wondered, or romance? She had no way of telling. There would be someone else listening, too, from a hidden corner on the second floor landing, and Brecken wished she could introduce Sho to the others, but the gap between the worlds still remained.

Voices and footsteps brought Anne Ricci and Michael Silva into the parlor. They greeted Brecken pleasantly, asked about her move to Arkham, settled on the couch. A knock at the kitchen door, which was level with the alley and thus suited to wheelchairs, brought Paul Czanek. His greetings were brief, and Brecken got little more than a nod, but the fire in his pale blue eyes was less hidden than Brecken had seen it before.

The other professors showed in the minutes that followed. Finally, Martin Chaudronnier and Miriam Akeley arrived together, the one stocky and graying, dressed in the under-stated elegance of old money, the other silver-haired and lean as a heron, wearing a black dress and a white sweater, moving awkwardly as though she'd been injured and had only begun to recover. Romance, Brecken thought, watching the two of them glance at each other. Maybe politics, too, but definitely romance.

Professor Satterlee spoke next, but by then Brecken was sufficiently keyed up that she couldn't process what the old woman said. Random phrases murmured themselves in the still air— "promising young composer," "first substantial work," "official premier with other works later on"—and then Brecken herself had to fumble through a few words of thanks and welcome, which she did without too much embarrassment.

Silence, then. She picked up her flute and glanced at the pianist, who paused, and began the quick flowing arpeggios that introduced the first movement of her concerto. *We live beneath the ground*, the theme said, and Brecken wondered briefly if anyone else would ever notice the bridge that she'd made, half by accident, between two disparate worlds.

Halpin Chalmers was right, she thought. There are always two realities, though they're not always the same two, not even for me. But whether it's Sho's world and mine, the baroque and the modern, the human and the eldritch, the terrestrial and the condition of fire—

I am the reconciler between them.

She raised the flute to her lips, began to play.

AUTHOR'S NOTE

This fantasia on an eldritch theme is the first of two volumes. The second, *The Nyogtha Variations*, will continue the story of Brecken and Sho, and tie up the loose ends I have deliberately left hanging at the end of this first volume.

Readers of the series *The Weird of Hali*, my other venture into weird fantasy, may find it helpful (or at least interesting) to know that *The Shoggoth Concerto* takes place in the same fictive universe as that series, but touches only peripherally on the tale of the Weird of Hali and its fulfillment. It takes place some five years after the events of *The Weird of Hali I: Innsmouth* and *The Weird of Hali II: Kingsport*, and the last chapter takes place at the same time as those parts of *The Weird of Hali IV: Dreamlands* that occur in the waking world.

Like my other weird tales, this story depends even more than most fiction on the labors of previous writers. H.P. Lovecraft, Clark Ashton Smith, Robert E. Howard, Henry Kuttner, and Frank Belknap Long all contributed raw material to the tale. So, on a different level, did Johann Joseph Fux, whose *Steps to Parnassus* (the textbook Mozart's father used to teach him counterpoint) helped me understand Baroque music, and the music department of the Providence Public Library in Providence, Rhode Island, which provided me with the background for Brecken Kendall's compositions. I also owe a debt to Sara Greer and Isabel Kunkle, both of whom read and critiqued the manuscript. I hope it is unnecessary to remind the reader that none of the above are responsible in any way for the use I have made of their work.